CECIL COUNTY
PUBLIC LIBRARY

O9-BSU-235

301 Newark Ave
Elkton, MD 21921

CLEAR
BY
FIRE

-------------- *A Search and Destroy Thriller* -------▪▶

JOSHUA HOOD

TOUCHSTONE
New York   London   Toronto   Sydney   New Delhi

Touchstone
An Imprint of Simon & Schuster, Inc.
1230 Avenue of the Americas
New York, NY 10020

This book is a work of fiction. Any references to historical events, real people, or real places are used fictitiously. Other names, characters, places, and events are products of the author's imagination, and any resemblance to actual events or places or persons, living or dead, is entirely coincidental.

Copyright © 2015 by Joshua Hood

All rights reserved, including the right to reproduce this book or portions thereof in any form whatsoever. For information address Touchstone Subsidiary Rights Department, 1230 Avenue of the Americas, New York, NY 10020.

First Touchstone hardcover edition August 2015

TOUCHSTONE and colophon are registered trademarks of Simon & Schuster, Inc.

For information about special discounts for bulk purchases, please contact Simon & Schuster Special Sales at 1-866-506-1949 or business@simonandschuster.com.

The Simon & Schuster Speakers Bureau can bring authors to your live event. For more information or to book an event contact the Simon & Schuster Speakers Bureau at 1-866-248-3049 or visit our website at www.simonspeakers.com.

Interior design by Kyle Kabel

Manufactured in the United States of America

10 9 8 7 6 5 4 3 2 1

Library of Congress Cataloging-in-Publication Data

Hood, Joshua.
 Clear by Fire : a search and destroy thriller / Joshua Hood.
   pages cm
 1. Special operations (Military science)—Fiction. 2. Suspense fiction. I. Title.
 PS3608.O5574C57 2015
 813'.6—dc23

                                                              2015000558

ISBN 978-1-5011-0571-5
ISBN 978-1-5011-0573-9 (ebook)

Clear by Fire is dedicated to the men and women of the armed forces, who put their lives on hold to fight for this great country during OIF and OEF. I wrote this book for you, and I sincerely hope you enjoy it.

CLEAR

BY

FIRE

CHAPTER 1

National Security Advisor Winfield "Duke" Cage nodded at the two Secret Service agents flanking the entrance to the White House situation room and adjusted the unfamiliar tie that was threatening to choke him.

The last time he'd stepped through this doorway, he'd quit as the chairman of the Joint Chiefs, effectively throwing away a career that had spanned two decades.

He'd sworn never to return. But that was under a different president, and while only eight months had passed, Cage was a different man, and the newly appointed national security advisor.

The room was smaller than he remembered but utterly familiar. The burnished wood of the massive table gleamed in the rays of the overhead lighting and cast its reflection on the flat-screens mounted to the walls. The blue and taupe carpet lay pristine, perfectly balancing the neutral coloring of the walls and the black leather chairs arranged around the room's perimeter.

His eyes drifted over the faces of the most powerful figures in Washington, men who were responsible for guiding their new president, and Cage wondered if he had enough in him for one last battle.

His aide, Jacob Simmons, made his way through the scrum of

onlookers and as he handed Cage the daily intelligence brief said, "There is a problem. We need to talk."

At six foot four, Cage was built like an all-pro tight end and towered over his short and stocky aide. The two men had been a team since their days at West Point, and their relationship had been tested in the cauldron of battle on more than one occasion. Simmons was the only man on earth whom Cage trusted, and during his brief exile, he was the only man who had his back. He was also one of the most capable intelligence operatives he'd ever known.

"Not now," Cage replied, catching the secretary of defense slipping toward him out of the corner of his eye.

"Duke, we have a serious problem," he hissed.

"Handle it . . ."

"Cage," Secretary of Defense Collins exclaimed, dragging his attention away from his aide.

"Mr. Secretary," he replied formally.

"I was surprised when the president told me he appointed you," he began condescendingly.

"Not as surprised as I was," Cage replied, taking the secretary's outstretched hand and shaking it firmly.

He knew that Collins had fought hard to keep him off the president's cabinet, and while Collins didn't have the balls to come out and say it, the secretary was already working on bouncing him off Capitol Hill. But this wasn't the first time someone had been after his scalp, and Cage was already a step ahead.

His ace in the hole was that he didn't have to be confirmed before Congress and therefore could only be fired by the president. As long as he kept the man happy, he was good to go. Cage felt the SecDef squeeze his hand as he looked searchingly into the ex-general's eyes. He was challenging him already and the day hadn't even started.

One lesson Cage had taken from his time in the Green Berets was that it was important to assert dominance among the pack as soon as possible, and he did this by slowly crushing his opponent's clammy grip until he could feel the thin, birdlike bones of the man's hand begin to compress against themselves. He pulled the man in close, as if to embrace him, and said, "Be careful, friend."

Just then the president walked into the room, surrounded by his top aides and chief of staff. Cage released his iron grip and stepped back as the leader of the free world looked at him and smiled broadly.

President John Bradley was thin and fit, with a deep tan and more than a passing resemblance to Robert Redford. The American public had been infatuated with his youthful exuberance and trustworthy gaze and he'd been elected in a sweeping landslide. Moving among those assembled, the president began working the room. He drew men to his side like moths to a flame, and Secretary Collins, like everyone else, was unable to resist. With one final stare, Collins turned his back on Cage and made a beeline for the most powerful man in the world.

"What the hell was that?" Simmons whispered, moving closer. "I thought we were laying low."

"Don't worry about him. Stick to the plan and he won't know what hit him."

"Look, we really need to talk. Something's come up in Kona."

Cage saw the president moving his way and wordlessly stepped forward, signaling to his aide that they would have to finish the conversation later. Despite his outward calm, he wished nothing more than to have a moment to find out what the hell was going on. Unfortunately, now wasn't the time.

"Duke," the president said, offering his hand and the famous smile that had gotten him elected.

The president was one of the few people Cage allowed to call him Duke. While it was a small thing to most people, the nickname was something reserved for those who had bled beside him in combat, and he guarded it jealously. The fact that Cage had fought with Bradley's father gave the president a free pass, but more than that,

Cage knew it was bad form to correct the President of the United States.

"Mr. President," he replied, taking his hand and shaking it warmly.

"I can't tell you how happy I am that you agreed to help me out."

"Well, Mr. President, I didn't figure you'd take no for an answer."

President Bradley had naively promised the American people that he would end the war in the Middle East while restoring the country's honor. But he needed Cage's help to make good on the promise.

"I'm just thrilled to have you on the team," he said, staring Cage deep in the eyes. "We have a lot of work to do."

Cage nodded as the president's chief of staff leaned in and said, "Mr. President, we are on a tight schedule."

President Bradley winked and, releasing Cage's hand, turned and walked back to his place at the head of the table.

CHAPTER 2

Mason Kane checked his watch and tried not to scratch the sutures sewn into the bottom of his arm. The neat row of black lines looked like a hairless centipede crawling its way toward his elbow, but worse than that, it itched like hell.

He was a wanted man, disavowed by his own country, the only American to earn a kill-on-sight order.

Mason knew the Mideast better than any Westerner, but he was running out of places to hide. The day before, a man he hadn't seen in years had tried to assassinate him in Kona, and Mason had come to Marrakech looking for answers.

The clock was ticking, and with every intelligence agency in the Mideast looking for him, irritated sutures were not a priority.

The Berbers had named the city Mur Akush, or "land of God," and from a distance the name made sense, but deep inside the medina, where Mason was waiting, there were no obvious signs that God had ever been there.

Zeus, one of few allies he had left, had warned him to let the situation "breathe" before coming to Marrakech, but Mason was tired of running and knew the game had changed.

There was only one way Decklin could have known where to find him. Someone had talked, and the amount of money it must have cost to scuttle the op in Kona told him that whoever it was had deep pockets.

Hate or greed was usually the only motive needed to kill a man, and it hadn't taken Mason long to figure out who was trying to smoke him. It had to be connected to Colonel Barnes, but he couldn't get his head around why the colonel was suddenly so serious about putting a bullet in his head.

He'd first met the colonel in 2006, after it became obvious that America was losing the war in Iraq. The president was looking for a win, and it was up to the Department of Defense to bring it to him. Their answer was the Anvil Program, an old concept ripped out of the CIA's playbook.

During Vietnam, it was called the Phoenix Program, and it had used Green Berets and the CIA's Special Operations Group, or SOG, to conduct asymmetrical warfare against an insurgency outside the military's legal boundaries of war. In the Middle East, all the CIA needed was the right man on the ground, and that's where Barnes came into the picture.

Barnes was a freshly minted colonel at the time of his appointment, and his marching orders were simple: Train a team to fight like the enemy, and then set them loose on the insurgency. Forget the rules of engagement, forget the media, just start stacking bodies—and that was exactly what they did.

Barnes was given the authority to handpick any soldier from any unit to accomplish his goals, and finding the right men was paramount. He pulled the file of every Delta operator, navy SEAL, and Green Beret he could get his hands on, and when he came across Mason Kane, he knew he'd found an operator born for this type of mission.

Mason had taken pride in being a soldier. He'd come from nothing, a half-breed who'd grown up on the streets, surrounded by pimps and dope boys. But the army didn't care that his mother was a drunk or that his father had abandoned him and had later blown his brains out with a cheap Walmart shotgun. The only thing the army cared about was whether he was good at his job, and Mason had been one of the best. There was a box somewhere filled with awards, and they all had citations that read, "For selfless service and bravery under fire," but Mason didn't care about that.

When the colonel found him, Mason was using his particular skill set to conduct deep-cover operations in Iraq. His ability to blend in with the civilian population and his mastery of Arabic made him a critical piece of the Joint Special Operations Command's eyes on the ground. He was everything the colonel needed and more.

Like the rest of the soldiers on the team, Mason had his demons, and it was only later that he realized the colonel sought out broken men.

Mason scanned the street. He knew he couldn't stay out in the open for long; too many foreign agents used Morocco as a base of operations. North Africa wasn't as stable as it had been fifteen years ago, and after the Arab Spring, many intelligence agencies were still focused on the region.

Slipping into one of Marrakech's many nameless narrow alleys, he pulled his Glock 23 from its holster and quickly screwed on a suppressor. It was bulky and made the pistol heavier, but it was better than the alternative. After jamming the Glock into his jacket pocket he headed to the three-story apartment building he'd been watching. It reminded him of East Los Angeles, where he'd grown up and learned to blend in. Being the only non-Latino boy in the barrio had taught him the value of keeping a low profile and that, combined with the dark complexion he'd gotten from his mother, helped him blend in among the natives of North Africa.

His feet scuffed over the worn cobblestones as a woman appeared at the edge of a balcony. She shook a threadbare rug over the metal railing and Mason shot her an annoyed glance as he stepped out of the way of the dirt shower. The woman ignored him and began to beat the tightly woven fabric on the metal railing with titanic blows that caused the rusted metal to shudder.

With a final disdainful snap of her wrist, the woman turned and disappeared into her apartment, allowing the American to continue to his destination.

Mason ducked as he walked under the low archway of the apartment building. Keeping a firm grip on the butt of his pistol, he carefully ascended the exterior stairs. The apartments were old and brown, just like everything else in the city. Chunks of flaky concrete had fallen out of the walls and masonry dust littered the cracked brickwork of the stairs.

Once he reached the third floor, he pushed open the thin metal door that led into the hall and made his way to a nondescript wooden door. Thick gray paint peeled beneath the flickering light, which struggled to draw power from the overworked grid.

Mason used a bump key to force the lock and stepped quickly through the door. The apartment was small and cramped and smelled like saffron and cooking oil. A small couch sat in the main room next to a neat pile of sleeping mats, while an overhead fan turned lazily above his head.

No one was home, and the American shut the door behind him and walked over to the sliding glass door. He slid it open and stepped out onto the balcony, looking down over the tightly packed neighborhood to see if anyone was watching before shaking the metal railing to see if it would hold. The bolts securing it to the wall were rusted but seemed to be in decent shape, so after a final check he climbed up and jumped over to the next apartment.

He pulled the pistol from his pocket and peered through the glass into the apartment. A cursory check around the edges of the door frame didn't turn up any wires, and once he was sure it wasn't booby-trapped, Mason slipped out a knife. He was about to pry it open when he realized the sliding glass wasn't locked.

The pungent smell of kif drifted out into the air, alerting him to the presence of his target.

So much for tradecraft, he thought to himself as he stepped through the window.

Mason brought the pistol up and quickly cleared the main room. Moving to the bedroom, the smell of hashish grew stronger, and he followed the smell to its origin before stepping into the small room.

"What's up?" he asked in Arabic.

The Algerian sitting on the bed looked up from the large hookah, his eyes wide with surprise. He reached across to the table for his pistol and Mason raised his Glock and said, "Don't do it."

The man ignored his warning, and just as his fingers were about to touch the weapon, Mason shot him in the hand. The suppressor didn't make the pistol silent, but it did muffle the report to a dull *thwack*.

The bullet hit Karim's hand below the knuckles and sprayed the wall with blood. He instinctively snatched his hand back to his torso and began to scream in pain.

"I told you," the American said with a shrug as he snatched the pistol off the table. It was a Russian Makarov and had been freshly oiled.

"Mason, I— I . . . ," he stammered in Arabic.

"I'll never understand you people. You clean your gun, then get high and forget to lock your back door. I guess you figured I wasn't coming back."

The man just stared at him blankly.

"Karim, I thought we had a deal. I mean, that's why Ahmed paid you, right? To make introductions and watch my back?"

Mason adopted a casual air as he scanned the room for any more weapons that the spy might have lying around. He thought he knew why Decklin wanted him dead, but he couldn't figure out why the Algerian had betrayed him.

"For the last six months, I've been running around every shit hole in Africa, dodging the Americans, the French, and your jihadist friends. Hell, everyone wants to kill me, and all you had to do was take the money and keep your mouth shut."

"That's what I've been doing, believe me," the man begged.

"Yeah, that's what I thought too, but then I ran into an old friend in Kona. How the hell did Decklin know I was there?"

"Mason, there has been a misunderstanding, let me explain—"

The American cut him off by holding the pistol in the air and slowly pointing it at the man's knee.

"C'mon, Karim, a mistake? You're going to sit here and tell me that Barnes's triggerman just happened to stumble into Kona and try to put a bullet in my head? You know how this works; we're both pros, so do me the courtesy of not lying to my face. I'm going to give you one more chance to tell me the truth, and then I'm going to put a bullet in your kneecap."

The man nodded as blood ran down his mangled right hand and onto his soiled gray shirt. Mason knew he was weighing his options.

As a child, Mason had been soft, and he'd paid for it. Growing up in a tough neighborhood meant that he had to get either stronger or smarter. He had taken more than his share of beatings, but that person was gone now, purified and hardened by the cauldron of war. There was nothing soft in him now, and if not for the constant struggle to keep his humanity, he could easily have been just like Decklin.

"I have no idea what you're talking about," the Algerian said finally.

Mason steadied the pistol and squeezed the trigger, firing a round into the Arab's kneecap. Karim was already screaming before the expended brass tinked off the concrete floor.

"Karim, you're smarter than this. Don't make me be an asshole."

"Mason, I swear to you—"

The American lined the Glock's sights up with his other knee and slowly moved his finger to the trigger.

"Okay, okay, I'll tell you. The man with the CIA."

"Vernon?" Mason asked.

He had never trusted the man, but he'd never expected him to sell him out—especially not to Barnes.

"Yes, there was never a job. This was all about delivering you to Decklin."

Mason stepped away from the bed, struggling with what he knew he should do next. Karim deserved to die, but the American was trying to get free of all the death.

He grabbed a towel off the floor near the door, and tossing it to Karim, he said, "I don't ever want to see you again. If I do, you're dead."

Mason took the back way out of the apartment. The heat of the day had not yet fallen on the city, and the streets were crowded as he headed toward the Gueliz district. The "new city" attracted American tourists and wealthy Europeans, and he walked as quickly as possible through the sea of faces without attracting any unnecessary attention.

He'd had a rough life but had never been one to blame his situation on others. Mason wished he could say that his mother had done her best, but that was a lie. The only thing she ever cared about was getting wasted, and while most kids had childhoods full of good memories, he had the sullen days and violent nights of an alcoholic's son. His mother might not have loved him, but she'd made him into a survivor from day one.

Tossing the Makarov into a trash bin, he took out his phone and dialed a number. A moment later a man answered in Arabic.

"Yes?"

"You were right, it was Vernon. Have you finished the download?"

"I'm just leaving. I will send what I have to your phone," the man replied.

"Good. He's at the Emirates Café. Bring the package with you."

Ten minutes later, Mason was standing in the shadows, near the front of the Emirates Café, scanning the documents stolen from Vernon's computer. A pair of sunglasses hid his dark eyes as he glanced at the target's table.

The glare made it hard to read the smudged screen, and he was just about to hold the phone up when something clicked. It had taken less than a millisecond for his brain to interpret the two words that his eyes had seen, and he frantically swiped backward until he saw them again.

"Operation Karakul," it read.

He felt his heart skip in his chest, and a wave of adrenaline washed through his nervous system. He was barely able to steady his finger enough to open the message.

Mason's time in Anvil had given him access to more classified data than the entire analyst division at Langley. It was important that his team could track threats as they evolved, and he had come across the name "Karakul" before—it was the code name for Hamid Karzai, the president of Afghanistan.

The e-mail was from Razor 5, which he knew to be the call sign attached to the Joint Special Operations Command, but it was the content that floored him. It was simple and to the point: "Razor 5 confirms Operation Karakul is a go. Prosecute target ASAP."

Mason couldn't believe it. His mind scrambled as he slipped the phone back into his pocket and stared at Vernon, who was sitting at an outside table in front of the café methodically wiping the inside of his empty glass with a white napkin.

"This motherfucker," Mason muttered, running his hand quickly over his dark, slicked-back hair. Flicking the cigarette into the street, he made his way to the front door and disappeared inside.

The surprise on the CIA agent's face when Mason appeared before him told the soldier everything he needed to know.

The Algerian had told the truth; Vernon had betrayed him.

"Sorry to drop in like this, but it's been a hectic couple of days."

Vernon smiled sickly and tried to stall by taking a sip of water. "It's good to see you. I was just . . . having some lunch. I didn't know you were back," the spy stammered honestly.

"You gave me a job and I did it. Now I'm back for your end of the bargain," Mason said as he studied the spy's reaction.

"Uhh, yes, of course." Vernon turned white and scanned the crowded café, looking for a way out and trying to tell whether Mason was alone.

The waiter approached, and Mason ordered coffee and hummus and lit a cigarette with a battered Zippo while the man squirmed across the table.

"You aren't going to order anything?" he asked innocently.

"No, I'm not really hungry."

Mason watched tiny beads of perspiration appear on the spy's forehead. His pupils dilated and he shifted often in his chair as he struggled to get comfortable.

Who the fuck is Razor 5? he wanted to scream at the man, but he had to play it cool if he hoped to use the spy. Vernon was a slippery son of a bitch who might have been short on brains, but he was long on cunning. In fact, he was slick enough to make a career out of what had started as a joke.

The first time someone suggested arming a drone, everyone had laughed, but Vernon saw value in the idea and managed to gather enough support to get his own team. Five months later, the room was packed as Vernon's armed Predator smoked a house full of jihadists. He went from zero to hero before the shrapnel ever hit the ground, and soon after, he was charged with populating the kill list the drones would use for targeting jihadists. It was a good job, with zero oversight, which made him a perfect match for Barnes.

How had he not seen it coming, Mason thought. Vernon and the colonel fit together like pieces of a puzzle, but he'd been so desperate, so eager to trust, that he had let his guard down.

Vernon was back to inspecting the glass when the waiter returned to the table, and Mason spoke to him in Arabic.

"He's afraid of germs," Mason said, blowing a cloud of smoke toward the glass.

"Fucking Americans and their germs," the waiter replied before walking off.

Mason slipped the sunglasses off his face and stared at Vernon. "We had a deal. I work for you, and you get me back to America. You remember that, don't you?"

"The deal is still on, I promise. This has to be a mistake. Let me make a call . . ." Vernon started to reach into his pocket and Mason slammed his palm down on the table.

"Hold on there, boss. If you are trying to call Karim, let me save you the trouble. I just killed him."

The man froze, his hand an inch from the light jacket he was wearing. Mason could tell he was trying to figure out whether Mason was going to kill him in the open or let him live. The agent loved war by proxy, but when the conflict was right in his face, he became very uncomfortable.

The waiter dropped off the plate of hummus, and Mason tore a strip off the pita bread and used it to spoon some of the hummus into his mouth. He knew just as much about Vernon as the spy knew about him.

"The job was compromised. I think you tried to burn me," Mason said.

"Now hold on, I don't know where you're getting your information, but someone is filling your head with a bunch of bullshit."

Vernon was reaching, and they both knew it. He was buying time—hoping he could regain control of the situation.

"Really? For the last six months I've put a fucking continent between me and Decklin. For all he knew, I was dead, but the moment I show up in Kona, there he is. Are you saying that he's clairvoyant or that I don't know what the fuck I'm doing?"

The spy tried to go on the offensive. "You had a bad op—it happens—but don't try to put this on me. Five different countries want you dead, including the US. Before you start making accusations, I think you might want to take a second to remember who your friends are."

"Friends like Barnes? Is that whose dirty work you're doing?" It was a gamble, but Mason couldn't give the man an inch of traction. He had to push him now, or he'd never get the truth.

"What?" Vernon was frozen by the question, and Mason knew he had him.

"I know what you're up to, and it's never going to happen," Mason lied.

Vernon stared at him, his mouth hanging open like a broken gate. The spy was stunned, but recovered quickly and pulled an envelope out of his pocket. Passing it across the table, he locked eyes with Mason.

"Look, I didn't tell you to grow a conscience and fuck up your life. You did that on your own, pal. You made a choice and it backfired. I'm sorry the world's not fair."

Mason reached for the envelope, which Vernon was holding down with the tip of his fingers. The spy felt a shift in the momentum; Mason still needed him.

"Do you know what they had us doing out there?" he asked.

"I don't know or care. Mason, you need to grow up. There's a war going on and you need to get over the past. I've read your file, and it's a sad story, but here's a news flash: no one gives a shit. The only reason you're not dead or locked away is because I want it that way." He lifted his fingers off the envelope and let Mason take it. "The only people who care about you are gone. The only record of your existence is in a file that I burned the day I found you. Remember that."

Mason slipped the envelope into his pocket as the waiter returned with the bill and a carafe of water. The young Arab sat the check on the table and began filling Vernon's glass. Mason reached for the check, bumping the waiter's arm, causing him to spill the water across the white tablecloth and onto Vernon's pants.

"What the fuck," Vernon yelled, pushing away from the table as water soaked his pants. Mason's hand flashed to his pistol at the spy's sudden movement, but he quickly regained his composure as the waiter set the carafe on the table and made a big show of blotting the water on Vernon's jacket.

"Jesus, Mason, what is this bullshit?" Vernon's face was red with anger as he tried to brush off the waiter's clumsy attempts to help him.

"Calm down, it's just water," he said as Vernon finally untangled himself from the zealous Arab.

Vernon sat back down, keeping his chair away from the dripping white linen, and looked accusingly at Mason. "That was some bush-league bullshit."

It was obvious that the CIA man thought he had done it on purpose.

"Look, I said I was sorry. It was just a little water."

"Yeah, but I'm the one who looks like he pissed his pants, not you."

"Fuck, maybe I just need to find someplace to hide out for a while and get my shit together," Mason said, a plan forming in his mind as he lit another cigarette and the other patrons turned back to their meals.

"You need to do something. You're falling apart on me. Go get laid or whatever it is you do. I'll make some calls and see if we can get you back in the States in a few weeks."

"You're right. I'm sorry for getting in your face like that."

Vernon looked across the table and studied him. Mason looked defeated, and that was exactly what the spy wanted.

"I told you that I would take care of you. You're going to have to trust me, okay?" Vernon's voice had softened, but it was all an act.

"I know. I'll take care of the check and then I'm going to get out of here. I think I need a new country. Can you get me some papers?"

"Where are you trying to go?" Vernon asked as he stood up. He wanted to get the hell out while Mason was off balance.

"Maybe up the coast. I've got friends in Libya," Mason replied, lowering his head in false defeat as his mind scrambled to connect the dots. He needed to get Decklin out in the open, and he hoped Vernon would take the bait.

"Let me see what I can do. Give me an hour," Vernon said, shouldering his assault pack and walking away from the table.

Mason finished the rest of his coffee and pulled a handful of crumpled bills out of his pocket and tossed them on the table. The waiter came back to collect the bill and looked down at the desolate American.

"Do you want some more coffee?"

"Yeah, I'll take another cup," Mason said as he reached into his jacket and pulled out a stack of fresh American bills from Vernon's envelope.

The waiter nodded, took the money from the American, and then placed a phone on the table.

"That was a nice switch," Mason told him.

"I know." The waiter smiled as he pocketed the cash and began clearing the table.

Mason had never trusted Vernon and had paid a great deal of money to keep the man under surveillance. The cloned phone was a result of that significant investment. Picking it up off the table, he ran his fingers across the small screen, clearing away a layer of dust. He needed to get out of the country but had to be sure that Vernon had taken the bait.

The American had learned the hard way that there were very few people he could trust. He'd trusted Colonel Barnes once and was still paying for that mistake. Finishing the coffee, he slipped the phone into his pocket and headed to the street.

CHAPTER 3

The middle-class neighborhood looked like a postcard sent from the god of suburbia. Stately trees and cookie-cutter houses stood watch over the men and women jogging up the impossibly black asphalt as Renee Hart turned down the street for the third time.

Sprinklers lazily baptized manicured lawns and pruned bushes while perfectly distributed drops of water sparkled brilliantly in the fading sunlight.

Renee frowned behind the wheel and squinted against the sun's fading rays as it slipped behind the Sierra Nevadas. She was living a nightmare, a Special Operations soldier lost in suburbia.

She felt out of place in the blue jeans and polo shirt she was wearing instead of her normal combat gear. Being in civilian clothes made her feel vulnerable, and her left hand slipped to the horseshoe pendant hanging from her neck, an unconscious grounding technique. Her mother had given her the simple talisman, and the sterling silver was worn to a glossy finish from nervous friction. It reminded her of the life she had left behind and the damage her decision had done to her tight-knit family.

It had been hard telling her mother that she was joining the army. She'd felt guilty as the tears spilled down her mom's face, but she had made her choice, and there was nothing more to talk about.

"You're giving up your future to follow a boy?" her mom had screamed at her. "You are going to regret this for the rest of your life."

Renee tried to tell her the same thing she'd been trying to tell herself. She wasn't doing this because her boyfriend had signed up. She wanted to tell her mom that she was afraid of college, and that after the awful years of being a terrible student, struggling with dyslexia, and feeling like an idiot in school, she felt this might be exactly what she needed. But she just couldn't quite get it out.

Finally, she found the address and pulled into the driveway she'd already passed three times. The white stucco walls and dark wooden trim were a drastic contrast to the dirty brown compounds of the Middle East, and the unfamiliarity made something as simple as finding an address incredibly difficult.

She knocked on the heavy oak door and a moment later a man's distorted face appeared in the lead-glass window. Her contact, Joseph Davis, worked for the Defense Intelligence Agency, and he was ruining her day.

"Hey, I didn't know you were coming by," he said, holding open the door for her to come in.

"We have a problem. I tried calling, but you didn't pick up," she said, getting right to business.

"I must have been in the shower. You got time for dinner? Annie's making meatloaf."

Renee looked around the pristine entryway, taking in the little touches that people fill their house with to make it a home. Joseph turned and walked through an open door, and she stepped in, careful not to track dirt onto the spotless terra-cotta tile.

Following him into the kitchen, Renee saw a fit brunette standing over the stove. The woman frowned as Renee walked in, and immediately a palpable tension filled the air.

"Annie, this is Renee. She flew in from Afghanistan to help us out at the office."

Renee could tell Annie didn't like her right away, but she was used to the injustice of women acting hostile around her. Wives were the worst. Female soldiers weren't supposed to look like she did, and the fact that their husbands were working long hours with the pretty blonde was interpreted as a threat. This was exactly why she preferred to stay in Afghanistan.

Relationships had never been her strong suit, and observing the couple gave her a glimpse into what she'd given up to pursue her career. Renee had always planned on getting married, and she knew vaguely that she was running out of time. Someone had once told her that a young girl's father is her model for future mates. If that was true, then it was no wonder she was still single. Her dad had only paid her attention when she stood in front of him and demanded it.

"Renee said she called, but I never heard it. You didn't hear my phone ringing while I was in the shower, did you?"

"Nope," Annie said, looking back down at the pot she was stirring.

She was a terrible liar, and Renee realized immediately that she'd probably heard the phone and most likely erased the call log.

"The target got a call. He was on the line for ten seconds before hanging up and deactivating his phone," Renee said, ignoring Annie's scowls.

"Shit, did you let the guys know?"

"I let them know, but apparently someone canceled the surveillance. No one is watching him."

"What the *fuck* do you mean it got canceled? We had authorization for the rest of the month."

"Joseph," his wife exclaimed, apparently surprised at his language.

"Sorry, baby. Look, I have to go," he said, grabbing his pistol from the kitchen table.

"I'll be in the car," Renee said. It was obvious that this was going to need some smoothing over.

She could hear the emotion in Annie's voice as she made her way to the door. Outside, she shook her head as she unlocked the Jeep with the key fob and climbed in. Renee could imagine what Joseph was going through inside. The job demanded flexibility and total dedication, which left little time for healthy relationships.

Renee had left Afghanistan forty-eight hours earlier and had already lost a day trying to get caught up with Joseph's end of the operation. Her team was counting on her to bring back actionable intel, and she was getting nowhere sitting in her new partner's driveway.

According to the intelligence report Joseph had sent up the chain, he had found evidence that her target was about to make a major buy, and she needed to know what was important enough to pull him out of hiding. Three months ago she'd come across an American soldier of fortune by the name of Decklin who was funneling guns and money for al-Qaeda affiliates in the Mideast. At the same time, the Department of Defense's intelligence division, or DIA, was investigating a two-million-dollar wire transfer that originated in Saudi Arabia and was traced to California. The recipient, a Dr. Keating, ran a company called BioCore, which had a handful of government contracts with the CIA and the DoD. Believing Decklin could be working with this Dr. Keating, Renee had been sent to California to assist the DIA.

Renee was frustrated as she sat in the Jeep, waiting for Joseph to join her. There was no time to waste; she had a job to do. When she was gone, Joseph could go back to domestic life, but right now they needed to move.

Renee had tried her hand at balancing work and love, and she'd failed miserably. During her first deployment, she had been naive enough to think her relationship with Jonas was the real thing. But the reality quickly became obvious. He had wanted her to be two people, an equal during the day but subservient at night. Their relationship had died before they ever left Kuwait, and Jonas had gotten himself transferred to another unit by the time they landed in Iraq.

Joseph worked for the Department of Defense, and according to his file, he had requested to come back to the States five times in the last two years. Being an operative wasn't exactly conducive to having a family, and Renee understood, but he still had a job to do. The fact that she'd wasted so much time driving out to his house annoyed her the most. Personal issues were a by-product of the job, but Joseph was coming with her one way or the other.

"Sorry to take you away from meatloaf," Renee said when he finally got into the Jeep.

"Just shut up and drive."

"There, there, little bear, national security comes first," she laughed as she backed out of the drive.

"Women," he huffed. "Since I'll be sleeping on the couch tonight, you mind telling me what the plan is?"

"Help me figure this out. Jim Green is the chief of station, right?"

"We don't call them that, we call them the agent in charge," he replied.

"Okay, well, as the agent in charge, why is he pulling your surveillance package? My guess is that he doesn't like taking orders from a girl, but I could be wrong."

"But the Riyadh transfer was legit. Hell, he signed off on it."

Renee had learned the hard way that men had a huge problem taking orders from a woman. As a member of Task Force 111, Renee was the tip of the spear when it came to tracking high-value targets for the military, but the job came with more than its share of bullshit. The Special Operations community was an all-boys club, and they felt that women were being forced on them. Since she had the dubious honor of being the only operational female in her unit, Renee was seen as the enemy.

The government had long ago cracked the network of accounts that rich jihadists used to finance terror cells, and the large amount of cash was cause for concern.

"I wouldn't think Jim Green would jeopardize his career for something so juvenile," Joseph said. "He can't wish to be the assistant agent in charge his whole life."

"Yeah, well, some people have a hard time seeing the whole picture. I've got someone working on the phone issue. The doctor might have shut off his work phone, but he doesn't go anywhere without being able to talk to his mistress."

"That's pretty slick, Renee."

"I try." Her phone rang, interrupting the conversation.

The caller ID read "Blocked number," which told her it was coming from a secure line. She knew immediately it was her contact in the NSA, a fellow Southerner whom she'd first met in Somalia.

"What's up, Sammy? Tell me you have good news."

"Yeah, I have the phone. He's on the freeway heading for the airport."

"I need to know where he's going."

"Well, I can't tell you that, I'm not a mind reader. Hold on." The muffled rustling on the other end told her he had placed his hand over the phone. Despite his attempt to block the receiver she could hear someone else talking in the background.

"Renee, he's getting a call on another line. We're trying to triangulate it right now."

"I need that phone."

She could hear a flurry of keystrokes and then another muted voice was talking in the background. "All right, I've got audio, just stand by for a second."

Renee pulled onto the freeway and headed toward the airport.

"Okay, he's off the phone and headed to 976 Mayweather. It's a parking garage just south of the freeway."

They were ten minutes out from the meet-up. Renee pulled over on the side of the road and had Joseph take the driver's seat so she could get her camera ready.

Renee plugged the address into the SUV's GPS and Joseph followed the red line right to a bunch of warehouses behind the airport. No matter what country she found herself in, it always seemed to get shitty around the airports. Renee checked the focus on the camera's lens as Joseph pulled onto a side street about a block south of the parking garage.

She got out and stood on the corner of the street. Through the camera she could clearly see the entrance. But once the targets went inside she'd be blind.

"I need a better spot," she muttered.

The target had picked a perfect place to conduct countersurveillance, and it was impossible for her to see anything from where she was. The parking garage dominated the high ground and had an excellent field of view of the only access road. Renee knew that if they left the concealment of the side street, they'd be caught out in the open.

There wasn't any time to move the Jeep.

"Do you want me to move or not?"

"Just hold on," she said.

Joseph was keyed up. Maybe it was the fight with his wife or maybe he was just tired, but the usually implacable agent was on edge. Surveillance was a passive art and required patience and proper positioning. His boss's chicken-shit move had cost them the positioning, and Joseph was straining her patience.

"There's Dr. Keating's car," Joseph said as a black BMW pulled into the lot.

Renee lifted her trusty Nikon and snapped a few shots of the car and the plate as it flew into the garage. The camera's sturdy black housing was dinged and scratched from countless operations around the Mideast, but it was still as functional as it had been the day she bought it. It was her safety blanket and one of her only real possessions.

She checked the images on the digital display just as a Chevy Malibu crept down the street and pulled into the target location. Renee knew she had to move or risk missing the meeting.

"This spot isn't going to work. Keep your radio on and don't do anything until I get back," she told Joseph.

Something told her not to leave Joseph by himself. The man was a solid partner and had spent his time in the shit, but she had a feeling he'd gotten sloppy since coming back from the Mideast.

But Renee knew she couldn't worry about him right now. She just didn't have any more time to dick around. She found an alley ten feet behind the Jeep and sprinted to the first fire escape she saw. Slipping the camera strap over her head, she jumped for the bottom rung of the metal ladder. It creaked under her weight but held as she pulled herself up. She scrambled up to an open window and slipped inside.

The building's interior smelled worse than the alley. The floors and exposed metal beams were covered in pigeon shit and a fine layer of dust, and insulation covered everything that hadn't already been looted. But a grimy window on the north side provided her an excellent vantage point on the garage.

Making sure that her shadow didn't flare across the glass, she took her position and brought the garage into focus. Once she was set, she slipped an earpiece into her ear and hit the transmit button on her radio.

"I'm good."

"Okay," Joseph replied.

The meeting was on the third level of the four-story garage. Two cars were pulled into the shadows, but the Nikon was set up for low-light shots and she could see everything despite the darkness.

She snapped a string of shots before giving Joseph an update. "I've got three guys pulling security, plus the two targets."

The three men had the swagger of ex-military. They were dressed in civilian clothes, but to the trained eye, it was just another uniform. Each man wore the huge Suunto watch loved by Special Ops troops. The watches were made in Finland and had replaced the coveted Rolexes of the Vietnam era.

Her target, Decklin, was dressed in a tailored suit and looked nothing like the Department of the Army photo that was in the database. He'd changed a lot since being bounced from the military and graduating from being a thug for hire to running his own team of ex-soldiers who sold their skills to the highest bidder.

The man got around, that was for sure, but what her boss back in Afghanistan needed to know was why he was here. Her team had lost him two weeks ago in Pakistan, and it had been a stroke of luck that the NSA had picked him up making a call in northern Mali before catching a flight to the States.

His dark beard and olive complexion gave him the illusion of respectability that his file adamantly contradicted. The man had a nasty reputation and the ability to move almost invisibly from one continent to the next. They called him the Ghost, and the nickname, like his reputation, was well earned.

Zooming in with the camera, Renee saw Decklin hand the doctor a bulging manila envelope and stand patiently as Keating counted the money inside. Zooming in with the camera, Renee saw that it was *a lot* of cash. He didn't trust the doctor, and like most men in the business, he paid half at order and half on delivery.

The doctor stuffed the envelope in his pocket and then popped the trunk of his BMW with his key fob. He lifted a heavy black Pelican case out and, after closing the trunk, laid it on the car. He popped the latches and opened the lid, revealing a row of silver stainless steel tubes.

"Package is in the open."

"How many does he have?"

"Looks like five or six."

"That's too many, we can't let them leave," Joseph said.

Renee heard the growing concern in her partner's voice, but their orders were clear. "We're not here for that. I need you to stay put," she warned.

The radio was silent.

"Joseph, do you copy?"

Through the camera she could see that the meeting was wrapping up. Decklin handed the case to one of his men and was shaking the doctor's hand when Renee noticed a subtle shift in his body language.

His posture became rigid, and his hand moved up to his head as if to tuck his hair behind his ear. It was an awkward movement and it didn't fit.

"What are you doing?" Renee said to herself.

She held her breath and waited.

Decklin's carefree attitude had been replaced by a military concentration. Something was wrong.

Focusing in on his ear, Renee discovered a small earpiece just as Decklin turned and looked toward where the Jeep was parked. She knew he couldn't see anything from the garage, but somehow they'd been compromised.

Renee ducked out of the window. Had someone seen her?

"Joseph, there's someone watching," she said as she leaned out with the camera and began scanning the garage for a spotter.

The radio was silent.

"Joseph, I need you to respond."

Her heart began beating faster as she scanned the top of the garage. The gray concrete whizzed through the lens like a landscape from a moving car. She was still waiting for Joseph's reply when she found the sniper.

He was laid out on the top floor near the shedlike roof access. If Renee hadn't been actively searching for him, she'd never have found his position. It was only the years of real-world combat experience that made her give the awkward outline a second glance.

"Sniper on the roof, northeast corner," she called out dutifully.

It had been a good five seconds since her last transmission and still the radio was quiet.

"Say again, I dropped the radio," Joseph finally said breathlessly.

"There is a sniper on the roof. Something alerted Decklin and the package is on the move."

"What?"

Something about his succinct reply had a guilty edge to it that Renee couldn't miss. "Joseph, what did you do?"

Renee watched the doctor's BMW pull out of its parking space and head for the exit. Decklin was a picture of indifference as he lowered himself into his car and closed the door. His reverse lights lit up the gloomy interior of the garage as Renee lowered the camera and backed away from the window.

"What the hell did you do?" she demanded, slipping out the window and onto the fire escape.

"I can see the target's car coming out of the garage," Joseph said, ignoring her question.

Renee slid down the ladder and dropped the four feet into the alley. The jolt from the short fall stung her feet like a thousand needles. It reminded her of when she was a kid and had "practiced" flying by jumping off the swings at school.

Coming around the corner, she realized that the Jeep had been moved. It was almost to the edge of the alley now and they had seen it.

She hopped into the backseat and snatched up the laptop that lay on the floor.

"What the hell did you do?" she demanded as she connected the camera to the laptop with a USB cable. "Why did you move the truck? Are you out of your mind?"

"I needed to be able to see," he said, looking at her in the rearview mirror.

Renee connected with the satellite uplink and began transferring the pictures to the secure server. She was fuming but needed to stay professional. As soon as her boss, General Swift, got the intel, her job in the States was over. She just hoped that Joseph's momentary lack of judgment hadn't spooked Decklin.

A small window told her the link was established, and she quickly typed out a message and sent the intelligence packet to Afghanistan. Renee was about to close out the computer when Joseph started the Jeep and put it in drive.

"What are you doing?" she demanded.

Looking up, she saw the doctor's BMW pull out onto the street. Decklin's Malibu was right behind it, but instead of following Keating, her target went left.

Joseph waited a few seconds and then pulled out after Decklin.

"Your mission is over. We've already had a soft compromise, do not follow them," she ordered.

"I've got my own orders," he said. "Jim just finished briefing the director, and he says that shit doesn't leave the city."

She wasn't surprised that the assistant station chief wasn't truly in charge. But this was bullshit.

The Malibu was three hundred meters ahead of them, and the engine roared as he mashed the gas to catch up. Renee held on to the headrest of the front seat. Through the windshield she watched the Malibu take a sharp right turn at the next intersection. Joseph was driving too aggressively to simply be tailing it.

He took the turn angrily and the sound of metal hitting the door drew her attention to the HK MP7 that lay on the backseat.

"You're too close, they are going to see you," she yelled at him.

He ignored her and lifted a radio from the center console. "We're moving north on Seventh Street. The target is in a dark Chevy Malibu."

"Check. We are moving to intercept."

"Holy shit, you guys planned this?" Renee couldn't believe it. They had pulled the surveillance package on purpose.

"Look, I would have told you, but since you guys aren't sharing all the intel, we had to make a move. There is no way we can let that shit get out on the street. There is no way we can track a nerve agent once it leaves the country."

"Joseph, listen to me, you do not want to fuck with these guys. Just stop the car, I can have Swift talk to your people," she begged.

"Not my call," he replied.

The Malibu slowed ahead of them and took the next turn gently.

She knew they were heading into the industrial center by the appearance of overgrown lots and dilapidated warehouses that had appeared almost out of nowhere.

It was the perfect place for an ambush.

"He's leading you into a trap," she said simply.

"We have agents all over the place. Your friend Decklin is about to get his ass shot off."

Renee slipped her pistol out of its holster. She seriously doubted what he was saying.

"Westbound on Third Street," Joseph relayed over the radio.

"Check, two minutes out," the voice replied.

"Joseph, it's not too late, just let him go."

The Malibu suddenly accelerated, cutting wide like it was about to head southbound.

"They are heading south on—" he yelled.

He couldn't see the sign and had to drop the radio to try to maneuver the car to continue pursuing.

"Repeat street name?" the voice asked over the radio.

Joseph hit the gas and turned the wheel, but at the last moment he watched the Malibu pull a hard left to cut back across the lane.

"Shit."

The Jeep was out of position. Renee reached for her seat belt as Joseph hit the brakes and pulled the wheel hard to the left. The back end began to slide out from under them as he punched the gas to get traction.

Renee caught a hint of movement out of her peripheral vision and turned her head in time to see the grille of a white panel van bearing down on them.

It hit the side of the Jeep and sent it spinning across the intersection. The impact knocked her across the backseat and into the door frame. The rear window exploded, showering the leather upholstery with tempered glass. Renee's head bounced off the passenger-side door, causing her vision to blur as the SUV was spun around a hundred and eighty degrees. She smelled cordite from the airbag deploying and heard Joseph grunt in pain. There was an overpowering smell of burned rubber and smoldering wires, and then everything went black.

She came to gradually. One by one her senses came back online. Renee smelled something burning and then she tasted blood in her mouth. Her brain told her it tasted like copper, but she still couldn't see.

She struggled to place the persistent dinging coming from someplace outside of her head. There was a burned, caustic smell in the air; the last time this had happened she'd just hit an IED in Ramadi.

Her eyes fluttered open. She was lying on the floorboards between the front and rear seats. Something hard dug into her back, and being jammed down in the floor made it almost impossible to shift away from the pressure.

Turning on her side, she felt the friction from the rough carpet burn her exposed skin. The movement sent a shard of pain through the back of her skull. Ignoring the screaming protest of her shoulder, she dug behind her until her hand closed around the butt of her SIG P226. A few tugs and it was free.

A tiny voice was yelling frantically from the mangled front seat. Renee collapsed onto her back, pistol in hand, and looking up into the front seat, she saw Joseph lying still against the steering wheel.

He was bleeding heavily.

A shadow appeared at his window. Renee struggled to focus and then the window exploded as the muzzle of an M4 punched through the glass. Her pistol came up, guided by the primitive part of her brain, and she fired two shots from her place on the floor.

She heard the man grunt as blood misted onto the spiderwebbed windshield. Reaching above her head and grabbing the latch, Renee pushed the door open with her head. The fresh air felt good as she twisted herself onto her stomach and clawed her way out of the Jeep.

A burst of rifle fire hit the Jeep like a handful of gravel being thrown against an aluminum building. She struggled to her feet as what was left of the windshield exploded into the air.

Renee wavered on her feet like a reed caught in a strong wind. Time was slowing down and the events unfolding around her were surreally disconnected. The gossamer fragments of glass danced in the streetlight as the steam from the Jeep's disabled radiator coiled skyward.

The Malibu screeched to a halt fifteen feet from her position, and the doors were flung open before the car was even in park. Renee brought her pistol up. The sight picture danced in front of her eyes, but she fired five quick shots into the car before retreating behind the SUV.

Stumbling over her feet, she fell to her knees. She turned awkwardly and fired again before the slide locked back on the empty magazine.

Dropping the magazine, she got to her feet and conducted a mag change without thinking.

Renee's training had taken over the moment she fired the first bullet. She was reacting without actively thinking, and it saved her life. Her head throbbed and her vision spun with each movement, but she wasn't going to die here. Taking a knee, she called to Joseph one more time. If the amount of fire pouring into the truck hadn't pulled him back to consciousness, then she assumed he was dead.

Looking back down the road, she saw the edge of a building that would give her cover. Renee knew she could make it, but she refused to leave Joseph behind.

Coming up to a crouch, she held the pistol at the ready as she cut the angle between her position and the van, which sat disabled on her left side. She stepped out and immediately saw a man crawling away from Joseph's door. His right arm hung awkwardly across his chest, while the muzzle of his M4 dragged on the ground.

She fired a single shot to the head and he went limp. Once her target was out of the fight, she was looking for the next one. Scanning over the sights, she moved forward at a crouch. A head appeared in the space between the two vehicles and she fired twice. The first round went wide, but the second hit her target in the shoulder and he spun out of her line of sight.

Knowing the .40-caliber rounds could punch through the van's thin exterior, she fired four more shots. Each round hit at chest level, with a three-inch space between them. She transitioned back to the Malibu, got an acceptable sight picture, and fired at one of Decklin's men before scooping up the rifle in her left hand.

Renee brought the M4 up and laid the rails across her right arm. Still holding the pistol in her right hand, she fired to see if the weapon was working. Before the round was ejected, she holstered up and grabbed the door handle.

It was hard work juggling the rifle and trying to wrench open the twisted door, but she managed to get it open and quickly yanked Joseph out of the driver's seat.

Something hard hit her in the chest and she stumbled back, leaving Joseph on the ground, as she lost her grip on the rifle. She was off balance and tumbled to the ground with a sharp jolt. Struggling for breath from the impact of the round, Renee scrambled for the rifle and hoped the trauma plate she'd added to her soft vest had been worth the extra bulk.

She heard screeching tires off to her left and a few quick gunshots filled the air as her fingers closed around the rifle's pistol grip. Renee grabbed Joseph by the collar and dug her feet into the ground as she pulled him toward the rear of the Jeep.

The volume of fire picked up to her front and she could hear the staccato bursts echoing around her as the shooters blasted away on full auto. Looking over her shoulder, she estimated there were two feet until she was in the relative safety of the back of the Jeep. Her breath came in ragged gasps as she dragged her partner's dead weight along the asphalt.

Ignoring the slamming doors, rifle fire, and screeching tires, she got him around the corner and collapsed in exhaustion. Renee heard sirens in the distance as she let go of the rifle and sat up to check for a pulse.

The side of Joseph's head was bleeding badly and there was a long jagged cut on his forehead. Two small holes in his chest had stained his shirt a deep crimson and despite the fact that she couldn't find a pulse, Renee began CPR.

"Friendlies," a voice yelled as she began rescue breathing.

A man appeared around the corner with a rifle at the ready. As soon as he saw Renee, he lowered his weapon and yelled, "I found them, get an ambulance."

She ignored him and the men who followed as she tried to save her partner. It wasn't until an EMT arrived on scene and they forcibly pulled her away from Joseph that she stopped trying to save his life.

CHAPTER 4

Cage strode purposefully to his office, trying to keep a calm exterior as Simmons spoke quickly from his right side.

"I don't have all the particulars right now, I just know he isn't dead," he said, reaching for the door to their office and pulling it open for his boss.

Cage smiled at his secretary, noticing the boxes still on her desk, and said, "Bess, I thought I told you to make sure you got out of here for lunch."

"Yes, sir, but there's so much to do. Secretary Collins has already called twice."

"We can worry about him later; go get yourself something to eat. I don't want to be blamed for not giving you enough time to plan your wedding."

Bess blushed, but Cage raised his hand disarmingly.

"I'm serious. Why don't you see if that fiancé of yours has time to buy you something to eat? The office will be here when you get back."

His secretary's eyes lit up as she snatched her purse out of the drawer and stood. "Are you sure?"

"Yes, ma'am, I'll see you around one, and don't worry, I'll call the secretary before you get back," he lied.

The two men walked into his office, and by the time he got to his desk, Cage was already loosening the tie around his neck.

"Close the door," he said, switching his cell phone off and tossing it on the desk.

Simmons ensured that Bess was heading out of the office before closing the door behind him, and when he turned to face his boss, it was as if a different man had appeared in the room.

Cage had his jacket off, and the starched white shirt strained against the muscles of his chest and arms. He might have been fifty, but the man was still just as built as the day he left the army.

"What the fuck is the problem?" he demanded as Simmons took a seat on one of the chairs.

"Sir, I have—"

"Jacob, don't start. If you can't handle those dumbasses in Bagram, then I will."

"Yes, sir, but—"

"Don't talk, listen," Cage said, getting to his feet.

Simmons had been with Cage long enough to realize that his boss was back in military mode, and it was more than obvious that he was pissed.

"How hard is it to kill one fucking man? We have the most advanced military in the world, with every intelligence asset at our fingertips, and those dumbasses can't put one man in the dirt. Tell me how the fuck this is happening."

"Sir, reports on the ground are saying that he slipped the ambush and then went to Morocco."

"He doesn't leave Morocco alive, do you understand me?"

"Yes, sir, I will let them know."

"Jesus, no wonder we are losing the fucking war," he said, moving to the window.

"Duke, what are we going to do about Collins?"

"Don't worry about him—that's my job. I need you to do what

you do best: collect intelligence and prosecute targets. If we can't get those inept motherfuckers to execute the plan that I put together, then taking care of Collins is going to be the least of our problems. What does the timetable look like?"

"There was a slight hiccup at the handoff; apparently someone at the DoD is having problems following orders."

"What happened?"

"They tried to grab the package and got their asses shot off."

"Is it going to come back on us?"

"No, sir, I know a guy with the local news. He wrote the story up as a narcotics operation gone wrong. Local PD is going to play ball, so there is no blowback on us."

"Who's taking point on the cleanup operation?"

"A guy named Green; he's the assistant agent in charge or some shit like that. He's clueless; the man couldn't find his asshole with two hands and a map. Duke, it's covered. Trust me."

"So what happens now?"

"Decklin gets the case out of the country, and the DoD will get the FBI to hit the doctor's. It will be a routine warrant, but the doctor will be taken out during the operation. It's too easy."

"Is that everything?"

Simmons hesitated before getting up, and Duke caught it.

"What else?"

"Sir, it's just a hunch, but—"

"Jesus, Jacob, I've got work to do, just spit it out."

"It's General Swift. I don't think he's going to play ball."

"Are you worried about him, or are you worried about yourself?" Duke asked honestly.

"Duke, you know I'm good to go, but I don't think the old man has it in him."

"Let me handle that. Swift will get in line, or he will be put in line. Trust me, it's going to work out."

"Yes, sir." Jacob smiled and headed for the door as Duke picked up the phone and dialed a number from memory.

"Nantz, it's Duke. The package is on the way to Barnes." He paused, listening to the man on the other end of the line. "Yes, I understand, but I need you to do something. Have the team test the gas. I want to see what Swift does."

CHAPTER 5

-------------------- California

The EMT had told Renee that she might have a concussion, but she had declined a ride to the local emergency room. She finally got back to her hotel room at three o'clock in the morning. Tossing the room key on the table, she set her camera and blood-spattered computer on the bed before heading over to the minibar.

The blood under her nails appeared dark brown in the light cast by the small refrigerator as she bent down to grab an airplane-sized bottle of vodka. Sparks of pain radiated out from the back of her skull as she stood upright. It hurt like hell, but the dizziness wasn't that bad.

She downed the bottle in one long gulp, hoping it would dull the pain. She was tired and looked longingly at the king-sized bed and inviting pillows but remembered an instructor in North Carolina telling her that she could sleep when she was dead.

She knew she still had more in the tank, so she tore her gaze from the bed.

Sliding the holster and pistol off her belt, she placed them next to the camera and laptop already resting on the bed. She pulled the bloodstained blouse over her head, tossed it in the trash, and headed to the bathroom.

Renee flipped on the light and turned the shower on full blast.

The mirror fogged from the steam of the hot shower, and Renee wiped her hand across the glass to see herself.

Gingerly she touched the bruise forming on her sternum. The dark red and blue welt was getting darker between her well-formed breasts, and it hurt to touch. The trauma plate had saved her life and she knew it.

"You look like shit," she said to her reflection.

Renee had been forced to learn doggedness at an early age just to keep up with everyone else. Looking back, her struggles seemed like such a little thing compared to where she was now, but back then, having to work twice as hard as everyone else had seemed so unfair.

Her mother had always told her she could do whatever she wanted as long as she was willing to work for it. While her father and brothers played outside, romping in the yard, she would watch them through the window as she sat at the table, drowning in schoolwork, just trying to keep up with her classes. She was a prisoner of her own weakness, and she swore that one day nothing would keep her down.

In third grade Renee's mom had gotten her a tutor named Maleeha. She was a middle-aged Pakistani whose husband worked at her mother's real estate company, and Renee was fascinated with the stories of her home. This was her first exposure to a life outside of Mississippi, and it was intoxicating. She would rush through her schoolwork and spend the rest of the time trying to learn Pashto from her tutor, a skill that would bear fruit later in life.

The day she arrived at basic training, Renee had been like an uncut jewel, waiting for the master's hand. Her drill sergeants had chipped away at the rough edges and smoothed and refined her strengths until she was polished and tightly anchored in her new setting.

Renee's first duty assignment was in PsyOps, where the time she had spent with Maleeha gave her a unique insight into the mind of women in the Mideast. The army was struggling to find a niche for women in the Special Operations community by setting up the

Lioness Program, which attached women to Special Forces teams in Iraq and Afghanistan. Renee had been in the army for less than nine months when she was chosen from a pool of applicants to try out.

She breezed through the selection course and soon found herself deployed, but it wasn't what she'd expected. The grizzled Green Berets viewed her as a burden, which she hated, and only used her when they had to. So Renee set out to make herself indispensable. Her halting grasp of Pashto allowed her to talk to the women in southern Afghanistan without a male being present, and she soon developed a rapport with the women of the region. Before long she had a network set up that fed her information from the local villages. The wives and mothers who came in contact with the Taliban would tell her anything she wanted to know, and her unit began to make real progress in the area.

When her deployment was over, the army sent her to the language school at Monterey and immersed her in Arabic. It was hard, and she hated every moment of it, but she knew that she had a toehold in a world denied to most women and she wasn't about to give it up.

After graduation, they sent her team to Ramadi, where there was an offensive under way. Despite her previous deployments, she had no frame of reference for her new role at the tip of the spear. The firefights were loud, savage, and in-your-face—like a knife fight in a dark alley. In her new unit, you either carried your weight, or you went home in a bag, and it was too much for many of the women she had graduated with.

Renee was an anomaly. She came alive in the cauldron of Ramadi. The first time she saved a teammate's life, dragging him to safety despite his bulk, everything changed for her. No longer was she a burden; she was now an asset who had proved her worth under fire.

Turning on the sink, she began scrubbing Joseph's blood from her hands and forearms. The manicure she'd gotten the day prior was ruined, proving how frivolous pampering herself really was.

Rinsing her hands filled the stark white basin of the sink with a rust-colored mixture of dried blood and soap. She reflected on the dead bodies, empty hotel rooms, and sand-filled tents as she dried her hands on the plush hotel towel. Death and loneliness were all she had.

Stepping into the shower, Renee was able to relax for the first time in hours. The cream-colored shower curtain acted as a shield from reality, and she'd happily have stayed in there for the rest of her life if she could have. She washed her hair and used the bar of soap to clean her body. Stepping back out of the water, she lifted the horseshoe pendant from between her breasts and used her fingernail to clean bits of dried blood off it.

She'd been told in training that seeing people die would get easier, but it wasn't true. Death left an invisible residue on the soul that no amount of water or booze could ever wipe away.

It was still dark when she woke up at five thirty a.m. Her body was working through the aftershock of yesterday's battle plus too many trips to the minibar to self-medicate. But Renee knew that you can't work out if you don't get out of bed. Dressing quickly, she got a drink of water before heading to the hotel's gym. She hated working out, but she dutifully stepped on the treadmill.

The news played on the flat-screen TV mounted to the wall in front of her. A perfectly groomed anchor was talking about the recent uprisings in Afghanistan. She increased the speed of the treadmill until she was at her seven-minute-mile pace and tried to read the closed captioning scrolling across the bottom of the screen.

American soldiers had unknowingly burned a pile of Korans, and retaliatory bombings and attacks on coalition bases were now on the upswing. Renee looked away and focused on her breathing.

It looked like it was going to be another bloody spring in Afghanistan.

Renee finished her four miles and grabbed a towel to dry the sweat off her face. She left the gym and headed back to her room to get ready for the day. By seven she had eaten and was on her way to the DoD office to grab her stuff.

From the outside, the industrial gray building the DoD was renting stood unobtrusively within the confines of the commercial district. The massive window was coated with a shiny silver veneer that distorted her reflection as she walked toward the main entrance.

Renee looked up at the cameras mounted along the apex of the overhang and felt a momentary jolt of self-consciousness. She scanned her ID at the front door and waited for the electronic lock to click open.

Once inside the foyer, she gave her badge to the security guard, who scanned it before allowing her to walk through the metal detectors. Her pistol caused the machine to light up, and the guard dutifully wanded her with the handheld scanner.

Everyone in the building carries a gun, but the poor security guard still has to go through the motions, she thought.

"You have a good day, ma'am," he said after completing the scan.

"Thank you, Austin," she said, smiling at the middle-aged man.

Her shoes clicked across the shiny marble tile of the lobby as she walked to the bank of elevators. Pushing the call button, Renee waited for the shiny brass doors to slide open before stepping in and pressing the round button for the third floor.

As the elevator gently rose, she looked up at the mirrored ceiling and ran her hands over her hair. She liked the way she looked, but it was a double-edged sword. Being a driven and attractive woman in an all-male world came with its own set of unique problems. If you were too direct, the boys thought you were a bitch, but if you were too sweet, they figured you were a tease. Her last mistake, Jonas, had liked the fact that she was independent, but as soon as it got serious, he wanted her to change. She had cared about him enough to ignore it at first, but if she was going to give up her career, it had to be for someone who accepted her just as she was.

Stepping off the elevator, Renee immediately noticed the usually sedentary office was buzzing with activity.

"What's going on?" she asked the secretary sitting at her desk near the front.

The secretary was a civilian and didn't care about much besides her thirty-minute breaks and being able to talk to her sister on the phone. She shrugged and left Renee to figure it out for herself.

The office space was set up in an open floor plan and was designed to promote productivity and teamwork. The only walls on the floor were made of glass and held a large meeting room to her left and a series of offices to her right. The offices belonged to the station chief and his underlings, and dark venetian blinds provided management with a sense of privacy, while everyone else sat in the open. A giant window took up the entire back wall of the office and framed the breathtaking California morning in floor-to-ceiling glass.

Renee walked over to the desk she had been temporarily assigned and called her boss, General Swift. He was a busy no-nonsense man who got right to the point.

"What the fuck happened?"

"Sir, they went off script, there was nothing I could do."

"Damn it, Renee, you know better than to get pulled into a fucking firefight in an American city. I've got shit going on over here that you wouldn't believe. I don't need another fuckup."

"Yes, sir, I understand."

"So, what's your plan now?"

"I'm going to grab my stuff. I told them to close the airports and train stations last night, and I'm hoping to get a fix on Decklin before he leaves the country."

"Keep me posted and don't fuck this up."

Renee hung up the phone and looked across at the conference room full of people in battle-dress uniform pants and ripstop shirts. They were having a briefing. But before she could join them the assistant agent in charge was staring at her from his desk, obviously pissed.

"Renee, where the fuck are the rest of the photos?"

"Jim, I released everything that was relevant."

"One of my agents is dead and you're still holding out on me?"

"Some of those photos are classified," she said, biting back her anger.

"This is bullshit. You're here to assist us, not get my people killed." He stood up from his desk, his face red with righteous anger. Grabbing a handful of papers off his desk, he shoved them into her hands as he stormed away. "That's the operation plan for today. We're hitting Dr. Keating's house in about an hour. He didn't go to work today and we want to catch him before he leaves the country."

"What about the airports? Did you alert them about my target?"

"Renee, this thing goes both ways. You help me and I help you."

"What does that mean?"

"It means that I passed your request up the chain of command. I thought you were advised of our procedure before you arrived," he said, mocking her.

"With all due respect, sir—"

He cut her off with an open hand. "Look, the doctor is the only lead that we have right now. If you want to come off of any intelligence that you might have, then we might be able to entertain some other options." He stopped in the open area between his office and the conference room and stared down at her.

Jim Green's ability to ignore the fact that his actions, or at least the actions of the people he reported to, had directly contributed to last night's fiasco didn't surprise Renee the way it used to. People wondered why they were losing the war, but Renee knew that despite public promises no one was interested in working together.

"I can assure you that I would hand over any *relevant* intel with or without clearance. Jim, I see what's going on here, and I think it's a huge mistake."

"Renee, I'm out of options. I have a dead agent and three dead bodies that I can't ID. The director wants results and that's what I'm going to give him. You really fucked us on this and now we're cleaning up *your mess*, so you can either show a little gratitude and sit in on the briefing or go pout at your desk. You choose, because I don't care."

Turning before she could answer, he walked into the conference room and pulled up a chair next to the station chief. "She's not going to give us anything else," Jim Green said as Renee walked into the room.

Everyone turned to look as she stood frozen in the doorway. Renee could tell they were already laying the failed operation on her. She knew she should pack up her stuff and leave, but something inside her refused to admit defeat.

The station chief turned in his chair and cast a dark look at her before telling the team leader to continue with the briefing.

Renee slipped into the room and stood with her back against the glass wall. A large picture of the doctor's house had been printed off the Internet and appeared to be the only imagery they were using. Random words and phrases were written haphazardly on the giant whiteboard that the image was taped to; the only thing tactical about the mission was the man with "Tac Commander" written on his shirt.

Renee had been here before. As one of the first women to fight in a Special Ops unit, she was used to the smug egotism that most men wore like suits of armor. She had two strikes against her before ever stepping in the room. The first was the fact that she was a woman in a man's world, and the second was that she was new. No one cared what the "new guy" had to say, especially if it was a woman.

She might not have been welcome, but she still paid attention as J.T., the team leader, briefed the plan. He was dressed in the latest Crye Precision gear, and the five-hundred-dollar outfit had been freshly pressed. The man had his pants bloused over his hiking boots, which made him look like a mall security guard. Renee didn't know the guy, but he looked like a total douche.

"We're going to approach the objective from phase line green." He used his left hand to trace the route on the map, but Renee couldn't see the tiny image and had no idea what street he was referring to. "Once we hit phase line blue we are weapons hot, and the plan is to stop short of the objective and set up an outer cordon. I want the breaching team ready, on my go, to hit the door, and I'll need the red team around the back providing rear security."

Despite the fact that she had actually been *inside* the doctor's house the day prior when she tapped his phones, no one bothered to ask for her input. So she slipped out of the room to call Swift again.

"Jalalabad TOC, Sergeant Wilson speaking. How may I help you, sir or ma'am?" the sergeant on duty at the tactical operations center answered.

"Sergeant Wilson, this is Razor 1 on an unsecured line. I need to speak with General Swift, right now."

"Ma'am, he's not here."

"Where the hell did he go?"

"He's at Bagram, some kind of meeting."

"Shit. I need you to find him and have him call me back. He has the number."

"Yes, ma'am."

The line went dead, and Renee stuffed the phone in her pocket and jogged to the elevator. She jumped into the crowded car, her mind racing as it made its descent.

The elevator settled after completing its four-story trip to the basement, and the doors slid open with a ding. Renee could see that the door to the equipment cage was still open, and she slipped into the secure area with the rest of the agents. She didn't have any gear, but luckily the army had taught her the importance of making friends with the supply and equipment personnel, and Renee always made it her mission to be on a first-name basis with them wherever she went.

While the strike team geared up and checked their weapons, she went straight to the armorer. The entrance to the arms room had a heavy metal door, like a bank vault, which was open. Once the main door was opened, the armorer had another metal half door that prevented people from entering but allowed them to receive weapons and gear that he passed through the open portion.

Renee leaned over the top of the door and peered in. She felt like a mother picking her child up from day care, but instead of a kid, she was trying to get a rifle.

"Hey, Matt, sorry to bother you," she said to the man seated at the metal desk set against the reinforced concrete wall.

"Renee, I hear you had a shitty night," the young, lanky man said as he bounced up from the desk.

"Yeah, I need a rifle for the raid. Can you hook me up?"

"No problem, do you have a requisitions form?"

"Jim Green didn't give me one, he told me to draw something from you."

After last night's shooting, she technically wasn't cleared to go out with the strike team until after her shooting review board. Even though she was in the military, she still had to follow the DoD's policies, but Renee knew there were always ways around the rules.

"I'm not supposed to give anything out without the form, but what the hell, you have the highest security clearance in the building. What do you want?"

"It doesn't matter to me as long as it's been zeroed."

The inside of the armory had a large metal workbench and a red tool chest against the far wall. Every other inch was filled with weapon racks, equipment, and body armor. Matt grabbed a decked-out M4 from the rack and checked to ensure it was unloaded before handing it over.

"I assume you need magazines and ammo too?"

"Please." She pulled the charging handle to the rear, even though he had just shown her the weapon was empty. It was rule number one and had been drilled into her head for the last six years of her life.

The rifle was equipped with an Aimpoint micro battle optic, which looked like a toy but was rugged and extremely light. It could run forever on a single battery, but Renee checked it anyway. She turned the knob all the way up, and after ensuring the bright red dot didn't flicker, she shut it off.

The strike team was loading up and she needed to hurry or they would leave her.

"Is the supply room open?" she asked, knowing she was pushing it.

Renee hated using her feminine wiles to get men to do what she wanted, but there was no way she was sitting this one out. She stuffed the mags into the plate carrier's pouches, which Matt had given her, and then with a look that was a mix between a pout and a promise said, "I need to get a flight suit and a radio too."

"Whatever you need, pretty lady."

"Thanks. If you're still around when I get back, I'll let you buy me a beer."

He blushed and handed over her helmet.

Renee jogged over to the last van and opened the passenger door. Before getting in, she jammed a magazine into the rifle's mag well and racked a round into the chamber. The driver arched his eyebrow as she pulled herself into the seat. "Rough morning?"

Slamming the door closed, she settled her bulky gear into the seat. The driver's name was Steve, and he'd been Joseph's friend and partner for a long time. Renee was glad to be riding with him. "What makes you say that?"

Steve had put in more than his share of "work" for the DoD and truly didn't give a shit anymore. He had three years until retirement and was the most laid-back man at the office.

The cargo door slid open as a squad of agents piled into the back of the van. He gave her a playful nudge on the shoulder as she put the helmet on her head and adjusted her ponytail.

"Don't worry about it. No one worth a shit blames you for what went down."

"Your boss does."

"Like I said, no one *worth a shit*."

He laughed and put the van in drive as Renee turned on her radio. The men in the back were psyching themselves up and basically dicking around as the convoy pulled out of the underground garage and headed for the street.

Renee had been on more operations than she could count, but they had always been with a team she knew and trusted. Nervousness crept coldly up her spine and into her stomach. She didn't know these guys, but she could tell they weren't switched on. If things got bad, Renee knew she would be on her own, with no one to watch her back.

She took a deep breath but couldn't shake the feeling that something bad was just over the horizon. Renee prayed that she was wrong but had learned long ago to trust her gut. She had to be ready for the worst.

CHAPTER 6

Sergeant First Class Jericho Harden was breathing hard by the time he made it to the ridgeline. The air in the Afghan mountains was thin, and the steep terrain made the five-kilometer movement seem like a marathon. He took a knee five meters short of the summit and adjusted his pack. The wide straps were cutting into his shoulders and a familiar tightness was forming at the small of his back.

Sliding the strap off his right shoulder, he dropped the heavy rucksack to the ground and pulled a Nalgene bottle out of the top flap, allowing himself a moment to enjoy the view.

The Hindu Kush Mountains of northeastern Afghanistan were awe-inspiring. As the cool mountain air rushed down from the snowcapped peaks above him and swirled against his sweat-soaked body, he wondered how many men had experienced this view.

He was sweating now but was well aware that his body temperature could drop very quickly out in the open. Replacing the bottle in his pack, he slipped a black fleece skullcap over his head before grabbing his radio and laser range finder. Looking behind him, he ensured that the rest of his men were pulling security before continuing up to the summit.

The night before, the colonel had received the green light on the operation, sending the team into a flurry of action. All the planning and time spent masking their movements had led to this moment, and Harden knew that they were about to show the world that the war was far from over.

The Kunar province lay protected in the shadows of the Hindu Kush Mountains, like a lush jewel nestled in the craggy embrace of some prehistoric god. Harden had listened to his boss, Colonel Barnes, tell of ancient armies broken against its treacherous peaks and impenetrable caves. Many men had lost their lives here, and he had great respect for this sacred place.

The mujahideen had broken the Russians in these mountains and had damn near done the same to the Americans. As Harden crept closer to the flat plateau, his eyes were drawn upward to the indifferent snowcapped peaks that marked the gateway into Pakistan. The treacherous mix of shale and granite crunched beneath his chest and elbows as he crawled closer to the edge and began setting up his equipment.

Taking a small GPS out of his pocket, he hit the power key and waited while it tracked the satellites orbiting in the exosphere. Putting his eye up to the optic, he looked down the steep ledge and into the valley below.

The fuzzy brown squares of the mud compounds came into focus as he twisted the knob on the back of the optic, and a moment later, he could make out the individual bricks of the target house. Two black and white goats tugged at the leaves of a small bush, while smoke rose lazily from the metal chimney.

His enemy had no idea.

Adieb Hakin stepped out of his house, his white headdress blowing in the light breeze. Walking over to the large woodpile stacked against the eastern wall, he grabbed an ancient ax and began splitting logs to feed into his *bukhari* stove. The stove was his family's only source of heat, and for centuries the Kunar region of Afghanistan had supplied the rest of the country with wood for the winter. Smuggling timber was illegal, but like everything else in the country there were ways around that.

He raised the ax high in the air and brought the iron head down on the log, neatly splitting it into two ragged sections. Harden hit a button on the top of the range finder, and the laser quickly calculated the distance.

"Seven hundred meters," he read off the digital display.

Harden lifted the hand mike and depressed the rectangular button on the side.

"Anvil 6, this is Anvil 7, target acquired." He lowered his eyes back to the range finder and gazed across the village, which had been at the base of these mountains for hundreds of years.

Adieb was a Taliban facilitator whose close connection with President Karzai had protected him while he helped kill hundreds of Americans. He was one of the president's untouchables, but Harden's mentor, Colonel Barnes, was about to change all of that. Harden had spent his career hoping for a commander like Barnes, someone who didn't give a shit about the brass and just wanted to win. He knew that his boss could make general one day, if he cared about rank, but Barnes had much higher ambitions.

"Anvil 7, this is Anvil 6, good copy. Stand by." The colonel's voice came across the radio net and Harden unconsciously let his gaze sweep to the far side of the village, where his boss was lying in wait.

Harden read off the coordinates from his GPS before pulling a protein bar out of his cargo pocket. He ripped open the brightly colored wrapper, took a bite, and chewed contentedly as he watched Adieb cut wood. Harden's only complaint was that he wished he hadn't left his water back with his gear. The protein bar tasted like dirt and was sticking to the top of his mouth.

A small cloud of dust appeared out of the east as he used his tongue to unstick the bits of chewed protein from his teeth. Spitting a bit of the bar on the ground, he fiddled with the focus knob, trying to make out the convoy that was speeding along the road.

He waited patiently as the cloud grew, until they were close enough to make out the first Toyota Hilux speeding along the unimproved dirt road. He counted four vehicles in all. Each one had five heavily armed men in the back. As always, the colonel was right.

As the second in command, he was the eyes and ears of the team, and it was a position he swore he'd never give up. He had learned a lot when Mason was Anvil 7, but the man had turned out to be a pussy, and Decklin, well, his time was cut short because he was a fucking psycho. Harden had waited, making the most of his time by learning what not to do from his predecessors. His only goal was to not screw up.

"Anvil 6, Anvil 7, the guests have arrived," he said, stuffing the wrapper back into his pocket.

"Anvil 6, roger that."

The trucks sped into the village and pulled up to the target house. Seven men jumped out and formed a tight perimeter around the first truck. They waited while the short thick man stepped out of the cab, with his famous black head scarf wrapped tight against the cold.

Children appeared out of nowhere and rushed the perimeter. The men stepped forward to stop them, but the squat Taliban commander raised his arms like a benevolent uncle and they stepped out of the way. The children ran to the man and grabbed on to his legs. They didn't care that he was a murderer; in fact, they probably relished it.

The commander made a big show of searching his pockets for something to give them as Adieb slammed his ax into the wizened stump and stepped outside the compound to greet his guests.

"Risk 1, Anvil 6, how copy?" The colonel's voice came over the radio as Harden stared at the most wanted Taliban commander in Afghanistan. The man didn't look like a terrorist as he lifted handfuls of candy out of his pocket and held them just out of reach of the squealing children. Harden didn't give a fuck about these people and shared the common belief that they were all terrorists in one fashion or another.

"Risk 1, go ahead, Anvil 6." The pilot's voice was thin and mechanical as it came over the radio.

Harden knew that the attack aircraft was somewhere in the area even though he couldn't hear it. He kept his eyes glued to the optic and the fat man showering the children with candy.

"Risk 1, I have a priority target at grid." The colonel read off the coordinates Harden had given him and waited for the pilot's reply.

"Good copy, Anvil 6, I'm two minutes out."

Harden knew the pilot had no idea what he was about to bomb, but the colonel had the correct identification codes and the pilot would prosecute the target under the assumption that it had been authorized. Procedure made the military predictable and all too easy to utilize, if you knew how to exploit the inherent technological weaknesses of the "green machine."

"Anvil 7, stand by," the colonel ordered.

He imagined the pilot punching the target grid into the onboard computer that fed the data to the thousand-pound joint direct attack munition attached to the aircraft's wing. The bomb's GPS guidance system would steer the munition down on the target from whatever altitude it was dropped at.

"Anvil 6, Risk 1, bombs away," the pilot said.

"Good copy, Risk 1."

The Taliban commander smiled as the children ripped the wrappers off the candies and stuffed them greedily into their mouths. He was recruiting the next crop of jihadists with a dollar's worth of melted sugar.

Adieb opened his arms wide for the customary embrace as the commander tousled the hair of a young boy and stepped free of the knot of young beggars. They knew he had more candy and ignored the bodyguards who tried to move them out of the way. He was just within reach of his trusted friend when the bomb hit.

The force of the explosion evaporated any evidence of the meeting in a huge flash. A geyser of black smoke and brown earth erupted from the massive crater, and a second later the sound rolled up the mountains until it reached Harden.

Wuuuummphhh.

"Anvil 6, Anvil 7, good bomb," he said over the radio as the inky black cloud rose high in the air.

"Risk 1 copies good bomb. I'm clearing the area, thanks for the work."

"That's what you think," Harden muttered to himself as he looked through the scope at the wreckage below.

"Roger, Risk 1, Anvil Out," Harden said over the radio.

There was nothing left of the trucks or the gate. A dull gray pall of smoke hung over the twisted remains of the compound as the women of the village rushed out to gaze upon the horror. For a brief second, before their plaintive cries rose heavenward, it was perfectly still.

From his perch on the side of the mountain the villagers looked like ants milling around an inverted anthill. While the mothers of the dead children looked for any remains with which they could enshrine their grief, the men gathered in militant knots just a stone's throw away.

Harden turned off the GPS unit and slipped it back into his pocket. Gravel crunched behind him as one of his men moved up to the edge with an M240 Bravo machine gun. At seven hundred meters, the village was well within its range. Swinging the range finder to the north, he saw Colonel Barnes and the rest of the team creeping out of the low ground.

Five minutes later, the colonel came over the radio as Harden forced a pair of earplugs into his ears.

"All Anvil elements, engage," he said simply.

Harden's gunner pulled the M240 onto his shoulder and squeezed off a short burst of 7.62s down into the village. The rounds slammed into the group of men just as a long burst erupted from Barnes's position.

The villagers were caught out in the open as the two gunners took their time raining fire into the village. Every few seconds a single shot from one of their snipers rang out, ensuring that no one made it out of the kill zone.

The rate of fire from the two guns slowed as the last of the villagers crumpled to the ground. A moment after that, the valley lay silent, as if nothing had ever happened.

CHAPTER 7

Mason took the precautions of a hunted man as he walked to the Internet café. He was pushing his luck by staying in the city, but crossing the border wasn't as easy as it used to be. Certain arrangements had to be made before he cleared out.

As he walked, the American used the grimy shop windows to check for tails. He constantly changed direction and cut from one side of the street to the other in an effort to thwart any pursuers.

Slipping between a group of tourists, he moved deeper into the heart of the city, but despite his hypervigilance, his mind began to wander.

His fall from member of the most elite unit in the military to one of the most hunted men in the world had been as sudden as it was final. The years of war had turned his soul callous, and he'd lost the part of him that his friends and family had known. Like many of the men who'd fought nonstop since 2001, he had been changed by horrors civilians would never know.

Mason had been married once, back when he had a chance to be happy. He had met Meg on a flight to North Carolina, and the chance encounter had blossomed into a relationship despite their differences.

He knew he never deserved her, but she supported him when he went through Delta selection, and after he was selected to join the unit, he rewarded her by proposing. She wanted a diamond that wasn't gaudy but was big enough to fill her friends with an innocent amount of envy. They planned a simple wedding in Florida followed by a honeymoon in Hawaii. But it never happened. Before he deployed, they stood before the justice of the peace. Afterward, he promised to make it up to her.

Six months later, when he got back, they went on their Hawaiian honeymoon, but he could never fit the dream wedding into the unit's schedule. The fights started, which surprised them both because they'd never really fought—before the war.

Mason didn't mind sleeping on the couch because, honestly, he didn't sleep much anymore. He promised if she could just hold out a little longer they would be a real family outside the military.

The next deployment to Iraq came four months after the first, and when he came home this time, it was to an empty house and a Post-it note that read, "I can't do this." Every room in the empty house smelled like her, but drinking seemed to help. After signing the divorce papers and putting the house on the market, Mason tried to move on.

He volunteered for the next deployment because he didn't want to stay in the States and figured that at least Iraq would be familiar, but he was wrong about that too. The country he'd left a few months before had imploded along the fractured lines of sectarian violence. The once-annoying insurgency had grown into a violent beast that roamed the cities and streets devouring soldiers and civilians alike.

His wife had been his foundation. She was the light that brought him through the darkness, but now she was gone and he was lost. Worse than being lost, Mason realized that he was a cliché. He was a "Dear John" whose girl had been stolen while he was away. When he slept he dreamed about her fucking some other guy whose hands and mouth touched places he would never see again. His war wasn't in Iraq; it was in the sweaty, twisted sheets of some other man's bed, and it was killing him.

One day he just stopped giving a fuck. Combat was the only thing that got him out of his head. What others called "heroic actions in the line of duty," he called a way out.

Stopping to light a cigarette, he casually scanned the faces milling around him. Nothing stuck out, but he knew better than to ignore his instincts. Making his way up the street, he could see the Internet café perched two blocks north.

On top of the café's roof was an ancient satellite dish whose exposed cables ran to a crudely patched hole in the wall. Inside, a dark-skinned Arab sat behind a small desk covered in cigarette ash and empty cans of Wild Tiger energy drink. Without looking up from the grimy television set, he peeled a cracked square of plastic from a stack and slid it to the American.

Mason looked at the faded number six written on the plastic and walked back through the dense haze of cigarette smoke until he found the assigned terminal. He passed the desk, continuing to the rear of the shop, where he located the exit, before returning to the computer. Taking a seat, he checked his watch and logged in.

The space was jammed with computer terminals and the people sitting in front of them spanned every nationality in the region. Arabs, Africans, and Asians sat side by side, blowing smoke into the air, while chatting over Internet phones in their native languages. It was a chaotic homogenization of culture and technology that was unique to North Africa.

Mason scanned the room as he waited for the computer to boot up. The connection was slow. He'd already been at the computer for a minute.

Being on the run was impossible without a network, and while Mason had been taught to kill in the military, he had learned to survive from his mentor, Ahmed. Like him, the Libyan was a fugitive, and a deep friendship had grown between them. Over the years Mason had been able to repay the man for saving his life, but he never forgot the debt he owed.

The Internet provided a level of ambiguity, but e-mail accounts could be hacked and traced, so he still had to be careful. Obscure chat rooms provided a way to hide in plain sight by using simple codes, and Ahmed had set up a list of such sites, which they rotated to avoid detection.

It had been a week since their last contact and the site Mason logged in to was for Nissan car enthusiasts. The Web page allowed people to chat on various blogs or privately message another member. After typing in his password, Mason composed a quick message explaining his need to get out of the country.

The message was addressed to "gearhead71" and Mason wrote, "I need a new brake job on my old truck and wanted to know a good time to bring it by the shop."

Leaning back in the plastic chair, Mason lit a cigarette as the phone in his pocket chirped. Vernon was making a call.

Mason plugged an earpiece into the cloned phone and, shoving the earbud into his ear, hit the answer button. On the same day he shook Vernon's hand to begin working for him, he'd broken into the spy's apartment and found the cache of burner phones that Vernon rotated sporadically. Mason hadn't had time to clone them all, but luckily the CIA man was lazy and soon tired of rotating the phones, which gave Mason the upper hand.

"Yes," a man's voice answered. Not someone Mason could recognize, but definitely someone in command.

The connection was bad and Mason assumed that whoever was on the other line was using a satellite phone.

"Are you secure?" Vernon asked.

"I wouldn't answer if I wasn't."

Mason leaned forward and closed his eyes against the babble of the room. He didn't recognize the voice, but he was immediately struck by the inherent command of the speaker's tone. This was a man used to giving orders.

"The target made it out of Kona, he's going to Libya."

"Libya." There was a long pause on the line.

"Yes, sir, is that a problem?" Vernon asked hesitantly. He was obviously intimidated by the man on the other end of the line.

"No. Are you sure?"

"Yes, sir, I'm sure. Look, I've released his file to the locals, so there's nothing to worry about. Is everything set on your end?"

"Does he know about me?"

"No, how could he?"

"Because he's a lot smarter than you are."

"Look, he has no idea what's going on. Trust me."

"I find that people who ask for trust are usually the ones who don't deserve it. Send Decklin to deal with him, and tell him not to fuck it up this time."

"Yes, sir, what about the drone?"

"As long as you have done your part, Barnes will take care of the rest."

"I loaded the override software, and the target's itinerary has been forwarded to the colonel."

"Get Decklin to Libya, and take care of this problem," the voice replied.

"Okay, I'll—" The line went dead before Vernon could finish his sentence and a second later the spy ended the connection.

Mason felt a chill creep up his spine as he tried to process the conversation. Obviously Decklin and Vernon were up to something, and it involved Barnes pretty deeply.

He'd heard rumors that his old teammate had sold his soul to the private sector, but it sure sounded like someone was putting the band back together. Decklin had many talents, but his lack of ethics was what made him valuable. There was nothing the man wouldn't do if he thought it would profit him.

Mason had learned this lesson firsthand.

The local intelligence apparatus was a joke, but if Vernon leaked the fact that he was in Morocco, there was no way for him to know who would come out of the shadows for a chance to take him out.

Mason's hand slipped subconsciously to his pistol. The bulge was reassuring but not practical in the tight confines of the Internet café. Checking his watch nervously, he decided to give Ahmed five minutes to reply and then he had to leave.

He lit another cigarette and felt his foot tapping nervously on the chipped concrete floor. Mason strained to see the front door. It was out of sight, hidden just off to his left.

The computer tab blinked suddenly and a small white envelope appeared at the bottom of the screen. He clicked it open and greedily read the message that appeared.

It read, "Can fit you in on Thursday. Do you need a ride home?"

Mason typed, "See you then—need a ride."

He hit the enter button, sending the message, and was about to log off when he saw that Ahmed was typing a reply.

His watch told him he'd been at the computer for six minutes.

The new message popped up at the top of the previous one, and Mason leaned in to read it.

"You're burned, get out now."

Fuck.

Mason quickly logged off the computer and moved to the front of the café. He handed the man the plastic card and turned his back to the desk while the shopkeeper checked the computer for the amount of time Mason had used.

A black sedan cruised slowly past the shop, its windows tinted dark against the sun.

Relax, you're good, he told himself.

The Arab was counting out his change and trying to watch the TV at the same time. He fumbled with the coins, dropping them on the floor with a curse. Outside in the street, the sedan had come to a stop near the curb.

Mason's hand reached for his pistol as a man with a cropped haircut got out of the passenger seat and looked down the street before closing the door behind him.

"Keep the change, my friend, I need to use your toilet anyway," Mason told the man in Arabic.

The shopkeeper handed him the key to the restroom and returned the bills to the register without taking his eyes off the Bollywood remake he was so engrossed in. Mason weaved his way back to the rear, passed the bathroom, and pushed on the back door. It was locked.

"Seriously?" he asked aloud, cursing himself for not checking earlier.

Mason searched for a latch; there wasn't one. The door had to be secured from the outside. He was about to kick it open when he noticed the welds on the door frame.

There was a small recess near the door, partially obscured by an empty crate of wire. Mason moved back to the bathroom, unlocked the door, and flipped on the light. The smell of shit and stale urine poured out, and he checked to see if the man was coming before closing the door and wedging himself behind the crate.

It was a bad spot, but it was all he had. Reaching into his pocket, he pulled out his knife and flipped the blade open with his thumb. Mason ducked down behind the box and prayed the dark corner would conceal him.

I should just shoot this asshole, he thought as a shadow appeared against the wall. He knew the suppressor would be too loud, though, and the last thing he needed was the cops on his back.

The man from the street slipped into his view, his light skin almost glowing against the dark walls. He was well dressed and had the deformed ears of a wrestler. Mason waited as the man slipped a pistol out of his jacket and shot a quick look back toward the computer terminals.

Mason could tell that it was some kind of Beretta knockoff, and that meant the man was local. He just hoped he was poorly trained.

The edges of the man's mouth turned up in a smile as he took a shooting stance in the middle of the door and slowly began to turn the knob with his nonfiring hand. Mason silently rose into a crouch as the door cracked open. With the knife at the ready, he stepped out of the shadows.

He was trying to time it so that he would slip behind the assassin just as the door came open all the way, but his hip gently bumped the crate and the subtle noise gave away his position as he stepped out into the open.

The man stiffened and, with his hand still on the knob, turned toward the sound. Mason brought the knife up, the blade aimed at his spine, but the man was already moving. He missed his spine, but sunk the blade into his back. Yelling in pain, the man turned abruptly as Mason shoved him into the bathroom, losing control of the knife as the pistol arced toward his face.

Mason tried to duck, but he was too close and he felt the jarring blow glance off his scalp. Dazed, the American stumbled backward as blood gushed from the wound. Recovering quickly, Mason got his hand on the man's pistol and forced the slide back with his right hand.

His attacker kneed him in the stomach and Mason gasped for air but managed to weakly hook the man's leg with his heel, trying to force him off balance. Despite the knife stuck in his back, the man easily avoided the trip and sent an awkward cross toward Mason's jaw.

Refusing to let go of the pistol, Mason lowered his head and took the punch on the top of his skull. His attacker cursed and began frantically pulling the trigger, but the weapon refused to fire. Mason took advantage of the fact that his attacker's finger was stuck inside the trigger guard and twisted hard on the pistol. Too late the man tried to free his finger. A second later Mason heard the fragile bones finally snap.

Ignoring the man's curses, he brought his elbow over the top and caught him in the chin. The assassin buckled at the knees and fell hard on his back. Mason heard the blade snap off as the man slammed into the filthy tile floor.

Mason's foot slipped in the pool of blood, but he caught his balance and drove his heel down on the man's throat. The man gurgled and his legs shot out as Mason crushed his windpipe with a sickening crunch.

Panting heavily, he closed the door behind him and checked to ensure his attacker was dead. Rifling through the man's pockets, he grabbed his wallet and phone and moved painfully over to the dirty glass mirror stuck to the wall.

He was bleeding from the gash on his forehead, and the left side of his face was caked in blood. Mason turned back to the corpse and ripped off a section of the man's shirt. Returning to the mirror, he did his best to clean up. He was sure the fight had attracted unwanted attention and he needed to get moving.

The American stepped out of the bathroom, broke the key off in the lock, and slipped his sunglasses on. The frames had been cracked in the fight, and they sat awkwardly on his face as he walked to the front. He had no idea how the man had tracked him to the café and couldn't be sure if any more assassins were waiting for him on the outside.

Mason headed for the front door, pausing for a second to look at the attendant, who had produced a rusted revolver from an open lockbox under the desk. The man's hands shook as he took in the American's savage expression and slowly placed the revolver on the ground.

Mason nodded at the terrified Arab, cracked the front door, and then stepped out into the street. Ducking off into an alley, he pulled out his phone and smashed it beneath his foot. They were tracking him somehow, and he cursed himself for not checking the envelope he'd gotten from Vernon before leaving the café.

"You're getting sloppy," he said to himself as he skimmed through the stack of bills, then paused to light a cigarette.

There was no tracker, and he breathed out a smoke-filled sigh, knowing there was one more thing he needed to do before he could leave town and this was as good a place as any to do it.

The American pulled a small pill case from his pocket. It was the same type found at any pharmacy in the States, except instead of pills, the case held a neat row of SIM cards. He removed the SIM card from the dead man's phone and slipped it into the compartment labeled "Friday." After replacing it with one of his own, he dialed the number to Vernon's work phone.

Mason had been on the ground in Iraq when the military realized the limitless possibilities of cell phone data. When he was in Task Force 120, they had techs attached who would hard-wire into the cell phone towers that the US was putting up all over the country and pull data usage and locations right from the source.

Mason had configured the SIM card to project one of the trunk lines from CIA headquarters in Langley, so when Vernon answered the phone he assumed that he was taking a call from his boss.

"Hello?" he said from across the city.

Mason didn't say anything; there really wasn't a need. As soon as Vernon answered, Mason typed a three-digit code into the phone and hit the send key. The code activated the detonator attached to the small charge in the CIA man's phone.

When the line went dead, Mason knew it was because the phone had just exploded.

CHAPTER 8

Cage's military bearing was the only thing that kept a smile from playing across his face as the DoD analyst worked through his PowerPoint briefing. He waited patiently as the man walked deeper into a trap that no one in the room knew had even been set.

"Mr. President," the man said as he used the small clicker to switch to a slide of the Mideast. "We believe that the conflict in Syria is burning out and that the recent up-swell in violence is simply the last gasps of a movement reaching the limit of its abilities."

"So you are telling me that there is nothing to worry about?" the president asked.

"We believe so, but we are taking steps to ensure the outcome we desire," Collins interjected smugly.

"What in the hell does that mean?" Cage said, unable to contain himself any longer.

"Excuse me?"

"I haven't heard anything that sounds remotely like actionable intelligence, so what exactly are you talking about? I assume that you have someone on the ground giving you real-time information."

"We are using signal intercepts and UAVs to gather intelligence."

"That's not going to be enough, and you know it."

"We have other measures in place," Collins shot back.

"Well, I think everyone would love to hear about them."

Collins looked at the president, hoping his boss would save him, but Bradley seemed to be agreeing with his security advisor.

"Duke's right, I don't think that's going to be enough. What else do you have?"

"We have a program in place that is arming and advising certain elements of the Syrian opposition," the analyst said hesitantly.

"Does the CIA know about this?" Cage demanded.

"This isn't a CIA briefing, it's a DoD brief," Collins interjected. "If you will let him finish, he might just answer all of your questions."

"Just a second, I'd like an answer to that," President Bradley said. "Like I told everyone yesterday, I want a broad approach to these problems. Why aren't you using the CIA?"

"Mr. President, the CIA doesn't have any assets in the region; we do. If we were to bring the Agency into the game at this point all they would do is get in the way," Collins said.

"Now, wait a minute," Director Hollis said from across the table. "My office hasn't been contacted in any way about what is happening in Syria, but I can promise you that arming the Syrian opposition isn't going to help anything, and for the SecDef to infer that we don't have any assets in the area is simply not accurate."

"So the DoD hasn't even bothered to consult the director of the CIA on the situation in Syria? I would think that that would be the first person I would notify. I mean, isn't that their job?" Cage said, waiting for Collins to step into his trap.

"That is exactly our job," the director of the CIA said, shooting a hard glance at Collins.

"I thought that I was perfectly clear about how I wanted these problems handled," the president said. "If we can't work together as a team, then I am going to find someone who can."

Collins bristled under the threat, his eyes narrowing in anger. Cage waited for the president's gaze to shift back to the front of the room before giving the SecDef a wink. Just as he expected, the man's face turned a deep shade of crimson as Cage got to his feet.

"Sir, I agree with you a hundred percent, and I believe I can speak for Director Hollis, who is mandated to handle these types of situations, when I say that we are playing with fire. The SecDef is way out of his depth, and it's going to bite us in the ass, I can promise you that."

"Here we go," Collins muttered.

"Secretary Collins, I think that your appraisal of the situation in the Mideast is as dangerous as it is shortsighted. Who's your man on the ground?"

"That is classified," Collins bellowed.

"Classified? How am I supposed to do my job when you're not sharing intel?" the director interrupted as Cage posted himself at the front of the room.

"Mr. President, if we assume that the violence in Syria isn't going to spill over into Iraq simply because we are giving weapons to a group of lesser terrorists, then we haven't learned anything from our time in Iraq," Cage said, holding up his hand.

He took a laser pointer from the table, pointed it at the screen, and shot a red beam at the border between Iraq and Syria.

"Right now we know that the rebels in Syria are receiving aid from Hezbollah and training from Iran, and that there is a movement building along the border that threatens northern Iraq."

"Mr. President, this is utter nonsense," Collins interjected.

"Is it?" Cage demanded. "Look at the map. In Syria, al-Nusra, a group we know is attached to al-Qaeda, is moving toward the Iraq border, while the Taliban is pouring over the Pakistani border, taking back key terrain in Afghanistan," he said, running the pointer across the map. "What happens if they move into northern Iraq and take Mosul or Kurdistan?"

"We can handle that when and if it happens," Collins shouted.

"You are arming these people while they are opening a route that stretches from Syria to Afghanistan. What the fuck do you think is going to happen?"

"He's right," Hollis echoed from his place at the table.

"This is bullshit, and exactly what I'd expect to hear from someone like you. Someone who wants nothing more than to keep this war going for another ten years," Collins said, getting to his feet.

"I'd love to hear what you think is going on," Cage demanded, baiting the trap he'd been setting since he walked back into the White House.

"Well, if you would let the man finish his brief instead of interrupting, maybe you could."

"Wait, Director Hollis, do you agree with Duke's assessment?" the president asked.

"Absolutely, sir, someone has to fill the vacuum we left when we pulled out of Iraq. This is a huge mistake, a mistake that could have been avoided with a little teamwork."

Collins was visibly shocked by the sudden onslaught and stood awkwardly near his chair. The rest of the National Security Council was obviously intrigued, and the president turned his gaze toward the SecDef in anticipation of his rebuttal.

"Tell me I'm wrong," Cage said simply.

Collins made his way to the front of the room, his analyst taking a step back as his boss took the pointer, and looked up at the map.

Cage smiled inwardly. He had forced the SecDef's hand and now the man had to either put up or shut up.

"Mr. President, I have been told by General Swift in Jalalabad that his men have made contact with the opposition in Syria and have begun setting up training camps with vetted members of the opposition. I do not have all the specifics right now, but I can promise you that everything is under control," he began haltingly.

"I've heard enough," the president said. "I want some answers by tomorrow morning; we can't keep going on like this. Duke, if you don't mind I need a word with you. The rest of you are dismissed."

There was a scuffle of papers and folders being shut as the Security Council grabbed their stuff and headed out of the room. Secretary Collins stood dazed, staring at the president to see if he had to leave as well.

"You too, Collins," Bradley said.

Once the room was clear President Bradley said, "Duke, I don't like this cloak-and-dagger stuff."

"Understood, sir," he replied.

"I want you to make sure the CIA has a handle on what is going on in Syria. I can't afford to be blindsided this early in the game."

"Yes, sir, what do you want me to do?"

"I need you to get to the bottom of this, make sure Collins isn't biting off more than he can chew. Find out what you can about this asset, and bring it right to me."

"Roger that, sir," Cage said as he turned for the door, a smile creeping across his face.

CHAPTER 9

-------------------   California

It took about thirty minutes to navigate their way through the morning traffic and get on the freeway. The communication over the handhelds between the team vehicles was its own traffic. There were so many electric voices that it just turned to static, and for some reason, it made her think of the time her father took her camping after basic training. They had rented a van, and despite feeling carsick, she pretended she was having a good time. All the while her dad tried to get the Ole Miss game tuned in on the ancient radio.

The campsite was near Natchez, Mississippi, a place so different from California that it might as well have been on a different planet. Compared to the pristine cityscape swishing by the raid van's window, the rustic desolation that lined the road of her memory was both depressing and uninspiring.

"So, how's the army?" her father asked, abandoning the static-filled radio with a sigh.

"It's fine; it's not bad now that basic is over." It was rare for them to be alone together, especially now, but Renee was trying to relax and enjoy the time with him even though she knew that the trip was originally planned for her brothers.

"You'll be all right. How hard is it to put a damn antenna out here?" he said, turning on the radio again and fiddling with the dial.

"I have an AM radio in my bag," she offered. "It's an emergency kind that gets a signal anywhere."

"Really?" She could tell he was interested and it made her happy. Renee jumped in the back and grabbed the small radio out of the pack her mom had bought for her. Extending the antenna, she dutifully turned the knob until the game came on.

"Dang, that is better," her dad said, turning off the van's radio and patting her knee with a smile. "You're such a smart girl, you know that?"

Renee smiled as she remembered the feeling of acceptance she had gotten from that pat on her leg.

The radio on her vest came to life, shattering the memory.

"Five minutes," J.T. said.

The men in the back conducted a final check of their weapons and gear and began standing up.

It was almost time.

The convoy turned off the main road and pulled into an upscale residential neighborhood. Renee could see the familiar two-story house appear ahead of them as the commander called, "One minute," over the radio. It sat on a slight incline at the end of the street, dominating the avenue of approach. Any element of surprise was lost the moment they turned on the street.

"That's the house right there." She pointed the target out to Steve, who took his foot off the gas.

"Damn, they're stopping right in the front *yard*," he said as the lead vehicles jumped the curb and began unloading their squads in plain sight.

"Stop here, it's too congested," Renee said.

She'd done this too many times to be nervous, but her instincts were telling her that something bad was about to happen.

Once their van came to a halt, the team jumped out and moved to take up their positions. Renee could see J.T. standing in the open, directing his men over the radio. She counted twenty men, dressed in MultiCam, swarming loosely toward the house. It was a goat rope, and she found herself praying that everything would go according to plan.

J.T. called the breachers up to the door before the cordon was set, and they moved up to the breach point without a security element.

The idea was to hammer the pick into the iron door and once it was open, use the "ram" to breach the wooden door behind it. It was slow, especially when the men didn't work together, and when the ornamental security door was finally forced open, they had been standing in front of the fatal funnel for ten seconds.

The "ram" was a heavy steel cylinder that had handles attached to the top. The breacher was too close to the door and couldn't get any power out of his hips. So the first hit glanced off the sturdy oak door.

"Hit it again," J.T. yelled over the net.

The man took a step back and hit the door right above the knob. The weakest part of the door was the locking mechanism, and the second blow tore it from the door frame with a groan.

The breachers moved off the porch as the point man moved up and tossed a flashbang into the open doorway. Instead of following it in, he waited for it to explode before entering the house.

"Get in there," Renee muttered as she slapped the dashboard in frustration.

They were doing everything possible to give whoever was inside the upper hand. By not "riding the bang" into the house, they had once again failed to grab the momentum.

The team looked rusty and unsure. They needed to be the aggressors, but instead they were waiting. Whatever advantages J.T. had hoped to exploit had been squandered from the moment they pulled up on the objective.

Finally the point man made the decision to push into the house. He made entry, followed by four assaulters. Just as the last man crossed the threshold, though, a massive explosion erupted in the entryway.

The explosion created a vacuum at the breach point, as the over-pressure sought the path of least resistance. The expanding gases hurtled out of the doorway in a ball of black-tinged fire. Renee watched as one of the operators was spat out of the doorway, a mangled heap of disjointed arms and legs.

As the smoke cleared, she could see that the shock wave had knocked the remainder of the assault team off the porch and singed the perfectly manicured azaleas that were planted near the front of the house. Burning wood and crown molding drifted slowly to the ground in the still morning air and then bright yellow muzzle flashes erupted from inside the house.

Windowpanes were punched out on the second floor as muzzles ported the glass and heavy machine-gun fire opened up on the team below.

Renee couldn't believe what she was seeing. Five members of the assault team went down as heavy fire raked over the rest of the team. The radio was useless due to the heavy amount of traffic, and she could hear men yelling for help over the gunfire.

Ignoring the general's warning to act as an observer, she flung open her door and stepped out into the street. Snapping her rifle up toward the house, Renee began firing controlled pairs into the upper window. She shot at the muzzle flashes but was unable to make out the shooters.

"Do we have any smoke?" Renee yelled at Steve, who sat wide-eyed in the front seat, watching the firefight unfold.

He was vapor locked, and Renee had to jump back into the van and punch his shoulder to get his attention.

"Steve, I need you to pay attention."

Shaking off the initial shock, he tried to focus on what she was saying.

"Do we have any smoke? We have to go get those guys."

"I think there's some gas in the back."

"Do something with this while I check." She handed him the rifle before sliding into the cargo area. There were two rows of benches mounted on the thin metal walls of the van, and they hinged open to reveal storage space beneath them.

Renee found some gas masks and medical bags in the first storage bench, and she tossed them on the floor as she opened the second bench. She could hear someone firing in the backyard, but she kept searching until she found a forty-millimeter gas launcher and a row of green ammo cans. Frantically she pulled each can up so she could read the label and dropped them back into a heap until she found one marked "CS."

The launcher looked like a huge revolver with a buttstock attached, and Renee snapped the breech open and began feeding munitions into the black cylinder. There were five chambers, and after she filled each one she locked the breech closed.

Taking a second to pull a mask over her head, she tugged down on the black straps until they were tight and placed her palm flat on the filter. Renee sucked in to ensure she had an airtight seal. She didn't want to gas herself, especially since the bulky mask already cut down on her field of view. Sliding the left door open, she hopped out of the van and moved up behind Steve, who was shooting over the hood.

Tapping him on the back, she grabbed her rifle before handing him a mask. A man appeared in the burned-out doorway of the house and tossed a grenade at the agents in the front yard. The frag went off with a deep boom ten feet from where J.T. was hunkered on the ground. The explosion sent clods of dirt and grass showering down on him, but still he refused to move.

Once Steve had his mask on, Renee grabbed his shoulder and pulled him close. "I'm going to deploy the gas and then we go," she yelled through the thick filter.

Her voice was muffled, but he nodded and hopped back into the driver's seat while she brought the launcher up to fire. Unable to see the sight, Renee estimated the range and fired the first gas canister at the front door. The propellant from the munition left a white trail as it arced toward the target, but the round hit high above the door and bounced out into the grass.

Adjusting her aim, she fired the next round right through the doorway. The munition struck the shooter in the chest as he raised his rifle to fire on the van and backed him into the house.

Renee shifted fire to the second story, arcing two more rounds into the shattered windows. She knew there were only two more canisters left and decided to put them into the grass at the front of the house before jumping into the van.

Steve shifted into drive as the caustic white smoke began rising from the ground. Renee barely had time to get set before he floored it.

Steve picked a spot between the house and the downed men, while Renee fought to close the right-side door the team had left open after jumping from the van. When he hit the brakes, she lost her balance and tumbled to the floor. The stock of her rifle hit her in the side of the face, knocking the mask loose and breaking the seal.

Renee could feel the gas slipping into her mask as she jumped from the van. As it wafted past the broken seal, it got trapped inside the mask and immediately attacked the sensitive mucous membranes of her tear ducts. Her eyes shut involuntarily against the pain. *It's not called tear gas for nothing*, she thought as her lungs began to burn.

Grabbing the closest man by the casualty evac strap sewn into his heavy vest, she dragged him to the van. She fought the overwhelming urge to vomit as the gas slipped down her throat. Renee felt her tendons straining and she was very cognizant that she could rip her bicep if she wasn't careful. Ignoring the pain, she continued pulling him toward the van, until Steve appeared and effortlessly relieved her.

Taking a moment to clear the mask, Renee held her breath before resealing it over her face. Once the tear gas made contact with her skin, it deposited the activated crystals, which fed off the sweat running into her eyes. The molten liquid found its way into her pores and burned like acid.

The wounded in the van reverted to survival mode instead of

helping their teammates get to safety. They fought over the extra masks like a bunch of children while another round of gunfire poured from inside the house. Wisps of black smoke were beginning to rise from the roof of the structure, and Renee realized that the munitions had started a fire.

I've got to get to the doc.

Her lungs were heavy as she ran to the edge of the house. Each breath was more difficult to catch than the one before, and her eyes were watering heavily. Renee slipped up behind what was supposed to be the perimeter team. The men had their backs to her and were struggling to pull their masks tight over their heads.

Renee was surprised that they had actually brought their masks, since the rest of the team couldn't be bothered with the extra kit. She reached up and squeezed the rearmost man on the shoulder to alert him of her presence. His body tensed under her light grip, and he turned awkwardly to see who had gotten behind him. If the situation hadn't been so grave, it would have been comical. The bulky mask robbed him of his peripheral vision, so much so that he was forced to turn his entire body to see over his shoulder. It was as if the mask had made his neck immovable.

Renee noticed the fear in the man's eyes and gave him a second to compose himself. The situation sucked and she could see that he had already checked out mentally. Using rudimentary hand signs, she motioned that she was going to move around to get a better look. But the agent shook his head vigorously and signaled for her to stay put.

Renee shoved him out of her way and moved up to the lead man, who was posted at the corner. The smell of smoke made its way past her filter, and she knew they were about to lose any chance of getting the doctor out alive.

"Are you going to do something or just stand here?" she yelled into his ear. Her voice was muffled and ragged under the gas mask. The agent had to lean his head back to hear, and when he shouted back at her, Renee had no idea what he was saying.

There was no point in talking. She was about to push him out of the way when he brought his muzzle up and turned back to his sector. Renee squeezed the back of his arm, letting him know she was ready, and waited for him to take the lead. She prayed he'd been paying attention while pulling security on the backyard, because she needed to trust him to lead her in.

Hugging the wall, they moved around the corner and toward the back door. Between the windows and the yard, there were too many angles for the two of them to cover. The threat could come from anywhere and it was her responsibility to cover the point man.

She was placing her life in the hands of a stranger.

Renee wanted to take the mask off. It made it impossible to get a good sight picture because she couldn't get her cheek to the stock of the rifle. If a threat appeared, she would be point shooting, which was not the preferred method.

The point man stopped suddenly in front of her, and his rifle locked on to a tree ten meters to their right. Slowly a member of the security element peeked out from behind the giant oak. He moved out just enough to get their attention but refused to leave the cover of the large tree.

She could see the bodies of two of his teammates lying motionless on their faces near the cover. The man made no attempt to help them but slowly raised an outstretched finger toward the second-story window adjacent to Renee. She looked up in time to see the blinds moving, and a barrel appeared, pointing at the tree.

The man ducked out of the way just as three shots splintered through the glass. The rounds sent bark flying off the tree while Renee lined up for a shot. She fought to bring the optic in line with the mask as her point man dropped to the ground. Flicking off the safety with her thumb, she fired a round at the target and cursed as it went wide.

The muzzle began pivoting down to address the new threat, forcing Renee to rip the mask off her face with her left hand. Firing two more rounds in an effort to keep her attacker off balance, she felt the stinging effects of the gas once again.

The gunfire from the window was ineffective, forcing the man to expose his body for a better shot. Renee centered the Aimpoint's dot on his chest and fired again. She allowed the muzzle rise to carry the three-round burst up his chest and watched his head kick back as the final round struck him in the forehead.

Reaching down, she grabbed ahold of her partner's vest and tried to drag him to his feet. They had lost the element of surprise, and she needed to get into the house before the defenders moved to the back. The agent was halfway to his feet and Renee was already pushing him forward. He dug his feet into the ground to halt his forward momentum, forcing Renee to dodge around him.

Snatching a flashbang from the man's kit, she saw the back door a few feet ahead. There was too much of a chance that it was booby-trapped and she just wasn't willing to risk it. Arcing past the door, she tried to steady the rifle on top of the bang she held in her left hand.

There had to be another way in.

Just past the porch, she found the floor-to-ceiling windows of the solarium. Juggling the rifle and the flashbang, she placed the muzzle over her left forearm and pulled the metal pin with her right index finger. Praying the flashbang was heavy enough to breach the plate glass, she hooked the metal munition through the window and into the room.

Renee punched the bottom corner of the window with her muzzle, and the large pane quickly shattered. Ducking her head, she stepped through the makeshift breach and waited for the explosion she knew was soon to follow.

It came in a white-hot flash of light and deep sound. The concussion reverberated off the walls and slammed into her like a kick to the chest. She'd spent years training with live flashbangs being thrown on top of her and knew she had to keep moving. Her body leapt into action on instinct.

Renee could almost hear her CQB instructor yelling the checklist of a proper room entry at her as she moved.

"Hard corner, primary scan . . ." She mirrored each step as she cleared the room.

The tile-lined solarium was empty, but she had a foothold into the house and showed no signs of stopping. Carefully stepping into the hallway, she snapped her rifle to the left. A man stood dazed and her safety came off as she fired center mass. She saw the blood mist onto the wall and was moving to her right before his body hit the ground.

Two doors stood open on either side of the hall. She needed another body but stood alone. There was nowhere for her to hide, and her left hand swept to her belt for the flashbang that wasn't there.

Shit, move.

Renee had learned the basics of CQB at Bragg, but it wasn't until she was sent to the Direct Action Resource Center, or DARC, in Little Rock, Arkansas, that she mastered the lethal art. Under the tutelage of Rich Mason and his Special Operations cadre, the wheat was separated from the chaff.

As heavy metal blasted from speakers attached to the catwalk, they would don their gas masks before entering the blacked-out kill house. Inside, role players armed with Simunitions waited in the shadows to teach them the difference between life and death. Knowing she'd had the best training in the world, she pushed forward.

She was well past the point of no return when she heard a scuffing sound to her right. She crowded the left wall and switched to combat clearing, a technique designed to maximize speed while giving the operator the best chance at survival.

The known threat in the room dictated that she clear that room first, and she dutifully turned her back to an open door. She was playing a numbers game now, weighing risk versus reward. She saw a foot in the corner of the room and was getting ready to take a shot when something slapped her hard in the back. The impact sent her reeling headfirst into the room.

Fighting to keep her rifle up, Renee heard another round zip past her head as she pulled the slack out of the trigger. Knowing she was in a bad spot, she tried to move out of the line of fire without getting hit again.

Fuck!

Renee was a split second away from shooting Dr. Keating in the head, but upon identifying her target, she released the pressure on the trigger.

She felt someone moving into the room behind her, and she turned her head in time to see an AK-47 pointing at her head before three shots punched through the man's chest.

Her unlikely savior appeared in the doorway, his gas mask still covering his face. The man she'd left outside had come in after her, and not a moment too soon.

The fire was raging upstairs and they could hear wood splintering as it was consumed by the blaze. Any second now, the roof would collapse and they'd all be trapped. Renee grabbed hold of the doctor's shirt and dragged him out of the room. Pushing him headfirst through the twisted door frame, she paused to check the pulse of the two mangled agents lying in the entryway hall. They were both dead and from the looks on their faces hadn't felt it.

Outside, the local police had made the scene and secured a wide perimeter as the upper floor of the house caved in. The smoke was dense around the front of the house and Renee pushed the doctor toward the van so they could get some fresh air.

Assistant Agent in Charge Jim Green looked totally defeated as he briefed police commanders and the federal agents who would be handling the investigation from now on. Ambulances carted the wounded off to the hospital as Renee pushed the doctor into the back of the van and slammed the door behind them.

She was sweaty, bleeding, and totally pissed off when she fit a pair of flex cuffs over the doctor's wrists, pulling them tight. Renee knew that it wouldn't be long before the Feds took control of their prisoner; there was no way she was going to retain custody of him after what just happened.

"Listen up, doc, because I'm only going to ask this once. If you lie to me I'm going to shoot you." She slipped the SIG from her chest holster and pointed it between his legs to make sure he got the point. "I want to know everything you have on whatever you sold Decklin two nights ago. You have less than a minute."

Dr. Keating looked over at Steve, expecting him to do something. When it was obvious the agent wasn't going to step in, he tried stalling. Renee's patience was already thin and she didn't have time for his games. She slammed the barrel across the side of his face before hitting him in the throat with the web of her left hand. Using the momentum of the throat strike, she slammed his head hard against the metal interior and squeezed.

"You're going to kill him," Steve said calmly as the doctor's face turned red. Renee knew what she was doing, and after a few seconds she released the hold on his throat. Keating gasped for air and tried coughing his Adam's apple out of the back of his throat.

Holding up his zip-tied hands in submission, the doctor managed to say, "Stop. I'll tell you what I know." Renee slipped the pistol back into its holster and glanced out the front windshield to see if anyone was coming. The scene outside was chaotic and no one was paying them any attention—*yet*.

"I was approached by an intermediary from the CIA about my research involving biologics. I was working on a new delivery system that would transport cellular data to the frontal lobe of the brain—"

"Frontal lobe of the brain? What the fuck are you talking about? The CIA doesn't give a shit about frontal lobes."

"I swear to you that I thought I was working for the government. You have to believe me. The whole situation was very straightforward until it was time to deliver. I was contacted and given instructions to bring the bio agent to the parking garage. That man yesterday gave me the second half of the money and then there was a lot of shooting. I had no idea it was going to be like that. I went home and there were four men waiting for me."

"Who was expecting delivery of the package? Where was it going?"

"I don't know. I swear it."

"You better tell me something if you want to leave here in one piece."

"Please, you have to understand, I thought it was legit. I'm not a bad guy—"

"Doc, save it."

"I heard someone mention a place called Kamdesh. That's all I know."

Renee didn't know if he was lying or not, and there wasn't time to find out, because the door of the van slid open. Jim Green stood there glowering, flanked by three men with "FBI" written across their blue windbreakers.

"Dr. Keating, don't say another word. You are now in the custody of the FBI," one of the agents said.

"Jesus, Renee, do you mind telling me what the hell you think you're doing?" Jim Green exploded as the FBI agent stepped into the van to grab the doctor.

"My job."

"What happened to his face?" one of the special agents asked.

"He fell."

"Cut the shit, Renee. I don't know what game you're playing, but I promise you that when the chief hears about this, you can kiss your career good-bye."

"When the chief hears about what?" a man's voice asked as Renee was stepping out of the van.

Everyone turned to see Chris Thompson, the deputy director of the Defense Intelligence Agency, appear with his aide.

"Sir, this woman is—" Jim Green began.

Chris held up his finger, stopping his subordinate in midsentence. "Gentlemen, I appreciate all of your help, but as you can see we have a great deal of work to do." He offered his hand to the FBI agent and, after a firm handshake, motioned for Renee and Jim to follow him.

"Sir, someone in our office will be in contact with you soon," the FBI agent said.

"Tell your boss that I'm still planning on coming over for dinner tonight, and thank you once again for your help." He continued walking over to a black Tahoe that was parked out of the way of all the commotion. His aide unlocked the truck and went around to the driver's side.

"Sir, I would like to brief you on—"

"Jim, save your breath. I think you've done enough today. It seems to me that you have a situation you need to handle until your replacement relieves you."

"But, sir—"

"Agent Green, shut the fuck up and get out of my face." He watched the crestfallen man walk away before turning to Renee. "I understand you saved a lot of lives today."

"It shouldn't have happened in the first place," she said honestly. The adrenaline rush was fading fast and the last two days caught up with her in a second. She was exhausted. There had been too much death and some of it was her fault.

"Maybe."

Chris opened the door of the Tahoe and motioned for Renee to get in.

The deputy director took a seat next to her and told his aide to drive.

"This fuckup is going to start a huge shit storm, and people are going to want some answers," the deputy director began. "Right now our lawyers are shitting bricks trying to figure out if this little operation was even legal, but that's not what I'm worried about." He paused as the driver navigated his way through the mass of cars parked along the road.

As they got closer to the outer perimeter, Renee could see news vans parked on the perfectly manicured grass of the upscale neighborhood. Their satellite masts were extended, and cameras and reporters were busy trying to beat each other to the scoop as trophy wives and homeowners gossiped and tried to get on TV.

It was a madhouse.

"I want you to know that Joseph was a personal friend of mine. Not many people know that we were partners when he first got the job. I say all of this so you will understand that what happened to him is a very personal matter. That being said, I've been contacted by General Swift, who wants you on a plane as soon as possible."

"Sir, I understand General Swift wants me out of here, but I—" Renee stopped talking as the man next to her raised his hand.

"This isn't negotiable, I'm afraid."

"I understand." She didn't, but it appeared the conversation was over.

The deputy director tossed a manila folder onto her lap and began speaking as she opened the cover.

"Renee, inside that folder is your standard nondisclosure agreement. If you sign it, you get bumped up to the boys' club; if not, then nothing changes. You go back to Afghanistan and get back to work."

Renee scanned the first paragraph before turning to the last page and scrawling her name across the signature line. There was no reason to read the whole thing; she knew what it said, and more importantly what it meant.

Thompson took the folder and stuffed it into his briefcase.

"You ever heard of the Anvil Program?" he asked.

"Rumors mostly," she began, "some black ops unit that Decklin was attached to."

"The Anvil Program is something we inherited from the Bush era, but unlike your run-of-the-mill Special Ops unit, this one was off the books. I'm talking next-level classified."

"So what does this have to do with Decklin and me? I mean, why are you telling me all of this?"

"Two hours after Decklin kills one of my agents, Colonel Barnes, and all his people, walk off the reservation; an hour later every hard drive with any information on the Anvil Program gets wiped out. We have no idea how it happened; all my guys can tell me is that it was an inside job."

"Okay . . . ," Renee said, waiting for the punch line.

"All we have left is this," he said, holding up a thumb drive. Deputy Director Thompson squinted his eyes and looked into the distance. "A man like Barnes doesn't just give up his career unless he's got big plans of his own."

CHAPTER 10

-------------------- **Kamdesh, Nuristan**

The pilot of the Mi-17 kept the helicopter in the fading sun for as long as possible before gaining altitude to clear one of the higher peaks. The Russian helicopter was a relic of the Soviet invasion and until recently had been used to ferry supplies from Kandahar to coalition outposts. A cracked manifold had sent it to the scrap yard, but after a new coat of paint and fresh Afghan army markings, the old warhorse was once again carrying troops into battle.

While the Serbian pilot focused on keeping the ancient helicopter in the air, his copilot kept an eye on the oil gauge. The instrument panel was faded from constant exposure to the Afghan sun, and the glass over the dials was covered with a thick film that partially obscured the white needle inside.

The crew chief's sweaty coveralls smelled of stale vodka as he squeezed past the soldiers lining the thin skin of the helicopter and made his way to the surprisingly neat row of oil cans bungee-corded below the gearbox. A metal can opener hung from a length of grime-coated rope, where it swung gently in front of Colonel Barnes's head. The man grabbed the silver tool in an oil-soaked fist and held it tight against the lid of one of the cans. He applied enough pressure to pop two quick holes in the lid before pouring the contents into the gearbox.

Colonel Barnes closed his faded copy of Marcus Aurelius to avoid the sporadic drops of oil coming from the lines that split off from the gearbox and watched the man toss the can out of the open observation window. He'd paid the crew well to transport his team to the target but would be greatly relieved when they were finally on the ground.

"Colonel, we're five minutes out," the pilot said over the radio in his heavily accented English.

Barnes's rusty Russian was better than the pilot's terrible English, so he had told the man to stick to his native tongue, but the pilot had refused with his trademark toothless smile. The colonel stowed the book in his cargo pocket and leaned forward to get a brief glimpse out of the cockpit.

His team was conducting their final gear checks as they neared the objective, and to his right Harden leaned forward and spat tobacco on the floor of the helicopter. Barnes tapped him on the shoulder and held up five extended fingers. Harden nodded and wiped the dip spit off his lower lip before passing the sign to the rest of the team.

The smell of jet fuel and burned oil filled the stifling confines of the cargo compartment, and as the pilot lowered the ramp, a welcoming flood of fresh air blew over the waiting soldiers. The colonel unplugged his headset from the helicopter's communication jack, switched to the team's internal channel, and checked the black Pelican case that sat on the floor between his legs.

He'd been skeptical that Decklin could deliver the weapon he'd asked for, but the man had proved more resourceful than he'd imagined. The vials of the untraceable nerve agent had arrived a day before they were expected, which gave Barnes the ability to push up his timeline.

It was supposed to be some potent stuff, but Barnes had never been the type to take someone else's word. He needed to see for himself, and that was exactly what he planned to do.

This would be his last operation in Afghanistan, and he planned on making it a memorable one. The war was winding down, and

America was tired of fighting a conflict with no foreseeable end. But as the United States was losing its resolve, the enemy was growing stronger and much more threatening. Men like him, the true believers, had been fighting the jihadists in one country or another since 2001, and there was no way they were giving up because the American people were losing focus.

The colonel had been given greater latitude to prosecute the fight than any man before him, but it would never be enough to win. He lived by the Clausewitz motto: "You must pursue one great decisive aim with force and determination."

Barnes was about to show everyone the depth of his determination, especially that piece of shit Karzai. Fate might have chosen that man to rule Afghanistan, but Barnes believed in making his own destiny. Karzai had done more to undermine America's policy in Afghanistan than the Taliban. He was a thief and a liar, and Barnes relished the idea of putting an end to his reign.

His attention swung back to the cockpit, where low ridgelines hid Forward Operating Base Kamdesh from his view. The FOB was a black site and its location wasn't on any of the maps most military commanders had access to. But Barnes knew that it lay just over the next ridge, hidden from prying eyes.

The copilot held up one finger and the colonel got to his feet, grabbing the case by its plastic handle. He felt the helicopter shudder beneath his boots as it began to slow. The pilot gently popped over the final rocky outcrop, swung the nose toward the landing pad, and flared for landing.

Stepping off the ramp as soon as the wheels touched the ground, Barnes kept his head low as the spinning rotors beat the loose dirt and sand into a thick cloud of brown dust. He knew his men were right behind him as he held his breath against the hot exhaust, and he stayed bent over until he was clear of the blades.

Two bearded Special Forces soldiers were sprinting down the hill toward the landing pad. One of the men had a rifle slung casually across his chest and was trying to keep his flip-flops from coming off his feet as he ran. He used his right hand to keep the rifle from hitting his bare knees, which protruded well below the tiny black shorts he was wearing. The other Green Beret was dressed in a tan tank top, cutoff fatigue pants, and unlaced boots. He was unarmed, except for an angry expression.

Obviously, they weren't expecting him.

Barnes could hear the engine being pushed to full throttle, and the two men running toward him waved their hands in an attempt to get the pilot's attention. The pilot ignored them and lifted the helicopter off the pad, pushing it toward the valley floor below.

The men were yelling something now, but it was still too noisy for the colonel to hear them, so he kept moving forward.

"This is a restricted base, you can't be here," the one man yelled as the distant thundering of the rotors drifted away. He stopped, hopping gingerly on one foot as a piece of gravel found its way between the thin sole of the flip-flop and the exposed flesh above it.

Barnes suppressed a grin and motioned that he couldn't hear them. Holding his hand to his ear, he continued to close the distance between them. Stopping two feet away from the Green Berets, the colonel placed the black case on the ground and made a show of searching through his pockets.

"I have orders here for . . ." The annoyed expression on his face deepened as he searched for the elusive papers. "Shit, I know it's here somewhere. Tell your captain that Colonel Barnes is here for the prisoner."

The soldier with the rifle had gotten the rock out of his foot and took a menacing step forward as Barnes's right hand disappeared around his back.

"You don't have clearance to be here," the man replied over the thick wad of chaw stuck in his cheek.

There was a subtle click as Barnes slipped the knife from its Kydex sheath at the base of his spine. The Green Beret turned to spit a long stream of brown tobacco onto the gravel pad as the colonel's blade sliced down into his throat. A look of utter bewilderment was frozen on his face as his hands rushed to his mangled throat. Thick jets of oxygenated blood arced through his fingers and onto the front of Barnes's uniform.

The colonel pushed him hard in the chest and took a step to his left. A metallic cough echoed from his rear as Harden fired his suppressed M4. The 5.56 round hit the second soldier in the eyeball, blowing the contents of his skull out of the back of his head.

He was dead before the expended brass bounced off the gravel.

"Move," Barnes ordered.

He pulled the knife from the man's throat and wiped the gory blade across the dead soldier's T-shirt. It wasn't the first time he'd killed an American, but for many of his men, this would be their first step down the dark path.

The Anvil Team moved up the hill and into the FOB's perimeter. As he passed the dead soldiers, his radio operator, Jones, delivered a rifle shot to each of the men's foreheads. They called it "moonroofing" and it was standard practice on the team to ensure a combatant was dead.

Barnes sheathed the knife and lifted the black case off the ground as suppressed gunfire erupted in the tranquil twilight. It was supposed to be a silent raid, but the detonation of a fragmentation grenade told him they had lost the element of surprise.

"So much for that," Barnes said as an invisible defender opened up on full auto. The long burst echoed off the rock face and bounced across the valley. The colonel handed the case to Jones and loosened the sling on his rifle in eager anticipation.

More gunfire rang out, followed by another explosion.

"Heavy contact, building two," someone said over the radio.

"Roger, moving."

At the top of the rise, Barnes could see two of his team firing into building two. Someone inside was engaging his men with a belt-fed machine gun, and the bullets tore chunks out of the plywood wall, filling the air with splinters.

A muffled yell rose over the din. "Frag out."

Barnes watched the grenade tumble through the air and land near the wall, where it exploded with a distinctive thump. Rounds buzzed angrily over the colonel's head and he turned to his left to see muzzle flashes coming from the commo shack.

Jones had a small gray box in his hand, and the digital readout on its face glowed red before blinking green.

"We're jamming," the black man said, putting the electronic jamming unit back into its pouch. He barely flinched as a bullet hit the gravel in front of him and ricocheted off with a whine. Raising his rifle toward the commo shack, he fired three quick rounds and started toward the building.

"Hold tight," Barnes said.

Firefights were perversely calming to him, like staring into the flames of a fire, and he found himself unable to look away. The colonel felt the goose bumps crawling up his arms with a chill, like a dose of the most exclusive drug.

Jones shrugged and clicked the push-to-talk button on his chest. "Contact, building four."

"Roger, red team moving."

The small incline that led up from the landing zone gave an unparalleled view of the FOB. The cluster of plywood buildings sat nestled in the shadow of the mountains, with the dominant terrain being the communications bunker, built atop an artificial hill. Whoever was holed up in the tiny shack could shoot down at his men but didn't have the angle to hit Barnes or Jones.

Looking at his watch, he noted that it had only been three minutes since he'd stepped off the bird. Harden had five more minutes to clear out the FOB before Barnes would step in. The colonel had learned from General Swift that it was always best to let your men do their job, and while most leaders wanted to get into the fight,

Barnes knew that his men were more than capable of handling the situation.

He knew that any decision made during the first ninety seconds of an engagement was usually too far behind the power curve to matter. It was only after the situation began to settle that a commander's orders could affect the outcome.

Reaching into his sleeve pocket, Barnes took out a can of dip. Placing a pinch of tobacco into his lip, he watched as three of his men jogged toward the commo shed.

The first man moved to the edge of a Hesco barrier. The cubes of felt and reinforced wire were filled with dirt and used to defend positions. Using the lip of the bastion to steady his rifle, the operator engaged the door of the commo shed.

Once the base of fire was set, his partners began maneuvering up to the building by successive bounding. It was choreographed chaos and beautifully executed.

Ensuring that he didn't cross into the line of fire, the first man moved in a shallow arc to the far side of the gentle incline and took a knee. Flicking the safety off his rifle, the soldier fired at the target while the second man sprinted up the middle. Once he was five meters in front of the other assaulter, he went to a knee, engaged the target, and allowed the other man to move up.

It had taken them less than a minute to close the distance, and he watched as his soldier prepared a frag. The other operator was sprinting to join his teammate, trusting the support position to deal with any threats that might suddenly appear.

One of his men yanked the door open, and a soft white light spilled out of the interior, bathing the breach point in a welcoming glow.

"Frag out," the radio crackled.

The explosion went off, muffled by the thin plywood walls, which bowed under the pressure. Three shots echoed inside, followed a moment later by three more.

"Building two clear."

"Building three clear."

"We need a breacher at jackpot," Harden said.

"Moving," came the reply.

Barnes stepped up to the top of the hill and watched the two men exit the commo shed. One of them popped a green ChemLight and dropped it at the threshold so that everyone knew the building had been cleared.

"Four's clear."

A loud thump rose from across the compound followed by, "Positive breach at jackpot."

Jones grabbed the black case and began walking to the center of the FOB. Barnes took a moment to watch the sun disappear behind the mountains. The deep red and vibrant oranges stood in stark contrast to the burned and bullet-marked buildings that lay before him.

"Jackpot secure. We have the package."

"Good copy. Anvil 6, Anvil 7, objective secure," Harden told Colonel Barnes over the radio.

"Anvil 6 copies all," he replied.

Barnes unbuckled his helmet and slipped the noise-canceling headset off his ears. He hated wearing helmets, and if it weren't for the need to stay in contact with his team he wouldn't have worn the headset either.

Placing the helmet under his arm, he headed toward building one. His boots crushed the shiny brass under his feet as he walked over a blackened divot made by a grenade.

The tan wall and tin roof of building one followed the same basic design as the rest of the black site, except that someone had spray-painted skulls on the exterior walls. Over the door someone had stenciled "The Scorpion Den" in black spray paint.

The "team room" was where SF teams spent their downtime. It was the modern equivalent of the Viking mead hall, minus the women and booze, where warriors gathered to share tales of battle and sexual conquest. A plate of food sat cooling on the table, and the last occupant had even paused the movie he'd been watching before the attack. It was an eerie reminder of the transience of life.

Jones was already inside, sitting at one of the tables with an open Toughbook computer attached to a satellite uplink. The black case sat open next to the computer and Barnes set his helmet, with the headset nestled inside, behind the case. He looked down at the metal cylinder inside with its eerie biohazard sticker on stark display.

The door to the team room swung open and Harden appeared, pushing a visibly frightened Arab in front of him.

"Mr. Hamzi, it's good to see you again," Barnes said as Harden forced the man roughly onto the couch. The colonel lifted the metallic tube out of the case and walked over to Harden. Jones was talking to the pilot on the radio as the Anvil Team second in command gingerly accepted the tube from his boss.

"The bird is inbound, sir," Jones said without looking up from the laptop.

"Good. Take a team down to the village and make sure everyone masks up. We don't want any cross-contamination."

"Yes, sir. The perimeter's set and I have Hoyt and Villa securing the commo shed."

"Sounds good to me. Make sure you get the video footage."

Harden nodded and left the room, while Barnes ran his hand through his blond hair and sighed as he walked over to the couch. Slipping the knife from its sheath, the colonel took a seat across from the Arab.

As he twisted the blade slowly in his gloved hand, the blood from the SF soldier was visible on his tan fingers. Barnes's father had taught him that the threat of violence was usually worse than the actual act. A man's fear was always amplified by the deep thoughts couched within his own consciousness.

As a child, he'd stolen his dad's shotgun and snuck out to the pasture to play cowboys and Indians. Swinging the shotgun from one grazing cow to the next, he pretended they were marauding savages attacking the peaceful homestead. In an instant, his finger brushed the trigger and the twelve-gauge went off, knocking him to the ground.

Dazed, he sat up in the dirt and gingerly touched his collarbone. He thought it was broken but immediately realized he had a bigger problem as one of the cows fell to its knees, a gaping hole in its flank.

He had rushed home to hide the shotgun, but there was no way to disguise the dying cow. An hour later, his father found him hiding in the barn. His father took him out to where the cow lay bleeding out from the double-aught buckshot that had torn open its side.

Barnes hadn't seen his dad pick up the broken piece of fence post as they walked across the pasture because he'd been too busy trying to come up with a plausible story. Suddenly, his mind was blank, and he couldn't take his eyes off the gnarled piece of wood in his father's hands. His tiny imagination ran full bore, quickly filling his mind with endless possibilities.

Fear had erased the carefully plotted story he'd come up with, and he confessed everything in a torrent of tears and pitiful gasps. Barnes didn't flinch during the beating and once his father's arm got tired, he handed the young boy a knife.

"Put her out of her misery," he'd told him.

The same fear was now in the Arab's eyes as Colonel Barnes leaned forward and held the blade of the knife inches from the man's face.

"You have a choice to make," he began, placing the blade on the man's face and slowly dragging it down his cheek. The razor-sharp edge split the man's skin easily, leaving a trail of fresh blood behind. "You can either sit here until I bleed you out, or"—Barnes pulled the knife away from the quivering man's face as one of his men appeared with a satellite phone—"you can call your brother and find out where the president's convoy is."

The blood from the cut began dripping onto the man's shirt.

Barnes had to reach forward with his free hand and slap him across the face to snap him out of his daze. The man jumped and greedily reached for the phone.

"Before you make the call," Barnes said, grabbing the man by the hair and twisting his neck around, "I want you to know that if you fuck this up, I am going to kill you, very slowly."

The Arab's face paled, and there was a rushing sound. Barnes looked down at the wet stain on the man's crotch before letting go of his hair, and he smiled broadly.

CHAPTER 11

"Can anyone tell me what the heck is going on?" the president demanded from behind his desk.

NSA Cage stood just on the edge of the tan carpet and watched as Secretary Collins stared down at the presidential seal embossed on the floor. Instead of waiting for the rest of his cabinet, the president had jumped on Collins's ass as soon as the two men came through the door. Cage knew that he was next, and the only intel he had was from an encrypted text from his aide, informing him that the DIA had decided against a warrant and instead launched a daylight raid against the doctor's house.

The agents had gotten their asses handed to them, and it was all because Decklin couldn't follow fucking instructions. The operation had resulted in a burned-down house and more than a handful of dead agents, and right now the media was having a field day.

Instead of feeling dread, Cage was suddenly optimistic. His instincts were telling him that there was an advantage to be had, if he could only figure it out in the next few seconds. He knew he had the space he needed to distance himself from the fallout and was in the midst of taking a deep breath when he noticed a man looking at him from the edge of the room.

"I don't want your excuse, I want to know what happened," the president yelled, slamming his open hand on the desk.

Cage would have loved nothing more than to watch his boss continue to savage Collins, but he was focused on trying to place the face at the other end of the searching gaze. He felt he could safely infer that he worked for the CIA, due to the fact that he was standing next to the director of the CIA, but anything more than that would have been speculation.

The man in question was dressed like a lawyer, with his gold-rimmed glasses and carefully pressed suit. Once the man looked away, Duke pulled out his cell phone and flipped on the camera. Ensuring that the phone was on silent, and the flash turned off, he shot a furtive glance around the room. Once he was sure no one was looking, he snapped a quick picture.

SecDef Collins stammered under the president's verbal onslaught, giving Duke time to attach the picture to an e-mail and send it to Jacob.

"Identify this man," he typed with his thumb before sending the text.

A few seconds passed before the phone vibrated in his hand, and he quickly read his aide's reply.

"Stand by," it read.

"So what you are saying is that your people thought it was a good idea to run an operation in broad daylight, inside the United States? Am I hearing you correctly, Mr. Secretary?"

"Sir, m-my people are looking into the circumstances right now," Collins stuttered, drawing Cage's attention back to the matter at hand.

"What kind of sideshow nonsense are you running here? I do not need this right now. I thought I made myself perfectly clear when I picked you for this job."

"Y-yes, sir, you—" Collins stammered, but was cut off by the president's open palm.

"Duke, what's your take on this?"

"Sir, I was totally in the dark on this one," he lied as Collins turned toward him, the fight gone from his eyes.

The SecDef was woefully out of his depth, and he knew it. If only Cage could figure out how to exploit the situation, he might be able to get the leverage he needed.

He knew that if he hit him too hard it would look petty, but Duke had never suffered fools lightly, and he realized that the president was expecting him to live up to his fearsome reputation. After all, eight months prior he had marched into this very office and called the last man sitting behind the massive desk a "fucking idiot."

He decided at that moment to use the CIA as his ally. It was no secret that the two agencies were engaged in a bitter battle over available funding, and if he could be seen as sympathetic to the Agency, he might be able to sink Collins.

"Sir, I believe the director of the CIA will agree with me that whoever authorized this operation went beyond whatever authority was given to him."

Director Hollis nodded his head in agreement as the bespectacled man to his left turned his searching gaze on the national security advisor. "I agree, and I would like to add that if there was any intelligence linking the targets to any terrorist organizations, my agency should have been read in before it got to this point."

Secretary Collins took a visible step back and brought his hands up in an effort to shield himself from the two-pronged attack. "If either of you are insinuating that I had any knowledge of this operation beforehand, then you are crazy. My sources on the ground had no idea that this was going to happen," he squeaked.

"So you do have sources that you're not sharing? I thought we were on the same team, Secretary Collins," Cage said calmly.

"Why you . . . ," the man spat, his face red with anger. "Who do you think you are, standing there—?"

"Enough," the president yelled, jumping to his feet. "You screwed this up, and you have until the end of the day to fix it. Do you hear me?" he said, rounding his desk and pointing at Collins.

"Mr. President, please—"

"No, that's the end of it. I'm not going to stand here and listen to this . . . *shit*. Either you get control of your people and start sharing intel with the team, or pack your bags."

It was the first time the men had heard the president curse, and for a man famous for his aversion to profanity, it spoke volumes. The room fell silent as they waited to hear what was to follow, but President Bradley had gotten control of himself, and after a short pause said, "That will be all. I want a full brief by the end of the day. Everyone out."

Cage felt the phone in his pocket vibrate and was turning toward the door when the president said, "Duke, you stay."

Cage turned back toward his boss and cast a quick glance at the man in the gold glasses as he walked past him. He was sure he knew that man and wanted nothing more than to check his phone, but he restrained the impulse and moved to the head of the room.

President Bradley looked tired as he moved back to his chair, digging into his pocket as he took a seat. His hand emerged with a wad of bills, and after selecting one off the top, he leaned forward and stuffed it into the open mouth of a jar hidden behind a picture of his wife.

He moved the jar to the middle of his desk, and Cage noticed that it was more than halfway full of random bills.

"My daughter, Layla, and her mother made this for me," he said, turning the jar so that Cage could see a note taped to the front. The makeshift label read, "Daddy's swear jar."

Cage couldn't help but smile as the commander in chief slid the jar back and forth between his hands. The most powerful man in the free world took it as a personal loss that he had to put money in the jar, and his irritation was evident as he finally leaned back in his chair and placed his hands on the top of his head.

He looked tired, and his first week in office wasn't even halfway over.

"Did you really tell the vice president that you were going to rip his face off and wear it as a mask?" President Bradley said after a moment.

Cage was caught flatfooted by the question, and his mind raced back to the fateful day eight months prior.

"Uh, yes, sir, it wasn't my proudest moment."

"Aww, cut the 'sir' crud, Duke. My dad told me that you were the best officer he'd ever served under and a man I could trust."

"Your father was a fine soldier, sir. I wished more than once that I was more like him."

"He used to tell me stories about the two of you in Somalia. Y'all really got after it, didn't you?" he asked, letting his famous Southern drawl slip into the conversation.

"It was an experience," Duke replied honestly.

"My dad told me that bringing Collins on was a mistake, but obviously I didn't listen. He told me that no matter how many good things I do, I will always be judged by the bad. He said you were a perfect example of that."

"Your father was a fine man. I was sorry to hear about his passing."

"I tell you what, that cancer, it doesn't care who you are or what you've done. When it gets its claws into you, it's over."

"Yes, sir. You know my wife, Connie, she . . ."

"It's been a rough year for you, hasn't it, Duke?"

Cage nodded, feeling a knot forming in his throat. In the past eight months he had lost the two constants in his life. He'd lost his career and the one person who kept him balanced. Leaving the army had been hard, but losing Connie had changed him, made him harder. "It hasn't been easy, sir."

Cage looked at the man seated before him and felt a tiny jolt of guilt rise up. There was a time when that little pinprick would have made its way to his heart and found fertile ground for it to grow, but that was a long time ago. Cage knew the cancer hadn't killed his wife. She had given up the moment their son's body came back from Iraq, and when she got sick, there was nothing left for her to fight for.

The day he'd put his beloved soul mate in the ground, Cage had stood at the edge of the hole, staring down at the coffin lying amid the freshly turned earth. The tears had refused to come, until the soldiers and men he'd bled with filed by and in a silent gesture of respect tossed handfuls of dirt onto the lid of the casket.

The simple, unprovoked gesture opened the floodgate for tears that had been bottled up for so long, and he wept uncontrollably before God and everyone. After the procession had filed by, Cage grabbed a final handful of the cold earth in his hands and, sealing a promise he'd made on her deathbed, tossed it down into the hole.

Looking up at the president, he felt the guilt fizzle out in his chest as he steeled himself for what was ahead. If the man looking up at him had any idea of what was coming over the horizon, he would have put Cage in the darkest hole on earth, but he didn't. All he saw was the patriot who had fought with his father, a scarred warrior who'd spent his life fighting for a country that was unaware of the cost.

Ten minutes later, Cage finally freed himself from the president, and once he was clear of any prying eyes, he pulled out his phone. He clicked on the text message and felt a chill creep up his spine as he looked at the man staring up at him.

"Shit," he cursed as he called Simmons.

"Yes, sir?"

"How bad is it?"

"Sir, it's not good. The picture you sent to me is of David Castleman, and he runs some kind of counterterror apprehension team called Task Force II. All I could find out was that they are working in Africa right now."

"So, why the fuck is he here?"

"Sir, according to General Nantz, they are tracking Mason Kane, and I assume they think he's somehow connected to this."

"Shit, is this going to come back on us?"

"Sir, I'm trying to find out everything I can without going through official channels. I've already talked to General Swift and he swears that Decklin was not told to leave any stay-behind force when he left."

"You tell Swift that if he doesn't handle this in the next forty-eight hours, then he's a dead man."

"Yes, sir," his aide replied.

Duke hung up the phone and walked over to the window, his mind racing to connect the dots. Things were getting out of control, and if his men didn't get a grip, he was going to start putting bodies in the ground.

CHAPTER 12

M ason stood on the outskirts of the bazaar, taking in the smells of the dirty bodies filling the enclosed area. Smoke from charcoal braziers drifted in the gentle breeze and mixed with the smell of meats being grilled. The market was packed with wide-eyed tourists enthusiastically bartering for anything they could take home and display over their suburban mantels. Locals scowled at fat Europeans and fatter Americans whose pale skin and expensive cameras annoyed the shopkeepers. The city had been founded on trade and the modern generation held true to their forefathers' innate ability to separate a foreigner from his money.

But he wasn't here for trinkets. He needed to find Ahmed, his contact, the one man besides Zeus whom he could actually trust.

Ahmed had schooled him in the art of tradecraft and taught him that it was the subtle cultural differences that could blow your cover and label you as a foreigner in North Africa. He snapped to when he spotted a sleek Mercedes stop by one of the tea merchants. Ahmed had arrived.

Mason moved into the crowd, dodging the packs of sweaty Westerners who were blissfully unaware of the world that turned around them. Ahead of him, Ahmed was swearing loudly at the merchant's overpriced tea.

"That price is ridiculous for these dried leaves. They aren't fit for my bathwater, much less to drink." Ahmed waved his hand dismissively in the air, while the wizened Algerian stood with crossed arms and a look of total disinterest.

"You Libyans wouldn't know good tea if it was given to you on a golden platter. Why are *you* wasting my time?"

"*I'm* wasting *your* time? In Libya you would be flogged in the street for this. You take advantage of honest Muslims, in the face of Allah, with no shame at all." Ahmed raised his arms in disgust and moved away from the tea merchant, who continued shouting insults until he was out of earshot.

"Perhaps I can buy you some tea, my old friend." Mason spoke in Arabic from Ahmed's side.

"Ah, Mason, I wondered how long you were going to make me wander around this dreadful place until you finally showed up." The two men embraced warmly in the midst of their chaotic surroundings.

Ahmed held Mason at arm's length, a paternal frown slipping over his countenance as he looked at the freshly sutured wound on the American's forehead.

"Still getting into trouble, I see. One would hope that you've gotten better at sewing yourself up by now."

"Could have been a lot worse if you hadn't given me the heads-up," Mason replied honestly. "How did you know?"

"A little bird told me," he laughed.

The two men began walking through the crowded stalls. Ahmed pulled a light blue handkerchief from his pocket and unfolded it with a flourish. Casually, he raised it to his face and dabbed the perspiration beading up on his forehead. Mason realized that the simple gesture was actually a signal to the men watching after their boss.

"I see that you have not lost your edge." He'd been unable to locate Ahmed's security detail, even though he'd arrived an hour early for the meeting. The man was a legend in the intelligence world for a reason, and while he was no longer actively employed by the Libyan intelligence service, Ahmed was still a very powerful man.

"You can never be too careful these days. I know of a place we can go—away from all these *tourists*." Ahmed spat the final word out like it burned his mouth. Like many in the region, he had no love for Westerners.

Grabbing Mason's arm, he led him toward the illegally parked Mercedes. The driver opened the door as they approached, and the two men settled into the luxurious leather interior. The air conditioner felt good, compared to the midday heat, and Mason allowed himself a sigh of satisfaction. Ahmed gave the driver a street name, and the German car pulled away from the curb.

Ahmed had been one of the contacts he used when deployed to Libya under Barnes, and the man was a fountain of information. The country was falling into chaos, just another domino in the chain of events they would later call the Arab Spring. The people were tired of Gaddhafi, who happened to be Ahmed's boss, but the clever Libyan realized the writing was on the wall and quickly changed sides.

While conventional generals were focused on Iraq and Afghanistan, there were officers inside the Special Operations community who had a separate and very secret mandate. Iraq had offered a unique foothold into the region, and while most people thought the war was about oil, the real prize was Iran. It became obvious that a frontal assault wouldn't work on the country that had vexed America since the Reagan administration, but if they could isolate it from all of its allies, it might just implode.

Libya was first on the list, and Gaddhafi, a man who had benefited as much from Iran as he had from his huge reserves of oil, had to be eliminated. Mason's job was to stir the pot, and Ahmed, realizing what was about to happen, gave him the spoon. The spy told them where to find the dictator, and helped Mason fix his position and maneuver the mob that would eventually kill him.

Thirty minutes later, they were sitting inside a small café waiting for their tea to arrive. The café was a holdover from a more elegant time. The marble tile, dark wood, and burnished brass furnishings gave it the appearance of a European salon.

Mason offered Ahmed a cigarette while casually checking the exits for the quickest escape route. He knew Ahmed's men were discreetly pulling security in the area, but he never relied on others to protect him.

"I cannot believe that you still smoke those foul things," Ahmed said, his face crinkling in disgust at the offered cigarette. "You Americans might not be the most cultured people, but you have excellent tobacco. Put that away and have one of mine." Mason returned the offending pack to his pocket, slipped one of the American cigarettes from Ahmed's battered silver case, and lit it with his Zippo.

Mason took a deep drag, trying to remember the last time he'd had a Camel.

Smoking might have been a bad habit, but it was all he had left, and he planned on enjoying it for as long as possible.

"I can't tell you how long it's been since I've had one of these."

"They are much better than those nasty French Gauloises you carry around with you, but I'm very certain you did not come all this way to talk about tobacco."

"I have to go to Libya."

Ahmed nodded, motioning with his cigarette for Mason to continue. "For the file, I assume? Do you think that is wise?"

Mason felt the first spark of self-doubt as he studied his mentor. Ahmed was a slight man and barely five foot seven; one could even call him diminutive. His aquiline nose, dark brown eyes, and salt-and-pepper beard gave him a cultured, almost urbane air, but it was all a clever façade. Beneath the day-to-day trappings was the iron will and fastidious mind of a vicious predator who had lulled more than one man to an untimely death.

"The American I was working for, the one with the CIA, he made a call to someone and I have no idea who it is. Somehow this is all connected to Barnes, and the Anvil Program, but I can't get my head around it. Someone has to be pulling Barnes's strings, and whoever it is must be all the way at the top. The only intel I have is at the safe house."

After breaking with Barnes, Mason had needed some insurance to protect him from the military. He'd used a program to hack into the colonel's personal computer and downloaded most of the hard drive before the breach was detected. If he was killed, Ahmed was supposed to send it all to the American press. But while he was still alive he needed to get to the laptop, which had been stashed at one of Ahmed's safe houses. He desperately hoped it would give him some answers.

Ahmed let out a paternal sigh and watched the smoke curling up from the end of his cigarette. After he'd gathered his thoughts, he fixed his steely gaze on his American pupil.

"You have been working for your American masters for too long, my friend. I warned you about the CIA. I told you that man wasn't going to give you a free pass back to America, did I not?"

"I'm just trying to get the hell out of here."

"How have you lived so long being this naive? If it wasn't so sad, I would laugh." Ahmed threw his hands in the air and shrugged his shoulders in a manner that showed his bewilderment with the whole affair.

Ahmed had been a Gaddhafi loyalist, and a colonel in Libya's intelligence service. The man had run more black operations than any other agent. His claim to fame had been an operation in Switzerland, where he'd used a banker's family as leverage to gain access to funds the United Nations had frozen. He had developed quite an impressive network of contacts—until the Americans came. Regime change cost him everything, and when he became a fugitive, the United States placed him on the terror list. Like Mason, he could never return home, but unlike his American friend, Ahmed only fought for those who paid him the most money.

"It's not something I would expect you to understand."

"What I understand and what I *know* are two separate things. I know that your own men tried to kill you. I know your country doesn't care about the Arabs and that your president doesn't care how many must die to protect its interests."

Ahmed fell silent, the painful memories getting the best of him. When he spoke again the Libyan's voice was low and hard.

"You and Zeus are what's left, and they will take you too if given the chance."

Ahmed had been around the block more times than he could remember, but the day Zeus brought Mason to his house, the Libyan had found himself at a total loss. He hadn't believed the American's story at first, but while the wounded American slept, he had checked with his sources and was shocked to find that Mason had been telling the truth.

He couldn't believe that so many men had ignored the colonel's visible descent into madness. The Libyan had asked Mason over and over how the American soldiers could have stood by and watched Barnes shoot a six-year-old girl in the head and then massacre the rest of her family.

Mason watched the emotion slipping over his friend's face. Ahmed was by no means soft but there was a deep reservoir of sadness inside him, fed by horrors most men would never know.

The waiter appeared with their tea and the two friends lifted their cups in silence. Mason took a moment to enjoy the complex aroma of the brown liquid before taking a sip. The key to good chai was the delicate mix of tea, sugar, and milk. Much like life, success lay in the balance.

Good tea encourages the mind to wander, but unfortunately all of Mason's good memories were gone. The thought of returning to Libya evoked a powerful stirring inside his soul as painful memories poured out.

Unwelcome images and sounds rushed past their barriers, like flames seeking oxygen. He could feel himself falling backward into his own mind, and his heart began racing in his chest.

On that desperate day, he could hear the static from the radio as he tried to make contact with his team. He smelled the red dirt and the copper scent of blood in his mouth. Rounds cracked low over his head. Some were so close he could hear them cutting through the air, while others ricocheted off the pile of bricks in puffs of dust and broken concrete. The rebels began flanking his position.

Oh shit, not now.

Mason was fighting for his life one second and the next he was back at the table, his heart rate jacked through the roof.

He caught Ahmed watching him from across the table and felt ashamed of the weakness that must have been written across his face. Mason struggled to decipher the Libyan's expression and then it hit him: it was compassion.

"Ahmed, when the uprising started in Libya, do you remember how quick we turned on Gaddhafi?"

"I assume by 'we' you mean your government?"

"Yeah."

"I remember telling him not to trust your president, but he assured me that he had certain . . . How did he say it? Oh yes, 'assurances.' "

"What does that mean?"

"It is funny you put it that way, because that is what I asked him. You must realize that the man was utterly deranged, out of touch with reality. I told him that my job was to protect him and the country, but he was so certain that—"

"Certain about what?" Mason asked. He suddenly felt like he was on the verge of a great discovery, and all he had to do was coax it out of the notoriously closed-lipped spy.

"He was certain that the Americans needed him. One of your generals was flown in, a week before the riots began. He had a closed-door meeting with the president, but I'd had Gaddhafi's offices bugged long ago, so I was privy to the entire conversation."

"What did they talk about?" Mason willed himself to calm down; he had always had his suspicions about the operation and knew deep down that someone besides Barnes had been calling the shots.

"He assured the president that your government would do everything in its power to support his government."

"So he lied," the American said.

"Of course he lied. A week later, your drones were hitting our communication installations and knocking out the power grids. We were unable to use our aircraft and then your Anvil Team appeared."

"Our mission was to cut the head off the snake and get out without anyone ever knowing we were there. We were to make it look like the rebels killed him. Those were our orders. I knew they didn't come from Barnes, because the whole operation was way too elegant. The colonel is a hammer, and whoever was in charge knew exactly how much force to use and exactly who to talk to."

"The war was never just about Libya, or Gaddhafi," Ahmed said patiently. "The man who met with the president wanted to disrupt the whole region."

"Do you remember his name?"

The café hummed with the frivolous conversations of the other patrons, recounting the day-to-day minutiae of their lives. The world's ability to ignore what was right in their faces was amazing. The Mideast was in turmoil but right now, in that café, no one cared. There was a storm building on the horizon and he felt like he was the only one who could see it.

Ahmed appraised Mason as he patiently finished his cigarette, and finally said, "I will get you into Libya; as for the man you seek, you need to look much higher if you wish to find him."

CHAPTER 13

The Gulfstream G650 thundered toward Afghanistan at 620 miles per hour, and as the engines hummed through the night air, Renee Hart turned her attention back to the computer in front of her.

She wanted to find Decklin so badly that she was willing to overlook the fact that Deputy Director Thompson was using her to save his own ass. It was his fault that there was some psycho running around with a suitcase full of nerve gas, but what troubled her most was how General Swift fit into the scheme of things.

Thompson had promised to get her the access she needed and advised that Swift would be told to leave her alone, but something wasn't right. She wasn't used to keeping things from her boss, and the fact that she was being asked to do so raised certain red flags. Somehow, her boss was right in the middle of Barnes and the Anvil Program, and Renee was still trying to figure out how far the program reached.

The thumb drive repeated some of what the deputy director had already told her but went into more detail on Anvil's original mandate of working off the grid to find, fix, and finish terror cells wherever they presented themselves. The major problem was the fact that everything about the program was totally illegal, but no one seemed to care as long as they were getting results.

In the beginning, the newly minted unit was designed by the

CIA, but someone jockeyed hard to pull it under the DoD. Once Barnes took command, he began cutting all communications with his bosses at the Pentagon and opened a secret channel with the CIA to get ahold of their drone program.

The CIA didn't have the red tape that the DoD had, and with the right clearance from the upper echelon, Barnes could prosecute any target he wanted.

The colonel fascinated Renee, and she pored through the pages looking for any information she could get her hands on.

He came from a blue-collar family in Montana. Growing up poor, he had spent more time working on his father's ranch than studying, and his grades were a reflection of his priorities. However, his SAT scores were off the chart.

He attended Montana State on a full scholarship and had graduated from the College of Engineering with honors, but then, inexplicably, he enlisted in the army.

Somewhere along the way, someone realized that Corporal Barnes had a great deal of potential and submitted him for Officer Candidate School, and after twenty-four months in the army, he was minted an infantry lieutenant. He decided to join the Green Berets as soon as he made captain, and was given command of an A-Team just as the war in Afghanistan was kicking off. In another stroke of luck, he was one of the first Americans on the ground.

Captain Barnes was attached to the CIA's Jawbreaker team, and his exploits on the ground were legendary.

He had managed to stay in theater, in one capacity or another, from 2001 until the present. He never went home and never took a break. He was working almost entirely for the CIA, running missions in Iraq, when he came to General Swift's attention.

Barnes, now a major, was seen as the bearer of the sacred torch of democracy, and General Swift expected him to illuminate the dark path to victory. No one had time to notice the subtle but furious narcissism that was growing within him.

The man was magnetic and dangerous. General Petraeus called him a "warmonger," and Barnes wore the title like a badge of honor. He had nothing but disdain for the generals who sought to garner Iraqi affection. For him, the way to victory was through total war, and while his methods were barbaric, they were effective.

He was running Task Force 120 when he was given command of the Anvil Program.

Iraq was turning into a bloodbath and the men running the war kept throwing more bodies into the grinder. The victory they had held up a few months before had turned to ash in their hands, and the old president had needed a "win" to sell to the American public.

With no yardstick to measure success, they used a body count to prop up the faltering conflict. Barnes's team provided more bodies than most of the coalition forces combined. JSOC (Joint Special Operations Command) rolled the classified figures into their weekly briefs in an attempt to right the foundering ship. It was all about results, and the old president had laid it out: "Leave Barnes alone." The golden child was safe to sink deeper into the darkness, and no one was watching over those men he pulled down with him.

Then, according to the document, something odd happened. Sometime during his last days of office, the previous president suddenly ordered the DoD to pull the plug on the program. The sudden shift in policy intrigued Renee, especially when she read that the former chairman of the Joint Chiefs of Staff had lost his job over a confrontation stemming from the decision.

Had the president realized that they were losing control of the Anvil Program, or was it something else? Either way, the decision to cut the program had a profound effect on the balance of power in Washington, and Renee wondered if this decision had pushed Barnes over the edge.

Renee scrolled through the documents, pausing to study the last picture taken of Colonel Barnes. He was standing next to a building, its sandy exterior scorched with the black scars of expended munitions. She recognized the building as the house where they had shot it out with Saddam Hussein's two sons.

The picture captured Colonel Barnes in all his glory. He stood with a wry smile in front of the smoldering building, his body armor stained black with blood and dirt, his rough beard and close-cropped blond hair framing a cold and brooding gaze. Renee enlarged the picture and stared at his eyes. There was a powerful savagery in them, like a grass fire fed by a harsh wind.

She breezed through the remaining documents, looking for anything that she could use. Most of the files were incomplete, and it seemed that whoever had saved the documents had done so while they were being deleted. It wasn't much to go on, and she still couldn't get a firm grasp on the overall picture.

She was about to close the computer when she noticed an offhand memo from Barnes to Swift entitled "Objective Massey" that grabbed her attention. Renee remembered that the Third Ranger Battalion had conducted the raid along the Syria-Iraq border and stumbled across huge amounts of intel linking Saudi Arabia, Syria, and Libya to terror cells in Iraq. The documents reinforced the growing idea that Iraq and Afghanistan were just the first steps in a much wider war.

Renee's eyes burned from lack of sleep and she had to close the laptop, but she couldn't stop thinking that the memo might be the key to this whole thing. Barnes was telling her something, but she was too exhausted to see it. Whatever it was could wait until after she had gotten some sleep. Digging a pill bottle out of her bag, she popped an Ambien out into her palm and swallowed it with a sip of water.

The jet prepared to land at Jalalabad Airfield eight hours after leaving Ireland. Renee felt the steward shaking her awake and slowly opened her eyes. She'd been dreaming, and the transition back to the waking world was a journey she didn't want to take.

Groggily, she sat up, the side of her face damp from a light sheen of sweat. Renee took the offered bottle of water and allowed her empty gaze to wander around the cabin. Opening the cap and taking a drink from the cold bottle, she remembered staring at a slumped form behind the wheel of a smoking vehicle. Just like the nights before, when she finally pulled the person free, she was staring at herself.

Light blue carpet stretched from the bulkhead to the rear of the cabin and offset the dark brown leather of the plush chairs and sofa. Even the cool air that circulated through the cabin smelled expensive. It also caused chills to run up her arms as she finished the last of the water. The steward asked if she needed something to eat, and she forced a cheery smile.

"Yes, please."

She slid open the window shade and watched the flaps deploy as he returned with a sandwich wrapped in cellophane.

"I thought you could use this too," he said, and kindly handed her a Red Bull.

"You're a lifesaver."

She could feel the pressure change in her ears as the jet descended for their final approach. Unwrapping the cellophane, Renee took a bite of the turkey sandwich, savoring the flavorful sourdough bread and crisp lettuce.

"Don't get used to the VIP treatment, girl," she said to herself as the jet touched down and taxied to one of the private runways.

Her first deployment to Afghanistan had taken three days and spanned three countries. She had ridden in a tiny seat, jammed between two bulky soldiers on their first deployment. Their nervous chatter had annoyed her, but not nearly as much as the rough ride of the transport.

Renee's hand slipped back to her lucky necklace, and she idly slid the pendant back and forth across its chain as she chewed. Her first tour had changed her. The violence and deprivation of combat had blasted away at the facets of her humanity. When she learned that her father had suddenly taken ill, her first thought was what to do about the mission that was coming up. By the time she got to a phone, he'd passed away, but by then death was so commonplace that it took a day for the tears to form.

The key to being a good soldier, her first squad leader had once told her, was the ability to suffer through anything while continuing to push forward. In Iraq, they called it "the suck," and like a good soldier, Renee had embraced its suffering. She knew now that while a good soldier merely embraces suffering, a great soldier always asks for more.

Renee opened the frosted silver and blue can of Red Bull and washed down the remains of her meal. By the time the plane rolled to a stop, she had fixed her hair and was wearing the smile that everyone expected of her.

The sun was just beginning to rise over the Tora Bora Mountains as she thanked the steward and stepped off the plane. Renee's eyes glanced over the rusted-out hangar that had once been used to repair Russian attack helicopters. It was too small for the larger cargo planes and had bullet holes stitched across the metal siding from when the United States had taken the airfield.

Grimy windows covered in dirt and cobwebs muted the sunlight from the outside, and the concrete floor was stained with oil and jet fuel. Renee saw a man with a closely trimmed Mohawk leaning against a late-model Chevy Suburban that sat running a few feet away from the nose of the jet.

Tattoos covered both of his deeply tanned arms before disappearing into his sleeves. A white scar extended from his scalp down the right side of his face and over his jawbone. As Renee's feet settled onto the hangar floor, two more thick-necked men got out of the truck and walked around to meet her.

"Well, if it isn't Kevin and the famous Z-boys. I hope you have my gear," Renee said.

"Yes, ma'am, it's in the back. I hope you haven't gone soft after hanging with all those California surfer boys," the burly Mohawked man replied with a smile. Taking two giant steps forward, he grabbed Renee up in a big bear hug.

"I wasn't even gone a week. Put me down. I'm supposed to be in charge."

It felt good to be home.

"I hear you made quite the impression back in California," he said after setting her back on the concrete floor.

"It was an experience," she replied.

Renee had handpicked the Green Beret to be her team leader. It was a decision she had never regretted. A true warrior, Kevin had the innate ability to find the enemy on even the most mundane missions. No matter how heavy the fighting got, his team always made it back home. An offhand comment by an army officer had earned them the name "Zombie Squad" after he said the team "took more hits than the undead." The nickname stuck, but for brevity's sake was cut down to "Z-boys."

"Good to see you, Bones," Renee said, greeting another familiar face, who had gotten his nickname because of his striking resemblance to Phil Mickelson's caddie.

This was her home, among warriors whose sacrifices left their bodies scarred and their eyes blank and distant. The men of the Zombie Squad had the unique swagger born from self-awareness. Outsiders assumed their aloofness was a result of arrogance, but what they never saw was their deep warmth and love for their brothers in arms.

"Is this the new guy?" she asked, moving to the rear of the truck.

"Yeah, his name's Tyler. We got him after Milo was smoked at Gardez; he's good people." Introducing herself politely, she took in the scruffy beard that hid the boyish face but failed to mask the man's steely gaze.

"Ma'am," he said, his lower lip bulging from a large pinch of dip.

Renee looked down at his hand, which was rough and covered in the scar tissue indicative of a bad burn. His ring finger had been partially amputated and the words "nice try" had been tattooed below the missing knuckle.

"Welcome to the team."

Renee tossed her bag into rear of the truck and grabbed an M4 from the duffel that lay open. Pulling the charging handle to the rear, she ensured the weapon was clear and on safe before inspecting it. Once she was satisfied that the rifle was serviceable, she began checking the rest of her faded gear.

"Renee, the general wants to see you right away," Kevin said.

"Yeah, I was hoping to get a shower first. Can't it wait?"

"Uhh, no. He told me to come and get you—not that I wouldn't have anyways," he stammered.

"What's going on?" she asked, zeroing in on his uncharacteristically serious tone.

"A CIA black site got hit last night. Someone sent us a video."

"Black site? I didn't know we had any more of those in country."

"None of us did."

Renee slammed the rear doors, wondering if it was connected with either Decklin or Barnes or both. "Okay, let's go see the old man." She shrugged and moved to the front of the truck.

Jumping into the passenger seat, she slid on a pair of dark Oakleys and cranked up the A/C. The sun was halfway to its apex and already burning brightly in the east. Kevin pulled out of the hangar door, which had been slid open for Renee's arrival, and she could see the heat already beginning to form a mirage above the black asphalt of the tarmac. The flight line was alive with the frantic bustling of man and machine, and through the air-conditioning vents she could smell the distinctive odor of burning jet fuel.

Jalalabad never slept. Like Bagram to the west and Kandahar to the south, "Jbad" played a huge role in supplying the war effort. Cargo aircraft were constantly ferrying in mission-essential equipment, personnel, and supplies, and as a result the base was always in motion. During the invasion, the small airfield had been at the epicenter of the covert war that was unfolding across eastern Afghanistan. When al-Qaeda and their Taliban benefactors retreated into Tora Bora, the base became a vital staging point for operations in the area. Its proximity to Pakistan attracted the majority of Special Operations soldiers and clandestine operatives, and unmarked aircraft became a common sight.

Kevin drove cautiously through the Hesco barriers that formed a protective wall around the Special Operations side of the base. Throwing the truck in park in front of a low plywood building, he told Bones and Tyler, "Stay put," before jumping out.

Renee walked up to the heavy steel door and punched her access code into the keypad. The lock clicked open and they walked into the tactical operations center, or TOC, where they were met with a flurry of activity.

Typically, only a skeleton crew manned the TOC during the day, since most missions took place at night. Obviously something big was going on and the large, open room was packed. Soldiers frantically pecked at computers lining the massive square table that sat in the middle of the room. The three large monitors hanging from the ceiling were alive with maps and lists of coordinates as information was posted for all to see.

The plywood floor was covered in a layer of fine grit called "moon dust," which hadn't been swept away, and the trash cans were overflowing with Styrofoam coffee cups and tobacco-filled spitters.

General Swift was standing below a monitor, with a phone in each ear, and a huge dip in his lower lip. The usually unflappable officer was stressed out, and seeing Renee walk in added to the already deep scowl on his face.

The video playing on the screen was in black and white and had a large targeting reticle in the center of the feed. Numbers designating altitude, airspeed, and heading told her that she was looking at the heads-up display of a drone.

"General Swift," she said from her boss's side.

The general held up a finger as he listened to whoever was on the other line. "Right now, all we know is that there was an attack on American forces near Kamdesh," he said in his gravelly tone.

His right fist held the phone so tight that his knuckles had turned white. Turning his head, he spat a brown glob of tobacco into an overflowing trash can.

"I understand that, sir, but we had no idea they were operating in the area. Kamdesh is not an operational FOB."

The way the general said the word "sir" made her smile. She'd learned long ago that a person's inflection when saying the word was one of the oldest yet safest ways of showing displeasure when talking to a ranking officer. He might have been saying "sir," but he sure didn't mean it.

"Roger that, I'll keep you updated." He slammed the phone down as Kevin approached with the coffee. "Thanks, son," he said, grabbing Renee's cup and taking a sip despite the dip in his mouth.

Kevin shrugged and headed back to the coffeepot to retrieve another cup.

"Some CIA dipshits have been running an illegal detention site at Kamdesh. They were using a Special Forces team as security and last night the FOB got hit. We have a Reaper en route now and about ten minutes ago, we got this." He pointed over to a staff sergeant staring at a laptop.

"General, I need to ask you something," Renee began.

"I'm a little busy right now."

"It's about Colonel Barnes," she spat.

General Swift's wide shoulders went rigid, and he turned slowly toward Renee. "What did you say?"

"I know about the Anvil Program, sir."

"General, I have the video up," the staff sergeant said from his place in front of the laptop.

Swift's eyes narrowed as he studied Renee. He was about to say something but decided against it.

"Renee, check this out," Kevin said from the table.

Renee knew she'd lost her chance and grudgingly moved to the laptop as the general picked up a phone and began dialing. "What do you have?"

"It's an unencrypted video that came in from the FOB," he said, hitting play.

The video was from a mounted helmet camera and was from the point of view of whoever was wearing it. The quality was clear but jumpy. She could hear the man's muffled breathing and it sounded like he was wearing some kind of mask.

The camera panned to a group of men wearing level-three chemical breathing masks. Their position overlooked a typical Afghan village, and the video perfectly captured a sixty-millimeter mortar that had been set up next to him.

"Hang it," he commanded as another soldier held a mortar round at the top of the tube.

"Fire."

The gunner dropped the mortar round into the tube, and they heard the metallic sound of the round sliding down before the mortar bucked as the firing pin hit the primer on the bottom of the round. A cloud of dust shot up as the round arced out of the tube with a boom.

"Hang it," the man said again.

Another round was held above the tube and on the "fire" command the sequence was repeated.

"What the hell is this?" Renee asked the sergeant.

"Some really fucked-up shit, ma'am."

The camera was turned to the village and someone off-camera said, "Splash," followed a second later by the round air-bursting over the target. She could barely make out the white cloud that was forming when the second round exploded near the first one.

The picture held tight on the cloud that was slowly spreading and drifting down onto the dirt-brown compounds. The villagers looked like tiny caricatures of people grouped together in clumps as they pointed up at the cloud.

After a few seconds, the helmet-mounted camera looked down at the black case, and Renee recognized it immediately as a military-issued Pelican case similar to the one she had under her bed. Inside the box two more mortar rounds sat, nestled in gray egg foam. The bright orange biohazard symbol painted on the body of the rounds stood out clearly.

"Oh no," she whispered.

She could feel her stomach knotting up as a sick feeling washed over her.

This was what Decklin was doing in California. Suddenly the pieces began to fit. She thought she might puke and got up to find a trash can but instead bumped into the general's drone control station, made up of a makeshift cockpit being helmed by two air force pilots. The terminals resembled a training simulator that pilots used before actually getting into an airplane.

The "pilot" sat on the left, in front of a bank of controls and screens, which allowed him to fly the drone. Next to him, the sensor officer had a similar setup, but instead of flying, her job was to operate the onboard targeting systems and cameras that made the Reaper so deadly.

The feed from the drone's heads-up display was linked to the giant screen that hung on the far wall, and Renee watched as the pilot banked the drone hard to the west.

Over his headset, he was talking with one of the air force's AWACs, the sophisticated aircrafts that provided command and control for coalition pilots in the area.

"Whiplash 14, this is Sentinel 3, readvise heading and altitude," a voice said from the speaker attached to the station.

"Sentinel 3, this is Whiplash 14, stand by." The pilot checked his heading before turning to the sensor operator. "Sensor, confirm heading, I think there's a problem with the compass."

"Heading is two nine zero degrees," the red-haired woman replied.

"Yeah, that's what I've got. I can't bring the damn thing around."

The pilot gently pivoted the joystick in his hand, but the Reaper refused to respond.

"Run a diagnostic check for me," he told his female counterpart.

"Flight systems green, navigations systems are green, uplink is . . . We have uplink failure."

"This piece of shit," he swore. "Sentinel 3, Whiplash 14, be advised that we have uplink failure. I say again, we have no control of the drone."

"Whiplash 14, I copy. Be advised you are leaving your operation box."

"What's going on?" Renee asked.

"Something is interfering with the drone. It's not responding," the female captain replied calmly.

"What in the hell?" General Swift bellowed from across the room. "Why am I getting calls that my Reaper is leaving the ops box?"

"The drone isn't responding," Renee replied.

"I can see that. Why is this happening?"

"No idea, sir, we are running diagnostic checks right now. Something is wrong with the signal," the male captain replied.

"Get that piece of shit back online, I don't need this right now."

"Whiplash 14, Sentinel 3, we are clearing the airspace until the drone gets back online. How copy?"

"Whiplash 14 copies."

"The frequency's jammed. It won't let me override it," the woman said, typing furiously on the keyboard in front of her.

"Where is it going?" Renee asked.

They ignored her as the drone leveled out and then gently waggled its wings back and forth. "Diagnostics are good, it's not a software problem."

A red alert prompt popped up on the Reaper's heads-up display. It read, "UPLINK TERMINATED."

"Someone has hacked the feed."

"Is that thing armed?" Kevin asked.

"Yes, it has the usual complement of Hellfire missiles," the woman replied.

The general snatched a phone off the cradle and violently punched in a number. He impatiently waited for someone to answer while yelling orders across the TOC. "Can someone find out where the hell this million-dollar piece of shit is going?"

"Can you disable the flight link?" Renee asked.

"No, ma'am, it doesn't work like that. If the guidance link is severed, they are programmed to return to base."

"Is there anything you *can* do? I mean, there has to be something in the manual."

"No, ma'am, someone is going to have to shoot it down."

"This is General Swift. I need to speak with the officer in charge. No, I can't wait, get him on the phone."

"Sir, it looks like the drone is heading to Highway One," a lieutenant said from the map attached to the wall.

"Yes, who is this? Captain Otto, we have a nonresponsive drone two kilometers west of Highway One. I need an immediate intercept with authorization for a shoot-down."

Renee could see Highway 1 appear on the horizon where it snaked toward Pakistan like a dull gray serpent.

"Bird's inbound, time to intercept five minutes," the general yelled without taking the phone from his ear.

"Whiplash 14, we have two F-15s moving in for intercept. ETA five mikes, how copy?"

"Roger, Sentinel 3," the pilot responded.

"What's that on the road?" Kevin moved forward to get a better look at the screen.

A line of SUVs appeared at the upper edge of the feed. The vehicles were moving at a high rate of speed and bunched tightly together.

"Sir, we need to find out if we have an asset on the road," Renee said.

"I'm on the phone with Bagram, waiting on an answer," another officer said from his desk.

Renee realized that her fists were clenched in anticipation, and she forced herself to relax. Her palms were red from where her fingernails had dug into her skin, and she wiped her clammy hands on her pant legs.

"Sir, it's Hamid Karzai's convoy."

"Shit. I need those birds expedited, now."

The Reaper cruised lazily at fifteen thousand feet, where it was invisible to anyone on the ground.

"Pilot, we have sixty-degree target lockout. Weapon and laser spin up," the sensor operator said.

Renee wasn't sure what was going on, but it didn't sound good.

"Sensor, check weapon and laser status."

"Status complete, weapons are hot. Laser and auto track are coming online. Laser status complete, laser is hot and tracking on heading three five zero."

"Initiate auto-destruct."

"Pilot, access denied. Master arm is hot, we have missile launch."

The reticle of the high-definition camera was focused over the second vehicle in the convoy. The feed showed where the infrared targeting laser was locked on to one of the vehicles as it moved unsuspectingly down the road.

"Pilot, impact in three, two, one." The missile appeared in the screen for a split second as it slammed into the roof of the target vehicle. The explosion obliterated the vehicle and washed out the camera in a giant orange burst of flame and black smoke. Before the smoke cleared, the sensor operator was speaking again.

"Pilot, laser is hot. Master arm is hot, missile away."

"Oh God," Renee whispered as the second Hellfire went streaking toward its target.

A deathly silence fell over the TOC as everyone focused on the unauthorized strike unfolding before their eyes. In the background someone aboard the AWAC was trying to confirm the first missile strike, but the pilot wasn't answering.

Renee was amazed at the sensor operator's cool. She reported the drone's functions with an unattached professionalism, void of any emotion.

The drivers of the convoys had been trained by American Special Operations and went into immediate evasive action on the road. Assuming they had hit an IED, the trucks sped through the kill zone. If they stuck to their training, they would stop and take up a defensive perimeter once they were clear. There was no way for them to know that a second Hellfire was hurtling toward them.

Renee had seen countless drone strikes in her time, but never one like this. The state-of-the-art UAV seemed to be functioning autonomously while losing none of its lethality.

"Pilot, impact in three, two, one," the woman said again.

The laser designator tracked its target as the vehicles sped down the road. It was two hundred meters away when the second Hellfire detonated. The impact tossed the vehicle in the air, where it tumbled like a scrap of tin before slamming into the ground in a ball of flames.

General Swift silently lowered himself into a chair, the phone cradled to his ear, forgotten.

"Sentinel 3, I confirm two unauthorized missile launches. We have two hits at grid . . ."

Renee wasn't listening. She looked over at the general, who'd buried his head in his hands in disbelief.

The feed suddenly shuddered and the picture violently corkscrewed on the screen as the drone tumbled toward the ground. The last thing they saw was an air force F-15 shoot past the Reaper after successfully hitting it with its twenty-millimeter cannon.

"How do you hijack a drone?" Kevin asked from her side.

"Someone has to be very familiar with our operating systems," Renee replied.

The enormity of the situation filled the room and slowly settled on the silent witnesses like an invisible weight. Everything had just changed.

"Sir, I just received another message on the secure network," one of the men said from his desk.

"What?" General Swift asked weakly.

"Another video, sir."

"Put it on the screen," Renee ordered, taking the initiative.

"Yes, ma'am."

A moment later the screen, which had gone blank after the Reaper was shot down, blinked to life. A blue box with a white "play" arrow appeared, and Renee watched the sergeant's cursor scroll over to the arrow and click it.

The video showed the inside of an American FOB. The gravel was scorched black in some places, and the walls of the buildings were pockmarked with bullet holes. The camera panned over a row of bodies before focusing on Colonel Barnes.

The colonel stood framed by the dark mountains in the background. The sky looked impossibly blue, with white clouds slowly drifting on an invisible breeze.

"General Swift," he began. "Do I have your attention now?" Barnes looked comfortable and supremely arrogant in his dirty camouflage uniform. His blond head was streaked white in the sunlight, and despite the dark sunglasses, he oozed a violent aggression.

"I advised you to heed my warning, but you wouldn't listen. Still the most clueless man in Afghanistan, I see. I would suggest leaving as soon as possible, before the natives find out that the Americans killed their president. Anvil 6 out."

The video ended, leaving Colonel Barnes's face framed on the large screen.

CHAPTER 14

The drive from Algiers to the Libyan border crossing at Ghadames took seventeen hours, and Mason tried to sleep for most of the way. The compact Toyota was cramped and smelled like dirty laundry and stale cigarette smoke. It was impossible for him to get comfortable, and he finally gave up the idea of going to sleep and just smoked.

His driver, a young Libyan, stopped before the border crossing to buy six cans of warm beer from a roadside vendor. Returning to the car, he asked Mason if he wanted one before popping the top and chugging the can.

Alcohol was illegal in Libya, which meant that it was hard to find but not impossible to get. Mason got out of the car to take a piss on the side of the road, and after he finished, he stretched his legs and surveyed the long line of cars at the border.

Ghadames had always been a prominent city because it had fresh water. Thousands of years ago, the arid crossing would have been packed with caravans waiting to water their camels at the oasis. Since the civil war it had become a hub for drugs being smuggled into the country and weapons coming out.

It was a dangerous place, but Mason's only concern was the 290 miles left to Tripoli. The driver tossed the empty can of beer out of the window and lit a cigarette before getting back on the road.

The driver cursed under his breath and honked his horn as he maneuvered the car onto a dirt bypass and snaked around the line of cars. He stopped next to a tan shack and honked his horn twice. A middle-aged soldier ambled slowly from the building, with the bored expression that only a civil servant can muster. His uniform was stained with sweat and bulged around the midriff as he made his way to the car.

"You again. What do you want this time?" he asked the driver, his hand resting on top of his leather holster.

"Uncle, you look tired. Are they working you too hard?" the driver asked with concern before handing over the sack of beer.

"This *fucking* job, all day I sit out in the sun and listen to these people. I've had enough, I tell you." He took the beer with a smile and patted the driver on his hand. "You are a good nephew, but next time bring me the American porno mags that I've been asking for."

His nephew smiled as the soldier bent down to get a look at Mason.

"Where are you going?" he asked.

"I have family in Tripoli and my mother is sick," Mason replied in Arabic. The soldier nodded and patted the top of the car, telling them that they were free to go.

The car pulled off and the driver asked Mason if he had his pistol ready.

"Yeah, why, what's up?"

"There are more checkpoints on the road ahead, but they aren't manned by the military. It should be okay, but you never know."

Mason slipped the Glock out of his waistband and placed it beneath his thigh, making sure it was out of sight. He ignored the sharp edges cutting through his pants and tried to enjoy the scenery as they drove toward the city.

They had to stop four more times before making it to Tripoli, and at each checkpoint the driver had to fork over a wad of wrinkled dinars to get past the militia guarding the road. The government might have controlled the borders, but the road was still in control of the rebels. Halfway to their destination, the driver pulled over at a bombed-out gas station and Mason switched cars. He thanked the man for his help before settling into the nicer Toyota Land Cruiser that would take him to the safe house. The American wondered if Toyota was the only company that imported vehicles to the Mideast.

"Maybe I should give all this up and set up a dealership," he thought to himself before dozing off.

His new driver woke him up outside Tripoli and pulled the SUV through the gate of a modest house on the outskirts of the capital. Mason grabbed his gear and stretched before walking up to the door.

Knocking twice, he turned the brass knob and pushed open the heavy wooden door. The interior of the house was dimly lit and filled with cigarette smoke. The floors were a rough concrete, and a large rectangular rug took up the middle of the large room, beneath an equally large table.

The furnishings of the house had obviously been picked off the street, because nothing in the room matched. A faded blue chair and two brown couches added an island of color in comparison to the whitewashed walls, and the chairs surrounding the table were mismatched and rickety.

Mason smiled as Zeus turned away from the table, the small black comb he used to brush his prized goatee still in his hand.

"Well, look who finally decided to show up. I was just telling Tarek that I thought you'd decided to live in Morocco."

The American looked over at Tarek, who was hunched over a computer, his strong shoulders and huge arms dwarfing the tiny laptop. Like Zeus, he had worked for Ahmed in the Libyan intelligence service, and after a visit to the United States he had fallen in love with the movie *Serpico*. Ever since, he had adopted Pacino's shaggy hair and thick beard, which he dyed black to cover the gray. Mason had bought him a leather coat, like the one Pacino wore in the movie, and despite the warmth of the night he still had it on.

Zeus embraced him as he dropped his gear near the couch, and kissed both sides of his face in the traditional Middle Eastern greeting. Mason nodded to Tarek, who made no attempt to tear his attention away from the laptop.

"What happened to your face?" Zeus asked, holding his friend at arm's length. "I told you about the whorehouses in Morocco, but you wouldn't listen."

"It's nothing," Mason replied.

"Let me guess, you got into a fight because you ignored your friend's advice. Am I right?"

"I handled it."

"That's not the point, my friend. One day you're going to go against someone faster or stronger than you, and then what? If you don't listen to me, you will never live long enough to get out of here."

"I got it," Mason said, annoyed at the scolding. "I see you've been busy."

He pointed to the table, which was covered in maps and photos, and a computer that had seen better days.

"When Ahmed said that his 'little prince' needed help, we dropped everything." He smiled at his own joke and pointed to Tarek. "Now, if I could only get this one to do some work, I might be able to get some rest. Tarek, you are being rude. Say hello to our guest," he snapped.

Tarek grunted from the computer. Mason could see that he was scrolling through a gallery of porn, which had become a national obsession since the Internet ban was lifted.

"Tarek, turn off that filth and get us some tea," Zeus commanded while lighting a cigarette. "I swear to you, your bombs will never do as much damage as your American pornography. It will be the death of this country."

Tarek cursed loudly when the video he clicked on refused to load and slammed the computer shut.

"I keep telling you that we need better Internet. How am I supposed to do my job when I must wait an hour to download anything?" He stood with a huge smile, popped the front of his leather jacket like he'd seen in the movie, and swept Mason up in a backbreaking hug. "He has been on a long journey. I am sure he doesn't want tea. I have something much better." Tarek released Mason and disappeared into the small kitchen. A moment later, he returned with a bottle of Johnnie Walker Red and three glasses. He poured a healthy amount of the golden liquid into the glasses before passing them around.

"To the return of a good friend." Holding the glass high, he slammed the contents down with a fluidity born of practice. Once all the glasses had been refilled, cigarettes were passed out and Zeus moved to the center of the table.

"So what do you guys have for me?" Mason asked.

"I hate to be the one to tell you, but the files you downloaded, they were all corrupted," Tarek said as gently as he could. "I thought I could fix them, but right now it's not looking good."

"Shit . . ." Mason felt the bottom fall out of his plan and prayed that Zeus had something.

"Don't worry, my pale friend, once again I, the almighty Zeus, have come through," the large Arab said with a flourish. "You didn't give us very much to work with, but we made it happen. There have been three Americans who entered the country in the last two days." He pulled three pictures off the top of the large stack and laid them out on the table with the flourish of a showman.

Mason leaned in to get a better look. The photos had been taken with a telephoto lens, and the date and time stamps were visible at the bottom. He frowned at the first picture and idly flicked his cigarette as he studied the eyes then the nose and ears. Mason knew that if they wore a disguise, these would be the hardest parts to change.

"I don't know this guy," he said before moving to the second image. After studying the second photo for a few moments, he shook his head and, using his forefinger, pulled the final picture to the center of the table.

As soon as he laid his eyes on the final picture a jolt of recognition rose up his spine like an electric shock.

It was Decklin.

Mason could feel his heart beating faster in his chest as he leaned in farther to make sure. Ash drifted from his lit cigarette and fell like gray snowflakes on the picture.

Mason stared at the image with a visceral hatred, focusing on Decklin's eyes, which looked like two piss holes in the snow. The man had ruined his life, and he felt the edges of the picture slice into his hand as his fist closed around it. How well he remembered every single detail of that fateful day.

He and Decklin were in the lead vehicle as they drove over the pitted Libyan roads toward the town of Sirte. They were following a low-level asset to the city, and due to the danger outside the vehicle, inside the cab of the truck the mood was tense.

"You shouldn't have gone against the colonel like that," Decklin said as he tried to keep the target vehicle in view.

Mason had been watching his teammate stew for the last hour and was relieved that he'd finally broached the subject.

"What did you expect me to do? He murdered those people."

"That's not your call to make. I'm telling you that you fucked up *big*."

Mason knew that Decklin really didn't care what happened to him. The man had hated him from the moment he joined the unit and had been waiting for him to fail since the first day. He could see the outskirts of the city ahead and would be glad to get out of the truck and stretch his legs. If Decklin knew that he'd reported the colonel, then he was sure that Barnes knew, and it made him uneasy.

Barnes had handpicked him to join the unit, and most of the senior guys resented him for that. While the rest of the team held Mason at arm's length, the colonel had taken a personal interest in him, even promoting him above guys like Decklin.

Turning on the colonel was the hardest thing he'd ever had to do.

The man was like a father to him, but he'd lost touch with reality, even if no one wanted to admit it. Barnes was more focused on Libya than Iraq or Afghanistan, and now that their team had been sent into the country to overthrow Gaddhafi, Mason was having serious doubts about how much more he could take.

The target vehicle made a turn ahead of them, and Decklin hit the gas to keep from losing it around the corner.

"Pay attention, you're getting too close," Mason said.

Decklin ignored him and cut the wheel to avoid a gaping hole in the dirt road. The maneuver put them too close to the wall, forcing them to take the corner blind. As soon as they made the turn, they saw the target vehicle speeding through a checkpoint that had been set up on the road.

"Contact front," Mason yelled into the radio as the Gaddhafi loyalists opened up on their vehicle from twenty-five meters away. Bullets shattered the window, peppering Decklin with glass as a burst from a PKM hit the engine block of the Toyota Land Cruiser and the truck shuddered to a stop. Mason brought his rifle up from between his knees, bumping the muzzle on the dash as he flipped the safety to full auto. Getting the rifle centered on his chest, he held the trigger down and sent a long burst through the shattered glass.

His ears were ringing, but adrenaline numbed the pain as he threw the door open and rolled out onto the road. Getting caught in a near-side ambush was something they trained for, and Mason knew that his team had to gain fire superiority if they were going to break contact. He could smell the gun oil burning off the rifle as he hammered through his first magazine and began looking for a better position.

"Moving," he yelled as Decklin ran to the rear of the vehicle and tossed out a frag. Once his teammate started firing, he sprinted across the road toward the cover provided by a dilapidated warehouse five meters away. Changing magazines on the run, he found a position along the wall and reengaged the blocking position.

Mason needed to keep his head down while the rest of the team moved up.

Jones was on the radio calling for an emergency extraction as the team flowed into the building, firing as they moved, and Mason counted each one as they passed him.

Decklin was the last man to make it across the street, and after Mason touched his shoulder and added him to his count, he tossed a smoke grenade out into the street.

The team was already finding positions to defend their small perimeter when Mason entered the building. Decklin was directing Hoyt to blow an improvised firing port in the wall with a breaching charge, and Mason began looking for work.

There was an open window on the south side of the warehouse and Mason took his position next to the opening just as the charge went off. He was turning to get Decklin's attention when he came under fire from an open field, outside the window.

Mason ducked out of the way as the heavy rounds chipped shards of brick off the windowsill that pelted him in the face. Firing two quick bursts at his attackers, he dumped the magazine out of the rifle and was slipping a fresh one into the mag well when he heard the unmistakable sound of a grenade bouncing off the concrete floor to his rear.

Tink, tink.

He could hear the metal body rolling toward him and, without hesitating, dove through the window. Mason hit the ground awkwardly. He felt a sharp pain in his shoulders as the explosion blew a brown cloud of shrapnel and stucco over his head.

Dazed and bleeding, he tried to get to his feet. Just then an AK round slammed into his chest plate and knocked him on his back. Lying on the ground, gasping for breath, he could hear the sharp crack of bullets breaking the sound barrier above his head. Concrete dust and rifle frag rained down on him as the rounds thumped into the wall behind him.

I've got to move.

Breathing in deep raspy breaths, Mason dragged himself behind a pile of rubble and began firing as two of the loyalists maneuvered on him. The deep, slow hammering of their AKs echoed off the buildings, and he could hear the rounds smacking into the precarious pile of bricks.

Mason's heart was pounding and his hands were slick with sweat. He knew, without a doubt, that the frag had come from *inside* the warehouse. Decklin had just tried to kill him.

Gaddhafi's men were swarming around his position like fire ants emerging from a disturbed anthill. The sun burned down on the back of his neck as he came up to a knee and snapped two rounds into a man who'd just broken cover.

Pivoting to his right, he fired four shots at two men who'd made it within twenty feet of his position and then ducked to prep a grenade. He felt slow and vulnerable as he ripped the pin from the grenade. He was aware of the cold sweat soaking the back of his shirt. Releasing the spoon, Mason counted to three before tossing it out.

The explosion was immediate and a wash of hot dust and grit exploded up and out. Mason stayed on his knees and scanned for targets. He leaned out beyond his cover and acquired a fat jihadist in a torn polo shirt who'd stopped in the open to fumble with an RPG. The man went down hard and Mason tried to get a good look at the battlefield.

Dented pickups were bringing men from the city, and as soon as one unloaded, another truck would appear. The new arrivals formed a rough perimeter from east to west, forcing Mason to find a new position. The only cover left was the low wall of a bombed-out shed a few feet away.

Bouncing up to a crouch, he flipped the selector to full auto and darted to the wall. He held the trigger down as he ran, and the HK416 hammered through half of the magazine before jamming. Diving into cover, he felt a heavy blow strike his leg. His lower body twisted out from under him and he slammed hard into the brick floor.

Mason wasted no time clearing the malfunction. The rifle smoked in his hands, threatening to burn his fingers as he slammed another magazine into the weapon and prepped his last grenade.

He prepared himself for a good death and swore to go down fighting. Mason tried to come up to a knee, but his leg wouldn't support his weight. Grabbing the wall with his left hand, he pulled himself up to a throwing position. Tossing the frag long, he knelt and keyed up his radio.

Nothing.

He switched through the radio frequencies, but they were all static. The firing in the warehouse had stopped, and he knew that his team had left him to die.

"Mason, you were saying?" Zeus's voice pulled him back to reality. The cigarette had burned down to the filter in his hand, and he mashed it into the ashtray and grabbed the bottle of Johnnie Walker Red.

Get your shit together.

Taking a pull off the bottle, he composed himself and asked, "Where is he now?"

"He is in Benghazi. We have a man on him, but there is a problem. According to the French, he is working for the CIA."

"Wait . . . what did you say?"

"According to my source, at the French embassy, this man," Zeus said, pointing at the picture of Decklin, "is a CIA agent."

The new development didn't make any sense. The CIA was still reeling from the Benghazi bombings and the secretary of state had directly forbidden any American involvement in the country. If the CIA had agents on the ground, they were operating without presidential approval.

"Do you have a problem killing a CIA asset?" he asked Zeus.

"Not especially, but is that wise? I thought you were trying to go home," the Libyan said with crossed arms.

Mason looked back at the picture and took another shot from the bottle. Once his resolve was set, he turned to Zeus.

"You and I both know that I'm never going home."

CHAPTER 15

-------------------- Washington, DC

"I don't understand how something like this is even possible," President Bradley yelled as he slammed his hand on the table.

"Sir, they are claiming it was a weapons malfunction, but the facts tell a different story," the national security advisor said, placing a black folder on the president's desk.

"Duke, what am I looking at?"

"Sir, this is a joint report between my office and Director Hollis. We believe we've found the SecDef's source."

"Go on," the president said, skimming the memo.

"Sir, we believe that Secretary Collins has been using Master Sergeant Mason Kane to run guns from Libya to Syria. Besides the fact that this is extremely illegal, and a job typically handled by the CIA, we have learned that Kane was once a member of a decommissioned DoD project called the Anvil Program."

"I don't know what that is, Duke. I have never heard of the Anvil Program."

"Sir, right now I think we need to keep it that way. If any of this gets out you're going to need plausible deniability. You shouldn't be held accountable for policies enacted during another administration."

The president looked at Duke for a moment, weighing what his most trusted advisor was telling him.

"Okay, I'll go with that for the time being. What do I *need* to know?" he asked.

"The DoD lost contact with Kane two days before the attack on Karzai and didn't bother to let anyone know."

"Jesus, where was his last location?"

"Afghanistan."

The president slumped back in his chair, his eyes raised to the ceiling as if he was seeking spiritual guidance. Duke almost felt sorry for the man, but deep down he knew he had to keep moving forward.

"Sir, the CIA had an officer keeping tabs on Kane, and yesterday I was advised that he had been murdered. Per CIA protocol, Director Hollis initiated an in-depth investigation on Kane, which has turned up some very interesting information. If you will turn to page two, you will see a list of accounts that are tied to the DoD's Special Actions Division. The CIA has advised us that this is how the DoD is funneling money to Kane. We tracked the funds to a Libyan national acting as Mason Kane's handler. A man we know only as Ahmed."

"So the United States was paying the American who assassinated the president of Afghanistan. Is that what you're telling me?"

"I'm afraid so."

"Jesus, what am I going to do?"

"Sir, I can fix this, but I'm going to need some room to work."

The national security advisor had the president right where he wanted him, and he knew it was time to drop the hammer.

"What do you need? Just name it and I'll make it happen."

"General Swift has flown to Bagram to meet with General Nantz, and they are in the process of setting up an operation to take out Mason and whoever else might be involved. Right now all of this is circumstantial, but—"

"Duke, do what you have to do. If you need a presidential order to go get this guy then that's what I'll give you. Just get it done."

"What about Secretary Collins, sir? I know we don't get along, but I don't want to be the guy who ends his career by accusing him of treason."

"Don't worry about that, just find Mason Kane, get the truth, and we can figure out what to do with the secretary after that."

"Yes, sir," Cage said solemnly.

CHAPTER 16

Renee sat in the hangar, staring at the flat-screen attached to the plywood wall with two metal hooks. Everyone not performing mission-essential duties was crowded in front of the TV, watching the story unfold on CNN.

A reporter was standing on the roof of the Kabul Hotel as dark columns of smoke billowed up from the whitewashed city behind him. An explosion went off in the distance, shaking the camera and causing the reporter to duck and cover his head.

A few moments later, he regained his composure, and he began talking into the camera. "With the death of President Karzai, US military troops are flooding into the city. We have received footage of an American soldier taking credit for the assassination, and right now, as you can see, the city is awash in violence."

The camera panned away from the gray-haired reporter as another car bomb exploded near the center of the city, followed by a long burst of gunfire. Renee could hear the faint screams of rockets as they arced in from the hills surrounding the capital.

"It is the largest uprising we have seen since the invasion, and things are only going to get worse, as world leaders rush to an emergency meeting at Camp David. Sources close to the president tell us that this could be the last nail in the coalition's coffin. In the wake of the Arab Spring, it appears that America will soon be supporting the war effort on its own."

"Shit," Renee swore as Kevin walked in and stared up at the giant television.

"The bird's ready, but we have to go now. They are diverting all the flights."

She nodded and grabbed her gear before heading out to the flight line. Renee had wanted to talk to General Swift before heading out, but the man had gotten on a flight to Bagram before she had a chance. Things were moving quickly now, and without the general there, they could get out of control fast.

Renee sat inside the UH-60 Black Hawk and let her feet dangle out the open door as the pilot lifted off. The wind whipping into the troop compartment caused her pant legs to snap and pop as the bird picked up speed.

The crew chief and the gunner rotated their 240 Bravo machine guns up and out, ensuring they had unobstructed fields of fire. Renee rested her hand on the black rubber case that held her level-three gas masks and wondered what lay ahead.

Two dual-rotored CH-47 Chinooks pulled up alongside the Black Hawk before the pilot pushed the throttles forward and thundered off toward Kamdesh. The pilot kept the bird low and fast, and as the landscape raced beneath them, she could make out the oblong shadow of the Black Hawk on the brown earth. Reaching an open spot on the outskirts of the city, the gunners test-fired the 240s by sending two short bursts into the ground before putting them back on safe.

Kevin sat to her right and looked relaxed as the pilot rolled and dipped the bird, changing speed and altitude in an attempt to confuse any asshole on the ground with a gun.

Renee swallowed hard as her stomach knotted up. The locals

loved to shoot at low-flying helicopters, and she knew it only took one lucky shot to ruin a perfectly good day. One of the lessons taken from Somalia and reinforced in Iraq was the fact that a slow-flying helicopter was a hard target to resist.

She could hear the pitch of the rotors change as the helicopter fought to gain altitude. The hilly ground gave way to the foothills of the mountain range and the blades struggled for purchase in the thinner air.

"Ma'am, I'm looking at the grid you gave me and there's no FOB on the map," the pilot said over the internal channel.

"Trust me, it's there," she said confidently.

"I'll take your word for it," he said with a shrug.

Renee ignored the pilot and switched over to the team channel. It was too loud to talk inside the helicopter and even if she yelled, they wouldn't hear her.

"I know that Kevin already briefed you, but I'm going to go over it again. General Swift doesn't want us to go to the village until it has been cleared by the bio team. There is a Special Forces team already on site at the FOB. We are going to link up with them while the other team secures the convoy. I don't think Barnes is still in the area, but if anyone sees anything, let me know."

"Roger," the team repeated in unison.

"Guys, we need to stay frosty."

"Renee, we've got this, don't worry," Kevin said as the rest of the team nodded.

She knew they were the best at what they did, but at the same time, she was beginning to realize that going after Barnes was not going to be an easy day.

Forty-five minutes later, the pilot decreased his altitude as he searched for the objective. The door gunners began actively scanning for threats as the trail helicopter lifted above them to provide cover.

Renee could see the small FOB through the cockpit windscreen. It appeared as a tiny brown square among the gray mountains.

AH-64 Apaches circled the FOB like angry hornets. She knew from the quick briefing that there were attack aircraft loitering out of sight, just in case. In a matter of two hours all available assets had been allocated to cover the FOB and the wreckage of Karzai's convoy. For the time being, the military was bringing its full weight to bear.

Despite the air cover, the gunners and the pilot called out possible threats as they thundered toward the gravel-covered pad. The pilot brought the Black Hawk low over the stone-filled Hesco barriers before dropping the bird down for a soft landing.

Renee hung the headphones back on their hook and, keeping her head low, scooted out of the helo, her feet crunching into the gravel. The rotors kicked up a cloud of brown dust, obscuring the area as the engines went to full power. The nose of the Black Hawk dipped forward as the tail came up and the helicopter leapt into the sky.

Kevin yelled to catch her attention and pointed with an outstretched arm toward two bearded Americans standing at the edge of the landing zone. Renee walked over to them, cleaning the grit out of her mouth with a drink from her CamelBak.

"Ma'am, I'm Sergeant First Class Miles and this is Captain Westin with the Third Special Forces Group. We had no idea you were coming out until we got the call from your pilot."

"Pleased to meet you, Sergeant Miles, and you too, Captain. How long have you been on site?"

"We received a call from the FOB late last night. It came over a satellite phone and said the base was under attack," the captain began as they walked off the pad and into the perimeter of the small FOB. "Someone back at headquarters made contact with us over the radio and for some reason, our commo guy waited thirty or forty minutes before sending it up the chain."

Renee counted ten men moving around the perimeter and an

additional seven-man gun team pulling security from the apex of the low mountain peak. The FOB was perched on the flat edge of the mountain face. It had an excellent field of view of the valley floor below, and she could barely make out the quarantined village off in the distance. Renee could see plumes of dust rising like clouds from the valley floor where the heavy Chinooks were landing.

Evidence of the attack was inescapable and the stench of death rose above the FOB like the aftertaste of violence. Blast marks from grenades scorched the gravel where they had exploded, and bullet holes stared like eyeless sockets from the exterior of many of the buildings. The sun glinted off the shiny spent brass and gave the momentary illusion of something valuable.

So this is what a crime scene feels like.

"How many casualties were there?" she asked as she surveyed the carnage. It felt wrong to be here.

"There was an eight-man element here, with one commo guy; all of them were KIA. We have no reports of enemy casualties and no blood trails, but we haven't cleared anything besides the perimeter. It looks like they hit them while they were still in their racks. The last stand was around the commo shed. We found a lot of brass outside, but we haven't located the phone anywhere." Captain Westin spoke like he was ordering dinner. There was no emotion in his voice and absolutely zero empathy. It was obvious he didn't care for the outsiders interfering in what he considered a Special Forces matter.

The commo looked lonely and abandoned at the top of the hill, and the door frame and walls were pockmarked with bullet holes and blast marks. Renee could tell that whoever held the building had not wanted to give it up.

"They must have brought in some outside talent for this one," Captain Westin was saying as Renee walked into the shack. "I honestly didn't think hajjis had it in them."

Somewhere along the lines of communication, word of who perpetrated the atrocity was not being shared. Either the generals hadn't released the information, or someone was already trying to cover it up.

Renee shot a glance at Kevin, who shrugged and shook his head. She'd play along and let the facts speak for themselves.

Walking through the door of the commo shed, she stepped gingerly onto the cracked and splintered floor. Jagged black edges had been burned into the plywood planks that lined the bottom of the building, and splattered blood was still visible on the wall where one of the SF soldiers had been hit.

"Who is this guy?" she asked, pointing to one of the bodies.

"His name is Specialist Kent. He was a communications guy we borrowed from headquarters."

The entry wounds to his chest and head were much smaller than they would have been if they had come from heavier-caliber rounds.

A layer of sand was spread over the pool of blood that marked the site of his death, but the blood had seeped through and stained the sand crimson.

The smell of cordite hung faintly in the air like incense from an ancient ritual, and as Renee moved closer to the desk, just a few lonely drops of blood marked Specialist Kent's final resting place in Afghanistan. She turned slowly, searching outward from the desk, hoping to see anything that would tell her what she already knew.

"You still think that the Afghanis did this?" she asked, scanning the efficient kill zone.

"Maybe the Iranians or the Pakis sent a team over the border," the captain said.

"Captain, how long have you been in country?"

"Uh, a little over two months."

"Do you have any other combat experience?"

"Yes, ma'am, I was with the 508 Parachute Infantry Regiment in 2007."

"Oh yeah, where were you?" Kevin asked, looking up from another body that lay off in the corner.

"I was at Kandahar. I was the supply executive officer."

"So you never got into the shit? Is that what you're saying?" Kevin stared at him, daring him to deny that he'd never actually been in combat.

"Well, uhh . . ."

"Listen, *sir*, were not talking about a bunch of National Guard guys guarding a checkpoint at Balad. These men were some badass motherfuckers, and there is no way they get hit in the middle of the night without taking somebody with them."

"Well, I've heard of things like this happening in the Korangal."

"What Kevin is trying to say is that somebody with a highly honed skill set did this."

"Ma'am, what's that over there?" Kevin was pointing to the corner just to the left of where Kent had been killed. It was a small white square of cloth covered in what looked like dirt. However, as she bent down closer she immediately knew what it was.

"I'm not sure that I'm following you," the captain said.

"Renee, what kind of brass is that?" Kevin asked.

"I've got 5.56 NATO and two 7.62s. I guess the 5.56 is from him?" she said, bending down to scoop up some of the expended brass off the floor. "What about the brass outside, Captain?" Renee asked.

"It's all 7.62s."

"What are you thinking?" Bones asked.

"The entry wounds, they are too small for an AK. I bet this brass was planted."

Renee walked over to where Kevin was squatting and looked down at the corpse. He was no Green Beret. The soldier's hair was cut low, almost to the scalp, and his body was soft and flabby.

"You have a Gerber?" she asked Kevin, who slipped the multi tool off his belt and handed it to her. She opened up the pliers and said, "Sorry about this, kid," and slipped the nose into the chest wound.

"What the hell do you think you are doing?" the captain said, exploding, as he stepped forward. Bones moved into his path and stuck out his hand.

"Chill out, sir." He looked to SFC Miles to see if there was going to be a problem and the seasoned warrior simply shrugged.

Renee dug around for a second before the pliers hit something hard, and then very carefully she pulled out a mangled 5.56 round.

"The bullet never lies," Kevin said softly.

She maternally patted Specialist Kent on the head and whispered another apology before standing up. Holding the bloodstained round up for the captain to see, she asked, "So who called Jalalabad and asked for the drone?"

"I can't believe you did that." The captain was pale as he looked at the bloody round.

"The drone, who called for it?" she asked again forcibly.

"The drone was vectored in after we couldn't raise the FOB via radio or satellite phone. It was sometime this morning, but I was told that there was an equipment issue and it never made it to the objective."

The lies had already begun in earnest.

Renee dropped the bullet and wiped the Gerber on her pants before handing it back to Kevin.

"Kevin, let the pilot know we're ready for pickup. Captain, you might want to call your headquarters and find out what really happened here."

"I'm not sure I'm following you." They had only been here five minutes and had already found signs that pointed to a well-coordinated unit.

Renee wasn't sure whether the man was playing dumb or didn't see what was going on. The fact that someone had managed to take out an entire SF team without taking massive casualties was a feat in itself, but when you combined that with the fact that the site wasn't even on the maps, it pointed to a leak somewhere at the top.

There was something bigger going on here, and she wasn't about to get caught in the middle if she could help it.

"Birds are inbound," Bones said as they walked out of the commo shed.

"We're done here."

They stopped short of the pad and turned to shield their faces from the sand the bird kicked up as it touched down. Sergeant Miles waited for the crew chief to motion the team forward, then grabbed Renee by the crook of her arm and helped guide her to the door.

The team loaded up, leaving Renee and Sergeant Miles hunched beneath the spinning rotors. He stuck out his hand and shouted, "I know someone who can find Barnes for you."

Renee leaned forward, caught off guard by the sudden gesture. She stuck out her hand, and he jammed a folded scrap of green paper into her palm. He waited for her to gain control of it and then quickly pulled his hand away. Clutching the note tightly, she climbed into the Black Hawk and took a seat on the floor as the crew chief signaled the pilot that he was good to take off.

The helicopter squatted as the torque from the rotors compressed the hydraulic shocks of the landing gear before it shot skyward. The pilot cranked the stick hard to the left, sending the helicopter screaming downward into the valley.

Renee looked at the green slip of paper she'd wadded up in her hand. It came from one of the waterproof notebooks soldiers carried. Written on it in black marker was "Mason Kane."

CHAPTER 17

The sun was setting over Benghazi when Mason and Zeus pulled the dusty BMW into the small garage of the safe house. They had been on the road for the last eighteen hours, and Mason's mouth tasted like the car's ashtray. Both men had taken an amphetamine tablet halfway through the drive, and their minds were sharp despite the fatigue of their bodies.

Mason knew he could go another day without sleep but hoped that Tarek's plan wouldn't take that long.

Once inside the garage, Zeus set about switching the car's plates, while Mason pulled a toothbrush and a bottle of water from his assault pack.

It was amazing how brushing your teeth could make you feel like a new man. And the house actually had running water and a Western bathroom. No holding himself over a hole in the floor. Life's little luxuries. Mason judged his reflection harshly in the bathroom mirror. He despised the cold, hateful eyes, which stared at him like a mongrel guarding a trash pile. The face looking back at him was a mask he wore to hide from the things he'd lost. He thought about the last time he'd seen his ex. He'd surprised her by coming home early, and they'd gone out to see if there was anything left to talk about, or if they could maybe even try again.

Mason had spent most of their dinner nervously drinking Jack and Cokes while she laid out the problems with their sham of a marriage. He'd listened, nodding his head occasionally, but it was a one-way conversation for the most part.

The first sign that he'd changed more than even he had realized came when the movie started. He was reaching for the popcorn when there was a huge explosion on the screen. He thought he was in control, but the deep rumble that came from the massive speakers lining the ceiling of the packed theater sent him sprawling to the floor.

"What are you doing?" she asked, clearly freaked out.

"Holy shit, that was real." He grinned drunkenly from the floor.

"Mason, what's going on?"

Mason looked around, a deep feeling of shame burning its way across his face. He was supposed to be tough, and here he was lying on the floor like he belonged in a psych ward.

He didn't care whose feet he stepped on as he climbed to the end of the aisle and staggered toward the exit. She tried to grab his arm, but he pulled it free with a jerk. He needed air.

"Mason, stop, where are you going?" She grabbed him by the back of his shirt as the glass doors banged against the outside of the building. At the curb he doubled over, his mouth stretched into a mask as he vomited.

"Oh, Mason. I'm going back in to get you some water. Just wait here. Don't go anywhere."

As soon as she went inside Mason pushed himself up and, fighting off the world spinning around him, stumbled into the shadows.

That was the last time he'd seen her. But he knew that it was better that way.

Mason heard Zeus enter from the garage and go into the kitchen, where he began banging around in the cupboard. Drying his hands, he flipped off the light and went to meet his friend.

"Do you have to make so much noise?" he asked, walking into

the kitchen. The Libyan was filling a black kettle with water, and he squinted as the cigarette smoke got into his eyes.

"Why does it matter? I'm making tea, not going to the mosque. Maybe you can make less noise fixing us something to eat."

"Who's going to pull guard if I'm cooking food?"

"The only people coming to this house are those that we bring here." Zeus might as well have added "idiot" to the end of the sentence from the way he said it.

"Well, shit." Mason shrugged and started searching through the cabinets for something to cook. Tarek had ensured the safe house was fully stocked with everything they could possibly need, including cabinets full of food. Mason found a box of rice, some beans, and dried dates. Throwing the rice and beans into a pot, he added bottled water and placed it on the gas stove.

They ate the simple meal and went over the plan one more time. The fluidity of the situation required the ability to remain flexible. Tarek was in charge of the surveillance assets who were tracking the target, and Mason and Zeus would handle the crash-and-grab.

Once they were finished, they checked over the gear Mason had requested from Ahmed.

Each man had an AK-47 with five loaded magazines and three Russian grenades. He had asked for folding stocks on the rifles, and that was it. There weren't any optics or fancy flashlights that might give them away. Low-pro body armor, a trauma kit, pistol ammo, and two flashbang grenades rounded out the kit.

Mason took his worn Glock 17 from its holster, dropped the magazine, and ejected the round in the chamber. Aiming the pistol at the ground, he pulled the trigger and locked back the slide. Once the pistol was disassembled, he used a frayed toothbrush to clean the dust and sand from the slide before pulling a barrel snake through the chamber and out the muzzle. A light coat of oil and the weapon was reassembled and loaded.

Next he laid out the five pistol mags, unloaded them, and

began disassembling them. After lightly oiling the springs and brushing out all the crap that had collected inside, he put them back together and reloaded them. After securing his pistol and magazines to his kit, he turned his attention to the last piece of equipment.

The Taser had been hard to find, but Tarek was a resourceful man. It was a Chinese knockoff and the voltage was higher than he was used to, but it would do the trick. The yellow pistol had been painted black so it wouldn't stick out, and Mason checked the cartridge and the self-contained probes to ensure that no paint had gotten into the mechanism.

Mason was finishing up his inspection when Zeus's cell phone rang. The conversation lasted less than ten seconds before he hung up.

"The target is on the move—Tarek will pick us up." Mason nodded, grabbed the vest from the table, and strapped it on.

Ten minutes later, Tarek pulled up to the house in a four-door Toyota pickup. He was wearing an assault vest covered by an open shirt and his cut-down AK-47 was strapped above to the cab's ceiling. Mason got into the backseat with the barrel of his rifle pointing down. His eyes darted to the portable radio in the center console as a voice called out Decklin's position.

"He is four kilometers from your location, traveling west in a white car," the voice reported over the accelerating engine.

"Any idea where he's going?" Mason asked Zeus, who was talking over the radio while Tarek drove.

"He has been driving around for most of the day, but now that it's getting late he could be heading to the apartment or to get something to eat. I have a position set up if he goes to the apartment, but if he doesn't . . ." Tarek shrugged as he looked into the rearview mirror at Mason.

"The target is checking for a tail. I am going to have to pass him off," one of Ahmed's men, Jamal, said over the radio.

"I have the vehicle. He is approaching the intersection. He is moving south now in the second lane," another man said.

"What is your location?" Zeus asked. The man answered and Zeus advised that they were two minutes away.

Mason's heart was pounding as the different cars radioed information back and forth. Somehow they had to catch him out in the open but away from anyone who might be watching.

"He just turned in the middle of the road. The target is moving north. I cannot get to him."

"Shit, don't lose him," Mason said.

The radio fell silent as Tarek passed a slow-moving van and gunned the engine. Mason was looking for the white car, but it was dark and he couldn't tell the color of the cars until after they had passed. Luckily, traffic was light, but it would be easy to lose a tail in the city.

"I have him. He's parked the car in an alley and is on foot moving southeast."

Mason was sweating in the backseat as he tried to picture Decklin's movements. The target could have been getting food or he could have been meeting with someone who'd notice if he didn't show up. He realized that his muscles were tensed up and he tried to make himself relax.

"Okay, he's going into the store."

Mason let out the breath he had been holding as the seconds ticked by. Working off the assumption that he would head back to his car, Mason began setting up the grab.

"Zeus, I say we take him at the car. If he gets mobile again, we could lose him."

The Libyan nodded and asked for the exact location of the alley. As soon as it came over the radio, Tarek made a quick turn and cut across oncoming traffic. Turning onto the next street, he continued west for a moment before slowing down.

"There it is." He pointed to the nondescript sedan parked at the edge of the alleyway. Two modest buildings on either side appeared to be closed for the day. Mason was looking for a place to set the ambush, but the car was parked in an excellent spot to prevent that.

"Okay, head down the street and turn around. We're going to have to wait until he comes to us, and then we hit him."

Tarek continued down the street. Mason couldn't believe he was about to attempt a drive-by with a Chinese Taser. If it didn't work, they were going to have to subdue Decklin before he could get to a gun.

"The target is coming out of the store with a bag. He is heading back toward the car."

"Keep us updated. We need to know exactly where he is," Zeus said.

"Ask him what he's wearing," Mason said from the back.

"What is the target wearing?"

"He has on blue pants and a gray jacket."

"Well, that's not very helpful. I hope these little prongs will go through the jacket."

Tarek turned the car around and was waiting fifty meters away from the alley. He left his lights on to avoid unnecessary attention, but he couldn't stay in the street for long.

"Target is one street away and moving north."

"If he doesn't go down, I need you to be ready with a flashbang."

Zeus set the radio in the center console and pulled a bang from his kit. Using his fingers, he bent the wires securing the pin to the spoon so it would be easier to deploy.

"Two hundred meters."

"It's on you. Tarek, don't fuck this up." Mason had the Taser out and flexed his fingers around the pistol grip. Rolling down the window, he twisted in his seat to give himself the best angle possible.

Tarek slowly inched forward as he mentally kept track of the distance. It was hard tracking someone without a visual, and if he was wrong they could pass him.

The radio crackled. "He should be coming out onto the street any moment now."

Mason was searching for the first glimpse of the target as Tarek pushed on the accelerator. A car behind them honked and flashed its lights just as Decklin appeared in front of them. The car was right on their ass and Tarek was afraid to let it pass.

"Shit, go around, you fucker," Mason said as Decklin looked up in preparation for crossing the street. They were about fifty meters away and running out of room. Just as the target was stepping into the street, the car passed and the driver stuck his hand obscenely out of the window.

Decklin threw his hands up and cursed in Arabic. "Watch where you are driving, fool," he said before slamming the palm of his hand on the rear quarter panel of the passing car.

He looked directly at Tarek, who was now cruising along, and then focused on his car. Sticking his right hand into his pocket, he extracted his keys as they pulled alongside him.

Mason brought the Taser up and extended it out the window as Decklin turned his head to look at the vehicle. His finger had already closed around the trigger and the two metal leads shot out with an audible *pop*. Zeus was preparing to pull the pin as they stuck into Decklin's leg, and the Taser sent a jolt of electricity down the wires.

Tarek slammed on the brakes, sending Mason's face into the headrest. Decklin jolted as the volts hit his central nervous system and then dropped like a stone. Zeus leapt out of the truck and was on him a second after he hit the ground. The Libyan hit him with a savage strike to the side of his head to ensure he was incapacitated before slipping a pair of flex cuffs out of his back pocket.

Mason could hear Tarek on the radio calling for Jamal to come get the car as he pulled a black bag out of his back pocket and slipped it over the target's head.

Lifting him over the bed of the truck, they dropped him in. Mason reached into Decklin's waistband and secured his pistol while Zeus slipped another pair of flex cuffs around his ankles and pulled them tight. Before covering him up with a tarp, Zeus stuck a hypodermic needle in the target's neck and pushed down on the plunger. Decklin wasn't going anywhere for the time being.

Jumping back into the cab, Tarek hit the gas. From start to finish they had spent less than a minute securing the package. The radio came to life a final time as one of the trail vehicles dropped someone off to get Decklin's car. Mason lit a cigarette before punching the back of Zeus's seat in triumph. It was the only emotion he showed.

Back at the safe house, Mason attached the camcorder to the stand and flipped open the small viewing screen. He could clearly see the man secured to the chair and the table to his right. Three buckets of water, two plastic squeeze bottles, a towel, and a fire extinguisher were laid out on the table next to the hooded figure.

Zeus walked in front of the camera and began questioning Decklin in Arabic. The American demanded to know where he was and why he'd been captured.

"You are spy of the Jews," Zeus began as he circled the man with a length of garden hose dangling from his hands. "You will tell me the truth or I will hurt you."

"I am not a spy. I work with the United Nations. There has been a mistake."

"Do not lie to me!" Zeus yelled as he whipped the hose across Decklin's legs. "We know who you are and you will tell us the truth."

"I swear to you."

The hose cut through the air with a buzz as Zeus brought it over his head and down on Decklin's legs with an echoing *thwack*.

Decklin shot straight up in the chair as the pain washed over him. Behind the hood his mouth opened wide and he screamed. Zeus waited for the man's scream to die out before hitting him again. Decklin writhed in agony as Tarek came behind him and applied a chokehold to his neck. Mason could hear him gasping for air as Zeus struck him again.

"You will not lie to me!" he yelled in his ear. Tarek let go before he passed out. Mason lit a cigarette as Zeus and Tarek took turns beating and choking him. Zeus's shirt was soaked with sweat after ten minutes, and he tossed the hose on the table.

The chair was constructed to pivot into a reclining position. Each leg had a pin that Zeus removed while Tarek held on to the top of the chair. Once they were removed, the chair pivoted backward until it lay flat. He bolted it into a metal pipe secured to the floor.

Zeus walked over to the table, grabbed a white towel, and tossed it to Tarek. As Tarek pulled the towel flat across the man's face, Zeus filled an old metal can with water from one of the buckets. Mason held his cigarette in one hand and grabbed an empty bucket with the other. Placing it on the ground below Decklin's head, he moved out of the way.

"I promise that no one knows you are here, my friend, and no one is coming to get you. The quicker you tell us what we need to know, the quicker this will all be over," Zeus whispered in his ear.

Decklin tried to speak, but his words were muffled.

"I don't want your lies right now, my friend. I want you to sit and think about your situation. I know how long a man can hold out. So why put yourself through the pain when all you have to do is tell me what I want to know?"

Zeus slowly poured water over the towel spread across Decklin's face. The water seeped through the thin towel and then made its way down his nose. Decklin could only hold his breath for so long before his survival instincts kicked in, and once his mind sent the panic signal, he opened his mouth to breathe.

They had to be careful not to drown him, so Zeus poured the water slowly and waited for Mason to tell him to stop. Mason would nod when enough time had passed. The towel would be taken off his face and Decklin would cough and sputter for air until the towel was reapplied and the process was repeated. Each time Decklin was given just long enough to clear his lungs and grab a few breaths before the waterboarding continued.

Mason had learned this technique from the CIA in Iraq. He'd been taught what a man could take and what signs to look for to avoid killing the subject. Before he had been allowed to lead his own interrogation, he'd gone through his own session of waterboarding.

The terror that came with the drowning sensations could break even the strongest man. He had seen it break most detainees after only a few minutes. Mason didn't have the time to systematically break this man down, and he knew that you could only beat on a prisoner for so long before they started lying. They would tell you whatever they thought you wanted to know if you hit them long enough.

Zeus stopped after the second session to refill the can with water, which gave Decklin enough time to catch his breath. His body was shaking and he was close to going into shock. As the Libyan approached with the water he yelled, "Okay, I'll tell you."

Zeus spoke kindly. "I want you to realize, my friend, that we know who you are and will tolerate none of your lies. The first lie that comes from your lips will force me to start over."

"I don't work for the United Nations, I work for the British government—I'm looking for weapons."

"Is that why you were in Tripoli? Were you looking for weapons? I told you what will happen if you lie to me."

"Enough of this. Set him upright. I'll get the truth," Mason said in Arabic. He didn't have time to play games with Decklin, and he knew all too well the training they had been through to resist this type of questioning. "My brother thinks that he can lie to us and we will not know. I guess I must show him how wrong he is." Tarek and Zeus quickly set the chair upright, allowing Mason to move an industrial light around and aim it at Decklin's face. He motioned for the hood to be removed.

"It's been a long time, Decklin." Mason switched to English and watched his old friend squirm under the powerful light. His face was bruised and bleeding and was beginning to swell. "You've been busy, I hear."

Decklin's eyes adjusted to the bright light, and as soon as he saw Mason's face his eyes opened wide with fear.

"Mason, shit, I—"

"You what, thought I was dead? Your friend Vernon tried, but it didn't work out. I'm trying to get my head around what's going on, but I'm not having any luck. I was hoping you could help me out." Mason walked over to the table and grabbed one of the squeeze bottles before turning back to the chair. "I'm going to be real honest with you, buddy. You're not leaving this room alive, so the only thing you need to focus on right now is how much pain you are willing to go through before I put a bullet in your skull."

He didn't have an ounce of sympathy for the man who had tried to kill him twice in the last month. If Decklin wanted to act like a hero, then Mason was going to make him pay for it. The American held up the squeeze bottle in front of his would-be assassin's eyes and let him get a good look at it before he squeezed the bottle and sprayed its liquid contents over the man's legs. The smell of gasoline filled the room. Mason took his Zippo from his pocket and held it up for Decklin to see.

"So, what's it gonna be?" The Zippo's lid clicked open with a metallic snap and he used his thumb to spark the flint. Slowly he knelt down and touched the lighter to Decklin's pant legs, which ignited in a rush of orange flame.

Decklin tried kicking his legs in an attempt to put out the fire, but they were tied to the chair. The smell of burning fabric mixed with the black smoke of the gasoline as the flames crept greedily toward his waist.

"Mason, pleaaaase . . . ," Decklin yelled as the fire burned away the fabric and licked at the exposed skin of his legs. Mason squeezed more gas from the bottle and the fire jumped higher as the accelerant nourished the flames.

"What's it going to be? You want to burn to death for that piece of shit Barnes?"

The smell of burning flesh hit Tarek like a slap to the mouth and he recoiled in horror at the sizzling sound.

Decklin was screaming, but the soundproof walls absorbed his howls. He pleaded with Mason for mercy, but his old teammate just watched. Fire had its place in healing and justice, but when Decklin passed out from the pain, Mason felt nothing.

Zeus stood by with the fire extinguisher, and when Mason told him to put the fire out, he sprayed the white chemical across the unconscious man's legs.

"Tarek, you need some water or something?" Mason asked in Arabic.

"No, I will be fine. I have never seen this technique." He was visibly shaken, but he was in control of himself.

"Mason, are you sure this is the best way? We can give him the drugs if you want." Zeus checked Decklin's pulse, careful not to brush against his blistered legs. "If we kill him, we get nothing."

"He'll talk, trust me. He once told me that his biggest fear was burning alive. Just give him the adrenaline."

Zeus picked up a syringe from the table and jabbed the needle into Decklin's neck. He was careful with the dose, giving him just enough to wake him up but not enough to blow his heart. The man jumped up in the chair, the veins in his arms bulging against the plastic restraints.

"Welcome back, bro. As I was saying, why don't you fill me in on what you and Vernon were planning?" Mason squeezed another spurt of gas over his crotch and then waited with the Zippo.

"What the fuck do you want to know?" he screamed.

"Why are you in Libya?"

"To kill you."

"Yeah, I know that part. Who's running Barnes?"

Mason made a menacing movement with the lighter and Decklin tried to squirm away, his eyes wide with horror. "I don't fucking know," he yelled.

"Suit yourself." Mason set the lighter to Decklin's gas-soaked crotch and stepped back as he went up in flames. "Maybe I won't shoot you. Maybe I'll throw your body into the street so the dogs can get to you. If you're lucky and they don't eat you, maybe some nice person will take you to the hospital. I'm sure they're real nice in Libya." Mason had to yell over Decklin's agonized screams. "You ever visited a burn ward?"

"Vernon was working for Colonel Barnes," Decklin screamed as the flames burned through his pants and sizzled his flesh. "He bought some chemical shit from a doctor in the States. He got the guy to weaponize it."

"Okay. So Barnes hooks up with Vernon; what's the next target? Who's running the op?"

Zeus stepped forward with the fire extinguisher, but Mason blocked his path.

"I don't know, I just picked it up and dropped it off. I swear." Decklin was beginning to hyperventilate, but Mason didn't care.

"Mason, he's going to die," Zeus shouted as he tried to get past.

Mason knew he was close and refused to back down.

"Fuck him. Tell me, damn it."

"He can't tell you if he's dead." The Libyan pushed Mason out of the way and mashed down the extinguisher's handle. The flames had burned a blackened hole in the man's crotch and lower abdomen. The stench was overpowering and bits of pink flesh were poking out of the terrible wound.

Mason didn't care how much pain the man was in. He was going to get the answers he needed or kill the man trying. Snatching the syringe off the table, he held it up in front of the man's face. Decklin's head lolled to his shoulder, his mouth stretched wide as he screamed.

"You want morphine, then talk."

"Mason, look what you did to me . . ."

"Where's Barnes?"

"He's in Pakistan," Decklin whimpered.

There was no fight left in the man's eyes. He was dying and everyone knew it. His beard was matted with blood and saliva, and the bottom half of his destroyed body was still smoking. Blood, fat, and melted fabric dripped from his legs and collected in a puddle near his feet.

"There is a safe house in the city with all my gear. It's got everything you want to know on it. Please kill me," he begged.

"Tell me the address."

Decklin was fading fast and softly told him the address.

"Who's running the operation? Someone is giving Barnes intel, who is it?"

"It's Swift, General fucking Swift," he panted.

The hugeness of the confession was not lost on Mason, but he knew he couldn't let up yet.

"What's the next target?"

"Syria . . . the computer . . . it's all there."

Decklin's head slumped forward and he passed out.

"What do we do now? More adrenaline might kill him," Zeus said.

"The pain will wake him up," Mason said as he capped the syringe and tossed it back on the table. "We need to get to the safe house. I can promise you that it's going to be wired tight."

"I'll go," Tarek said weakly from the corner. He'd seen enough and would do anything to get away from the grisly scene.

"All right, but be careful and take your time. Don't fuck this up, we need this information."

Tarek practically ran for the door. Decklin moaned for morphine from the chair and tried to raise his head.

Zeus ran over to the table and jabbed the needle into his arm before Mason could respond. The relief was almost instantaneous as the drug shot through his system.

The two Americans looked at each other while Zeus backed away.

"What the fuck are you looking at?" Decklin slurred.

"You always had to be a hard-ass bastard, didn't ya?" Mason lit a cigarette and moved around behind the man. Leaning down, he placed his hand gently on the man's shoulder. "You always had something to prove, but there is something that I have to know." Mason paused and took a deep drag before leaning in. "Was it worth it in the end?" he whispered.

Decklin looked down at his mangled body, and his shoulders shook with silent sobs. When he raised his head, Zeus could see the tears streaming from his eyes but was unable to hear his tiny reply.

Mason stood up behind him and gently pulled his old friend's head softly over to his chest. He felt disgust welling up inside him past the rage that had fueled the interrogation. In the reflection of the camera's lens he caught a brief flash of his hateful visage and almost recoiled in horror. Pushing the weakness away, he grabbed a handful of Decklin's hair and jabbed a knife deep into the left side of his throat. Bright arterial spray shot from the wound as he dug the knife across the man's windpipe.

CHAPTER 18

One of the "armchair commanders," a major Renee had never seen before, came flying out of the operations office, his mouth twisted in anger as she and Kevin and Bones made their way toward the hangar.

"Is that a hot weapon?" he yelled as he marched across the tarmac, his finger pointing directly in Renee's face.

"Yeah, we just got off a mission. Do you have any idea what's going on out there?" she asked, stunned by his blatant aggression.

"I don't give a shit about some ragheads outside the wire. What I care about is you securing that weapon."

"Ragheads? Have you ever been outside the wire?" she demanded.

"That's not the point—"

"Look," she said, raising her rifle up to his face. "Do you see that smoke covering the horizon? Do you know what's going on right now? An American drone killed President Karzai, and those 'ragheads' want blood, because assholes like you keep sticking your finger in their face. So unless you want to try and take my weapon away from me and unload it yourself, I suggest you stand the fuck down."

She stood there staring hard at him as his mouth opened and closed a few times in disbelief. Renee guessed that most people allowed him to bully them with his rank, but she wasn't about to take shit from a guy who had never fired a shot in anger. When it was obvious he wasn't going to say anything else, she walked through the hangar door and headed to the operations center. Swift still wasn't back, but there was plenty of activity.

Men in a mixture of civilian and military dress were crammed into the operations center, and she knew right away that this wasn't the place to address her team. Renee had been in Jbad long enough to recognize Tier 1 contractors when she saw them, and she wanted no part of what they were involved in.

Typically, these men were contracted by the CIA and the NSA to conduct operations illegal to the military. They were paid operatives who worked outside of military channels on operations never meant to see the light of day.

Renee motioned for her team to head back to their room, where they could talk in private.

Five minutes later they stood around the table in the privacy of their team room and Renee asked, "So, who is Master Sergeant Mason Kane?" She wanted to know now that she'd had time to cool down.

"From what I heard, he's a guy who decided to grow a conscience at the wrong time," Bones said from his place at the briefing table.

"Why is he labeled a terrorist?"

"That is the million-dollar question," Kevin said as he opened his knife and began cleaning his fingernails.

"There was a team around here, about the time you went to Iraq. Guys called them the Ghost Squad," Kevin chimed in. "Their colonel was handpicked by General Swift."

"You mean the Anvil Program?"

"They had a lot of names. One of those urban-legend things," Kevin said, looking up from his battlefield manicure.

"So, what do you know about him?" Renee was intrigued. "Joe Rumor" was the military's unofficial information channel. The information usually came from a private who overheard a briefing and passed it to his friends.

She'd always found that there was a kernel of truth in every story, if you were patient enough to search for it. More often than not, the rumor mill was more accurate than an intel brief.

"I can only tell you what I've heard," Bones said.

"Well, let's hear it."

"First time I heard about Mason Kane was in 2008. I was at Firebase Lilley, about four miles from the Pakistan border. The CIA was using the firebase to run counterterror ops into Pakistan. We received actionable intel that a high-value target was holed up in some compound across the border. He was using opium money to finance anyone willing to come across the border and hit coalition troops.

"We knew where he was but couldn't get clearance to take him out. The CIA didn't like that, so they made a call to some general named Nantz who was the liaison between the CIA and JSOC at the time. Long story short, Nantz sends one guy across the border to neutralize the HVT. Guess who it was?"

"Mason Kane?" Renee guessed.

"Yep. Two days later, the target's head shows up in one of those foam coolers you buy at the gas station. The dude who brought it was the target's bodyguard. Said he found his boss dead on the toilet, with a note telling him to take the head to the firebase or get ready to bury his family."

"Holy shit," Renee said with a whistle.

"Like I said, it's all rumor, but I ran across a guy I know who said that Mason ran into a bit of trouble about six months ago. Something happened on a mission they ran up north."

"What happened?" she asked, intrigued by the story.

"People said he flipped out and murdered a bunch of civilians," Bones answered. "Single-handedly got all the Special Forces kicked out of Wardak."

"I remember hearing about that," Renee said. "The rumor was that some Special Ops guy was cutting off hajji faces and wearing them around like masks."

"Yep, that's the one. Anyway, it was right around election time in Washington, and General Swift began taking a lot of heat. He was told to send a team to take a look, but what they really wanted was for us to sanitize the site before anyone could get a handle on the situation."

"So what happened?"

"Hard to say, because Colonel Barnes sent Mason to Libya before anyone could talk to him, and right after that is when he left the reservation and got put on the kill list," Bones said.

Renee rolled her eyes at the two men. They were like kids at camp telling ghost stories. "That's pretty convenient. So no one actually saw anything?"

"Rico did. He got to the site before the rest of us, said someone had pulled all the bullets out of the bodies and collected all the spent brass. When he went out and talked to the locals, they all said the same thing. A white guy did it."

"So?"

"So Mason's not white. If you look at his army photo, the guy looks like a haj," Kevin said.

"Well, then, it couldn't have been him," Renee said sarcastically.

"Who knows, but it didn't matter anyways because Karzai got what he wanted. He used this to say he couldn't trust the generals anymore and started going straight to Washington, cut Swift and Nantz right out of the loop."

"I don't get it," Renee said honestly.

"What's to get?" Kevin asked. "We lost a major asset when they pulled the Anvil Program, and Karzai got free rein to do whatever the hell he wanted up in Wardak. Shit, it was all hands on deck when Mason went on the run. The DoD had us jumping through our asses trying to find him."

"Yep, they said they had a fix on him in Pakistan, but by the time they sent people in, he was long gone," Bones added.

"Probably never there in the first place." Kevin spat his dip into a bottle while Bones nodded his head in agreement.

"When does Rico get back from the Pesh?" Renee asked.

Kevin's prepaid cell phone rang, cutting off the conversation.

"Yeah? Okay, I'm on my way," he said, closing the phone and getting to his feet. "Speaking of the devil, the gate guards won't let Rico on base."

"Again? This is getting old," Bones said, sighing.

"Well, we might as well make it a field trip."

Renee grabbed her sunglasses, clipped her pistol to her belt, and followed the two men out to the truck. It was a five-minute drive to the north gate, where two guard towers and a row of concrete barriers were the only things separating the American enclave from Afghanistan.

Kevin put the truck in park and hopped out, leaving Renee to watch from the front seat. Her gaze drifted over the green sandbags fluttering in the wind and the small mounds of dirt collected at the base of the plywood guard shack. A mass of dirty Afghanis pressed against the chain-link fence, yelling at the guards looking down on them. Rocks bounced off the thick bulletproof glass with sharp cracks, and a haggard sergeant fought to keep his soldiers from escalating the already tense situation.

She had tried so hard to make a difference, but she knew that everything good they had done was now ruined. One man had destroyed everything in the blink of an eye. Renee scanned the soiled robes and windburned faces of the locals until her eyes stopped on a gaunt man squatted down against the fence. He was staring at her through squinted eyes, and two soldiers stood over him with their M4s at the ready. The soldiers looked to be about nineteen or twenty, and one of them suddenly kicked dirt at a young Afghani shaking the fence with his hands. Some of the dirt landed on the man seated at his feet, and the soldiers smiled as a young Afghani suddenly grabbed hold of the fence.

"Fuck you, America," he yelled as he shook the fence.

The soldier took the butt of his rifle and slammed it on the boy's fingers with a fleshy thump.

"Get off the fence," he yelled as the boy made a gun out of his fingers and pointed it at the man's head.

"America die," he yelled back.

Despite the chaos, the man seated on the ground continued staring at her until she looked uncomfortably away. There was something noble in his gaze and she found herself unwilling to challenge it. Kevin was showing his ID to the sergeant in charge, and the NCO pointed to the man she had just been looking at.

Renee looked back at the man—he was standing up now—and finally realized that it was Rico. When he got to his feet he looked at the soldier who was still yelling at the crowd and walked past without speaking. After walking through the gate, the sergeant handed him an AK-47 and offered a curt apology before turning back to the crowd.

He kept his eyes down as he walked to the truck and opened the back door. "What's up?" he said in a mellow Southern California accent as he tossed his gear into the truck.

"Did they just kick dirt on you?" Renee asked, handing him a bottle of water.

"Yeah, it happens all the time. Kinda gives you a different perspective on shit, though," he said, slamming the door and taking a long drink of water.

"Maybe if you'd call ahead, we could have a car waiting for you next time," Kevin said as he put the truck in reverse and headed back to their building.

"Whatever, bro."

"So, whatcha got for us?"

"I think Barnes has already crossed the border. There's some bad shit going down in the tribal regions right now."

"What do you mean?"

A few minutes later, the team was back around the table and Rico was digging a digital camera out of a dusty bag. He hit the power button and, after blowing the grit off the screen, tossed it to Kevin.

The digital images were graphic. The first picture was from inside a building. A dark crimson pool of blood was spread out on a rough wooden floor. There were black scorch patterns from grenades and the walls were chipped from shrapnel. The next shot was outside and showed heads stacked together to form a hideous pyramid reminiscent of Mesoamerican human sacrifices.

Quite a few of the shots had been taken on the move, which somehow made the images all the more grotesque. Grainy out-of-focus heads sat atop hand-carved spikes. Expressions of contorted misery were frozen on the faces and someone had taken the time to display them for everyone to see. The last shot showed a row of staked heads framed by snowcapped mountains. A lone woman was on her knees at the foot of a wooden stake with her head in her hands. Rico had gotten close enough to capture the woman's grief as the severed head leered obscenely for the camera.

"How many heads were there altogether?" Bones asked as the slide show finally ended.

"I stopped counting at about two hundred and fifty, but every district center that I went to had at least fifteen to twenty."

"Were they all confirmed Taliban?" Renee asked.

"I don't know every Taliban fighter that lives in the area, you know, but I do know that every major commander or lieutenant there had his head cut off. Some of the warlords and a handful of the high-level drug bosses were among the dead. It was very systematic, like they had a list or some kind of intel. If that's not bad enough, the people I talked to said white people did it."

"As in American?" Kevin asked.

"That's what they said. The people who live in these areas haven't seen Americans like they do over here. You know, maybe a handful of raids have gone off in the area, but most of those were done at night. The average villager couldn't pick out an American if you paid them. Whoever did this"—Rico pointed to the camera for emphasis—"is definitely not playing by any rules that I've heard about."

"So what do we do now?" Kevin nudged Renee, who was wondering the same thing.

"Something's not right here," she began. "I mean, does anyone else think it's strange that all roads seem to come back to Swift, and all of a sudden he gets called away? What do we know about General Nantz, and how in the hell does someone like Barnes plan the raid on Kamdesh without help?"

"Someone is helping him," Kevin said, stating the obvious.

"I just don't see Swift sanctioning a strike on an American FOB. Just doesn't seem like his style," Bones added.

"Maybe he didn't go see Nantz of his own accord," Renee said, thinking out loud. Like Bones, she was having a hard time seeing her boss as a traitor. "Either way, we have three targets right now and zero actionable intelligence. I have no idea who this Mason Kane is, or how he fits, but we know that there is a connection between Decklin, him, and Barnes." Renee was trying to get a plan together.

"Rico, do you still have access to that CIA dude, what was his name?" Bones wanted to know.

"Smith, yeah, he still owes me a favor," Rico said.

"Is he the one out of Bagram?" Bones asked.

"He was, but now he's the station chief's liaison. You know how rank has its privileges."

"All right, guys, cut the shit. Rico, I want to know what the CIA isn't telling us. Find out everything you can without making it too obvious. Kevin and I will focus on Mason. Bones and Tyler, that leaves getting a fix on Barnes up to you. We need to work quick on this."

"We're on it," Bones said, and turned to walk away.

"Well, if you put it that way, I guess it's time to go to work," Rico said, getting to his feet.

"Hell yeah, let's do this," Tyler added.

"Hey, Rico, how about you shower first?" Renee said.

"You got it, boss."

Kevin looked at Renee as the meeting broke up. He was about to say something when the phone on Renee's hip vibrated. Holding up a finger to Kevin, she lifted the cell phone to her ear. "Yeah?"

"This is Captain Lane at the TOC. We just got a fax saying that Task Force 11 has located Mason Kane in Libya. I have no idea why they sent it to us, but apparently they are launching right now to grab him."

"Any idea where they are taking him?"

"Well, the fax originated from a site somewhere in Chad, so I assume they will take him back there."

"So no one else knows about this?"

"Looks that way."

"Do me a favor and hold on to that information for a while. I'm heading to the flight line now. I need you to get me a flight."

"Roger that."

Renee felt her heart skip a beat as she hung up and jogged toward her room to grab her stuff. This was the opportunity she had been waiting for, and Renee knew that Mason might be the key to what was really going on. Now all she had to do was get to him before he was transferred out of the country.

CHAPTER 19

Sergeant First Class Harden stood at a window of the World Health Organization hospital in Pakistan and stared out at the marketplace below. A hot breeze brought up the rank smells of the unwashed and the charcoal smoke of the food vendors.

The *azan*, or Muslim call to prayer, drifted from a mosque's loud-speaker. The muezzin's amplified voice drifted over Peshawar's city-scape in a rhythmic undulation that beckoned the faithful to worship.

It was ironic, he thought, that somewhere in the tribal regions, the last of the Taliban were listening to the same thing he was. Colonel Barnes's squad had just spent four days sending these men a message in blood as they moved from district to district, killing anyone associated with the Taliban, and he knew that the squad only needed to push a little deeper into Pakistan's violent tribal regions to completely destroy the last of their leadership.

It had been so easy to hack into the CIA and Pakistani Intelligence Service databases and take the information that they'd been collecting and storing for years. All the target data and operational information that he needed had been waiting for someone to use them, while the agencies that collected the data did nothing.

Drone strikes and limited military incursions into the area might placate their political masters, but while the generals sat on their hands, America was losing the war. As a soldier, he saw the needless deaths for what they were, a betrayal, and while others may have been content to sit idly by and wait for the troops to be pulled out, he had chosen a much different path.

Harden heard someone coming up the hallway behind him. He turned to see Jones walking toward him, dressed like a World Health Organization volunteer. The WHO was unknowingly providing them with a base of operations and the perfect cover.

This was one of the most effective hospitals in the region. A massive earthquake that was followed by a polio outbreak had opened the insular city to myriad foreign aid workers who utilized the hospital and its compound as a base to distribute medicine and inoculations to the region.

"The boss wants to talk to you." Jones had been working nonstop for the past two days, deciphering the data from the attack in Afghanistan. Harden hated computers and was glad that his teammate knew what he was doing.

"You almost done with your thing?" he asked as they walked down the hallway, through a narrow corridor, and out into one of the courtyards.

"Yeah, I'm just putting the final touches on it before I pass out for a few days."

Harden slipped his sunglasses off the top of his head and over his eyes as they walked out into the open. He hated the desert sun and wondered why they never got to fight someplace nice and cold. If the Cold War had escalated, the upside would have been the fact that they would have gotten to fight in a place that had more than two seasons and a lot less sand.

"I hope it works better than that Y2K deal that had everyone freaking out."

"What I'm working on is going to make that look like an annoying pop-up ad. Remember what happened the last time you doubted my Jedi skills?"

"Yeah, let's not talk about it," Harden said as Jones opened the door to the team room.

The team had chosen the most isolated location and claimed they needed it to safely store the camera equipment they were using for a documentary. People were always helpful when offered the chance to be on TV. However, the downside of their cover was conducting phony interviews with the staff. Harden had given that shit job to Hoyt because of his lackluster performance in Kamdesh.

The team secured the area by placing a small "shim" camera above the room's only door. The monitor sat offset from the doorway and there was always a member of the team "pulling guard." For added security a claymore mine was mounted directly into the door with the detonator stationed at the listening post.

The room had rows of olive-drab cots lining both sides. Industrial lighting hung from exposed rafters and gave the room an institutional feel. Every cot had a soldier assigned to it and his gear was stowed neatly at the foot of the aluminum frame. The canvas cots had been designed during the Vietnam era, and Harden hated them because they were a bitch to put together.

He'd been sleeping on cots like these for the last ten years of his life and he still cursed the design. Before he could sleep on it, he had to slide a metal bar through the end and stretch the canvas tight enough to lock the bar into the frame. No matter how many times he tried, he always ended up with bloody knuckles.

Harden knew something was up because instead of sleeping, the team was cleaning their rifles and checking their kits. A low table in the middle of the room was covered with ammo, grenades, batteries, and other articles of war. At the far end of the room, next to his cot, was a small area curtained off by three poncho liners hanging from olive-drab 550 cord. The cord was attached to nails that had been driven into the wall.

This was the colonel's area and the team stayed away unless summoned. Standing at the opening of the hooch, Harden fought the urge to snap to attention before making his presence known. He had been out of the regular army for five years, but the discipline ingrained in basic training never went away. After a moment he said, "Sir, you wanted to see me?"

Colonel Barnes's raspy but commanding voice emanated from within the enclosed area: "Come in."

The colonel's room was neat but spartan. Barnes allowed himself no comfort items, except for a handful of books and a cot. A dusty plate carrier hung from a nail sunk into the wall, and below that was his rifle. The battered HK416 had seen more than its share of use. The bluing was wearing off and specks of silver flecked the black weapon, giving it a worn appearance.

Barnes stood shirtless near the wall, with a satellite phone held in his hand. The muscles in the colonel's arm flexed as he switched the phone to his other ear and motioned for Harden to hold tight. Barnes was a big man and despite his age was in excellent shape.

Large veins snaked up his solid arms, tracing across the muscles like contour lines on a map. Broad shoulders framed two tattooed ravens, which perched like Odin's mythical companions over his pectoral muscles. The two black birds stood silent witness to his patchwork of faded scars.

"Yes, sir, I understand that, but Swift isn't going to play dead. We need to deal with him right now . . . I understand that, sir, but I respectfully disagree . . . Roger that, I'll take care of it."

Barnes tossed the phone on the bed and looked at Harden.

"Look, we're almost done here in Pakistan, but I need you to take a team to the Swat Valley and set up an ambush."

Harden had spent the last few days killing on a scale that even he was unaccustomed to, and he was tired, but he knew they weren't finished yet. After they had flown out of Afghanistan, the colonel had dropped him and half of the team off in the tribal region, and while the rest of the team set up camp here, they had decimated anyone who had ties to the Taliban.

"Yes, sir, what's the target?"

"General Swift is proving to be the coward I always knew him to be, and he is trying to work both sides. We are going to force him to commit by leaking our position as northeast of here in the Swat Valley. The boss is giving him one final chance to pick a side." The colonel pointed to the area, and Harden nodded his agreement. He was familiar with the terrain and it was perfect for an ambush. "I need you to take a team out tonight and recon the area; I'll bring the rest of the team to link up with you."

"I got it, sir. Anything else?"

"No, just get me the grids."

"What about the rest of the targets holed up in the tribal areas?"

"Looks like they're getting a reprieve. I believe that we will have worn out our welcome in Pakistan after we deal with this situation."

"I'm good to go, sir, but . . ." Harden trailed off, not wanting to step out of line.

"What is it, Harden?"

"I was wondering if you've heard from Decklin."

Barnes turned to him, his eyes burning brightly with resolve. "He's got his orders. If we haven't heard from him, it's because he's working or dead," Barnes said coldly.

Harden had befriended Decklin, as much as you can befriend a psychopath, when he first joined the team and had mentored him until his skill set surpassed Harden's own. He knew that if he had gone this long without checking in, it was because he was physically unable to.

"Are you worried about him?" Barnes's question was more of an accusation than anything else.

He knew that Barnes was testing him. Keeping the title of Anvil 7 and the responsibility that came with it was never a guarantee. He had learned from his predecessor that getting the job was the easy part. Keeping it was an entirely different ball game.

"I was just curious," he lied.

Barnes nodded and smiled coldly at his star pupil. "It's a heavy burden to carry, but don't ever allow yourself to take your eyes off the prize. We have had to sacrifice so much to get here. Every time I look over those mountains, I imagine all of those soldiers hiding behind their walls, afraid to take victory out of the enemy's hands. We are here because they are unwilling to do what is necessary to win, and that weakness has emboldened our enemy. They smell the fear like a shark scents blood in the water. Our enemy knows what they themselves refuse to admit—they are all dead men waiting for their time."

"Yes, sir, is that all?"

"Go get your men ready." Barnes turned back to the map and Harden pivoted on his heel and headed back to the cots. He found Boz, his squad leader, already packed and ready to go. Boz's long hair was pulled back in a ponytail and his long, gray-flecked beard made him look like an outlaw biker.

"We have a mission?" he asked.

"Yeah, we need to go scout an ambush site up in the Swat Valley."

"Fuck yeah, I love ambushes."

"Grab Hoyt and whoever else you need and tell them to pack for seventy-two hours. I don't think we'll be gone that long, but you never know. We need claymores, a long rifle, and all the rest of the usual shit. I'll brief the operations order once the team is up. I'd like to be ready to roll in an hour."

"Got it. I guess I'll use Scottie, he's good on the long gun."

"Sounds good, let's get it done."

Harden headed to his bunk to pack his shit and let his squad leader handle the rest of the team. He pulled a map out of his filthy assault pack and found the area Barnes had pointed out to him. From the map it looked like a good spot, but he would have to get eyes on the terrain to make sure. The maps were old and sometimes the terrain on the ground wasn't exactly what you expected.

The distance to the target was about two hundred kilometers, but taking the terrain, and the fact that they would be on foot part of the way, into consideration added to the time it would take. Looking at the map, he mentally began marking ambush sites, alternate sites, and possible landing zones. He needed a backup for every primary site that he chose as well as emergency egress routes, rally points, and direction of travel.

Thirty minutes later his gear was packed, his kit was loaded, and he was headed through the door and out into the courtyard, where the vehicles were staged. Scottie had already topped off the truck and stowed the fuel and water in the back. Boz and Hoyt opened the rear doors and took a seat.

Scottie took his place behind the wheel and checked the sawed-off shotgun that was stowed between his seat and the gear shifter. Once he was ready, he started the vehicle and headed out into the city.

CHAPTER 20

Libya

"How far to the highway?" Mason asked as he chased the bouncing flame of his Zippo with the end of his cigarette. The old Jeep swayed side to side on its ancient suspension. The flame dimly illuminated the utilitarian interior and slightly washed out the Libyan's night-vision device.

Zeus frowned and took his foot off the gas until Mason lit the cigarette and closed the lighter with a click. It was hard enough driving in the daylight, but trying to get out of the foothills under night vision really sucked.

It seemed like every time Mason was in Libya, the roads were washed out, and this time was no exception. As Zeus dropped the truck into another hole, Mason began to feel carsick from staring at Decklin's computer.

The PVS-14 Zeus was wearing completely distorted his depth perception, making it impossible to pick a safe path. Inside the cab, Mason struggled to keep the laptop stable, while Zeus fought to keep the wheel steady.

"Five kilometers, but at this rate that could take all day," the Libyan said grimly.

Mason's stomach demanded he close the laptop or face its wrath, and he was just about to comply when he recognized a name he'd known from the Anvil Program. Clicking on the tab entitled "Gen. Swift," Mason brought up a memo written to his old boss.

"Hey, listen to this," Mason said to Zeus as he began reading the memo out loud. "It's a memo from some general in Bagram to General Swift, the commander of Special Ops in Afghanistan. It's labeled 'Eyes Only,' which means Decklin definitely stole this copy."

"Good for him, what does it say?"

"It says, 'You are directed to utilize Anvil 6 to prosecute kinetic operations in Objective Lion.'"

"So, what does that mean?"

"It means that someone higher than Swift is pulling Barnes's chain. I bet there's another attack on the horizon."

"You're reaching," Zeus replied.

"Bullshit, I'm telling you the same thing I told Ahmed. Someone is running Barnes and now we have proof that he's running Swift too. They are both fucking traitors," Mason said, slamming the lid in triumph.

The American glanced at his friend, who appeared bored as he leaned forward in his seat. The green light from the night-vision monocular spilled out over his left eye and provided the only illumination in the Jeep.

Mason could tell he was skeptical, but the American knew he was onto something.

"So, what do you think?"

"I hope this old piece of shit holds out," Zeus replied as the front end disappeared into another large rut. Mason's hand shot out to the vinyl dashboard as Zeus punched the accelerator and cut the wheel to the right.

"It might if you stop hitting every hole in the road."

"It is a good truck. They don't make them like this anymore," Zeus replied as the tires caught and dug themselves out of the hole.

"Dude, this truck is like ten years old. It's not exactly a classic."

"Yes, but now they make them out of plastic. They aren't worth a shit."

"Look, I know we're getting close to breaking this thing wide open. You have to trust me," Mason said.

"It's not like I have anything better to do," the Libyan replied.

"If we can find out who is pulling Swift's strings, we have a chance to end this."

"Is that really what you want?" Zeus took his eyes off the road for a split second and shot his friend a searching glance.

The two men had naturally arrived at a brutal honesty that formed the foundation of their relationship. They shared everything, even blame, and kept no secrets from each other. It was the only way they stayed close despite the horrors they'd been forced to commit.

Mason admired the Libyan and felt that he needed the man more than Zeus really needed him. He knew that his friend was tired of fighting, but he never complained and never let him down.

The cab fell silent again, leaving each man to exorcise his own demons.

"Did you hear that?" Mason asked suddenly.

"What, did you fart again?" Zeus asked, rolling the window down in anticipation of the smell to come.

"No, it sounded like rotors. Get off the road!"

Zeus snapped the wheel hard to the right and bumped the Jeep onto a soft field, and scanned for a place to hide. They were caught out in the open, with nowhere to go, and all they could do was wait.

Mason stubbed out the cigarette and propped open the door. He'd already disabled the interior lights, but he still had to be careful. Lifting his night-vision device to his eyes, he scanned the horizon near the foothills off to the west. There was nothing but empty sky in every direction. Maybe his ears were playing tricks on him.

Zeus got out of the truck, AK-47 in hand. Checking the magazine by feel, he reassured himself that it was full before jamming it back into the magazine well.

"Mason, I see a ditch," he whispered in Arabic.

The American followed the Libyan's outstretched finger and saw a small scar cutting through the field to his left.

"Go. I'll grab the gear."

The NODs bumped against his breastbone as he let them hang from the black cord attaching them to his neck. Reaching into the back of the truck, he grabbed his pack and rifle before sprinting toward Zeus. There was no mistaking the sound of an approaching helicopter now. The pilot had used the mountains to mask his approach, but now the heavy rotors echoed off the open ground.

Mason jumped down into the ditch and grabbed the satellite phone from his assault pack. Tossing it to the ground, he smashed it with the butt of his AK.

"Get rid of your phone," he told Zeus.

The Libyan ripped the battery out of his cell phone and flung it into the darkness, then hunkered down into the ditch.

Mason put the night vision back to his eyes and looked up into the darkness. Someone was tracking them and this time Ahmed wasn't there to warn him.

"Fuck."

A black shape gradually appeared, skimming low and fast over the rolling hills to the west. Mason saw it drop to twenty feet off the deck and race toward them.

The MH-60G Pave Hawk skimmed closer, outrunning the sound of its rotors, and Zeus flipped his rifle to "fire." Mason knew there was no way they could do anything to the Special Operations helicopter with a couple of AK-47s, so he quickly pushed his friend's rifle down.

"They'll kill us," he said simply, tossing his own rifle to the ground.

The Pave Hawk buzzed low over their position, its hot exhaust and downdraft beating the ground as it passed. Through his NODs Mason could see the gunner's infrared laser come to rest on them as the pilot brought the bird around in a shallow circle. He knew that the laser was attached to an M134 minigun, and he had no intention of provoking the gunner to use it.

"How do you manage to piss off so many people?" Zeus demanded, tossing his AK into the dirt.

"Me? You were there too. Don't try to act innocent," Mason yelled back as the helicopter flared briefly before setting down.

Zeus leaned in to ensure that Mason could hear him. "You always get me into this bullshit."

"Try to act professional." Mason shoved him as a group of soldiers jumped off the bird and fanned out. Before dropping the NODs, Mason could see four more infrared lasers dancing over his chest as a team approached their position with rifles at the ready.

"You better be glad that your friends are here, or by Allah I would kick your ass," Zeus hollered, shoving Mason back.

"Oh, really . . ."

"You two, shut the fuck up," one of the soldiers commanded as he placed his barrel into Mason's face.

"Uhhh, okay," Mason replied, looking up at the man he could barely see. "So, what's going on?"

"Keep your mouth closed," he said as two of his teammates reached down and roughly pulled the two men out of the hole.

"Hey, go easy, I've got a bad back," Mason complained as he was tossed to the ground. He felt a knee in his spine as they slipped plastic flex cuffs around his wrists and pulled them tighter than necessary. One of the men jammed a muzzle into the back of his skull, and the American prayed the operator had his finger off the trigger.

"Get him up," a voice commanded.

The two men jerked him painfully to his feet by grabbing his secured arms. Mason was able to get his legs underneath him before they nearly pulled his arms out of their sockets and stood grinning at them in the darkness.

One of the men flashed a red-lens flashlight into his face. The soldier's night-vision goggles were flipped up on his helmet, and the green hue that glowed out of the eyecups barely illuminated his dark beard and cold eyes.

He held up a picture and compared it to Mason. A moment later he clicked the small disk on his chest and spoke into the microphone that jutted out in front of his mouth.

"Hunter 6, jackpot." He took his finger off the talk button and turned back to the helicopter.

"What about the other guy?" one of the men asked.

"Bring him too."

A soldier pulled a black bag out of his cargo pocket and pulled it over Mason's head. Mason was guided back to the bird and felt his head being pushed down under the rotors before being forced into the Pave Hawk. The door was slammed shut and he heard the rotors spinning up as the helicopter jumped into the night sky.

Mason had no idea who these men were or where they were taking him. He was glad that they hadn't shot Zeus and left his body in the desert, but he felt bad that he'd gotten his friend caught up in another shitty situation.

His mind ran over the possibilities. If they had wanted him dead, they wouldn't have taken him, but that didn't mean anything. Right now there were too many unknowns, especially the identity of whoever was working behind the scenes. Depending on what they knew, Mason felt that he was in for a bad experience. He knew what he had been willing to do to get Decklin to talk, and there was no doubt that whoever was waiting for the bird would do the same, if not worse, to him.

CHAPTER 21

-------------------- Faya-Largeau, Chad

The Pave Hawk's wheels hit the tarmac with a rubbery thud, and Mason felt the bird's hydraulic struts compress as the pilot began shutting off the engine. He had no idea where he was and the only thing he could see was a tiny sliver of daylight at the bottom of the black bag.

The door to the Special Operations bird was thrown open, and he felt a pair of hands grab him and yank his body out of the door. The toes of his boots scraped against the ground as strong hands dragged him across the pavement and tossed him into a truck.

A body bumped into his shoulder in the artificial darkness and then the door slammed.

"I told you this was a terrible idea. You know I hate being tortured," Zeus hissed from his side of the backseat.

"Calm down," he replied in Arabic.

"How am I supposed to remain calm? This bag smells of rotten assholes." They had placed an operator between them, and the man told them to shut up, and Zeus fell quiet for a moment, then whispered, "I have to go to the bathroom very badly."

"Can you stop crying for a second and act like a professional? I'm trying to figure out where we are."

"How are you going to figure out where we are when we have

bags over our heads? These men are going to chop off our dicks and leave us in the desert to die."

"What are you talking about?"

"That is what your CIA does. I have heard all about it."

"If you two don't shut up," the voice from Mason's left yelled in Arabic, "I *am* going to stop this vehicle and chop off both your dicks." Both men fell quiet and Mason tried to get a sense of where they were.

The silence didn't last long. Zeus was nervous and unable to stay calm.

"I told you they were going to cut off our dicks," he said.

"What is it with you and getting your dick cut off all of a sudden?"

"I don't know," Zeus whispered back.

"Well, shut the fuck up about it."

"I can't."

"That's it. Stop the car, Mike," the man seated between them exclaimed.

"Mike, don't stop the car. My friend is nervous," Mason said quickly, trying to get some control over the situation. "Zeus, will you shut the fuck up? Look, guys, I think I've been pretty cool up to this point. I let you put a bag over my head and zip-tie me and do all your little spy shit, but let's not get crazy."

"Mr. Kane, no disrespect, but we have our orders," a new voice said from the front seat. "If you two could just sit back there and enjoy the ride, I would really appreciate it."

The vehicle was quiet except for the sound of the engine, which droned on as they drove. Mason didn't feel any bumps, so he knew they weren't going off road, and the speed was constant, so he assumed they weren't in traffic. He was almost certain that they were driving around in circles on a base somewhere close to Libya.

The vehicle slowed before coming to a halt. The mechanical sound of a door motor creaked in the background as his door was pulled open from the outside. The overhead lights allowed Mason to see through the fabric of the mask. It was like looking through a fogged window, but he was able to see the outline of a man reaching in to grab him. Strong hands yanked him roughly from his seat, and he scrambled to get his feet under him. A heavy grip clamped onto his shoulder as he blindly struggled to get his balance. Once he was set, he felt the man pushing him across the floor, which squeaked under his shoes.

Mason was confident that they were in a hangar.

He knew he needed these little victories to keep him alive. Knowing you were in a hangar didn't mean much in the scheme of things, but everything that boosted his confidence would help when things got rough.

A door opened to his front, and his escort pulled up on his shoulder and said, "Watch your step."

He lifted his foot up tentatively and was guided over a step up and into a hallway.

The temperature dropped a few degrees, which suggested an office or at least a space that had air-conditioning. Mason was pushed down a hallway, and he hoped they were going someplace to talk and not the alternative. Another door clicked open, and he was pulled into a room and pushed down into a chair.

The seat was cold under his butt, and he could feel a change in pressure as the door shut and locked with an audible click. He was in an interrogation room, but the absence of the usual shit-and-piss smell calmed his nerves. This was not the place where the hard questions would be asked.

Sitting in silence, Mason had no way of keeping track of time. All he knew was that his butt was falling asleep and he couldn't get comfortable. The metal chair had been altered and led him to believe that he was in a CIA holding facility. The CIA loved stress positions, and one of their favorite techniques was to cut an inch off the front legs of a chair so that you had to constantly fight to keep from slipping forward. He'd known guys to spray wax on a metal chair before an interrogation just to screw with the detainee.

He was sliding himself back into his seat for the hundredth time when the door opened and footsteps scuffed across the floor. The bag was pulled off his head, and he blinked against the bright lights of the room.

Mason's eyes adjusted slowly and the first thing he saw was a wooden table in front of him. A medium-height man, in a starched white shirt and black pressed pants, ambled slowly around into his field of view. He tossed the black bag on the table, followed by a thick manila folder, which landed with a slap.

The man took a seat. His shirt was open at the collar and his thin gold-rimmed glasses, perched on a bony nose, gave the man a banker's air. Mason could handle muscle-bound goons and the thick-necked interrogators who spat on you when they yelled, but this guy immediately made him nervous.

"Good evening, Mr. Kane. I apologize for any theatrics on the part of my associates, but we have a few topics we need to address. I hope you understand."

Mason stared at the man. He was going to let him do all the talking until he could get a handle on the situation.

"My name is Mr. David, and I've been looking for you for quite some time," he said, peering at Mason over the top of his glasses.

Mason remained silent, and the man opened the file and began casually turning pages.

"May I call you Mason?" he asked without looking up.

"Yes," he finally replied.

"Good," he said, managing a thin smile. "Mason, you have had a very extraordinary and distinguished career. According to your file you were one of the youngest men to ever pass Delta selection. You have remarkable ability with languages and are fluent in Arabic, Pashto, Dari, and Spanish. Everything was going according to plan until that night in Wardak." Mr. David looked up from the file folder, crossed his hands, and looked at Mason. "Would you mind telling me what happened?"

"It's not in the file?"

"Oh, it's in the file, but I think it only fair to hear your side of the story."

"I was a member of the Anvil Program, and I believed that some of Colonel Barnes's methods were not in the best traditions of the United States government."

"You were in Afghanistan at the time?"

"Yes, sir."

"And what exactly was the problem, in your opinion?"

"Colonel Barnes killed a local family when they wouldn't give him information on a Taliban network that was operating in the area."

"So you believe that he murdered these people in cold blood."

"Yes, sir, I do."

"And you had a problem with that?"

"Yes, sir, I had a problem with that."

"So for brevity's sake, you reported the allegations to General Swift, and what was the result?"

"They tried to kill me."

"Who are *they*?"

"Barnes, the team, Decklin. Pick one."

"And where did this occur? In Libya?"

"Yes, while we were on an operation."

"But you survived, and after that the situation got decidedly worse. When did you decide to start killing employees of the CIA?"

Mason didn't like where this was going. "What do you mean?"

"Well, I am curious: at what time did you decide that it would be a good idea, for a man in your position, to torture an Algerian national, put a bomb in your handler's cell phone, and cut off another man's head in Libya? It's a simple question."

Fuck.

"I guess it happened around the time they decided to kill me," he replied.

"It seems that a lot of people are trying to kill you. I wonder why that is."

"I've been told that I have a smart mouth," Mason replied honestly.

"Right now the CIA has a problem. We seem to be suffering from major incompetence among the operational elements in the theater. The last two station chiefs in Libya and Somalia are probably working at Walmart right now as greeters, and we have had to shut down our intelligence operations in the area. I've been watching you since we discovered you were communicating with Vernon, and I believe you can help me. But honestly, you hardly have a choice, really." All signs of the banker who had been sitting in front of him moments ago had vanished. The man's eyes had hardened and his face was filled with determination.

"Since the attack on Benghazi the CIA's operational footprint in North Africa has been reduced to zero. Right now we are unable to recruit assets, gather intelligence, or conduct operations in most of the countries where terrorism is thriving. And now with Hamid Karzai's assassination things have gone from bad to worse."

"Wait, what did you say?"

"The president of Afghanistan was assassinated with a drone. The people of Afghanistan blame the Americans and have begun a massive uprising."

"How the fuck did that happen?"

"Our best guess is that Colonel Barnes has decided to prosecute this war on his own terms," the man said.

"So, what do you want from me?"

"We'll get to that in a moment." He slipped the glasses back on his face and returned to the papers before him. "According to your files, you have a problem with authority but are extremely capable. Your handler Vernon categorized you as, and I quote, 'a valuable weapon who will continue to operate in any capacity as long as properly motivated.' Is that true?"

"I accomplish the mission assigned to me in a timely and efficient manner." Mason felt he needed to toe the party line until he got a better grasp on the situation's dynamics.

"That is a very cute answer. However, your records indicate that this is actually true."

"Sir, what exactly do you want from me?" Mason felt like he was at a job interview, but the flex cuffs told him otherwise.

"Well, Mason, your credibility in the United States and the Middle East is at a very low point. We are blind, deaf, and dumb right now, and my only salvation is a man accused of treason and acts of terrorism. Your friend Zeus has ties to Hezbollah and al-Qaeda, and you yourself are a known associate of quite a few terrorists.

"Right now the team needs a win, and I think that you two would fit the bill. I can offer you the same deal that Agent Vernon proposed. Except this time I can promise we'll follow through on it. No more false missions. You get Barnes and I've been authorized by the president to take you off the terror list and welcome you back into the fold."

"So you want to be my friend, is that what you're saying?" Mason was getting tired of the games, and if he was going to hang, then he'd rather get it over with.

Before the man could reply, the door to the room opened and a man stuck his head in. He motioned for Mr. David to come out into the hall.

"Please excuse me, I'll be right back."

"Can I have a cigarette, in the spirit of cooperation?"

"I'll see what I can do."

Mason was examining his flex cuffs when the door opened and an attractive woman walked into the room. The sterile uniform she was wearing told him instantly that she was not with the CIA.

"Did Mr. David need a bathroom break?" he asked.

She smiled without humor and pulled a knife from her pocket. Walking over to Mason, she slipped the hook of the blade into his flex cuffs and cut them free. Tossing a pack of cigarettes on the table, she made her way to the empty chair.

"My name is Renee," she began.

"Are you with the CIA too?"

"Nope, I'm with the military," she said, taking a seat.

Mason pulled a cigarette from the pack and looked around for a lighter. Renee leaned over the table, lit the smoke with his Zippo, and then tossed it on the open file.

"Thanks," he said after taking a drag.

"Mason, I don't have time for bullshit, so I'm going to get right down to it," she said, pulling her pistol out and placing it on the table. "I'm running a time-sensitive operation right now and either you can help me or I'm going to put a bullet in your head."

Surprised, Mason looked down at the pistol and then up at the woman's face. He cocked his head to the side and took another drag from the cigarette.

Who in the hell was this woman? Mason wondered, about to call her bluff when she picked up the pistol and aimed it at his head.

"I think I'm being detained by the CIA, so you might want to get in line," he said, trying another approach.

"I'm not worried about the CIA. You have five seconds."

Mason was pretty sure she wasn't bluffing.

"How can I help?" he asked with a shrug.

"You used to work for Colonel Barnes and a man named Decklin."

"Yeah, and?"

"Where are they?"

"Barnes is probably out killing children, but Decklin is dead."

"What?"

"I know for a fact that Decklin is dead," Mason said slowly.

They sized each other up in the silence that followed. Mason had no idea who this crazy chick was. He assumed she was either military intelligence or with the DoD. The fact that she knew more about him than he did about her put him at a disadvantage, but what really worried him was that she probably worked for General Swift, and that complicated things.

Renee had expected a monster, but the man sitting in front of her appeared at ease and confident. He oozed a subtle charm and self-assuredness that was common among Tier 1 soldiers, but there was an underlying intelligence in his eyes that was disconcerting.

"So Barnes has finally shown his true colors?" Mason asked, breaking the silence.

"Looks that way."

"Well, he killed Karzai, so it can't be all bad."

"He also murdered the inhabitants of two villages and decapitated most of the Taliban in Pakistan."

"Besides the villagers, I don't see what the problem is. Karzai was a douche."

"We don't murder people. I would think that you, of all people, should respect that."

"I've got Decklin's computer. If you can get me out of here, I'll kill Barnes for you."

"I'm sure you would, but can I trust you?"

"I guess we just have to find out."

CHAPTER 22

Mr. David walked back into the room. He didn't appear to mind that Mason was no longer secured or that Renee was sitting in his chair. Closing the door behind him, he placed his hands in his pockets and relaxed against the wall.

"So, who's in charge here?" Mason asked as he looked from person to person.

"That is an excellent question," the man began. "Ms. Hart, does General Swift know that you are utilizing fake identification papers to gain access to a secure facility?"

"I doubt it, but I'm sure he has more important matters to deal with."

"Well, unfortunately for you, we follow protocol here, and unless you have the proper documentation, I'm going to have to escort you off the premises."

"Try it," she said, aiming the pistol at him.

"Looks like a Mexican standoff to me," Mason joked.

"I need to borrow your detainee for a while. I hope that's not a problem," Renee said.

"There are some people in my organization who will have a problem with that."

Renee smiled and got to her feet, still holding the pistol on Mr. David. "Mason, get up, we're leaving."

Mason stayed seated, casually finishing his cigarette. "So does General Swift know you're here?" he asked.

"What?" He could tell she hadn't expected the question by the look on her face.

"You know, General Swift, your boss. Does he know that you're about to kidnap an American citizen, or is he taking orders from someone too?"

Renee stared at the American, refusing to back down, even though her brain scrambled to find the logical conclusion of his questions.

"If I may . . ." Mr. David pulled his hand out of his pocket and held up his index finger in a silent bid for caution. "I think you will find it difficult to leave this facility without garnering a great deal of unwanted attention. There is a way in which we can all get what we want if we can just take a moment to clear this up."

"I don't have time for that. I need to get in contact with my team."

"So, he doesn't know you're here?" Mason asked.

"Mason, get up, and follow me. You too, Mr. David," Renee commanded.

The two men shrugged and let themselves be led out of the room.

Once out in the hall Renee pushed the agent into one of the interrogation rooms and made sure the door was locked.

Mason kept walking along the hall, looking into each of the rooms, ignoring Renee's instruction to follow her. Finally he found the one he was looking for. He opened the final door and was greeted by the sight of Zeus chained to a metal table.

"Hey, man, this place sucks. I figured we should probably leave," he said with a cocky grin.

"Who is that and why is she pointing a pistol at you?" the Libyan asked calmly in Arabic as Mason and Renee stepped into the room.

"She's our new friend," Mason replied, searching for the key to his chains.

"But she's a woman," Zeus said as she approached the table.

"You're very perceptive," Renee replied in Arabic.

Taking the lock in her hand, she put the pistol back in her holster and pulled a metal pick out of her back pocket. Sticking it into the lock, she ignored Mason, who'd picked up a metal chair and lifted it over his head.

"Watch out, I'm going to smash it," he said.

The lock popped open in Renee's hand and she looked at him and rolled her eyes. "You're going to smash the lock with a chair?"

"I think I like her," Zeus said as he stood and rubbed his wrists.

Renee set the lock on the table while Mason gently set the chair back on the ground.

"Hey, whose team are you on?" he said.

"She is very pretty," Zeus whispered.

"Yeah, well, she wanted to leave you here, so don't forget who your real friends are. Besides, she works for Swift."

"Will you two shut up and follow me?" she commanded as she slipped out the door.

Mason frowned and followed her out into the large hangar, which was empty except for two black Suburbans.

"Do we have time to get my stuff?" Mason asked as she checked the first vehicle to see if it was unlocked.

"Are you serious?"

"I was just asking."

Renee found that the second truck was unlocked and hopped into the driver's seat. She sat looking around for the keys until Mason pulled down the visor and they fell into her lap. Renee shot him a dirty look and started the vehicle.

"Zeus, look in the back, see if they left any weapons," Mason said as Renee put the car in drive and pulled up to the bay door. She looked at her watch nervously and waited for the door to open. Someone shouted from the office area on the second floor of the hangar and she cursed as the door remained closed.

"Shit."

"Some rescue," Mason said as he hopped out of the truck and ran over to the control panel on the wall. He punched the green arrow on the top of the panel and the door motor kicked on with a metallic grunt. Renee pulled forward as the door crept open and Mason extended his middle finger to the man running down the steel stairs.

"Go, go," he said as he hopped in the truck and slammed the door.

"I found this," Zeus said, holding up a tire iron in the backseat.

"Great, that's a lot of help," Mason said to the shrugging Libyan.

Renee punched the accelerator and pulled out her phone as they sped out into the sunlight. Mason squinted and cast a quick glance around the base as she dialed a number and hit send.

"We're on our way and need to leave fast," she said.

"This isn't going to end well," Mason warned her as he glanced over his shoulder.

The base appeared brand-new, but had no distinguishing features that would tell him where they were. All of the buildings were corrugated metal and had been painted an earthy brown. The heat shimmered off the roofs as they reflected the sun's rays, and Mason wished he had his sunglasses. Up ahead, he could see the dark asphalt of the runway and a row of Pave Low helicopters parked neatly in a row.

"There is a truck coming this way," Zeus said from the backseat, and Renee glanced to her left to see another black Suburban racing toward them.

"Doesn't look like they are going to stop," Mason said as she gunned the engine and clenched the wheel.

A man leaned out of the window and waved his arm at their vehicle as the driver tried to close the distance.

"Put your seat belts on," she said, ignoring Mason.

They were a hundred meters from the gate that led to the flight line when their pursuers fired a warning shot over the front of the truck. Mason couldn't hear the rifle go off, but he saw the flame spitting from the muzzle.

"Uhhh, they're shooting at us."

"Relax, it's just a warning shot."

Mason opened the glove box, hoping to find a pistol, but there was nothing inside but an owner's manual and an air gauge.

"I hope you have a plan," he said, slamming the glove box shut.

"Just enjoy the ride," she replied as a burst hit the hood of the truck and bounced off with a spark.

A white Gulfstream sat on the tarmac barely two hundred meters away. Renee shot through the open gate, knocking the side mirror off the truck as she did, and Mason turned to look at the truck trying to catch them.

Three men with rifles ran out of a metal shed near the small control tower and fired at them as Renee cut the wheel and ducked behind a row of cargo trucks. The engine roared as she mashed hard on the gas and barely missed a ground crew loading a small prop plane.

"Holy shit, you're going to kill someone," Mason said, grabbing the dashboard.

"Will you shut up and let me drive?"

Slamming her foot on the brakes, she skidded the truck to a halt beside the waiting plane and jammed it into park. Hopping out, she made her way toward the stairs and waited for Zeus and Mason.

"Can you two hurry the fuck up?" she asked, pulling her pistol from her waistband and aiming it at the rapidly approaching SUV. Mason and Zeus sprinted, and she followed, her pistol at the ready. She stuck her head into the cockpit and was about to tell the pilot to go when she felt a barrel push against her neck.

CHAPTER 23

It had been almost eight hours since Harden had used the unsecure phone to place a call, and according to their sources on base, an operation was in the works to take the bait.

It was a waiting game now. Jones had just called their final grid up to the colonel, and the rest of the team was resting in the shade of their security position, double-checking their weapons.

The valley was more of a long depression than anything else and lacked the well-defined attributes of similar terrain in Afghanistan. A river had once flowed out of the mountains to the north, and its course had cut a shallow trough through the rich landscape. Dark green grass and multicolored wildflowers flourished in the rich sediment deposited by its waters, and the majestic pines dotting the high ground provided much-appreciated shade.

Interspersed among the lush vegetation were sporadic patches of smooth stones and stoic gray boulders, carried down from the mountain peaks. At first glance, the granite rocks appeared to offer ideal cover and concealment, and that was exactly what Harden wanted them to think.

The only usable landing zone was to the southeast of his position, where the wide, grassy plain could accommodate the heavy helicopters. Harden had studied the same satellite imagery that they would be using, and he knew that the valley was invisible until you were actually on the ground. Whoever was coming would naturally be funneled into his kill zone, with nowhere to run.

Kevin stood in the center of the unoccupied tent, holding a black laser pointer. Studying the terrain model on the floor, he waited patiently for the pilots to finish up their briefing. His stomach twisted in knots, but he did his best to hide the nerves.

The model was basically a large rectangular sandbox that he'd set up to replicate the topographical features of the team's objective. The primary infiltration route was a length of red string that snaked from the helicopter landing zone, or HLZ, all the way up to the target location. Every alternate landing zone, rally point, and phase line was represented with its own symbol so that every member of the team had a visual understanding of the mission.

He had done his best to be as thorough as possible, but he couldn't shake the nagging feeling that he had missed something.

Five hours earlier, an NSA signal-intercept bird had "pinged" a satellite phone in northeast Pakistan. The sophisticated aircraft had recorded a conversation in English and, after running it through voice-recognition software, the analysts felt sure that the phone belonged to Anvil 7. An hour after the intercept, there was a satellite photo of a small house nestled in the shadows of the wooded mountain peaks.

Finally, they had actionable intel, but Kevin wasn't buying it. It looked staged, but with General Swift in Bagram, his executive officer told Kevin to get his team ready. All available assets were tasked to the operation, including a joint CIA/Special Operations strike team, which had just arrived in country.

Major Toms, the XO, listened in silence as the pilots finished up their brief. He had no real idea as to what was going on and that was why he wanted Kevin to brief the infiltration and assault plan.

Kevin had never worked with the major before. He'd always been more than happy to let Renee deal with the brass, but she had fallen off the grid, and her phone kept going straight to voice mail. When he and Bones had suggested pushing the operation twenty-four hours, they were ignored, and all they could do now was pray for a miracle.

The lead pilot finished up his part and turned the floor over to the major.

"Kevin, it's on you," he said.

Aiming the red dot on the terrain model, he took a deep breath and dove in.

"Teams one and two will infil via CH-47 to HLZ Barney, and as soon as we are secure we will be moving out along the primary infil route until we reach phase line one." The red dot traced the route along the edge of the valley until it came to the phase line, which was marked with black string and a Post-it note with the number 1 written in black ink.

"At phase line one the strike team, call sign Striker 6, will break off and move to the high ground, while my blocking team will continue to the rally point, which is about a kilometer from the target. We will hold here until Striker 6 has set up overwatch at phase line two."

"What happens if we take contact before making it to our overwatch site?" a bearded operator on the Striker team asked, looking up from his notepad.

"The birds will need to clear the airspace to refuel, but we will have an AC-130 loitering across the border if we need it. Flight time will be ten minutes, and the major will establish comms with the pilot prior to departing phase line one. We're going to have a Predator on station with Hellfires if we need it, but intelligence is pointing to a clean infil."

"So if we get hit, we're on our own for ten minutes?"

"Look, I know it sounds like we're going in naked, but the mission dictates a high degree of stealth. These guys have shown a very sophisticated ability to use our air against us. To mitigate this we are keeping all aircraft outside the operations box until we need them. Trust me when I tell you that if we need the air, it will be there."

"What if they've already left when we get there?" Bones asked.

"We're using satellite and a high-altitude Global Hawk to keep an eye on the situation. If anything changes we'll know. If there aren't any more questions, I'll continue with the brief."

The briefing lasted for another hour, and Kevin felt like he'd been put through the wringer when it was over. He had covered as many variables as he could think of, but there was no way to conceal that this plan had been hastily constructed.

The mission was simple. The two teams were going to fly in under the cover of darkness and move into position before the sun came up. At first light they would attack the target house, grab any intel, and have the birds pick them up at the objective.

Everyone wanted more air assets, but the brass was wary of another incident. If things got real bad, Kevin would use a satellite radio to vector a flight of F-15s into the area. He thought it was a shit plan, but it wasn't his call.

The briefing broke up and everyone began to filter out so they could conduct final preparations. The major gave Kevin a pat on the back and told him, "Good job," before leaving the tent. Bones and Kevin were left alone to see if they'd missed anything.

"Where in the fuck is Renee?" Bones asked.

"Dude, I've been blowing up her phone, but she's not answering. Fuck it, let's get our gear and be done with it," Kevin said, feeling less confident by the minute.

Back at their building, Tyler and Rico were going over the map they'd laid out on the card table. As Kevin joined the two men, Bones grabbed an open box of MREs and began stripping them from their bulky packages.

"Any changes?" Tyler asked.

"No, we're still on."

"You heard from Renee?" Rico asked.

Kevin shook his head and stared down at the map.

"We have a few hours until we have to be at the flight line. Is there anything I missed?"

"The whole thing seems simple enough, but I've been in the valley before and it's not a place you want to go without a shitload of support. The terrain looks pretty straightforward on the graphics, but I guarantee you it's going to be rough. I just hope those CIA dudes can keep up."

"That's the least of our problems," Bones said from the corner, where he was stuffing ammo into his assault pack. "They won't let the gunship clear Afghanistan until we call for it."

Rico shook his head with a dismayed smile, but they were all professionals and would do their jobs without question.

Kevin walked away from the table and went to check his gear one last time. He pulled the phone out and hit the send key, automatically redialing the last number. After a brief delay, the phone rang once and then went straight to voice mail.

Fuck, Renee, where are you? he thought.

CHAPTER 24

Renee looked around the shiny conference room, taking in the faux hardwood flooring and the muted gray walls, before returning her accusing stare to Mason. He was sitting at the dull gray conference table, seemingly unconcerned that a moment ago she'd had a pistol jammed in the back of her head.

Obviously, the rescue attempt hadn't gone according to plan. She was so exhausted that at the time it had seemed like a good idea, but Renee was rapidly realizing she'd overstepped her bounds. They had taken her phone, which pissed her off almost as much as Mason's nonchalant attitude.

Renee turned her gaze back to the window and saw the white Gulfstream sitting just outside the hangar, where they'd been forced to leave it.

Mason leaned forward and whispered across the table, "Don't be upset, it was a good plan."

"What do you mean?" Zeus asked him. "It was a terrible plan and never would have worked."

"You're not helping. Can't you see that she's upset?"

"Well, lying to her isn't going to make it better," he whispered back.

"If one of you bothered telling me that Mr. David was hiding with a gun, we would be on our way by now," Renee spat, unable to keep her calm any longer.

"You had a gun," Mason replied defensively.

"I thought you were some badass Tier 1 killer . . . Just forget it."

"I don't think it's fair to put this all on me. We were doing just fine before you showed up," Mason replied.

Mr. David entered the room, flanked by two burly men in sterile MultiCam battle uniforms. The lack of unit identification told Mason that they were Special Operations, and if he had to guess he would say they belonged to Delta.

He could tell Renee was pissed, but he was having a hard time seeing her point of view. Mason watched as one of the men took a defensive position near the door, his hand resting on the butt of his pistol, while Mr. David walked to the front of the room.

"I hope everyone has calmed down since our last meeting," he said simply. "I would like to introduce Major Anderson. Mason, I believe you two met last night."

Mason stared at the man, ignoring his cocky nod. He hated officers and made no attempt to hide it.

"While our current relationship is not ideal, I find that it is quite fortuitous. The major has just informed me that a mission is being launched in the next few hours in an attempt to take down Colonel Barnes. It seems they are tracking a cell phone in the Swat Valley and have decided to prosecute the intelligence without utilizing normal channels."

"What does that mean?" Renee demanded.

"It means that Barnes has set up a trap for a bunch of dumbasses," Mason replied.

Zeus raised a finger to correct Mason, and the American nodded sheepishly.

"My fault, Zeus. I meant to say that General Swift and Barnes are setting up a trap for a bunch of dumbasses."

The Libyan nodded his assent silently, and Mason murmured his thanks to the man for correcting him.

"Well, those dumbasses happen to belong to me," Renee said, not buying that her boss was involved in what was going on. "Are you just going to let them walk into a trap?" she demanded, getting to her feet.

Major Anderson spoke up. "If you could relax for a moment, ma'am, I think you might be able to see things from our point of view. We reached out to General Swift, but the general is denying knowledge of the operation."

"Of course he did. What, did you expect him to admit that he was working with Barnes?" Mason asked.

"General Swift is a great man, and I have had the honor of serving with him for many years, so why don't you save your bullshit?" Major Anderson yelled.

"Think what you want, buddy, I'm just telling you what's actually going on."

"Either way," Mr. David interrupted, "we know that the assault will take place tonight and we are planning to use it to our advantage."

"You're going to use my men as bait?" Renee asked.

"Hell yes he's going to use your men as bait. What do you think this is, a Boy Scout convention?" Mason said.

"Why don't you shut the fuck up," Renee snapped.

"This is a very complex situation, ma'am," the major said. "The mission is going to go no matter what; all we can do is try to capitalize on what is being put in place. We are certain that some, if not all, of the Anvil Team will be on the ground. We have an obligation to neutralize these men, no matter what the cost."

"Let's say you're right and the colonel is there. How are you going to deconflict with the team on the ground so you don't get your ass shot off?" Mason asked, kicking his feet up on the table, as he got comfortable.

"Well, that's not my problem, because I'm not going," Major Anderson replied with a smile. "Mr. David has decided to send you two heroes to take care of this for us."

"Wait, how did I get involved in this?" Mason demanded.

"Because you killed one of my men and are a wanted terrorist. I figured that you would jump at the opportunity to avoid a bullet to the back of the head," Mr. David said.

"Well, shit."

"Hold on a second," Renee said. "If he's going, then I'm going. After all, it's my team on the ground."

"I wouldn't advise that, ma'am, this is going to be nasty. No place for a lady," the major sneered.

"I don't give a shit how bad it's going to be," Renee said honestly. "If my men are there, then I'm going."

"Do I have a say in this?" Zeus asked.

"Unfortunately not," Mr. David said, ignoring the Libyan's curses.

"So, what's the big plan?"

"Well, if Renee insists on joining you, the plan is for you three to be dropped off to the north of the objective with a radio and a laser designator. If the colonel or his team is at the objective, you are going to lase the target for a drone strike."

"A drone, are you serious? Do you know what he did with the last drone we sent after him?"

"We are well aware of his capabilities. We will keep the drone off station until it is time for the strike."

"That's a terrible plan. What if they aren't there, or what if we walk into an ambush and need more than a drone to break contact?" Mason asked.

"If it was easy, everyone would do it," the major observed.

"Good point. I guess we'll need some gear."

CHAPTER 25

-------------------- Swat Valley, Pakistan

There was zero illumination over the landing zone when the Pave Hawk was brought into a hover. The pilot worked the controls with an ease born of thousands of hours, and through the radio he gave the command, "Deploy ropes."

His copilot craned his neck to the right, catching sight of the infrared ChemLight attached to the free running end of the rope, to ensure that at least fifteen feet remained in contact with the ground.

In the back, the crew chief popped a green ChemLight attached to the top of the rope before pulling down hard. Once he was sure the rope was locked into place, he stepped out of the way and let Renee position herself in the door.

As soon as she disappeared, Zeus stepped up and, after ensuring his rifle was well secured, slid into the darkness.

Mason took his time feeding the rope through his boots. He'd had bad experiences fast-roping in the past, and he didn't want another broken ankle. Once he was satisfied, he swung out and away from the open door, turning to face the bird as he descended.

The downdraft from the helicopter blades beat against the top of his head, and Mason ignored the urge to grip the rope tightly between his hands. Despite the heavy leather gloves, he could already feel the friction burning his palms, and he was relieved to feel his boots slam onto the ground.

Quickly stepping out of the way, he flipped down his night vision and took a knee. The pitch of the rotors deepened as the pilot brought the helicopter to full power. The heavy rope was released from the rope bar as the helicopter disappeared into the night.

Mason waited for silence to return to the valley before moving. The infil had gone according to plan so far, but he knew they were still vulnerable. Jagged rocks and imposing boulders offered the enemy countless positions, and the lack of moonlight meant that his NODs were almost worthless. He needed to get them moving or risk compromise.

Taking the compass from his chest rig, he shot a quick azimuth to the west before moving up to Renee. Mason had chosen a route that would take them over the mountains and into a position that would allow them to overwatch the valley. Both he and Renee had agreed that the primary target was bullshit. Barnes was too smart to show his hand, and they were working under the assumption that this was an elaborate trap.

"Are we good?" he asked.

"Yeah, take point," she replied.

Mason stepped off, keeping his eyes open for a way up into the foothills. According to the map, they had more than two kilometers to travel and not a lot of time to get there.

Kevin took a seat on the nylon bench and turned his rifle so that the muzzle was pointed at the floor. The utilitarian interior of the large helicopter wasn't much to look at, but he'd been in enough Chinooks to know what to expect.

The crew chief checked the exposed hydraulic lines, which ran along the top of the troop compartment, as the gunners loaded their machine guns in preparation for takeoff.

After conducting his final preflight checks, the crew chief moved back to his position on the ramp. Kevin plugged his comms into the onboard radio. The operator watched the man take a seat behind the 240 B mounted to the ramp and snap himself into the helicopter with the thick bungee cord attached to his harness.

The dual-rotored helicopter lurched forward, and Kevin listened to the pilots contact the tower as they moved down the tarmac.

The flight across the border was short and Kevin could feel the "go pills" kick in when the Chinook was fifteen minutes out from the LZ. The amphetamines crept into his blood, filling him with renewed confidence, and by the time the pilot called the five-minute warning, he was ready to go.

The Chinook's descent caused a slight queasiness in his stomach. The pilot kept the nose up while the gunners poked their heads out of the gun ports and monitored the descent.

Kevin checked his rifle and flipped his NODs down over his eyes before yanking the cable from the comms box. The adrenaline spike that came with every mission caused a familiar tingle in his stomach. It was go time, whether he was ready or not.

The crew chief stood at the ramp as the helo flared and dropped its rear wheels into the high grass of the LZ. By the time Kevin felt the wheels hit the ground, he was already moving toward the ramp. He ducked under the hot exhaust and passed through the blowing dust and grass as he cleared the ramp. Moving out to the six o'clock position, Kevin took a knee about ten yards from the spinning rotors and brought his rifle up.

Behind him the second Chinook came in as the lead helicopter leapt for the sky. He braced himself as the rotors beat the ground and leaned forward against his knee to keep from being pushed over. It took less than a minute to unload both birds and when he looked over his shoulder, he could see both teams arrayed in a tight 360-degree field of fire.

"Let's move out," the major said over the radio.

Rico took the point. The tritium dial of his compass glowed green in the darkness, and for a brief instant he could make out his friends' profile before he snapped the case closed and headed out.

Kevin gave him room before forming his element into a wedge and stepping off. In the center of the two teams, the major was having trouble keeping track of his lead elements and he ordered everyone, "Turn on your IR strobes." Kevin fumbled with the beacon, which was the size of a box of matches, and after turning it on, stuffed it into his battle shirt pocket.

The blinking lights were invisible to the naked eye, but through night vision, the team flickered like fireflies in the darkness. He imagined Rico grumbling up front as he looked over his shoulder. His teammate had spent most of his army career as a scout sniper and hated having the strobe giving away his position.

The terrain made it extremely difficult to make any real headway, and Mason was sweating through his shirt, despite having gone less than five hundred meters. His sling was already digging into his neck, and his calves burned from fighting against the ridgeline's gravel-covered edges.

He should have heard the heavy Chinooks by now, and he began to worry that they were moving too slow. Taking a knee in the soft shale, he checked the GPS strapped to his wrist while Renee slipped up behind him.

"Are you lost?"

"No, but we should have heard their birds by now."

"What do you think?" she asked.

Mason knew roughly where they were by the terrain features, but just to make sure, he pulled a small laminated map from his chest rig. He moved as close to the rock face as possible before using a small red light to conduct a map check.

"We are about a kilometer away," he said, pointing to their position on the map. Mason had used the satellite images to mark a few trails he'd seen, but it was hard to find them in the dark. "If we can find this trail, we should be able to make up some time."

"It's up to you."

Mason forced himself to his feet and, after ensuring that Zeus was ready to move, stepped off. The rocky terrain dictated short, choppy steps, which slowed his pace and made his legs burn. Even though he was in excellent shape, the steep grades and thin air were sapping his energy. Sweat ran down his forehead and made the stitches itch, and he carefully wiped the sweat from his brow, wincing at the still-tender wound.

He searched for any sign of the trail as he moved, and luckily the stars burned brightly overhead, offering Mason just enough light to see a tiny discoloration in the rocks ahead of him. He assumed the off-colored path had been worn smooth by countless goat herders taking their flocks down into the lush valley below. If he was right, it would cut a lot of time off their route, but if he was wrong, they would be too far out of position to help the teams moving into what he was sure was an ambush.

On the valley floor, Rico checked his azimuth and made a small correction before calling his position back to Kevin. Despite growing up in the city, he had a natural spatial acuity, which allowed him to navigate without using a map. It seemed odd to everyone else, but after studying a terrain model, or a map, he was able to visualize what the ground looked like in his head with a staggering degree of accuracy.

"Be advised, we are five hundred meters out from phase line one. I'm killing my IR to conduct a recon of the area."

"Negative, we're running behind," the major said over the radio. "I want to keep moving for another two hundred and fifty meters."

"Fucking dick," Rico swore to himself. He was used to Renee and Kevin letting him do his job and was spoiled by the fact that they always listened to him. This was his first time working with the major, and it was rapidly becoming evident that he was a huge micromanager. The valley was beginning to narrow and the gentle terrain they had been traversing was changing around them. Just like Kevin and Rico had assumed, the terrain wasn't jiving with the photos they had used to plan the mission, and the plan they were adhering to needed to be modified.

"We need to hold up. It's getting narrow up ahead," he called back.

"Roger that," Kevin replied, not waiting for the major to answer.

Kevin held up a closed fist and his team spread out in defensive positions. Rico's beacon suddenly switched off.

"Cut your strobes," he said over the radio as he settled in to wait.

The grass looked dry as he took a knee, but after a few seconds, he could feel moisture soaking through his pants. He was used to being wet and uncomfortable, and as long as his feet stayed dry, he knew he'd be okay. Digging a Clif Bar from his cargo pocket, Kevin ripped the wrapper open and stowed the trash. The high-calorie bar would keep his energy up, but it quickly absorbed the spit in his mouth. Fumbling in the dark, he reached for the hydration tube and placed the bite valve in his mouth. The water was warm at first but got cooler as he drank.

Looking at the sky, he flipped up his NODs and wiped his brow with the back of his gloved hands. The stars blinked and shimmered across the heavens like millions of diamonds on an infinite jeweler's mat. It was humbling to be so small in such a wide space, and Kevin was struck by the fact that most people would never experience a sight like this.

Mason's back was tight at the base of his spine, and despite not wearing any body armor, he could feel the heat rising from beneath his shirt. He mentally checked off another hundred meters and after some quick math, he figured they were less than two hundred meters from their objective.

He stopped to pull the Nalgene bottle from a pouch on his chest rig and drank deeply. Some of the water spilled out over his chin, and he briefly considered pouring some over the back of his neck. The pads of the lightweight bump helmet were soaked with sweat and felt wet against the crown of his head. The helmet wasn't even ballistic, so it offered no protection from bullets, but he wasn't going to hold his NODs in his hand, so he'd been forced to get one.

He heard Renee moving up behind him, and as he stowed the water, she took a knee to his rear. Leaning in, she asked, "How far?"

"Maybe two hundred meters."

Looking over his shoulder, he saw that she was sweating but didn't seem to be in bad shape. Being around a woman awakened a long-forgotten protectiveness in him and the sensation felt strange. He barely knew anything about her, but he'd immediately recognized a steely resolve in her that made her special. Mason hadn't cared about a woman since his wife had left him, and he sure hadn't stopped to think about one, but for some reason, Renee was different.

"We need to move," she said.

Turning to check on Zeus, he noticed that she had her own compass out and was confirming their location against the GPS attached to the stock of her rifle. As the Libyan moved to follow, she squeezed past Mason and took up point.

Mason waited for his friend to catch up and noticed that the man wasn't even sweating.

"Aren't you tired?" he asked.

"I grew up in the mountains, my friend. If I could only keep you two from taking so many breaks, we would probably be there by now."

"I have to make sure we're going the right way."

"That never stopped you in the past. I see the way you have been looking at her."

"Shut the fuck up," Mason whispered back.

"There is no shame in it." Zeus smiled before pushing past Mason and moving to catch up with Renee.

CHAPTER 26

Kevin moved up the front of the element as soon as Rico advised that he'd found a spot with good cover. He gave the signal to move out and kept his eyes open for the IR ChemLight marking the rally point.

Just like Rico had said, the terrain began to narrow imperceptibly, and a shallow bend had to be negotiated before the team reached the rally point. Kevin could see the ChemLight's subtle glow where it lay nestled among the tall grass, but he was concerned about occupying the low ground.

He had to count the entire element into the rally point before making his way to the center of the defensive perimeter. When he got there, Kevin found Rico and Bones arguing with Striker 6.

"What's up?" Kevin asked.

"We need to get out of this low ground," Rico said.

"Look, my men are already out there. Just let them do their job," the CIA man said.

"Major, it's your call," Kevin said as Toms made his way to the impromptu meeting.

"We are going to stick with the plan and let the strike team get in position."

Rico shook his head in disagreement and the meeting broke up, leaving Kevin to placate Bones and search for Tyler.

The radio crackled. "Striker 6, I found us a way up."

"Damn, that was fast," Kevin said as Bones motioned for Tyler to join them.

"Are they even going to set up security?" Rico demanded in a low growl. "These cheese dicks are going to get someone killed."

"What's up, boss?" Tyler asked as he ducked down next to Bones.

"Look, I don't—" Kevin began, but was cut off by an explosion outside the perimeter. He instinctively ducked his head into his shoulders as dirt rained down on their position. Beyond their perimeter someone was screaming, and then a burst of fire erupted from the high ground.

"Contact two o'clock, forty meters," someone yelled as the machine-gun fire cut into the strike team.

Rico and Bones spread out, ducking behind cover before returning fire. Kevin turned around and, after flipping his selector to full auto, unloaded a magazine toward the threat. After three quick bursts, he pulled a smoke grenade from his kit and tossed it as far as he could.

Mason was startled by the sudden explosion and paused midstride. Realizing the ambush had just been initiated, Renee darted off the path and began scrambling up the rock face in an attempt to see what was going on.

"Zeus, get her," he yelled as she scrambled out of sight.

Pebbles and dirt rained down from the low cut, and the Libyan threw his hand up to protect his eyes. He staggered back toward the edge of the cliff face, his arms still shielding his eyes, and Mason had to jump forward to steady his friend.

Just over the ridgeline, the sound of heavy fire mixed with the deep concussion of the grenades going off.

"We're too late," Mason said as he steadied his friend and turned his attention to where he'd last seen Renee. Mason clambered up the rugged incline, which leveled out, revealing the valley floor below them. Zeus followed him up, and the two men watched as the firefight unfolded a hundred meters to the southwest of them.

Frantically, he searched for Renee. *Did she fall off the mountain?* he wondered. "Fuck, where did she go?" he asked out loud.

Mason was about to descend when Zeus grabbed his arm and pulled him back down.

"What?" he demanded.

"Mason, just lase the target and let's get out of here."

"What about her?"

The Libyan shrugged and Mason went to pull his arm free but stopped suddenly. Zeus was right.

"Damn it." He pulled his pack off his back and grabbed the bulky PEQ-1 laser designator out of the bag. The SOFLAM, or Special Operations Forces Laser Acquisition Marker, had made a name for itself during the invasion of Afghanistan. It was a rugged, easy-to-operate piece of equipment that allowed the operator to locate and designate a target for laser-guided munitions. Weighing in at eleven pounds, it had the ability to lase a target over twenty-three kilometers away.

Mason quickly ran through the test program while trying to shut Renee out of his mind.

Harden had watched the men file into their rally point and waited patiently to spring the ambush. Hoyt had carefully emplaced a handful of Italian antipersonnel mines in a shallow arc around the south side of the boulders, and he watched a soldier step on one as a squad left their perimeter. They were moving toward the high ground, just like he'd planned.

Boz had found the mines in Pakistan, and after careful inspection he'd assured Harden that they were serviceable. Apparently he'd been wrong.

"Those pieces of shit," he said to himself. Looking over his shoulder, he could barely make out Jones hunkered beneath a poncho liner. He was using the makeshift hide site to conceal the light from his computer while monitoring two radios. He used the computer to track any air assets coming on station while scanning the radios in case he needed to jam a particular frequency.

Harden was about to spring the ambush when one of the mines finally went off, and Hoyt opened up his 240 Bravo. The long burst echoed angrily off the rock face and sent fifteen rounds screaming into the valley. Holding the buttstock tight to his shoulder, Hoyt raked the rounds over the strike team caught in the open.

He had taken all the tracer rounds out of the ammo belt and instead of night vision, he was using a thermal optic to engage targets. The thermals picked up heat signatures and displayed them in shades of gray. Natural objects, depending on how much heat they retained, were gray, and people appeared dark black.

Boz had stacked a pile of forty-millimeter high-explosive rounds next to his position. He raised the M79 grenade launcher into the air and arced a round toward its target. The launcher looked like a fat sawed-off shotgun, and after firing, he broke open the breech, picked out the empty casing, and quickly slid in another round. It was an old weapon but still as effective as it had been in Vietnam. Boz liked it because it was light and didn't weigh down his rifle. He focused on getting the second round into the dead space behind the rocks, but a bullet snapped over his head and he ducked down as he fired, sending the grenade short.

Harden ignored the rounds buzzing around him, and shouted at his men. "Shift fire onto those dudes in the open. You aren't hitting shit. Hoyt, keep their heads down, I don't want them moving on us." He paused to lift up his radio and said, "Scottie, are you going to kill anybody today?"

"Stand by, Anvil 7. I'm just waiting for a shot," Scottie replied.

"Look harder. I don't want to be here all night." He paused and yelled back at Jones, "Is anybody trying to crash the party?"

"There is a Predator in the area, and someone down there is calling for air support, but I've got the lines all jammed up."

"Keep it up. I don't want any surprises."

Renee scrambled for a way down the mountain. Her team was taking heavy fire and she needed to get into the fight. The machine-gun fire and random explosions bounced off the rocks like the strikes of a blacksmith's hammer. She was overwhelmed by her impotence and felt a wave of guilt slipping into her mind. Renee tried to adjust her NODs to get a better view, but her foot clipped a rock and she tumbled face-first into a small depression.

Twisting in midair, she managed to land on her back, and the fall knocked the wind out of her lungs. Renee stared up at the sky, then realized that she must have knocked her night vision off its mount, because she couldn't see anything. Trying to catch her breath, she felt a sharp pain in her back. The screams of the dying rose like an invisible fog and drifted up to her ears. A brief hush fell over the mountain as she forced herself onto her side. Using her hands, she swept the dark earth for her lost NODs.

"Damn it," she yelled in frustration as the automatic fire picked up again.

"Hey, that dude is moving down there," Harden said without taking the thermals from his eyes. Hoyt was changing the belt on the 240, and after slamming the feed tray cover closed, he yanked back on the charging handle and slid it forward before pivoting to acquire the target.

The man was about to dive into cover when Hoyt stitched a quick burst across his back.

"He's down now," he said as he shifted onto another target. The men caught in the open were sitting ducks, and he was surprised that some of them were still alive.

"Boz, why aren't you shooting?" Harden demanded.

"I'm out of rounds," he replied.

"You're totally out of ammo? Way to be a burden."

Boz shrugged in the darkness and Harden was about to cuss him out when Jones interrupted over the radio.

"Hey, boss, that Predator's loitering just out of range. He's not getting close enough for me to lasso."

"What's it doing, just hanging out?"

"I can't tell you, but someone learned their lesson."

"All right, let's wrap this shit up," he said over the radio. The drone was making him nervous and up till now they'd been lucky.

A single rifle shot rang out, distinctive from the rest of the gunfire, and Scottie keyed up on the net: "You have a tango moving up to your three o'clock, I have no shot."

"Boz, go take care of that." Harden heard him grunt as he slid back a few feet and moved out with his rifle.

On the ground there was a heavy burst of fire as Barnes's team broke cover and began maneuvering on Kevin's pinned-down unit. The colonel directed his gunner to lay down a base of fire and waited to advance his team. He'd heard Harden's call and something in his voice was unsettling. Barnes had no intention of being caught out in the open and began to urge his men forward.

Hoyt heard the machine gun in the valley go into action and waited for it to stop firing before he fired another burst. The technique was called "talking," and as soon as one gunner ceased fire, the next would start shooting. The method conserved ammo and ensured that the defenders were pinned down.

Harden felt the thump of a grenade going off and Boz keyed up on the radio. "This guy's done. I'll stay over here and clean up." Anvil 7 stretched his cramped back as he watched the lethal dance unfold below him. He knew it would be over soon.

•   •   •

Renee had given up her fruitless search and clawed her way out of the hole she'd fallen into. Her nails were cracked and her fingertips were bleeding from the jagged rocks, but she didn't care. Focusing on the muzzle flashes from the high ground, she could barely make out another group of men firing from a second position. She had to do something.

Renee was surprised to feel warm tears sliding down her cheeks. No longer worried about her own safety, she moved closer to the edge and peered over the cliff. She was trying to judge the distance to the floor when the sole of her hiking boot lost traction and she slipped off the side of the mountain.

CHAPTER 27

Tyler yelled out, "Another mag," his voice barely carrying over the rifle fire. Somehow Kevin heard him, though, and stopped shooting long enough to pull a fresh magazine from his kit. He waved the mag at Tyler, who motioned for him to throw it.

Kevin tossed the magazine and realized he'd underthrown it as soon as it left his hand. Tyler, seeing that it was going to fall short, took a step out of cover. Just as he was about to snatch it out of the air, Tyler's head snapped violently to the side, and he tumbled to the ground.

"Man down, man down," Bones yelled as Kevin stared in horror.

"Shiiit," Kevin yelled as an unseen grenade tumbled into the perimeter and exploded in a rush of pressure and dark smoke.

Kevin felt the shrapnel pepper his face and arms as he was blown off his feet. Fragmentation grenades are designed to explode up and out, and he'd been in just the right position to avoid the brunt of the jagged metal housing, which sliced through the air.

Sitting up, he could feel the warmth of his blood as it seeped down the front of his face. His right eye had already swollen shut and his eardrums whined from the pressure. Everything slowed down as his brain tried to process the scene.

He watched Rico toss out a canister of smoke and saw the spoon separate from the canister body as it arced through the air. Bullets poured into their position and threw up tiny puffs of dirt as they impacted all around him. It was as if the near-death experience had given him a second sight that allowed him to pierce the darkness and chaos around him.

As he struggled to his feet, his hearing slowly returned and he could hear Major Toms yelling for air support over the radio. Bones was waving at him to get down, and Kevin realized that he was walking toward Tyler's body. The horror on Bones's face was clearly outlined against the dark surroundings, and Kevin wanted to tell him that it was going to be all right.

He was just raising his hand to tell his friend that he was okay when something smacked into his leg with the force of a sledgehammer. Kevin was confused. He felt no pain but was falling as his leg buckled underneath him. In his mind, he was falling through a pool of molasses. It took forever for his head to hit the ground, and he felt his helmet strike something hard as it bounced off the ground. His leg was numb, but looking down he saw that his pants were soaked with his own blood.

"Am I hit?" he asked in disbelief.

"Sniper at our ten o'clock," Rico yelled as Kevin's mind suddenly cleared, and he realized he was lying out in the open.

"Oh God," he moaned as the pain rushed past the endorphins and pierced his body like a hot knife. He didn't want to die, not here, not like this.

Using his hands, he clawed his way out of the kill zone. Another round hit him in the back, forcing him forward as the ballistic plate absorbed the damage. Inch by inch he dragged himself to cover, and once he was safe, he snatched the tourniquet off his chest. Forcing himself up into a seated position, he wrapped the sturdy nylon just below his knee and began tightening the windlass until the blood stopped.

He was out of breath and weak from blood loss when he finally secured the tourniquet and rested his head against the rock. Unbuckling his helmet, he laid it on the ground and began pulling his gloves off. Kevin wanted to rest and figured if he could catch his breath he'd be okay. As the firefight unfolded around him, he began pulling magazines and his final grenades out of his kit and laying them next to the upturned helmet. Taking a drink from his CamelBak, he looked around.

A man he recognized from the briefing had a bandage tied tightly around his leg. He was so close that Kevin could see the blood staining the white gauze as he fired at an unseen target. The expended brass tumbled from the ejection port and landed in a shiny pile to Kevin's right. A high-pitched scream announced an incoming RPG, which hit the man's position and exploded.

Kevin turned his head as shards of rock and bone filled the air, and when he looked back, the man was gone.

Bones was cursing as he engaged the unseen enemy, and out of the corner of his eye, he could see Rico beating the butt of his rifle against the ground. A casing was jammed against the bolt face, and his friend savagely slammed the rifle in an attempt to break it free.

"Get back in the fight," he told himself.

Using his rifle as a crutch, Kevin forced himself to his feet. His right leg tried to buckle under the weight, and he was forced to lean his body against the rock to get a steady position.

Bones tossed a frag and yelled for Tyler. When he didn't get a response, he ducked down and began searching for his friend. Kevin could see his shoulders sag when he saw the man lying facedown in the dirt. There was no time to mourn the dead as the remaining men fought for their lives.

Another RPG screamed in from the darkness. It skipped off the ground and detonated in the air above their perimeter. Bones went down and Rico sprinted from cover to help his friend.

As he moved, he was hit in the side, but he kept moving until he was hit again, this time above the knee. Rico's leg shot back, and he hit the ground hard, just as another grenade dropped into the perimeter.

Shadowy figures appeared out of the darkness, forcing Kevin to twist himself around to cover Rico. Using his thumb, he flipped the selector switch to full auto and fired without bothering to aim. Just as the bolt locked to the rear, he was hit in the chest, and he let himself fall to the ground. Grabbing a fresh magazine from the pile next to his helmet, he slammed it into the magazine well and released the bolt forward.

Firing one-handed, he was reaching for his final frag when a figure appeared above Rico. Kevin tried to swing his rifle around, but it was too late, and the man put two rounds into Rico's face.

"Fuuuck yooou," he yelled, sweeping the rifle across the attacker in a wild arc. The bullets went high, and Kevin watched the man's rifle snap onto him and fire.

CHAPTER 28

Renee was falling forward, away from the mountain. She could see the black expanse of the valley below her, and a jolt of adrenaline shot up her spine. The rifle swung wildly on its sling as she tumbled downward. With a sharp jolt, she was suddenly left dangling in thin air.

It took her a second to realize she wasn't falling, and when she finally looked up, she saw Mason hanging out over the ledge. One of his hands held on to a protruding rock, while the other was stretched over the edge and locked on to the drag strap sewn into the top of her kit.

Mason yelled to Zeus, "Hold my feet."

He could feel himself slipping, but he refused to let go of Renee. The Libyan grabbed his ankles and struggled against the combined weight.

The American had wanted to do nothing more than to set up the laser designator and call in the strike, but he knew he'd never be able to live with himself. Zeus had shrugged when he stowed the designator in his pack and set off to find Renee. It was a matter of blind luck that they had seen her fall into the shallow depression. Luckily, they had found a way down, and just as he was about to get her attention, he saw her stumble and pitch off the cliff.

"Pull my legs," he yelled over his shoulder.

Zeus set his heels in the shaky gravel and pushed hard while keeping a firm grip on his friend. Mason could feel his belt buckle digging in the dirt as he inched away from the edge, pulling Renee with him.

Finally, she was able to get a foothold and support her own weight. Grabbing Mason's forearm, she used her free hand to climb back onto the rocks.

"Holy shit, I thought you were dead," Mason panted as she collapsed next to him.

"Me too," she said weakly.

Mason dropped his pack and pulled out the SOFLAM for the second time that night. After screwing the tripod into the bottom of the laser, he set it up on a rock and centered the reticle on Barnes's men. Once he had an acceptable sight picture, Mason hit the button, which "painted" the target. The designator beeped once, telling him it was locked on.

After ensuring he had the remote switch in his pocket, he zipped his pack and tossed it over his shoulder. The laser would toggle itself on and off to conserve batteries, but they needed to be able to use the radio to call it in.

"We can't stick around here any longer," Zeus said matter-of-factly.

"Renee, we have to go," Mason said.

She was staring down at the final stages of the assault and ignored him. There was almost no fire coming from inside the perimeter, while Barnes's men fired and maneuvered until they were within grenade range.

"Renee . . . ," he said again, placing his hand on her shoulder.

"I know," was all she said.

They had four kilometers to cover to get to their extraction point. Mason had marked their last position on his GPS and moved quickly to get out of the jammer's range. He'd placed Renee in between him and Zeus, and periodically he checked over his shoulder to ensure she was still moving.

He'd known the woman for less than a day but was impressed by her resiliency. Mason had never been a misogynist, mainly because women had raised him, but he vividly remembered the first time someone introduced the issue of women in Special Ops. The general consensus of his team had been that women had a place in the kitchen or in the bedroom. It had been a joke then, but Mason had serious reservations about letting them into their warrior community.

Renee had managed to prove him wrong in less than a day.

The woman had more balls than most men he'd met, and the fact that she hadn't broken down after what she'd witnessed in the valley told him everything he needed to know. A part of him already felt a deep connection with her, but the warm feeling seemed wrong, and he tried to push it out of his mind.

They slowly descended a steep grade that gently leveled off onto the low ground. With the mountains behind them, Mason checked the radio, depressing the talk button. It was static-free.

Motioning for Zeus to halt, Mason took cover behind a jagged mound of dirt and stone and brought the radio up to his mouth. Using his left hand, he pulled the PEQ-1's remote targeting device out of his pocket and hit the arm button.

"Steeler Base, this is Steeler 7, be advised we are clear of the objective and target is painted." He held the radio to his ear and waited for a response.

"Steeler 7, this is Steeler Base. Good copy. Continue to primary extraction point. Be advised, Reaper is on station."

"Roger that, Steeler Base. Target is hot, I say again, target is hot."

"Stand by, Steeler 7."

Mason looked around at nothing in particular as he waited. Both Renee and Zeus were pulling security, leaving him free to deal with the radio.

"Steeler 7, Steeler Base, rifle on two Hellfires, how copy?"

"Good copy. Be advised we aren't going to be able to provide damage assessment."

"Roger, continue to exfil, Steeler Base out."

Mason stowed the radio and moved to Renee's position. He hoped the fact that two missiles were on their way might ease her mind.

"Missiles inbound," he said.

She didn't take her eyes off her sector, and the only response she gave was a slight nod of her head.

"We need to move out," he said after a moment.

Mason had expected some reaction, but she hadn't given it to him and he knew that the two missiles hurtling toward their target would never be enough to matter. Neither one would ever know if the Hellfires had even hit their targets.

"We'll get the guy who did this," Mason promised.

He wasn't sure why he told her that but knew she needed something to focus on. Mr. David knew who'd led the team into the ambush, and he was going to tell them whether he wanted to or not.

Renee got to her feet, and when she looked at him, it was impossible to tell what she was thinking. Her impassive face might as well have been carved out of marble. Standing in the darkness, she waited for Mason to lead them out.

Renee paused and looked wistfully at the rock face towering over them. Men like Barnes didn't die from missiles. Good men were all too easy to kill, while evil men seemed to pass unscathed as they doled out their violence.

She greedily devoured the moment, noting the stillness of the air and the light scent of raw earth and musty vegetation. She savored the stinging void in the pit of her stomach and the accusing voice that blamed her for the men's death. The misery would be her fuel when tired and her blanket when cold. Renee willingly shouldered the burden, and as she turned to follow Mason, she set her mind to a day when she would lay it beside Barnes's lifeless body.

Lowering her head, she resolved herself to put one foot in front of the other until that day finally came. She was so deep within herself that she almost didn't hear the low, rolling explosions of the Hellfires detonating on the back side of the mountain.

CHAPTER 29

Renee hadn't said anything during the helicopter ride out of Pakistan, and Mason was worried. She'd stared out the small window and idly toyed with the necklace she wore until they landed. When Mr. David met them at the flight line, there was pure hatred in her eyes, and Mason had thought it best to send her and Zeus to their assigned rooms while he briefed the new boss.

"Well, that was a failure," Mr. David said once they were alone.

"I told you what was going to happen, but you CIA fucks think you know everything. There is something bigger going on here, and you wasted a lot of good men to find out what I already told you," Mason replied angrily.

"Anything else you wish to get off your chest?"

"I want to know who's running this circus. Is it you, or are you working for Swift too? There has been a lot of Agency bullshit going on and I'm getting sick of it," Mason said, grabbing the man's arm as they walked toward the hangar.

Mr. David stopped walking as Major Anderson took a step toward Mason.

Mason didn't back down from a challenge. He stepped up to the major, his hand easing down to his pistol. "I've had just about enough of your shit. I know who you are, and I know what you're about, so why don't you cut the crap and make your play?"

"Fuck you," the major replied, stepping up to Mason's face.

"Stand down, Major," Mr. David commanded.

Mason felt the anger rising up in him and didn't care about the consequences. He was tired of this paper tiger's bullshit, and he was ready to put an end to it.

"Major Anderson, I gave you an order," Mr. David commanded again.

Mason could see him trembling, like a dog on a tight leash. Then the spell was broken and he took a step back.

"This isn't over," he said before turning on his heel and heading toward the hangar.

"You have an innate ability to alienate anyone wanting to help you, do you know that?" Mr. David asked.

"I don't need your kind of help."

"Come with me," he said.

Mason took his hand off his pistol and followed the man into the hangar. Instead of going into the conference room, he continued down the hall to a door guarded by two contractors. The men were dressed in plate carriers and sterile MultiCam uniforms, and both of them had rifles slung around their necks.

Mr. David showed them his ID card and then punched his code into the keypad. Mason heard the lock click open and they stepped through the door. Two more contractors were posted on the inside, their hands resting on the rifles slung around their necks.

The two men were obviously ex military and appeared to be in their late thirties. Both of their faces were deeply tanned and lined by the desert sun, and there was an aura about them that Mason immediately recognized. The silent sentinels held his gaze for a moment, and he knew they were sizing him up. The first man gave him a barely perceptible nod before turning his attention to the room.

The place was dimly lit, with gray carpet matching gray walls.

Vents in the ceiling pumped cool air into the room as a pale analyst studied the monitors and televisions that kept them in contact with the region.

The CIA man punched his code into another keypad and they walked into yet another hallway. Mason was losing his patience when the agent stopped at a small window cut into the wall.

"Take a look," he said.

Mason shot the man a look that conveyed his annoyance and peered through the glass. He was not prepared to see General Swift handcuffed to a table, very much the worse for wear.

"Well, look who it is. It's about time someone started listening to me."

The general sat rigidly at the table, an arrogant look on his face. Mason wanted to put his fist through it, and he could feel his heart beating faster as the rage built up in his stomach and spread through his veins like lava.

"Look, you don't have to believe everything I say, but obviously I'm not far off if you have him in custody. Give me five minutes with him and I'll find out what's going on for you."

Mr. David stood staring into the room. Mason could tell he was wrestling with his next course of action, and all he had to do was close the deal.

"I can promise you that whatever you think you know about this man doesn't come close to the facts. He's a murderer and he's the only one who knows who's pulling all the strings."

The spy took a deep breath and held it for a second as he weighed his options. "Do it, but do not do any permanent damage."

Mason nodded and stepped into the room with a smile.

The shock that replaced the stoic exterior of the general disappeared as soon as Mason closed the door behind him.

"Bet you weren't expecting me to come through that door."

"How . . . ?"

"Doesn't matter. What does matter is how much pain you're willing to go through before you tell me what I want to know. You see these walls?" Mason asked, bumping his fist against the thick gray foam that lined the cell. "How many of these have we built around the world?"

The general lifted his chin with a smirk. "I built one just for you back in Jbad. It's brand-new," he said.

"Well, that's a shame, because neither one of us is ever going to see it."

Mason approached the general ominously and placed his hand on the man's shoulder as he moved around behind him.

"It's been a rough week, for both of us. Did you know that your friend Decklin tried to kill me again?"

"Too bad he didn't finish the job."

"Yeah, he was thinking the same thing when I poured gas on him and lit him up like a roman candle. I still have the tape, if you want to see it."

"Fuck you."

"He said that too before I cut off his head and put it in a box."

"You're a sick son of a bitch," Swift replied.

"Maybe, maybe not, but one thing I don't do is kill fucking innocent women and children." Mason leaned in close and grabbed him around the neck with his left arm. He sank the rear naked choke in deep and used his right arm to tighten the pressure as he lifted the general out of his chair.

"You didn't see the pictures, see what your gas did to the children. I want to know how you sleep at night," he yelled into the general's ear.

He could feel the general's feet kicking against the table as he cut the blood flow off to his brain. He counted slowly in his head and then released the pressure before the prisoner passed out.

As Swift sputtered and gulped for air, Mason grabbed the back of his head and slammed it into the table. He fought to control his rage as the general's nose exploded in a pool of red.

"Tell me!" he yelled as he slammed his head down again, before reapplying the chokehold. "I know about Libya and Operation Lion. All I need is a name, and we can stop this shit."

He let the general go and moved back around the table. The general's nose was bent to the side and obviously broken. Blood covered his chin and the front of his tan shirt, and there was already a dark bruise around his neck, but what surprised Mason were the tears coursing down his cheeks.

"You find a conscience all of a sudden?"

"I never knew about the gas. I would never have gone along with it if I had known."

The proud warrior sagged in his chair. He was right on the edge, and Mason knew it wouldn't take much more to break him. He'd never liked the general and knew that despite the façade that had gotten him promoted, the man was a coward.

"I don't care if you knew or not, you're still a murderer."

"Fuck you, Mason."

"What is Operation Lion?" Mason asked, balling up his fist.

"It's the plan for Syria," the general spat. "We found files linking Iran, Syria, and Saudi Arabia to the jihadists in Iraq. After the surge, we knew the war was going to be wider than we originally thought—"

"Who is 'we'?"

Swift raised his chin and spat blood on the table before telling Mason, "I want a deal."

Mason instantly grabbed him by the front of his shirt and flipped the chair down to the floor. He placed his boot on the man's throat and pressed down. The general tried to grab his foot, but his hands were still chained to the chair, and he lay there choking as the blood from his broken nose poured down his throat.

"You want a deal? Is that what you want? Who is running the show? Tell me and I won't let you drown in your own blood."

"Gen— General Nantz . . . He's working with the CIA," he stuttered as Mason lifted his boot off the man's windpipe. "He planned it all."

"Where can I find him?"

"Bagram, he's in Bagram."

Mason looked down at the defeated general with disgust. Finally, he headed out the door, his mind already focused on the task ahead.

Outside, Mr. David looked flustered as Mason closed the door behind him.

"I need a plane to Bagram, ready to go in an hour," he said simply.

"I'll get on that," he replied, regaining his composure.

Mason left the hangar and walked toward the row of white-painted modular houses. He had gotten his second wind and was bolstered by the new information, but he needed to check in with Renee before leaving.

The "mods" were basically trailers set up to house five separate rooms. Each one was made of aluminum with a corrugated steel roof and windows cut into the side. The housing area was the military's version of a trailer park, but it was a huge improvement over the tents he'd used during the invasion of 2001.

He walked up the metal staircase and pulled the door open. A long, dimly lit hallway lay before him, which smelled of Pine-Sol and Windex. The smell was universal to the military and spoke volumes about the soldiers' discipline. His boots squeaked on the spotless linoleum floor as he walked down the hall. Most of the doors were open, which meant that those rooms were unoccupied, and he continued walking until he came to a room with a closed door.

He stopped, collecting himself, and after taking a breath, he knocked.

After a few seconds, Renee pulled the door open and stuck her head through the crack. "Yeah?"

"I was in the . . . I mean, I stopped by to see how things were going," Mason stammered.

"I'm fine," she said as she closed the door.

Mason stood in the hall for a second, not sure what to do. He started to turn and leave, not because she didn't want to talk to him, but because he was suddenly nervous.

"Get your shit together," he told himself as he knocked on the door again.

"What do you want?" Renee asked as she pulled the door open, but refused to move out of the doorway.

She'd just gotten out of the shower, and her hair was still damp and full of the distinctively feminine bouquet of her shampoo. Mason's eyes danced over the form-fitting T-shirt she was wearing and continued down to the short Ranger panties that barely covered her shapely legs.

"Can I help you?" Renee asked defiantly as he tore his gaze away from her body.

It had been a long time since he'd been this close to a woman and he found himself feeling intimidated.

"I, uhhh . . ."

"Yeah, you said that already, and I told you that I was fine."

She moved to close the door and Mason's hand shot out to check its movement.

"You need to cut me some slack. I'm trying to help you."

Renee let go of the door and crossed her arms beneath her breasts as she stepped back. The shower shoes on her feet were still wet, and they squeaked against the tile floor as she moved.

"Why do you think I need your help, because I'm a woman? Is that what this is all about? You don't think I can handle this shit?"

"No." Mason was getting pissed at her little attitude and heard his voice going up. "It has nothing to do with that."

"Then what?"

"Renee, you don't have to do this."

"Do what?"

"Act this way. We were there together, remember? And guess what, this thing isn't over yet. So I suggest you get your shit together, because there is no way I'm going to let you jeopardize my life or Zeus's life."

Tears welled up in her eyes, and she turned away from Mason and retreated into the room. He stepped inside and closed the door behind him.

"Look, I'm sorry, I didn't mean—"

Renee turned to him suddenly, and before he knew it she had grabbed him up in an embrace. He could feel her sobbing against his chest.

Mason was confused. One minute she was mad and the next she was crying. He had no idea what to do, so he reached down and patted her on the head.

"It was all my fault. I let all of this happen," Renee sobbed.

"It's not your fault. This is what Barnes does."

"I— I couldn't stop it . . . I had to watch them die . . . ," she stuttered through the tears.

"Renee, there was nothing you could do. You have to know that."

Mason knew that his words didn't matter. They were hollow attempts to assuage a wound that only time could heal, but he felt obligated to say something.

"I killed them," she whispered again before looking up at him.

Mason generally distrusted women, mainly because every woman who was supposed to love him had quit, but somehow Renee was different. He'd known her for only a few days, but he felt he could trust her.

"Look, get some sleep, and in the morning, when you're rested, it's up to you to decide if you want to finish this."

Renee looked like she was about to hug him, and Mason stepped backward, almost tripping over his feet. She smiled and said, "What, are you scared?"

"No, it's just, look, I . . . ," he stammered. "Just get some sleep, okay?"

He turned and headed for the door, leaving her standing in the middle of the room. Mason steeled himself for what was ahead as he stepped out into the hall. He was going to get the answers he needed—no matter what the cost.

CHAPTER 30

Colonel Barnes stood in front of the mirror and carefully cut his blond hair with a pair of scissors. The hair fell into a plastic bag, which he'd taped open over the sink, and he shaped his hair until it was as close cropped as he could get it.

The bathroom smelled of cleaning products and fresh soap. A ceiling fan rotated lazily above his head, blowing clumps of his shorn hair across the cool tile floor and onto his bare feet. He noticed a smear of dried blood on his forearm as he pulled a pair of latex gloves from a small box and stretched them over his hands.

The ambush had left him with a feeling of invincibility, which added fuel to his resolve. Still, he knew that his blond hair would only attract attention, now that he was out in the open, and he was going to use dye to remedy that.

He released each glove with a snap before grabbing the plastic bottle of hair dye. Staring at himself in the mirror, he shook the plastic bottle vigorously and noted with pride the rippling muscles in his chest.

This is my destiny, he thought.

Twisting the cap of the dye bottle, he felt it snap free in his hands and then dipped the applicator into the inky liquid. He was careful not to spill it on the stark white sink as he began applying it to his hair.

He worked the dye in from front to back until his hair was dark black, then replaced the lid and tossed it into the bag. The applicator and the brush followed, and when he was done, he ripped the bag free and tied it off.

He let the dye set for the allocated time before stepping into the shower. He turned the water on without waiting for it to warm up. The excess dye swirled around the drain like black rivulets of dark blood. He thought of the men he'd lost to the Hellfire strike, which had knocked him unconscious. Fate hadn't been finished with him then. In fact, it had another blessing in store. After they left the valley, the World Health Organization had given them seats on a transport from Pakistan to Jordan.

It was all coming together, just like he'd been told.

Three hours later, the team stood around the van they were taking across the border. They were waiting for the order to load up. Boz had just finished a protein bar and was taking the plastic wrapper off the Listerine he had bought in Jordan.

"Is there some ingredient in that shit that I don't know about?" Villa asked, watching him swish the blue liquid around in his mouth for the third time that day.

Boz had already gone through one of the travel-sized bottles and had been forced to open this one before the day was even over.

"Who knows, but for the longest time I thought it was vodka or something," Harden said. "The man should have been a dentist."

Barnes stood by himself, waiting for Jones, who had crossed the border the day prior with Hoyt, to send in his latest update. He'd considered his options and decided he didn't want to go north in search of another crossing. Without knowing who was in control of the checkpoint, he could be walking into a trap. When the phone finally rang, Jones didn't do much to help his decision.

Jones advised that he had a good vantage point on the crossing but that there wasn't any traffic coming from the Syrian side. Hoyt assumed that someone had cut the road and that al-Qaeda was letting people in but refused to let anyone out.

Barnes hung up the phone and called Harden over to him. Explaining the situation and lack of intel, he decided that they would dismount short of the border crossing before nightfall and conduct a recon before continuing on. Harden nodded and went to brief the team.

The civil war in Syria had brought every major terrorist group in the Mideast to the war-torn country. The violence and lawlessness meant that it was unsafe for most reporters, and therefore he didn't have to worry about his men showing up on the news.

Barnes sat in the front while Scottie drove, and if traffic stayed light they would arrive at their drop point fifteen minutes after the sun went down. He grabbed a map from the visor and checked his position on his wrist GPS. Once he found his location, he began searching for a good place to stop the van.

"Scottie, in another five kilometers I need you to pull off the road and head into the desert. Harden, you stay with the van and I'll take Boz and Villa up for the recon. You guys go ahead and kit up."

"Roger that, boss." They had bought the van from a smuggler who had built compartments into the seats that were virtually impossible to find. Villa and Boz moved off the bench seat and depressed the hidden lever that opened one of the compartments. The two men began pulling kit bags out of the hiding spot and laying them on the floor.

"I got your kit, sir." Boz handed the colonel's kit bag to Harden, who stood up and switched seats with him.

Barnes squeezed his large frame into the back of the van and slipped into his plate carrier. Instead of the HKs they were going to use AK-47s that had been modified to take a suppressor. He didn't want to leave NATO brass around the objective—not that it mattered. The 7.62 magazines that they were carrying were bigger and heavier due to the size of the round, and Barnes had made sure that everyone had a rig that would carry the magazines.

The colonel checked his optic to make sure it was working. He had never liked the EOTech, so he used an Aimpoint M68, which did the same job but had a dot instead of a reticle. They had modified the rifles because unlike the M4s, the Russian rifles didn't have rails to mount hardware. Boz had solved the problem by welding a small rail forward of the bolt, which allowed the team to mount optics onto the rifles.

The van came to a halt at the predetermined spot and the team conducted a quick radio check. From his position on the other side of the border, Jones was monitoring the same channel while Hoyt used thermals to scan the area.

"Anvil 6 is stepping off time now. How copy?" Barnes asked as he led the team away from the road.

It was common for Muslims to stop on the side of the road to pray, so the van wouldn't draw any attention. What would draw attention was three armed men running across the desert, so they made sure to push far enough out of sight that they wouldn't be detected by any passing motorists.

"Yes, sir, I read you. Our position is about one kilometer northeast of the checkpoint. We couldn't get any closer without being compromised, and there has been no traffic from this end for the last two hours."

"Roger that."

Barnes used the GPS to navigate away from the target before swinging wide and coming in from the south. He could see the road in the distance as it snaked east of him. According to the map the road would open up into a Y, and there would be a metal guard tower on a hill next to the intersection.

The terrain was flat and the sandy ground had been packed hard, making it easy to walk. Barnes could see low-lying shrubs and tufts of grass through his NODs as his feet gently scuffed the ground. He wasn't even breathing hard when he saw the guard tower rising over a low set of hills.

As they quietly slipped across the border, Barnes realized that he could have easily driven across without anyone seeing anything. However, in the back of his mind he knew that a plume of dust coming out of the desert might have drawn attention. The terrain was beginning to rise beneath their feet as they moved into the hills, and when they were five hundred meters out he called a halt.

"Be advised, we are five hundred meters from the objective."

"Check, boss," Harden replied.

"You must be in the low ground, sir—we can't see you from here."

"Roger that, we're moving out."

Barnes pivoted and touched Boz on the shoulder before he moved off in the darkness. He kept to the low side of the hill for as long as he could before he began working his way up at an angle. They made their approach carefully and avoided silhouetting themselves on the crest of the hill. The moon was beginning to peek out over the horizon, and they were close enough to the target to hear voices and smell the guard's cheap tobacco.

"Sir, we have you now. We aren't observing any movement."

Barnes keyed his mike but didn't say anything. In Vietnam, long-range reconnaissance teams referred to this as "breaking squelch." The technique allowed them to communicate nonverbally when talking could compromise them.

He pointed at Boz and motioned for him to set up on the hilltop. Boz nodded and began low-crawling toward the crest of the high ground. Once he reached a good vantage point, he keyed the radio, signaling that he was set. Barnes and Villa moved silently from their position and approached the target.

The colonel crawled as close as he could to the edge of the hill, and since no one had bothered to cut the grass he had plenty of concealment to work with. He was able to move all the way to the edge without any effort. He took a moment to relax as he looked around. Five feet below him was a metal shack made out of corrugated tin. He could see light filtering out of the west side of the shack, and he assumed there was a window over there.

"Boz, give me a sit rep?" he whispered.

"I've got one military-age male. He doesn't appear to be wearing a uniform."

"Roger that. Stand by for my count." Barnes motioned for Villa to follow him as he slid back down the hill. Reaching flat ground, he used the dead space between the hill and the shack to mask his approach. The sound of laughter emanated from inside the small building, and he was positive that they hadn't been compromised.

It was almost too easy.

He signaled to Villa that he was going to flank the building. Villa responded that he would hold on the east wall and breach on his signal. The silent conversation took only a second due to the countless missions they had run together. Keeping low, Barnes moved to the rear of the shack and out of sight.

A telephone line fed into the shack from a pole to his left, and he assumed they had access to a phone and maybe an alarm. He'd have liked to cut the phone line but didn't have the time. Carefully, he peeked into the window and got a partial layout of the room. Barnes saw four rebels inside, sitting around a table they had made from ammo boxes and an old pallet. The concrete floor had seen better days and was covered in dust and trash.

He could tell from their mismatched clothing that the men were definitely not Syrian regulars.

"Villa, we have four crows that I can see. Wait until I engage before you breach."

"Roger."

"Boz, give me a ten count on my mark. Ready, mark." Barnes began counting in his head, and when he reached five he stood up and moved across the window. One of the men inside caught the movement and got to his feet. He looked to be in his midtwenties, and as he turned his head back to the table, Barnes slipped his finger into the trigger guard and flipped off the safety with his thumb.

The M68 optic had an infrared setting, which allowed him to aim while wearing NODs. However, the light coming from inside the shack washed out the aiming dot and flared his night vision. Due to the offset between the barrel and the optic, Barnes had to center his point of aim above the rebel's forehead, so the round would impact where he wanted.

When he reached ten, he pulled the last bit of slack out of the trigger and sent a round through the man's frontal lobe. The colonel was already on his next target before the round blew the man's brains out the back of his skull. Working from left to right so he wasn't in danger of hitting Villa, he settled his dot on the next target and fired. The bullet impacted as the door crashed open and Villa engaged the other two men from the doorway.

Barnes watched his soldier step into the room, arcing his rifle toward the window as he moved. Villa's muzzle began sweeping down at an angle, and the colonel moved around to the front side of the building in case he fired. As soon as he cleared the corner, he heard two more shots from inside. Pushing through the open door, he stepped in behind Villa, who was holding on a man sitting on the floor.

Villa had fired two rounds low into the sitting man's abdomen, to avoid hitting his boss as he moved. Keeping the rounds at a downward trajectory avoided a possible friendly-fire incident. As soon as Barnes came through the door, he raised his rifle and fired a shot to the dying man's head.

"Nice shooting, I didn't see that guy."

"No problem, boss, I didn't want to splash you."

Barnes slapped his soldier on the shoulder and keyed his radio. "Boz, we are secured. We have five crows down."

"Roger, Anvil 6. My guy is down and we have no movement."

"Jones, are we good?"

"Roger that. We didn't even hear the shots, but it sounds like you owe someone a beer."

"As soon as I receive your allotment I will be sure to pay up."

"Hey, boss, sounds good to me."

"Harden, you can bring the van up."

Barnes moved Villa out to set up a blocking position in the east, and he headed across the road to block the northern approach. He found a spot that offered cover and a good vantage point, and he took a knee.

Jones came over the radio. "Sir, I have movement coming your way. It looks like twelve military-aged men and they are all armed."

"Villa, do you have eyes on them?"

"Yes, sir, they're about two hundred meters away. It looks like they came out of a ditch or something."

"Harden, we have company. I need you to black out your lights and conduct linkup."

"Anvil 7 moving."

Barnes left his position but stayed on the far side of the road. Moving in a crouch, he dropped into the low ground and began hand railing the road. He couldn't see the enemy, but he needed to flank them.

"Boss, you want me to roll 'em up?"

"Stand by. Harden, what's your location?"

"We are back on the road about five hundred meters out."

Barnes clawed his way up the steep embankment to make sure he had moved far enough past the rebels before he clicked his radio. "Villa, it's on you."

Villa waited until they were within fifteen yards of his position so that Boz would be able to cover him if he had to break contact. He had no idea where the colonel was but was sure that he was lurking somewhere. The sound of the van's engine was faint but growing as it sped up the road.

He wanted to let them get closer, but they would hear the van soon and he didn't want to spook them. The first shot broke clean and impacted center mass on the lead rebel. The second round followed a microsecond behind the first and caught the man in the throat as he stumbled forward. Rolling his shoulder into the stock, Villa applied positive pressure to the butt plate for better recoil management.

Villa snapped off two more shots and waited a split second for the optic to settle. The colonel popped up and he saw him prone out on the road and begin engaging targets. Barnes fired so fast that the suppressed rifle sounded like it was on full auto as he tore into the ranks.

Villa deliberately aimed low as he fired, which allowed him to stay on target despite the muzzle rise. Movies depicted operators only shooting at the head, but Villa liked shooting at the pelvis. It was a great target because there were a lot of good organs and veins in the area, and guys tended to bleed out faster if hit low. It also provided a natural transition from one target to the next because it accounted for the increased muzzle rise created by the 7.62 round.

Barnes wished he had a frag, but since he didn't he clicked his hand mike and said, "Moving." He came up to a crouch, moved about five meters closer to the rebels, and fired off a burst before he ducked back off the road.

Boz snapped two shots from the hill, but he was close to the effective range of the rifle and the rounds landed short and ricocheted off the ground. "Keep them down. I'm moving," he said across the radio.

Villa opened up with a burst as the rebels finally reacted to the ambush and began returning fire. Without night vision they couldn't see who was shooting at them, so they just started spraying lead everywhere.

Barnes had wanted to avoid a firefight because he didn't know who else was in the area. He saw the van fly through the checkpoint and pull off near the tower. Scottie jumped out of the driver's seat with his long gun and sprinted toward the metal steps of the tower.

Harden had his rifle out but wasn't sure where his team was, so he didn't engage.

"Boss, the natives are getting restless and we have guys wearing Hezbollah yellow moving out into the street. I suggest that you start wrapping it up."

"Roger that." Barnes dropped his magazine and slipped a fresh one from his kit and into the mag well. Racking the bolt, he began crawling forward along the low side of the road. One of the rebels popped his head up and Scottie fired from the tower. The rebel's head pitched violently backward before he slammed into the ground.

Boz's voice came over the radio. "I'm coming up on your right, V." Scottie fired again and the colonel heard the round's dull thump as it hit flesh.

"Anvil 6, stay low, we're going to move on these fuckers." Villa fired a four-second burst into the rebels' position, and Boz ran a few feet past him before diving to the ground. He began firing almost immediately to keep their heads down as Villa jumped up and bounded around him.

Once he was set, he ripped off another burst, allowing Boz to move up. They were so close now that he stayed in a crouch and fired as he moved up. The entire ambush had lasted three minutes and all the rebels were down.

"You two clear through. Harden, you and Scottie bring the van up." Barnes hopped to his feet and doubled back to retrieve his magazine. "Jones, I assume we can't come through your way."

The van pulled up as Villa and Boz were checking the bodies. He watched Boz fire a round into a rebel's face before continuing.

"I wouldn't risk it. There's a company-sized element loading up into a couple of technicals and heading your way."

"That's a good copy. When you have a chance, go ahead and move out. We are going to find a way around."

"Roger that."

Barnes waited for Boz and Villa to get into the van before he jumped in. He did a quick head count before telling Scottie to move out. Harden already had a route planned and told Scottie to get off the road and drive south. They took it slow as they navigated the terrain, but once it flattened out he was able to pick up the pace. The dust made it hard to see even with night vision, but Scottie was a pro at driving in shitty conditions.

"Anvil 6, we are clear and heading to objective one," Jones finally reported.

"We will see you there."

It took them an hour to skirt the settlements and get back on the main road. Harden navigated while the men topped off their magazines and conducted a brief after-action review.

"Villa, I messed up not picking up that extra guy in the house. I didn't have the angle I thought I did," Barnes began.

"No worries, boss. I should have picked up that ditch and I should have had a better position off the road. You saved my ass by flanking those shit bags."

"Hoyt and Jones should have picked that up on the way in and reported it," Harden said from the front.

"I think I did pretty badass saving everyone. I wish these AKs didn't suck so I could have kept the high ground," Boz said.

"Boz, don't you need to brush your teeth or something?" Scottie called from the front seat.

"You just keep driving and maybe one day when you grow up, you can go on missions with the big boys."

Barnes waited until the laughter died down before he spoke.

"I want you all to focus on the days ahead. All of our sacrifices have brought us here and our actions will finally turn the tide. While others have given up on the cause, you men have answered the call, and for that I am eternally proud. If I must die to change the world, I will at least take my enemies to hell with me."

The air was electric as he paused to look at his men. They knew what was at stake and were ready for whatever lay ahead.

Barnes let the silence speak for itself. The colonel's placid exterior hid the caustic hubris that had been driving him for the past six years. He was good at masking his intent, but the fact remained that his pride demanded the blood sacrifice that his team was about to pour out on the world. All the lofty talk about duty and honor clouded the issue and took the spotlight off the simple fact that Barnes would kill as many people as it took to break the back of radical Islam. It was his belief that it was America's role to pacify the region, and he was more than willing to go from country to country to achieve his goal.

Harden told the colonel that they were coming up on the outskirts of Damascus and would be arriving at the safe house that Dekker had purchased for them a few days earlier. The team was looking forward to a few hours of downtime before the final push. As they descended from the hills, they could see the lights of the ancient city sprawling out before them.

Scottie had stowed his night vision and was back to using the headlights as he merged into the light traffic. He was glad that the house wasn't in the heart of the city, because Syrian drivers were terrible. When they were ten minutes out, Harden was able to get Jones on the radio.

Jones told him that they had a green light to come to the house, and Harden began directing the driver through the maze of streets. The house was located in a residential area that was close enough to the target area without being right in the middle of the bustling city.

Barnes felt the tingle of anticipation as he drew closer to his destiny. Tomorrow a new war would begin, and there was no one that he would have to answer to.

CHAPTER 31

Bagram had changed since Mason was last there. The airfield had doubled in size, but it was still eerily familiar. It made him anxious to be back in Afghanistan, and a sense of fear washed over him as he shouldered his assault pack and set out to find his prey.

He pointed out the Joint Special Operations headquarters, which looked exactly the same as it had the last time Mason had seen it. It was a small building surrounded by a concrete wall, and the sight of it made him feel very exposed as he unconsciously felt for the pistol on his waist.

The compound's wall was made from Jersey barriers that had been stacked three rows high. The barriers looked exactly like the ones you would find at a construction zone or on the freeway. The wall was about ten feet tall and topped with razor wire. The only other security that he could pick out, besides the guard, was a camera mounted on a wooden pole near the entrance.

A guard sat out front, in a green plastic chair, enjoying a cigarette while basking in the sun. His rifle was leaned against the concrete wall to his left, but he didn't seem too worried about anyone bothering it.

"Are you sure that's it?" Zeus asked, looking for the additional security that he assumed he was missing.

"Yeah, that's it."

Zeus shrugged and told Mason to stay where he was. The American opened his mouth in protest, but his friend was already walking casually toward the guard, who seemed to be more interested in blowing smoke rings than doing his job. He was able to get within five yards before the guard lazily got to his feet. Zeus showed him his identification card and the two men began talking.

Zeus was careful to keep his head down and away from the camera while he spoke to the guard, and after a few minutes the Libyan turned and walked back to Mason's position.

"That young man is very polite for an Egyptian. He knows the man we are looking for and told me that he had a very long night and is sleeping in his room right now. Allah always smiles on the faithful."

"So, what are you thinking? Should we go wake him up?"

"I don't want to be rude, but we are pressed for time."

"Well, let's do it."

They found a line of Toyota Hiluxes parked near the edge of the compound, and Zeus spotted a set of keys in the third truck he checked. Mason got in the passenger seat, while Zeus drummed along with the CD playing in the cab.

"I like this band, the lady has a good voice. Who is it?" he asked as he drove.

"I don't know. It's some kind of teenybopper shit. Do you have any idea where you're going?"

"Yes."

"Are you going to tell me?"

"Not until you tell me the name of this band."

"I told you that I don't know." Mason hit the eject button on the CD player and pulled the silver disc out of the deck. "It says Lady Gaga. Like I said, I've never heard of it. If you don't tell me where we're going, I'm going to throw it out the window."

"Put it back in and I'll tell you."

Mason slipped the disc back into the stereo and hit the play button. "Done."

"We are going to the modular housing."

Zeus slowed the truck to a crawl as he approached a row of modular housing. The "mods" were metal trailers that had been converted into barracks and each had an address attached to the upper-right corner of the building. Once you found the correct row the numbers ascended from front to back.

Mason dug through his assault pack until he found a lock-pick set, a pair of gloves, and a cell phone. He wouldn't have the luxury of conducting the interrogation the way he wanted, so he was going to have to improvise. He lifted out four black zip ties before closing the bag.

"He told you all of this in a ten-second conversation? How did he know where to find the guy?"

"Just because he guards the CIA's front door, it doesn't mean he's loyal to the Americans. I would expect you to understand this better than anyone."

"Good point," Mason said before handing the zip ties to Zeus.

The American stepped out of the truck; his boots crunched over the gravel as he slipped between the metal trailers. He kept walking until he realized that Zeus hadn't told him the number he was supposed to look for. Stopping at the edge of one of the mods, he waited for Zeus to catch up.

"What's the number, dickhead?"

"It's that one right there."

The building was exactly the same as the ones they were staying in, except that these were painted a dull tan instead of white.

"It's room number three." Zeus spoke as he slipped on his gloves.

They moved to the stairs, opened the door, and stepped into a hallway that ran the length of the trailer. As they stopped to let their eyes adjust, Zeus held up five fingers, telling Mason it would be the last room before the bathroom.

Moving slowly down the hall, Mason motioned for Zeus to stay put while he moved into the bathroom. He paused long enough to ensure that no one was inside and then stepped casually through the door. A quick check under the stalls told him that no one was using any of the toilets, and then he headed to the shower area. It was empty and he stepped back into the hall.

Zeus gave him the thumbs-down sign, which meant the door was locked, and Mason took a knee next to the doorknob and carefully inserted the pick into the lock. It had been a while, but after a few seconds of screwing around with the tumblers he managed to disengage the lock and ease the door inward.

Zeus had his pistol out and stepped slowly into the room, and Mason drew his Glock and followed. It was dark inside and the two men waited for their eyes to adjust before moving any deeper. Directly in front of them were two beds pushed against the wall, with two wall lockers forming a neat cube. The lockers effectively cut the room into four sections, making it impossible to see the other two beds.

On the back wall there was a desk and an AC unit that hummed in the dark as it struggled to keep the room cool. Zeus could see the two beds closest to him didn't have linens on them and he nodded to Mason that he was ready to move. As the two men moved deeper into the room, they could make out a faint glow coming from a window that had been covered by a poncho liner.

Mason moved along the left side of the room until he came to the opening between the wall lockers. He could see a man sleeping in a bed to his right, and he stopped with his pistol up to signal Zeus that he had a target. Zeus moved up to the left side and once he visually cleared his area, he lowered his pistol to give his friend the right of way.

Moving directly toward the bed, Mason popped the hard corner formed between the bed and the lockers. It took only a split second, but once he saw that it was clear he pointed his Glock at the sleeping man and waited for Zeus to tell him it was clear.

Zeus moved up behind him and squeezed his shoulder, which told him he was free to move. General Nantz's mouth was open slightly as he snored on his back, and Mason inserted the barrel of the pistol into the man's open mouth. In one smooth motion he forced the pistol to the back of the man's throat until he gagged.

The general's eyes shot open while his brain processed what was happening. Zeus leaned in and whispered, "If you move, my friend is going to kill you." Then he flipped on the small lamp sitting on the desk. "I want you to get up slowly and move to the chair. Nod if you understand me."

Nantz nodded carefully and slowly sat up in the bed. Zeus grabbed the general's pistol off the camp stool that sat next to the bed and shoved it into his waistband. Once the general was standing, Mason used the pistol like a bit to guide him until the backs of his legs touched the edge of the chair. He gave Nantz a nudge with the pistol, and the man lowered himself into a seated position.

"Place your hands on the arms of the chair and do not move them, or I will shoot you in the face. Nod if you understand." Once again he nodded and lowered his arms. Zeus zip-tied the spy's arms to the chair and then bound his legs together at the ankles. After he was secure, Zeus moved around behind him and slipped another zip tie around his throat. Slowly he clicked the male end of the tie through the female until it was tight enough to be uncomfortable but not affect his breathing.

"I am going to take the gun out of your mouth. If you make any noise, my friend is going to choke you. You need to know that I didn't bring any cutters with me, so if you make him tighten it, we can't get it off. Nod if you understand." Mason waited for the nod before slipping the pistol out of the man's mouth.

"Before you start talking, I want you to listen. We know who you are and the orders you've been giving General Swift. We know that you compromised a team that launched yesterday and that they are all dead. All we want is information, and if you tell us what we need, you will never see us again. If you lie to us, we are going to hurt you. There is a kill team at 365 West Union Street waiting for our call. If you are uncooperative, they will kill your wife and your children. Nod if you understand."

Drops of sweat appeared on the general's forehead and dripped down his face when he nodded. His pupils dilated from the adrenaline dumping into his system. The fight-or-flight response was in full effect, but Nantz wasn't going anywhere. Zeus slipped past him and began searching his bed and the area around it. The Libyan pulled open his wall locker and began tossing the contents onto the floor.

"I need you to pay attention to what's happening right here. I don't need you to worry about what my friend is doing. I am going to ask you some questions now. I know your first instinct is to lie, but I want you to fight that. What do you have Swift doing for you in Syria?"

The general stared him right in the face and lied. "I don't know what you're talking about."

Mason didn't say anything. He just moved to the back of the chair and tightened the flex cuff around his neck a few clicks. Pulling the phone from his pocket, he began typing in a series of numbers. He waited for a few seconds, then began talking.

"Saber 6, you are a go to enter the house."

"Wait, I'll tell you. You have to understand what's going on over there while we are stuck in this shit hole. It's for the good of the country, you have to believe me. I'll tell you everything you want to know. Just don't hurt them."

"General, you probably have two minutes until they have your family."

"Ask me anything. I swear, I'll tell you. Just don't hurt them."

"Where is Barnes?"

"He is outside of Damascus."

"What's the target? You're wasting time."

"There's a mosque in Damascus that he's going to use to draw the terrorists into the city. Just like Najaf, Barnes is going to blow up the mosque and let them flood in. Everything I have is in the wall locker. Please don't hurt my family."

"You have thirty seconds."

"There's a hidden compartment in the back with a thumb drive. Everything that I know is on that drive."

"Fifteen seconds."

"That's all I know, I swear."

"Ten seconds. Tell me how to find him."

"I swear to God I don't know."

"You're running an operation in another country and you expect me to believe that you can't talk to your men? That's bullshit."

"We have a secure server that allows us to communicate. The address and the password are on the computer. Please, I swear to you."

"Saber 6, stand down," Mason said into the phone. He'd bluffed and won, but he wasn't sure it would matter.

"Can you keep them safe?"

"I need the password to this computer," Zeus said from the bed, where he had booted the computer and inserted the thumb drive, which had been exactly where Nantz said it would be.

"It's Pusher 79810."

Mason wasn't listening. He didn't care what Nantz had on the drive. Right now all he cared about was killing him. Placing his hand on the general's shoulder, he waited for the signal from Zeus. The Libyan looked up from the computer and nodded. Mason bent down and grabbed the zip tie.

"I want you to know that if I ever get back to the States, I'm going to kill everyone you care about." Nantz tried to say something, but Mason was already pulling the zip tie as tight as he could.

The general's legs shot out as his brain told him that there was a big problem. He tried to get his hands to his throat, but they were tied down, and the only thing he could do was twist and turn in his chair as the oxygen was slowly cut off.

Mason turned the chair so he could look into the man's eyes as the light faded from them and Nantz fell still.

"Do you have everything you need?" Mason asked.

"Yeah, I'm good."

"Okay, help me cut him loose." The two men cut the tie from the dead man's legs before cutting his arms free. Dragging the man to the wall locker, Mason grabbed a pair of medical shears from Zeus's back pocket and cut the zip tie from his neck.

"What are we going to do about this shit?" Zeus asked as they folded the general's body into the locker and forced it shut.

"I'm going to call Mr. David, and let him handle it," the American replied.

Zeus began wiping down the room. Mason pulled out the phone and held down the speed-dial key. Moving to the bed, he closed the laptop and put the thumb drive in his pocket.

"I didn't expect to hear from you this soon, Mason. Is there a problem?"

"More of a situation. I need a cleaning crew sent to building D 2280, room number three. Tell them to check the wall locker. And someone needs to start checking manifests on anything that carries passengers out of Pakistan. Barnes has to get to Syria with all his gear, and it's not like he can buy a ticket and check his weapons with the baggage guy."

"Got it, get back here now."

"Roger." Mason hung up the phone and pointed to the flight line. Barnes already had a jump on them, and he wasn't sure if he could catch up in time.

Hope they have an exit plan, Mason thought to himself on the way back to their vehicle. It was going to be a shit show for who-ever won the lottery of finding the dead general shoved into a wall locker.

Zeus started the truck and pulled away from the modular hous-ing, both men scanning for any obvious witnesses. They were just two contractors going about their day; he was sure no one was paying attention.

"What about Renee?" Zeus asked as he tried to keep under the posted speed limit. Their adrenaline was still pumping and he fought the urge to speed.

"Shit. We can't worry about that right now. Call Tarek and tell him to meet us in Syria," he said, handing the phone to Zeus.

Mason could hear Tarek jabbering in Arabic but couldn't make out what he was saying. He just heard the conversation from Zeus's side: "Tarek, Tarek, shut your mouth and listen. I don't care how much sleep you've gotten, I need you to go to Damascus. Mason said he'd give you ten thousand dollars if you meet us there . . . Yes, that is what I thought. We will see you soon."

"Why do I have to give him ten thousand bucks? Why can't you pay him?" Mason asked when Zeus handed him back the phone.

"If we were looking for a terrorist for my country, I would pay him, but we are not. Besides, you have plenty of money left."

"That's bullshit, Zeus. You don't even have a country."

"Well, if we are being honest, then neither do you. Unless you believe the fairy tale your latest CIA boyfriend told you."

"Wow, thanks," Mason said.

Mason knew he was never going home; he'd come to grips with that fact a long time ago. But he knew he needed to call Renee; after all, it was her men who had gotten slaughtered.

"What?" she asked after a few rings. Her voice was clouded in sleep.

"Renee, I . . ." Mason didn't know what to say now that he had her on the phone.

"You tell me where you are, or I'm going to kill you. Do you understand?" Renee didn't sound tired anymore, she sounded pissed, and Mason wondered if Zeus could hear what she was saying.

"Uh, we're going to Damascus and—"

"I'll see you there," she said before hanging up.

"Yeah, I think that's a good idea," Mason said to the empty line. He nodded his head like he was listening and then said, "Yeah, okay, I'll see you there."

"She hung up, didn't she?"

"What? Why would you say that?"

"Because the green light means it's connected, and the red light means there isn't an active call."

"Just shut up and drive."

CHAPTER 32

The fact that the clock was ticking down didn't seem to bother Zeus, who was snoring peacefully on the couch. Mason, on the other hand, was worried, and while the Libyan slept, and Renee and Tarek combed through Nantz's computer, Mason knew they were running out of time.

Renee had actually been waiting on them when they landed, and it was a good thing because she brought a bag full of cash with her, compliments of Mr. David. Mason thought she looked great, waiting at the hangar, and wondered about giving her a hug. Renee had answered the question for him by tossing him the sack of cash and telling him to get in the car.

By the time they got out of the airport and to the apartment, Mason had doled out ten thousand dollars in bribes. The CIA had no assets in Syria, and they were forced to rely on Ahmed's network of agents and fixers. His men covered North Africa and the Mideast and could get Mason anything he might need, for a price.

Tarek arrived before the sun came up, and as soon as he saw Renee, he forgot about everything. Luckily, she knew a thing or two about computers, and she and Tarek began working on Nantz's and Decklin's laptops. He was explaining the program he had written to search both drives when Mason decided to head down to the souk for supplies.

The city appeared calm, but Mason knew that in a war zone things could go to shit at a moment's notice. He began looking for any signs that the government was in control of the area, and when he didn't see any soldiers, he began checking for escape routes.

The market was already bustling with locals buying the groceries they would need for the day. Mason loved the early mornings and the feeling of promise that came with them. Everything was fresh and possible, and he felt renewed as he bought a carton of cigarettes. As he was slipping one into his mouth, the smell of fresh coffee drifted like an unspoken promise across the market and grabbed his attention.

Living in North Africa for as long as he had, Mason understood that making good coffee took time, and you were rewarded if you waited. He followed the rich, earthy smell until he came to a merchant who was roasting his beans over an open fire. The American told the man what he wanted, then waited patiently while the coffee merchant used a mortar and pestle to grind the beans into a fine powder.

Mason had done some investigating into the subject. Coffee had come from Syria to Constantinople in 962 AD, and legend had it that one of the first coffeehouses had been opened by a man from Damascus. While every Middle Eastern country had its own style of coffee, the Turkish style was likely the best.

As the American watched the man grind the beans, he realized that he was looking forward to sharing this with Renee. His wife had loved coffee, and every morning after his run, he would grab her a cappuccino and a bagel before heading in to work. The simple gesture never failed to make her day—that is, until the trouble started. Then he would find the coffee and the untouched bagel in the trash when he got home. He watched the merchant pour the powdered grounds into a plastic bag, surprised at the unwelcome memory, and then paid the man before grabbing a few more things for breakfast. Ahmed had taught him how to properly make the region's coffee, often saying, "Good coffee should be black as hell, strong as death, and sweet as love."

Back at the apartment, Mason used a stainless steel *cezve*, basically a pot with a long handle attached, to heat the cold water. As soon as the water was hot enough, he added six spoonfuls of ground coffee and three spoons of sugar and stirred until the grounds sank. Lowering the heat so that it wouldn't boil, he stopped stirring and allowed the water to extract flavor from the ground beans.

The key was in the foam that was beginning to form around the top of the metal pot. Mason had to constantly adjust the heat to retain as much as he could.

Once the coffee began to boil, he removed it from the stove to let the mixture settle. He repeated this step three more times before turning off the gas stove and removing the pot.

While the coffee cooled, he grabbed four glass cups and a plate. Filling the plate with a layer of figs and sweet breads, he prepared himself for the final challenge. Equally distributing the coffee's thick foam was the hallmark of a true master, and some coffee shops sold just the foam, which cost more than two cups of coffee.

Carrying the coffee and the food into the den, he placed them on the table before grabbing a cup for Renee. She gratefully took the cup and flashed him a smile. He went over to the couch Zeus was sleeping on and kicked it, waiting for his friend to sit up.

The Libyan rubbed his eyes and reached for the glass with a grunt. After taking a sip, he smiled and took the cigarette offered by his friend.

"This is really good. Did you make it?" Renee asked from the table.

"Yeah, a friend taught me how to do it."

"You're a man of many talents," she said, getting up from the table and walking over to him. She let her hand brush his and Mason felt his face grow hot.

The phone on the table rang, cutting off the conversation, and

Tarek checked the number before answering. "Yes?" He nodded as the caller spoke and then handed the phone to Mason.

"Hello? Good morning, Ahmed, how are things?"

"Mason, your friends crossed the border last night at Ramtha. There was a gunfight at the crossing and they killed a bunch of rebels. One of my men was able to track down their safe house. It's in the suburbs of Damascus."

"Where are they now?"

"They left the safe house five minutes ago in three vehicles. My man is following them. They appear to be heading into the city."

"Ahmed, I need to know where they are going."

"He won't lose them, but I suggest that you get ready. There is a lot of chatter coming out of Aleppo, and I believe that July is going to be a bad month."

"I owe you."

"Well, what else is new? I have my people standing by if you need them."

"Ahmed, we are going to need more than that. All we have are small arms and I'm going to need something bigger. If they are going operational, I'm going to need them soon."

"I can have someone meet you. Call me when you are ready."

"Thank you." Mason hung up the phone before handing it to Tarek. "Barnes is here and on the move. Ahmed has a man on them but doesn't know where they are heading."

"Both of these computers speak of 'target alpha.' Only one of them goes into any detail. Decklin's computer had an encrypted folder that I almost missed. Whoever is doing their computer work is quite competent, but not more so than I am," Tarek said with relish.

"Does it give a location?"

"No, they are much too sophisticated for that, but the folder was called '*Hafeedah.*'"

"'Granddaughter'?" Renee said as she took a sip from the cup.

"It has to be the Sayyida mosque," Mason added.

"It would make an excellent target," Zeus replied as he stood and stretched, the cigarette smoking from between his lips.

"What does that mean?" Renee asked, looking at Zeus.

"According to Shia tradition, the Sayyida Zaynab Mosque contains the grave of Muhammad's granddaughter Zaynab bint Ali. She was captured after the Battle of Karbala and forced into exile in Egypt after the death of her brother," he began. "Since the 1980s the Shia faithful have made mass pilgrimages to the site in honor of her strength and sacrifice. It's a very important site to them."

"So Barnes is trying to eradicate terrorism all by himself?"

"It's our best guess. We need to move," Mason said, jumping in.

He finished the last of his coffee and grabbed his bag, while Zeus stuffed a sweet roll into his mouth.

As soon as the Libyan started the car, Mason dialed a number into the new phone Tarek had gotten him and waited.

"We are on the move. Where can we meet you?" he said as a man answered in Arabic.

"Go to the tobacco shop," Ahmed replied. "Zeus knows where it is. We will be waiting for you there." The line went dead, and Mason told the Libyan where the meet would take place.

Damascus's history was one of occupation. Almost every country in the region had ruled the city of 2.4 million people at one time. The broad streets were laid out much like Paris, with wide straight avenues and large concrete medians. Traffic was a nightmare due to the countless minibuses that provided the main means of public transportation. The buses didn't run on a set schedule or service regular stops. Passengers would tell the driver where to stop, and he would simply pull over and let them out.

The civil war had caused an influx of people from the countryside and from other cities like Aleppo. The ancient city was bursting with refugees and their cars. Getting from one place to the other was definitely an exercise in patience. Unaware that the small car weaving through traffic was trying to stop a bombing, the city went about its business.

Zeus cursed as his feet bounced between the clutch and gas pedal. Buses and cars didn't bother signaling before they switched lanes because they knew if they gave any warning they wouldn't be let over. Mason braced himself as a minibus cut them off, causing Zeus to slam on the brakes. His knuckles were white as he hung on to the "oh shit" handle for dear life.

The Libyan shot him a dirty look that accused him of being a terrible passenger. Mason shrugged and tried to relax by lighting a cigarette. Tarek was sleeping like a baby in the backseat, and Renee pulled a hijab over her blond hair and shot him a smile.

It took them thirty minutes to reach the store, and Ahmed's men were posted outside the shop with rifles at the ready. A man with an AK-47 approached their vehicle with his rifle up. He looked at Renee, sitting in the back, before motioning for Zeus to roll down his window.

"We are guests of Ahmed," he said simply, and the man motioned for them to head around the back.

The Libyan followed the drive to the rear of the building as another one of Ahmed's armed men swung a large bay door open and motioned for them to drive the car inside. Zeus squeezed the sedan through the doorway before putting it in park.

Ahmed was walking around the large storage room with a satellite phone held to his ear. He held up one finger and yelled into the phone as his eyes played over Renee.

"What do you mean, they are coming? Why do I pay you so much if it takes you this long to give me information? The government is helpless. They couldn't stop a parade." Ahmed slammed the phone shut.

"I guess we have a problem?" Mason asked him.

"Yes, we have a big problem. One of my sources has confirmed the rebels are launching an offensive to take Damascus. Who is this beautiful creature?" he said, offering his hand to Renee.

"Renee, this is Ahmed."

"It is my pleasure to make your acquaintance," he said, taking her hand and lightly kissing it. Mason had seen the urbane version of Ahmed many times, but this was the first time it had made him a little jealous.

"Thank you for your hospitality," she said in Arabic, causing the Libyan to arch his brow in delight.

"I am sorry that we couldn't have met under better circumstances."

"Okay, that's enough," Mason said, taking Renee by the hand and pulling her away from his mentor.

"Ahh, so you are the one I have been hearing about? The first American woman to join their elite commandos."

Ahmed smiled before becoming gravely serious.

"Why have you brought her here? This isn't a place for a lady."

"She can take care of herself, I promise you."

Ahmed only needed to glance at her stony face to realize that might well be true. "We need to leave this place before it gets too dangerous."

"I can't do that, and you know it."

"Mason, the man you are looking for is going to die out there, and so will you if you don't come with me. I know you have a death wish, but are you willing to sacrifice her life?"

Renee spoke up. "It's not his decision. The man we are after killed my men, and I can't let that pass unavenged."

"I understand you have suffered, child, but this is not a fight for you," Ahmed said soothingly.

"I'm not leaving and neither is he," she replied.

"Leave it to you to find a woman as stubborn as you are. Fine, but it is on your head," he said, pointing to Mason.

The storeroom was lined with shelves and boxes. In one corner the wooden shelves had been modified to conceal a set of stairs that led down into a small basement. Ahmed turned and headed down the stairs. As they descended, Mason saw a single bulb hung from the ceiling, which cast enough light to reveal a space filled with neatly stacked wooden crates. In the center of the room was a large table covered with a respectable assortment of heavy weapons and ammo.

"Nice setup," Mason stated as he approached the table.

Zeus strolled around the table like he was buying vegetables off the street. He picked up a few items and looked them over before setting them down and moving on. Near the end of the table he found a canvas backpack with three RPG-7 warheads nestled inside. He checked the safety wires attached to the noses of the warheads, then began looking for the launcher.

While Mason was filling his assault pack with Russian grenades, Renee lifted the top off a wooden crate and found an RPG-7 launcher inside. The model had been designed for paratroopers and allowed the operator to break the launcher into two pieces. It still had the packing grease on it and was already mounted with the two-power optic.

Holding the two pieces aloft so that Zeus could see them, she snapped the launcher together and checked the optic and the flip-up sights.

"You have a good eye," Ahmed said approvingly.

"Tarek, go get the rag to clean off the grease," Mason said, looking at Renee.

Tarek gave him the finger, but he ignored him and smiled as Renee twirled the launcher like a child with a new toy.

"I was saving this for a special day, but seeing as how my shop probably won't be around for long, feel free to take it." Ahmed knelt below the table and lifted an M249 light machine gun from the floor. He set the machine gun onto the table with the flourish of a magician who has just pulled a rabbit out of a hat.

"Where did you get that?" Zeus asked as he walked over to the machine gun.

"Oh, I traded a man two boxes of medicine for this and hadn't gotten around to selling yet."

The M249 squad automatic weapon, or SAW, had a cyclic rate of fire of seven hundred rounds per minute. It could effectively hit a man at eight hundred meters, but the max range of thirty-six hundred meters allowed the operator to engage a larger target much farther away. Zeus ran his fingers lovingly over the cool metal before lifting it off the table.

He rotated the weapon toward the ground at a forty-five-degree angle. Carefully placing the muzzle on the concrete floor, he used the barrel and bipod for support. Squatting down, he flipped open the feed tray cover and performed a functions check. Unlike Soviet-designed machine guns, the SAW was not made of stamped metal and had tighter tolerances. If the weapon wasn't properly maintained and cleaned, it would jam, which was not a good feeling in a firefight.

Ahmed also had the barrel bag that came with the weapon. The green bag held an extra barrel and two hundred-round cloth pouches. Mason lifted three ammo cans of linked 5.56 onto the table and pointed to the ammo pouches.

"Hey, Zeus, you know what we called those in the military?"

The Libyan slammed the feed tray cover closed and lifted the weapon off the floor by its buttstock. "Ammo pouches?"

"Nope, they're called nut sacks."

"Don't be gross," Renee said as she grabbed an AK-47 and checked the action.

"What? It's true," he said, shrugging.

"I think that if your government allowed more women in your army, there would be less . . ." Zeus struggled to find the right word.

"Gayness?" Mason suggested.

"Yes, that is the word I was looking for. Gayness."

"Boys and their toys," Renee replied, grabbing a stack of magazines and looking for something to put them in. "Well, look at that, are these real?"

She was holding up a Chinese chest rig, which had been made famous by the Rhodesian army during the bush war. The simple rig was one of the most effective pieces of kit ever developed, and Mason walked over to have a look.

"Yeah, they look real, and there's a whole box of them."

Mason grabbed one for himself before shouldering the assault pack and heading for the stairs. He passed Tarek at the top of the stairs, ignoring the rag he showed him.

"Stop messing around and load up the gear," Mason said.

Tarek sighed and headed back into the basement, while the rest of them began loading their weapons into the car.

Ahmed tried to persuade Renee to stay with him, but she was busy loading the empty magazines. He turned his scowl on Mason, who stood before him, looking at the ground. The American knew all too well that Ahmed didn't approve of his obsession with revenge. "Ahmed, I thank you for everything that you have done."

"It is not too late."

"If I don't go, a lot of people are going to die."

"People begin dying the day they are born, and in our world they die every day. This has always been about you."

"Maybe, but it's too late to turn around now."

Ahmed's eyes watered as the two men embraced. He kissed both sides of the American's face and tried to shake the overwhelming sense of guilt that he was feeling. "What about you, Zeus? I believe that you still work for me." Zeus looked away, unable to meet the man's gaze. "Are you and your little friend going to defy me after all of this time?"

"I am just doing what you would do." Zeus towered over the man but looked vulnerable standing there.

"I always knew he was a bad influence on you." Ahmed smiled and patted the large Libyan on his arm. He was proud of them, but his heart still grieved. "Be careful and watch out for Tarek; he was never good at anything but computers."

Mason waited as the two men went to the car and began kitting up. Turning to Ahmed, he said, "You told me once that our paths are known only to God. If it is his will, I will see you again."

"*Inshallah*, if God is willing," Ahmed said. The two friends embraced a final time before Mason moved to the car and opened the door.

Renee looked at him from the backseat as Mason strapped the chest rig to his body. She reached forward for his hand, and he grabbed it briefly before looking at Tarek.

"You know that you can stay," Mason said.

Tarek ignored him and began loading the SAW.

Zeus turned the key and looked in the rearview mirror. He watched as Tarek expertly laid the rounds across the bolt face before slamming the feed tray cover closed. Leaving the bolt forward, he looked up and caught Zeus's eyes in the mirror.

"I cannot let you have all the fun."

Zeus smiled as he put the car in gear and headed onto the street. Mason had a map out and was trying to determine where they were.

"You might as well put that away and enjoy the ride. I know where we are going."

"Okay. So, where are we going?"

"We could take the airport road. It will take us to the mosque, but it is not safe. I think it's best to stay off the main roads and stick to the Shia neighborhoods. If we get stopped, we have a better chance of talking our way out."

The farther they drove from the center of Damascus, the more the war appeared around them. Traffic was thick heading into the city, and there were black clouds of smoke on the horizon. Bursts of rifle fire echoed throughout the city, and the cars and buses that filled the roads were loaded down with people's possessions.

"They will close the roads soon. And when they do we are going to be trapped."

Mason tried to call Mr. David, but the spy didn't answer. Mason slipped the phone into his pocket, put a magazine into the rifle, and jacked the bolt to the rear.

Where is he? he wondered.

CHAPTER 33

------------------------------ **Damascus, Syria**

Ten miles away, Barnes had his own problems. They had left the safe house in the al-Hajar al-Aswad district early and headed north on the M5. The plan was to move away from the target to shake any tails and then loop back south. Having spent the last ten years in the Middle East, Barnes should have been used to traffic, but he wasn't.

The early-morning traffic was moderate until they reached the southern bypass, where it looked like a parking lot. Scottie must have taken something, because he was too high-strung to sit still and he kept trying to weave through the traffic. When he wasn't attempting to drive up on the curb, he was cursing at every car that wouldn't let him over. His constant movement was starting to give Barnes a headache.

"Colonel, I think something's up," Harden said from the front seat of the van. Jones came across the radio from the lead vehicle before he could answer.

"Sir, it's starting to look like these people know something that we don't."

A familiar tension electrified the air, and the city felt like it was on edge. No one was panicking yet, but it was only going to take a small nudge to push the people over the edge. The team had been inside

Fallujah before the marines assaulted the city. They had watched the residents flee like rats off a sinking ship.

Barnes had picked Syria because his plan was to destroy the future of radical Islam by attacking the roots. Destroying the mosque would ignite another Shia versus Sunni clash, which would fill the city with fighters. Every major terror organization in the Mideast had representatives in either Damascus or Aleppo, and all he had to do was draw them out. Once they were in the open he could infect and kill them.

Even the suburbs that made up Damascus were filled with Iranians and Iraqis who were either sympathetic to the cause or actively participating in the movement. In his mind there was no such thing as collateral damage in Syria—the whole country was fair game.

Barnes caught a glimmer of light off to the west, and as he turned his head he heard a deep rumbling explosion. He could see a black cloud already drifting up over the buildings as automatic rifle fire chattered sporadically in the distance.

"Boss, the airport road is blocked," Jones said over the radio.

"Where are you?"

"We are two kilometers away from phase line green, but we won't be getting through this way. What do you want me to do?"

"What's your grid?"

"Stand by." Jones pulled out the GPS unit and read the grid off to Barnes.

Barnes pulled the map out of his kit and marked Jones's and Hoyt's location. Checking the coordinates on his wrist GPS, he marked his position. He realized that Jones was only one and a half kilometers in front of them.

"Can you get off the road? There is an intersection that will take you south through Midan. Then we can cross over onto the 110."

"Roger that."

Harden was already telling Scottie to turn south on the road that was coming up. He didn't think it was a good idea, but he nodded and turned into a suburb. The roads were narrow, but there wasn't as much traffic. Harden told Scottie to slow down so that the other vehicle could keep up. Behind them Boz and Villa were driving the van that carried the bomb they were going to plant outside the mosque.

"Boss, I made the turn and I'm heading southbound," Jones said.

"Stand by for rally point grid." Barnes consulted the map he was using to track their movement through the city. He used a red alcohol marker to trace their route on the laminated map. They were making better time now but were way off the planned route. Once he found a good spot, he called the grid over the radio. Barnes wanted to get back on the main road as soon as possible. He didn't want his people caught in the middle of whatever was going down.

"Sir, we are going to intersect with you in another five hundred meters. Hoyt, watch that guy . . . ," Jones said. "Contact front, contact front."

"Shit," Scottie said from the driver's seat.

"Contact at grid 4952/1021. We are in heavy contact—will advise." Jones was calm over the radio despite taking fire. The colonel located the spot on the map quickly while Harden entered the grid into his GPS.

"Harden, get us there."

"Roger that, sir."

"Head east for two blocks," Barnes told Scottie while Harden waited for his GPS to update. The driver pushed the pedal to the floor. He cut east on the first street he came to.

"Okay, I'm tracking. They are two streets over, come in from the south." Barnes looked back out the rear window to ensure the van was still following. He didn't want to lose them, but it wasn't a good idea to bring a bomb into a firefight either.

"Next left, slow down, Scottie," Harden commanded calmly. Barnes had his window down and his rifle up and ready to fire. The sound of small-arms fire was growing to a crescendo the closer they got.

"Right there." Barnes popped the door before the vehicle came to a stop. He could see men darting out into the streets with their rifles blazing. A firefight at this range had all the earmarks of a disaster.

"I see them." The street was crawling with rebels as men streamed out of the alleys and buildings and converged on the intersection.

Harden brought his HK up just as Scottie hit the brakes. The car slid to a stop. Barnes rolled out of the back and fired off a long burst of suppressive fire. Two armed rebels heard the car screeching to a halt and were cut down as they turned to investigate.

Barnes checked quickly for the van, which had stopped short. He caught a glimpse of Boz jumping out of the back with the 240 Bravo and moving up to the edge of an alley. There were men sprinting up the alley, and he could see one of them was armed with an RPG. Firing on the move, he hit the lead man in the chest. As the man went down, he discharged the rocket into the sky.

Boz made it up to Scottie's position, laid the machine gun across the hood of the car, and ripped a long burst into a mass of men attempting to move on the downed vehicle. The windshield was riddled with bullet holes, but there wasn't any blood immediately visible.

Barnes turned up the volume on his radio. He continued firing down the alley until the bolt on his AK locked to the rear and he was forced to transition to the pistol. Firing five quick shots with the Glock, he ducked into cover as a squat unshaven Syrian in a black tracksuit fired a burst from the hip.

He heard the rounds whizzing past him as he holstered the pistol and snatched a fresh magazine from his kit. They were within ten meters of his position when he got the rifle back into action and reengaged the men moving toward him.

"Be advised we are in a shop to your nine o'clock," Jones said over the net.

Harden moved up the left side of the street and posted himself at the edge of the wall. The scene was beyond chaotic, with men firing everywhere. He needed to get his men out of here. He engaged targets as they presented themselves, but with Barnes busy in the alleyway, he had to step up and control the fight.

Jones and Hoyt were hunkered down in a shop trying not to get shot as the firefight raged in the street. The door they had kicked open was riddled with bullet holes, and fragments of glass littered the floor.

"Frag out," Jones yelled before tossing a frag out into the street. The two men ducked down under the windowsill and waited for it to detonate. The explosion sent more glass crashing to the floor and peppered them with the fragments. Brushing it out of his hair, Hoyt sank to a knee and returned fire.

Jones got to his feet quickly just as Harden yelled that he was tossing a smoke canister to cover their exfil. He waited for it to start billowing up in the street before moving past his teammate. Jones slapped Hoyt on the ass as he passed, in case he didn't see him moving, and then retreated farther into the shop. As soon as he located the back door, he set up covering fire so Hoyt could move.

Harden was telling them to hurry over the radio as Hoyt ran past Jones and set up near the rear door. "Friendlies coming out," he yelled before tossing the door open and taking a peek outside. He could see the colonel engaging a target down the alley. Before stepping into the street, he made sure Jones was on his tail.

Jones stopped at the door to change mags while Hoyt moved up to cover Barnes. The colonel heard the heavy rifle barking behind him and turned to look over his shoulder.

"Let's go, let's go," Barnes yelled as Hoyt picked up his sector of fire. "All Anvil elements pull back to the vehicles," Harden called out over the internal net. The level of fire from the rebels had abated, but there was still a lot of movement around the periphery of the block.

Jones moved out from the shop with the laptop bag in one hand and his rifle in the other. Heading to the car, he tossed the bag into the backseat and told Hoyt to get into the van.

"Yeah, put me with the bomb, that's real cool," Hoyt yelled sarcastically. Villa collapsed back a few feet before turning to cover Boz.

"I'm set," Villa yelled. His teammate lifted the machine gun off the car and moved back to the van. The colonel had another frag prepped and tossed it down the alley before moving up to the car. He got a quick head count and waited for the van to get turned around.

"Let's get on out of here," Harden said once he slammed the door shut. Scottie put the car in reverse. As soon as the vehicles were clear, Barnes hopped into the backseat of the car and told Scottie to "punch it."

"Holy shit, that was intense," Scottie said as he sped past the van and took up the lead position. "You guys need to learn how to fucking drive."

"I need your empties," Barnes said. He opened a green ammo can and started pulling out preloaded magazines. Passing a handful to Harden, he refilled his kit and began loading the empty magazines from a can of 7.62 ammo.

"What happened, Jones?" Harden asked as he handed Scottie four full magazines.

"We made a right turn onto the street, and there was guy with an AK in the middle of the road. As soon as he saw us, he opened up. It was on after that."

"Get us on the main road before it gets ugly," Harden said without looking up from the map.

"It's going to be real fun trying to fit everyone in this little-ass Toyota Camry." Scottie grinned.

"Right now that's the least of our worries."

They pulled onto 110 heading south and they could see the Syrian army moving north along the road. Attack helicopters buzzed low above the buildings and began firing rockets down into the neighborhoods. Harden was looking for a way around an army checkpoint up ahead when an RPG skipped across the road.

"Shit, you want me to hold up or what?" Scottie asked.

"Get us off the road. We're a kilometer out from the target,"

Harden said. Scottie pulled the car onto the median and watched as another RPG sliced across the street and hit the checkpoint.

The soldiers followed the white trail of the rocket and began firing machine guns at a building a hundred meters to their left. They continued shooting until another rocket hit their position. Then they turned and fled.

"Are you serious?" Scottie asked out loud. "No one even died, that's just embarrassing."

"Fuck it. Let's go." They all had their windows down. Scottie put the car back in gear and accelerated down the street. He swerved across the median, into oncoming traffic, before swinging back into their lane. Luckily most of the cars on the road were stopped, and the two vehicles were able to pass around the checkpoint without any issues. The final phase line was less than a quarter kilometer away, and they knew there was no way Barnes was going to call off the attack.

Zeus and Mason were stuck on the southern bypass in a line of cars stretched along the route to the 110. Even though most of the traffic was heading north into the heart of the city, the roads were congested as vehicles began turning around in the street. An army checkpoint was on fire next to a brick building ahead of them. Sandbags gave off black smoke as they burned.

The government had artillery in the hills around the city. They could hear the large shells cutting through the air as they flew overhead. One of the shells fell short and impacted a residential area off to the west. The explosion rocked the car and kicked up a huge plume of smoke and debris. The rebels in the street turned toward the explosion as another shell detonated with a crunching thump. Zeus kept his head down as he drove.

"This neighborhood is primarily Shia. I hope the fighting stays north of here."

"There's another checkpoint ahead," Renee said from the back.

The cars in front of them were being stopped by a group of fighters wearing yellow Hezbollah headbands.

Mason looked up from the phone, annoyed that he couldn't get ahold of Mr. David. He saw that the traffic on both sides made it impossible to turn around, and he knew they were stuck. Tossing his rifle into the backseat, he ordered Tarek to cover it up with his blanket. If Lebanese guerillas suspected anything, the men would be executed in the street.

"Shit," Mason said.

Zeus calmly waited to pull up to the makeshift checkpoint while Mason slipped his pistol out of its holster and stuck it under his leg. The Libyan had the window down and came to a stop as one of the fighters stuck his head in.

"Where are you going?"

"We're heading south. The rebels have cut the road and are attacking the army checkpoints."

"I know that, but why are you heading south? The fighting is the other way."

Mason lit a cigarette and tried to stay calm as another guerilla strolled arrogantly toward his side of the car and looked greedily at Renee in the backseat. Things were about to get ugly.

"Look, my friend. We have a job to do, and we would like to get past if we may."

"How do I know that you aren't with the Brotherhood?" Zeus was trying to find an answer when the man shoved his rifle through the window. "Where are you from?" Mason moved his hand nonchalantly to his pistol and prayed that if he started shooting Zeus would hit the gas.

"Is that your commander over there?" Zeus pointed to a man in camo fatigues sitting on a folding chair. "Tell him that I need to talk to him. He knows who I am."

"You know that guy for real?" Mason asked as the rebel looked back toward his boss.

"Fuck no, just follow my lead," Zeus said quietly.

"We are going to die," Tarek whispered from the backseat.

"Stay calm," Renee said, placing her hand on his shoulder.

"Either you bring my old friend over to me, or let me go talk to him. It's your choice. I assure you, he will not be happy if I am not allowed to speak to him."

The Hezbollah fighter looked confused but allowed Zeus to open the door. Swiftly grabbing a stack of cash from the center console, he asked Mason to pass him the cell phone before getting out of the car. The Libyan walked confidently down the road and called out a greeting to the commander. He held his arms wide open as the man slowly got to his feet with a bemused smile.

Zeus embraced the man. The rebel at Mason's window lowered his rifle and walked on to the next car. He could see Zeus pointing back to the car while holding up the phone. The commander nodded as the Libyan passed him a stack of bills and began dialing a number into the phone. The commander smiled and slipped the cash into his pocket before taking the phone.

As he lifted the phone to his ear, Zeus turned and flashed Mason the thumbs-up. The commander talked on the cell phone for a few minutes before handing it back to Zeus. The two men embraced warmly, and Zeus trotted back to the car with a large smile. Mason could see the Hezbollah commander yelling to his men, who began piling into a white pickup, preparing to move out.

"Allah is with us today, my friend," Zeus said as he jumped into the car and put it in drive.

"Did you just bluff that guy?"

"Holy crap, I thought they were going to kill us," Renee exclaimed.

Zeus raced through the gears, accelerating to catch up with the white pickup, which had sped off in front of them. Seven Hezbollah fighters were holding on for dear life as the driver swerved back and forth across the lanes of traffic, making a path for them to follow.

"Sort of. When it looked like Gaddhafi was going to lose control over the country, Ahmed thought it would be best to find alternate means of employment."

"You mean he wanted to save his ass."

"Yes, of course, but what do you expect? He had contacts in Lebanon who thought he worked for Hamas. Ahmed convinced certain people that he had infiltrated the Libyan intelligence network and began selling them intel on Israel. The whole thing was rather preposterous, but Ahmed pulled it off."

"So how did you turn that interesting tidbit into the little performance we just witnessed?"

"Well, the money helped, and I just prayed that he knew of Ahmed."

"What was your plan if he didn't?" Renee asked.

"That much money has a way of changing a person's mind." Zeus smiled.

Mason shook his head in amazement as he retrieved his rifle from the backseat. Up ahead, two more pickups waited on the median. The fighters held on for dear life as the drivers jumped the curb and took the lead.

"Ahmed told him that the Muslim Brotherhood had hired Westerners to blow up the mosque," Zeus said with an evil smile.

"That was smart. Who knows, we just might make it out of this."

"Abdul is the Hezbollah commander for the city," he said, pointing to the white pickup that had already sped off. "He will be extremely motivated in ensuring Barnes fails in his task."

"I just hope we find Barnes first," Renee said.

Mason felt a wave of relief now that they were moving. He had seen checkpoints like these in Darfur and knew what type of men manned them. When law and order fell away, it was always the "freedom fighters" who did the most damage. In Africa, he'd seen more rape and murder than any one man should ever have to witness.

Looking up at the rearview mirror, he locked eyes with Renee.

She smiled at him, and he wondered if she knew of the danger they had just avoided.

"You don't have to worry about me," she said, leaning forward.

"Oh, really?"

"I'm a big girl, and I can take care of myself."

"I know. But if it's all the same to you, try to stay close."

She reached over the top of the seat and gently squeezed his shoulder. They had both found something in each other that they had been missing, and it scared Mason.

Up ahead, the lead pickups darted into oncoming traffic and blocked the road. The convoy cleared the intersection. The drivers of the blocking vehicles honked their horns and flashed their lights as they weaved their way back up to the front.

A truck passed, the bed loaded down with heavily armed jihadists. Mason wondered what Toyota would think about the fact that their pickup was the vehicle of choice for the new freedom fighters. It would be a great commercial, for the right audience.

"We're getting close," Zeus said.

The last truck crossed the median and sped past the convoy on the wrong side of the road. A yellow flag snapped in the breeze from its place on the roll bar as civilian drivers fought to get out of its way. At the last minute, the driver jumped the median and pulled into the center of another intersection.

"I don't think that flag is such a good idea," Tarek observed from the back. Zeus was about to reply when he saw a jet of flame and a cloud of dust kick up across the street. A moment later, an RPG slammed into the pickup, flipping it over in the middle of the road.

"Contact front," Mason yelled, bracing himself against the dashboard as the truck in front of them locked up its brakes.

Zeus jerked the wheel hard to the left and hit the gas to avoid hitting a Hezbollah fighter who'd been flung from the bed of the truck. He slammed his foot on the brake, which locked up. The burning truck spun on its roll bar in the middle of the street.

"Hold on," Zeus yelled. The truck in front of them dodged right into their path.

Time slowed. Zeus punched the gas in an attempt to avoid a collision. Mason felt the car shudder as the transmission slipped. They slammed into the steel bumper of the pickup. The impact sent Mason's head crashing against the windshield. Their vehicle stalled and came under fire.

Bullets shattered the windshield. The American could feel blood dripping from a gash on his forehead. He sat dazed, staring through the smoke wafting up from the crumpled hood. Another burst of fire raked the car. Shaking his head, Mason tried to focus. His vision was blurry, and he was having trouble getting the door open. He slammed his shoulder against the door frame while pulling up on the latch. The door groaned before finally opening.

Falling out of the car, he felt a hand grab him from behind. Mason let himself be pulled away from the mangled car. He felt hot brass falling onto his neck. Looking up, he saw Renee firing one-handed as she dragged him to cover.

They had driven right into an ambush. Heavy rifle fire was pouring in from fighting positions dug along the far side of the road. Mason's vision cleared slowly. He could see a squat brick building to his nine o'clock, which had a reinforced position set up on the roof. A heavy machine gun, most likely a DShK, was firing at their vehicles in long, slow bursts. The heavy .51-caliber rounds chewed up the lead trucks as a green flag with crossed swords snapped in the wind above the gun. It was painfully obvious that the Muslim Brotherhood was in control of this block.

The Hezbollah fighters scrambled for cover and began to return sporadic fire. Tarek pulled the SAW out of the backseat and laid it across the hood of their car. Holding the trigger down, he fired off a long burst at the roadblock set up on the other side of the intersection. Bodies of civilians and fighters littered the roadways as both sides fired indiscriminately.

Mason stumbled to his feet and brought his AK up to bear. He saw the gold dome of the mosque five hundred meters down the street.

"Zeus, there it is." He pointed.

"I'm a little busy right now."

"I need more ammo," Tarek yelled.

Renee ducked low and sprinted to the trunk of the battered car. She placed the muzzle of her rifle on the lock and fired a round through the mechanism. Fighting against the mangled trunk, she pried it open and snagged two ammo cans out of the back. Using her left hand, she tossed the first one to Tarek before coming under fire.

Mason staggered over to her and returned fire at a position across the road. Pushing her to the ground, he grabbed the last ammo can and lobbed it toward Tarek.

"Get the RPG," he yelled as he steadied his rifle on the roof of the car. Taking his time to get a good sight picture, he fired two more shots. One of the rebels hit the ground.

Renee leaned into the trunk to reach the RPG launcher and the rockets, which had slid to the back of the cargo area. She yelled to Mason, "My belt's caught—it got caught on the latch."

A bullet whizzed past his head with a hiss. He ducked down as the next round dinged off the exposed metal and ricocheted with a menacing whine. Scraping his knees on the ground, he fumbled with Renee's belt until it finally came loose. Mason tried to pull her free of the car, but she scrambled back to retrieve the rockets.

"What the fuck do you think you're doing?" he yelled as she ducked down beside him with a wink.

"Someone has to get us out of here," she laughed.

"You need to be careful," he yelled back.

"Yes, dear," Renee replied as she snapped the launcher together.

Mason dropped the empty magazine and pulled a fresh one from his kit. He slammed it into the rifle. Renee expertly slid a rocket into the launcher and locked it in place with a twist.

The amount of fire pouring into the kill zone made it difficult to find a target. Bullets zipped into the vehicles, sending shards of metal and clouds of glass flying into the air. A bullet hit the tire of one of the pickups, causing it to hiss as it deflated. Renee peeked out from behind the car, looking for a target. Mason was about to tell her to try to clear the road when more trucks sped into the intersection from the west.

"Technical," Zeus yelled out at a flatbed pickup. A Soviet KPV-14.5 antiaircraft gun mounted in the bed swung into view.

"Right there," Mason yelled to Renee.

"I've got it, get out of the way," she replied as she stepped out of cover. "Back blast area clear," she yelled before pulling the trigger.

Mason jumped out of the way. The booster charge engaged, sending a jet of hot exhaust out of the back of the launcher. The rocket rushed from the launcher. A split second later the main charge kicked in, leaving a trail of white smoke as it hurtled toward its target. He could tell right away that it was off target.

"Move," he yelled, grabbing Renee by the shoulder as he pulled her away from the car. His rifle smacked against his knees, but he was focused on getting her to cover since they'd given away their position. "Zeus, fall back," he yelled.

Mason looked over his shoulder and caught a brief glimpse of the youth manning the KPV. The tails of the green head scarf tied around his forehead snapped in the air as he struggled to pivot the huge gun. The muscles in his thin, ungainly arms strained beneath his faded Beastie Boys T-shirt as he stood on tiptoes to reach the trigger. Manhandling the heavy weapon until he was aiming at the mass of stalled vehicles, the young jihadist pressed down on the butterfly trigger and fired. The gun's heavy recoil shook his rail-thin body, giving the impression that he was having a seizure. However, as the bullets hammered into the position Renee had just vacated, a toothy smile played across the youth's acne-marked face.

• • •

Scottie had a full head of steam as he shot around the corner and sped toward the target. Downshifting, he expertly worked the wheel. The back end of the dented sedan snapped around as they came out of the curve, and he smiled. Harden grabbed on to the dashboard. Despite the pungent odor of the overheated brake pads, Scottie knew the car would hold up and wasn't worried when the needle of the faded tachometer jumped to five thousand RPMs.

Scottie was determined to make it to the mosque. If they wanted him to go slow, then they were going to have to take him out of the driver's seat. Red brake lights blinked on and off ahead of him, and cars slowed down. Hopping the median, he swerved into oncoming traffic, shifted gears, and cut back into his lane. He was having the time of his life and had totally forgotten about the van trying to keep up with his nimble vehicle.

"You realize that there is a bomb in the van, right?" Jones said, leaning forward over the armrest.

"You want me to slow down so we can get fucked up?"

Jones looked out the open window, taking in the burned-out vehicles and scattered shell casings lining the road.

"No, you're doing good."

"That's what I thought," Scottie yelled back.

"Take your next left and then a right turn," Harden cut in. "The target will be five hundred meters to the south."

"Roger that." Scottie whipped the car wide in preparation for the sharp turn. He felt the tires struggling to grip the road as he drifted smoothly around the corner.

Explosions and small-arms fire echoed all around them. As the symphony of war rose to a crescendo, they raced through the urban wasteland. The buildings muffled the direction of fire, making it impossible to get a fix on their point of origin.

Harden had abandoned the idea of his driver slowing down. He had to keep looking up from the map, which he'd positioned in his lap, because Scottie's erratic driving evoked waves of nausea.

Colonel Barnes swayed in the backseat as Scottie expertly handled the turn. He was calmed by the realization that he was closing in on his destiny. More than any man before him, he was going to change the face of this ancient city forever, and single-handedly solidify his place in the pantheon of conquerors.

Barnes harbored no qualms whatsoever about putting civilians to the sword. He saw them as savage enablers who provided the jihadists with an unwavering infrastructure, and their reparations were well past due. The world was about to take notice, he thought as the car slipped around the final turn and immediately came under fire.

"Back the fuck up," Harden yelled as a bullet knifed through the windshield and thumped into the colonel's headrest. Barnes twisted to see the hole, where his head had just been, as Scottie yanked up on the emergency brake and spun the car in a 180-degree circle.

"Go, go, go," Jones yelled, shaking the back of the driver's seat with his hands.

The car shook as the engine redlined. Scottie released the emergency brake and pushed in the clutch. His right hand shot to the gear shifter, and he slammed the sedan into first before mashing on the gas. The tires squealed on the pavement, and the sedan shot forward.

"Watch out," Harden yelled as the van careened around the corner.

The van's large bulk filled the windshield. A collision was imminent. Scottie could see Boz fighting the wheel in the front seat of the van and braced himself for impact. The sound of squealing brakes followed the bomb-laden vehicle as it fishtailed out of his line of sight. Then a sickening crash echoed over the gunfire. The van slammed into the concrete wall of a shop.

"They wrecked out," Jones yelled.

"Contact front," Boz yelled over the radio as they came under fire.

"Damn it," Colonel Barnes yelled, punching the back of the seat in anger, and Scottie slid the sedan to a halt.

Boz still had the talk button depressed, and everyone in the car could hear the staccato chatter of a rifle firing inside the van. Villa's muffled voice was yelling Hoyt's name. Then the radio went dead.

Colonel Barnes was out of the car before it stopped. His rifle came to his shoulder as Harden threw the car's door open and followed him. He could see smoke drifting from the engine compartment of the van, the twisted rebar poking out of the smashed wall as he ran. Barnes knew an errant round could set the bomb off, but he still harbored an ember of hope that they could make it to the target.

The driver's-side door cracked open. Boz leaned out of his seat, dazed, and pushed it all the way open. He tumbled to the ground but remained in control of his rifle, which he began firing from his side.

Shots rang out from inside the van, followed by a muzzle striking the windshield, as Villa tried to get a better view of his attackers. Harden sprinted to catch up with the colonel, who went straight to the back doors of the van and pulled them open.

The cargo compartment was covered in blood. Barnes stepped up onto the bumper and saw that Hoyt was on his back, bleeding heavily from his chest. He ignored the man and checked the bomb's components as his soldier weakly raised his hand for help.

Villa wedged himself through the narrow space between the two front seats and jumped into the back of the van. His foot slipped on the bloody metal floor, causing him to bang his knee as he tried to open the sliding door.

"Help him," he yelled at the colonel, who refused to look up from the bomb.

Cursing, Villa grabbed the handle and slid the door open before grabbing Hoyt by his drag strap. His rifle bumped against his groin as he carefully lifted Hoyt's upper body out of the van. The heels of the man's boots hit the pavement with a thump, and Villa dragged him around to the back of the van, where Harden was yelling at his boss.

"Get out of there. We have to go," Harden ordered, but Villa gently laid his teammate on the ground and ripped the first aid pouch from his kit.

Harden could see the pale edges of Hoyt's femur poking out of his pant leg as Villa pressed down hard on his chest. Blood squirted from beneath his palm from the pressure on the wound.

"I need some gauze," Villa yelled as the colonel reached out of the van and slammed the doors shut.

"What the fuck is he doing?" Jones demanded breathlessly, running to the side of his fallen comrade.

"Forget about him. Focus on Hoyt," Villa said as Harden dumped the blowout kit on the pavement and began rummaging through the medical supplies.

"Move your arms," Jones said, pulling out his knife and cutting the plate carrier straps off Hoyt's shoulders. As soon as he pulled it clear, he could see the uneven rise of the man's chest, which was indicative of a collapsed lung.

As they fought to control the bleeding, the ragged sound of Barnes trying to start the mangled engine crept over the gunfire.

"Help me roll him over," Jones said as the colonel fought to get the van started.

"I can't find an exit wound," Villa yelled.

Out of the corner of his eye, Harden could see Scottie shooting over the hood of the car. He grabbed a plastic tube off the ground and expertly pulled out a long, thin needle. Using his fingers, he worked his way down from the chest bone, probing for the intercostal space between the ribs before deftly inserting the needle into the chest cavity. He was trying to relieve the pressure in the man's lungs, but he knew it was hopeless.

Barnes had abandoned trying to get the van started and suddenly appeared on the right side of the van.

"Leave him, he's dead," he ordered harshly.

The men ignored him and continued working to save their teammate's life. Barnes brought his rifle up in a smooth motion and fired a single round over Villa's shoulder and into Hoyt's forehead. Harden scrambled backward at the sudden gunshot and reached for his weapon. Villa stared at the small hole in his friend's forehead, trying to figure out what had happened, and Barnes grabbed his shoulder and pushed him out of the way.

A deathly silence fell over the small group as the realization of what had just occurred sank in. Barnes lowered his rifle and calmly said, "Get up, the mission's not over."

Mason pushed Renee to the ground as the KPV pummeled the car, blowing holes the size of a fist in the thin metal. The gunner walked his fire down the side of the car before pausing to inspect the damage, and Renee fought to reload the RPG launcher.

Tarek and Zeus were huddled near the rear of one of the disabled pickups. While Zeus was trying to get Mason's attention, Tarek engaged the technical with the SAW. The Libyan tried to pull his countryman to safety, but Tarek brushed him off and darted from cover.

Laying the light machine gun over the hood, he fired off two long bursts at the gunner and knocked him off the gun.

Mason heard him yell in triumph and was stepping out to see what had happened when he heard the sound of a heavy impact to his rear, followed by automatic fire. Renee felt Mason's grip on her shoulder loosen and finally got another rocket into the launcher.

Zeus sprinted toward Mason in a crouch as Renee got to her feet and moved to a better position. Taking her time, she lined up the shot and closed her finger around the trigger. Mason jerked his head in her direction. The rocket leapt from the launcher and rushed toward the technical. Another rebel was just getting the gun back into action when the RPG slammed into the wheel well and flipped the truck into the air.

Renee yelled in triumph and turned toward Mason with a huge

smile on her face. Mason was looking back toward the front of their position with an ashen expression. She knew immediately that something was wrong. Ditching the launcher, she looked between the open space of the two vehicles to see Tarek sprawled in the open in a pool of his own blood.

Huge chunks had been taken out of his chest and part of his head was missing. Somehow, his hand was still clutching the mangled SAW.

Mason started toward his dead friend, but Zeus grabbed his arm. Renee watched the American try to fight him off.

"Get the fuck off me," Mason yelled.

Zeus yelled back at him, but Renee couldn't make out what he was saying over a sudden upswell in rifle fire. She could see the Libyan pushing Mason back toward the rear of the trucks when an explosion went off to her six o'clock.

"Mason," she yelled as rounds began pouring in from the rear. She managed to find cover just as a neat row of holes appeared along the wall she'd just been standing next to.

The American saw her go to the ground and ran toward the rear of the mangled convoy. His heart beat heavily as he broke free from Zeus and ran over to her.

The Hezbollah commander, Abdul, was firing over the bed of the truck. Mason dropped to Renee's side.

"They are behind us," she yelled, but he ignored her and checked to make sure she was okay.

"You need to stay down," he yelled.

"We have to get out of here," she said as another salvo thumped into the truck they were using as cover.

Mason conducted a mag change, and Zeus took a position next to Abdul. The Libyan fired off four shots before his rifle went down. Mason moved to cover his friend.

"Stay down," he yelled at Renee as he looked to see who was shooting at them.

He saw a bullet-riddled van against the side of the building, and a car that was facing north down the road. A man was firing at them from the trunk of the sedan. Mason pointed the reticle over the man's chest and fired. When he shifted to the next target, his finger froze on the trigger. Mason immediately recognized the bearded face that appeared through the optic. It was his old teammate Jones.

Jones ran back to the sedan in disbelief. He couldn't believe that Barnes had just murdered one of his own men, and it was only his deep-rooted discipline that enabled him to follow orders. Behind him, Villa stared open-mouthed at his gore-soaked hands and at Hoyt's lifeless body.

"What the hell just happened?" Scottie yelled at him as he fumbled with the door.

His hand paused on the latch. Villa was just turning his head to answer when Scottie lurched backward before tumbling to the ground.

Jones turned to look for the shooter when a round shattered the side-view mirror near his head. He hit the ground and low-crawled around the car, where he found Scottie sprawled against the door with a gaping head wound. Blood and brain matter were sprayed against the side of the car. Jones stared at the large exit wound peeking out of his hair.

"Scottie's down. We need to move," he yelled over the radio.

"Yeah, no shit," Boz replied.

"Break contact, all elements break contact," Harden yelled, getting to his feet and pushing Boz toward the car.

Mason lowered his rifle and flipped the selector on safe. The man he'd just shot in the head was down, and his mind was racing over the problem before him. The van lay less than ten meters in front of him, its front end buried in the thin concrete of the building. He knew he would have to break cover to check it out. He wanted Zeus to back him up.

"Zeus, its Barnes's van," he said, pointing past the pickup.

"What?"

The rifle fire made it impossible to communicate, and as they were yelling back and forth, Renee moved to Zeus's side, eager to see what was going on.

"Tell her to stay back," he yelled, pointing at the woman and raising a closed fist.

Zeus glanced over his shoulder just as Renee crept past him, moving parallel along the east side of the pockmarked building.

"Shit," Mason yelled as she moved into the open space to his right.

His rifle at the ready, Mason sprinted toward the van, hoping to get there before anyone saw Renee. The front sight of his AK bobbed up and down, in time with his steps. He swept the rifle to the left and right, searching for threats as he moved.

Villa had moved back up the driver's-side door of the van to lay down suppressive fire so that the rest of his team could break contact. Mason could only see the top of his head through the shattered window, but he was able to see the barrel of his rifle snap toward Renee as he acquired his target.

Mason fired four shots through the door before ducking around the front of the van. Zeus jogged to catch up with Renee. Mason saw him grab the back of her shirt and pull her behind him. The American tried to get his attention and signaled for him to take her back to safety, but the Libyan had just pulled a frag from his kit. After pulling the pin, he tossed it to the north.

Mason didn't wait for the explosion. He moved around the front of the van and squeezed between the front end and the crumbling concrete wall. The van's bumper pressed into his thighs as he forced his body through the narrow space and looked through the open cargo door.

Clearing as much of the inside as he could, he stepped up into the van. It was empty. His boots stuck to the coagulated blood covering the floor. He ducked low to clear the ceiling, and his boots made a ripping sound as they tore free of the tacky blood.

Two large artillery shells were fastened to a wooden pallet, which was ratchet-strapped to the floor. His heart skittered as he took in the wires and blasting caps drilled into the unstable ordinance. This was not a good place to be.

He had to make sure Villa was down before worrying about the bomb. He slipped his rifle through the space between the two front seats and wedged himself into the cab of the van. The van's windshield was riddled with bullet holes and was impossible to see out of. Bright arterial blood stained the center console, and he could see more blood on the inside of the driver's-side door.

Taking a knee on the driver's seat, he leaned out and saw Villa lying on his back with his hand clutching his throat. Dark blood seeped through the fingers, and his tan face was ashen. Mason raised the rifle with his right hand while holding himself steady with his left and fired a round through the man's forehead. Before Villa's head hit the ground, the American was pulling himself back into the vehicle.

The improvised bomb was expertly crafted from two 105-millimeter artillery shells daisy-chained together and attached to a complex detonator. On top of the shells was a silver tube, which had a small gouge cut in the casing. Mason could see that an errant round had caused the gouge. There was no way to know if the container was still intact or if it was leaking.

He slipped the AK's sling over his head and swung the rifle out of his way so he could get to his knife. Flipping the blade out of the handle, Mason cut the two black zip ties securing the biologic to the bomb and stowed his knife.

Crouched over in the van's cramped interior, he held the metallic casing up to the dim light filtering into the cargo compartment. It was lighter than he'd expected, but he knew it could easily kill everyone in the area.

Gunfire erupted to the rear of the van, causing him to shove the metal cylinder into his pocket and get back into the fight.

Flinging open the rear door of the van, he saw Boz standing in the middle of the street firing at Renee's last position. Mason's left hand found the wooden forearm of the AK and raised it up as his right hand found the trigger. The rifle wasn't even to his shoulder when he fired the first round, which was low.

The 7.62-millimeter bullet skipped off the ground and grazed Boz's foot. He yelled in pain and swung the barrel of his rifle at the new threat. As he turned, Mason fired again, hitting the man in the side of the chest and through the jaw.

Blood misted into the air as Mason stepped out of the van, his rifle following the wounded man downward as he fell. He kept firing until Boz had hit the ground.

Jones was firing at Zeus and Renee from the side of the car. Mason snapped off two shots before his rifle jammed. The bullets went wide, and he was trying to get to cover when a round caught him square in the chest.

Mason stumbled to the west side of the van. More bullets peppered the concrete wall as he ducked behind cover. Chips of brick and mortar peppered his face, sending dust into his eyes. Still, he ripped the magazine from the rifle and pulled on the charging handle to clear the jam. He could feel the blood running down his side as the mangled casing was flung out. He struggled to catch his breath. Blocking out the pain, he inserted a fresh magazine and chambered another round.

Mason saw Jones pop up near the trunk of the sedan and fire two short bursts from his rifle. He was raising his AK-47 to take a shot when he caught movement across the street. Two men were running for the entrance to the alley. As the last man turned to call Jones to him, Mason recognized Harden.

Mason fired at Jones, knocking him to the ground, and then swung his rifle toward the alley. Harden stopped and propped his

HK against the concrete corner. The scene seemed to unfold in slow motion to Mason as his finger closed around the trigger. Harden fired two shots. Mason pulled the trigger hurriedly to the rear, rushing the shot.

He thought he saw a flash of blood, but the man was gone in an instant. The American had just started across the street in pursuit when he heard someone yelling his name.

Casting a glance over his shoulder, he saw Abdul yelling into a radio. Renee's knee was pressed on Zeus's chest. Mason felt his blood run cold as he stopped in the middle of the street. He let his rifle fall to his chest as he stood in the open, staring at the Libyan's blood-covered shirt.

"Oh God, no," he heard himself mutter.

Forcing his legs to move, Mason ran over to the Libyan and dropped to his knees. Zeus had been hit near the shoulder and blood poured out of the wound.

"Zeus . . . Jesus . . . c'mon, you're fine," Mason stuttered as he looked down at his friend's ashen face. His breathing was shallow and ragged, and Mason prayed the bullet hadn't hit something vital. "Get a fucking truck over here," he yelled at the Hezbollah commander, who was still screaming into the radio.

"I can get up, I'm fine," Zeus said weakly, trying to get his feet under him.

Mason felt his heart ripping in his chest as he began plugging the hole with gauze in an effort to stop the bleeding.

"Fuck . . . Zeus, I'm so sorry," he said, tears welling in his eyes.

Abdul appeared with a pickup, and Mason yelled for someone to help him lift his friend into the back. Renee helped pull the Libyan to his feet and ignored his feeble groans as they laid him gently in the backseat of the truck.

"We have to go," Renee was yelling, but Mason wasn't listening. He looked down at the last friend he had in the world and then walked toward the sedan.

"Mason, the bomb," Renee yelled, but Mason didn't care.

He heard the truck behind him as he moved in an arc across the street until he could see Jones, lying on his side. Mason snatched the Glock off his hip, and his old teammate scrambled for his rifle.

"Look at me, motherfucker," Mason yelled as he came around the car, the Glock up and firing. The round hit the man in the back of his leg. Jones went down but continued to crawl to his weapon.

Mason fired again, hitting the man in the ass.

"You want to die running away like a bitch?" he yelled.

Jones flipped himself over and stared up at Mason.

"Was he worth it?" Mason asked before shooting the man twice in the head. Holstering the pistol, he reached into the car and grabbed the black laptop and an assault pack that lay on the floor. There was a map lying in the passenger seat. He snatched it up, then rushed back to Zeus and Renee and jumped into the backseat of the truck.

They were jammed tight in the backseat, and Renee was putting pressure on Zeus's wound as the Libyan's head lolled from side to side. The American yelled at Abdul to get them out of the blast area and then began searching for something to treat his friend's wounds. The backseat of the truck was littered with trash and dirt-caked wrappers but not a single medical supply.

Unzipping the assault pack, he dumped it on the floorboard at his feet. A radio, food, batteries, and a small trauma kit fell out. The American bent forward to scoop up the olive-drab kit. He took a penlike auto-injector of morphine out of the jumbled pile of supplies and pulled the plastic cap off the front. He placed it on the Libyan's leg and depressed the button on the end. A heavy-duty spring fired the needle into Zeus's leg with a snap and injected the powerful pain med into his bloodstream.

Mason had to almost climb onto his friend to inspect the wound. The bullet had gone clean through, missing his vitals, but the wound was still bleeding heavily and his clavicle was broken. Mason checked to make sure both lungs were intact, and then, unrolling the gauze, he began packing the wound as gently as he could while Zeus grunted and squirmed away. Suddenly there was a large explosion behind them.

He could hear the men in the back of the truck yelling. He looked out the back window to see the extent of the damage. The truck was about four hundred meters from the blast, but the men were still being pelted with debris and shrapnel. A dark brown cloud rose above the buildings and expanded outward from the overpressure. Orange flames were visible along the outer edge of the huge crater. Thick black smoke billowed up into the dust cloud as a deep rumble tore through the city block.

Abdul was chattering angrily on the phone, while Mason took a pressure bandage and wrapped it tightly over the gauze.

"What's he saying?" he asked.

"He's on the phone," Zeus slurred.

"Well, you're good as new," Mason replied as he retook his seat.

"I can't believe I got shot." The Libyan's head lolled to the side. He looked at Mason with dilated pupils, slightly slurring his words. The morphine had hit him quickly, leaving him pain-free.

"Hey, welcome to the club," Mason joked.

"They are all dead," he said seriously.

"I know."

"So many more will die now."

The narcotic had put him in a somber mood, and a single tear collected at the corner of his eye. Mason placed his hand on his friend's head and tried to block out the pain welling up inside him.

"No, my friend, they won't," Mason said.

He'd totally forgotten about the metal cylinder in his pocket. Frantically he pulled it out of his pocket.

"Oh shit," he said as he pulled it out and began looking for a bottle of water. He found one in the almost empty assault pack and quickly unscrewed the top. Ignoring Zeus's questioning look, he slowly poured the water over the gouge in the casing and watched for any bubbles. After repeating the process two more times without seeing any signs of leaks, he let out a huge sigh and smiled at his friend.

"How did you . . . ?" Renee asked, a wave of relief flooding her face.

CHAPTER 34

Mason's adrenaline was long gone. He was drained and slumped in the back of one of Hezbollah's Toyotas being driven away from the battle zone.

Tarek's death sat like a burning ember in his chest. The man had been so young and full of life, and Mason felt responsible for everything. It seemed that everywhere he went, people died. The only change was that lately they were people he actually cared about. There was no one else to blame for his failures. Despite his good intentions, he was even more of a liability than he had been before. At least when he was on his own, he was only hurting himself. And Barnes was still alive.

The truck slowed and pulled into a neighborhood adorned with yellow Hezbollah flags. It was their base of operations in the city. After the commander passed through a checkpoint, manned by young men hardened by the war, he pulled the truck into a bombed-out building.

"Where are we?" Mason yelled into the cab.

"Our stronghold," said a soldier as he cut the engine.

Mason nudged the prone Zeus awake. He had to drag the groggy and injured Libyan out of the truck. Blood had seeped through the bandage, and he needed to find a place to change it. As he and Renee steadied Zeus between them, Mason cast a longing glance back at the city before following the soldiers into the building.

It was a wreck, even by the standards of war. Sandbags were stacked against the walls and jagged sections of rebar jutted out at acute angles. All around them, Hezbollah men and women moved with a sense of purpose. They were filling sandbags, cleaning weapons, or preparing rations in a makeshift kitchen. Maps of the city hung on the walls, and ancient-looking radios were stacked on a low table in the corner.

The sun would be going down soon, and burn barrels were being set up in preparation for night operations.

The Americans propped Zeus on an ammo can and while a medic was looking at the wound, they were all surprised to hear a familiar voice greet them.

It was Ahmed.

"Looks like you are still alive, my friends."

Mason smiled, embraced his old friend, and said, "Tarek didn't make it."

Ahmed placed a hand on his shoulder and gave it a gentle squeeze. "He was a soldier, just like you. Allah set his fate long ago, my friend."

"I managed to get this." He handed the silver tube to Ahmed, who looked at it with a frown. "I checked it for leaks. I think it's still secure."

Ahmed held the tube up to the light and inspected the shallow gouge in the smooth metal tube. Running his thumb over the jagged crease, he shook his head while judging the weight in his hand.

"It is amazing that such a thing could kill so many people. There is still much to do," he said as Renee went to look for ammo.

"What else is there to do? Barnes is gone."

Ahmed's laugh bounced off the walls as he closed his hand around the silver tube. "Gone? Where is he going to go? Does he have wings that would allow him to fly away? No, my friend, he is most definitely not gone." An icy tone entered Ahmed's voice, and Mason felt a surge of hope.

"What do you mean? He got away. I couldn't stop him."

"Abdul, the commander here, is a crafty man. It is amazing how fear motivates."

"What the hell are you talking about?"

"Come with me. There isn't much time."

Fifteen minutes later Mason was sitting in the bed of a pickup heading back to the blast site. The sun was slowly dipping below the horizon. The street was eerily quiet as the call to prayer spread out over the battlefield. The fighting had stopped as the faithful prepared to pray for the dead and for those who would die.

Mason was thinking about the conversation he had just finished with Ahmed. The old spy had told Abdul that whoever aided his friends aided him. Finding the Lebanese commander had been a blessing, and Ahmed had made sure to take advantage of the chance encounter. He had offered Abdul half a million dollars if he found Barnes but advised him that if the American got away, his family would pay the price. It was a terrible bargain for a terrible time, but when Ahmed wanted something, he made sure to offer proper motivation.

Mason had lightly kissed Zeus on the head as his friend lay asleep on a cot. The medics had treated his wound and given him another shot for the pain. Abdul had a doctor en route under heavy guard. Zeus didn't even move when Mason bid him farewell. He knew that if he said good-bye to Renee, she would demand to come with him, and he wasn't ready to tempt fate with her life.

"Look after Renee for me," he told Ahmed as he stepped through the broken arch that led to the courtyard.

A truck sat idling in the open, and after a final farewell, he had jumped into the bed of the pickup. Now they were headed back out into the city.

Abdul's men moved into the area, motivated by their commander's sudden zeal. Since the Syrian army was busy trying to regain al-Hajar al-Aswad, Hezbollah had free rein to do as they pleased. The fighters had blocked off an entire mile northeast of the mosque and reported that Barnes was trapped somewhere inside the perimeter.

The truck slowed to a halt near the site of the explosion. All that was left of the battle was a huge crater and piles of concrete and twisted metal from the vehicles. Mason walked past the blackened hole and reverently approached the spot where Tarek had died. The explosion had erased all but the memory of his friend.

The bodies of Barnes's men had been stripped naked and propped along the wall of one of the buildings. After their gear and clothing had been removed the corpses were riddled with rifle fire, leaving them almost unrecognizable, except for the paleness of their skin.

Mason was by himself again, and it was a fitting end to the journey. He walked solemnly to the corner where Harden had shot Zeus. Running his hand over the pockmarked wall, he was barely able to make out the faint trace of blood before he crept up the alley in search of his prey.

Very soon the evening prayer would be over and the fighting would continue. He knew that Barnes would wait until darkness before moving out. There was no way he would risk certain death by moving in the daylight. As the sun dipped out of sight, Mason heard scattered small-arms fire rising up around the city.

Staying in the shadows, Mason placed his night vision over his head and waited for Abdul's men to begin. It was quiet and still in the street. Emaciated dogs ambled from alleyways in search of food.

A breeze came out of the east, carrying with it the distinctive *clink* of a mortar round being lowered into the tube. Seconds later he heard the light *thump* of the round leaving the tube, and then silence. The eighty-two-millimeter high-explosive mortar blasted with a resounding *crummmmmp*, and a burst of orange light lit up the stillness.

More mortars were fired into the area. He imagined there were two or three mortar teams working off in the shadows. If they knew what they were doing, the plan would work. But if they were off target, things would go to shit fast. The plan was simple: The mortar crews would beat the bushes while the rest of Abdul's men waited for anyone to come running out. Those who stayed in the maelstrom belonged to Mason.

It wasn't the most cutting-edge plan, but as long as everyone stuck to the script, it should work. However, with the first shriek of an inbound 107-millimeter rocket, Mason realized that someone had decided to take it up a notch.

The Type 63 rocket launcher is nothing more than twelve metal tubes mounted to a launch platform. Hezbollah had learned the hard way that stationary rocket sites had an extremely low survivability rate and had begun mounting them to trucks during the last war with Israel. The rockets were a cheap but effective way to blanket a wide area with an indiscriminate number of high-explosive rounds. The Soviet design philosophy of "more bang for the buck" was appealing as long as you weren't on the receiving end of the deal.

Mason had given explicit instructions to Abdul on how the "fire missions" should be prosecuted. He had even taken time to mark a "no-fire area" where he planned on setting up an overwatch position. Apparently no one had bothered to listen to that part of the briefing, because as he approached the chosen building, it took a direct hit from a rocket.

As he ducked to avoid debris from the shattered building, he knew he needed a basement or at the least some overhead cover. He could see a shop across the street that was unscathed by the recent fighting. Scrambling away from the flying debris, he kicked open the door and dove inside.

The shopwindow shattered as a mortar round exploded in the street. Mason quickly scanned the interior of the building through the noxious dust and smoke. Staying low, he glimpsed a metal ice cooler next to an equally ancient cash register. Old steel coolers were lead lined and would hopefully withstand an indirect hit.

Another rocket came screaming into the impact area. The high-pitched wail of the mortar was unforgettable. There was no way to tell where it was headed. He managed to dive into the metal cooler as the rocket slammed into the shop and pulverized the brick wall. Mason felt the cooler shift violently as debris bounced off the steel exterior and slapped it across the floor. The impact sloshed the stagnant water that filled the bottom two inches of his makeshift bunker up to the top of the lid and down into his face.

Mason felt his clothes soaking up the nasty liquid as he tried to spit the brackish water out of his mouth. It felt like he was in a metal trash can and someone was beating on it with a bat. He prayed that the cooler wouldn't become his casket.

When he heard the explosions starting to move more to the south, he tried to push the lid open, but something heavy was holding it down. Managing to contort himself inside the claustrophobic confines of the metal box, he got his legs up and began pushing on the lid. The weight on top of the cooler combined with the worn rubber seal around the edge made it airtight. He struggled to breathe. He could feel his spine grinding against the metal floor and his thighs were quivering as he tried to get some air. Finally the lid budged open about an inch, and Mason greedily sucked in a lungful of air.

"C'mon, biiiitch," he yelled as the sweat began rolling off his forehead and into his eyes. The more he pushed, the more carbon dioxide settled near the bottom of the cooler. The angle of his body was putting pressure on his diaphragm. Mason could hear concrete beginning to slide off the lid as he summoned a final burst of strength and forced the box open. His legs were shaking as he lay soaking wet in the bottom of the box and sucked gulps of air into his lungs. Looking up, Mason could see a huge hole above his head and the dark sky peeking into the shattered shop.

After a few moments, he shakily climbed out of the cooler and tentatively swung his leg over the edge. Huge blocks of stone and brick fragments were scattered everywhere. The cash drawer of the vintage register stood open. Smelling like a wet bum, he took a few small steps and tried to shake the lactic acid out of his muscles. It had seemed like such a good plan an hour ago.

From inside the destroyed shop, Mason could see muzzle flashes erupting in the night as a firefight broke out along the eastern perimeter. Rifles cracked in the distance, followed by the heavier chatter of the crew-served weapons. Creeping out into the street, he was greeted by a veritable wasteland. Through his night vision, the city block was now just an abstract collection of right angles and the skeletal frames of shattered buildings.

Moving to one of the only freestanding buildings in the area, he slipped inside and "dirty-cleared" the bottom floor. If there had been more time, he could have afforded to be more thorough. But right now, time was just as powerful an enemy as Barnes. Once he found the staircase, he ascended to the second floor and crept over to a shattered casement.

Waiting was the hardest part of an operation, and patience definitely was not one of his strong suits. Digging in his assault pack, he grabbed a bottle of water and took a small sip. Swishing it around in his mouth, he spat it onto the floor before taking a deep gulp. It was very still outside his makeshift hide site, except for the distant rifle fire. Doubt began to creep in like an uninvited guest as he stared out of the detritus and his mind began to play tricks on him. Objects began appearing more human the longer he waited. He had to force himself to focus. Cursing, he wished he had brought a thermal scope with him.

At first Mason wasn't sure if he had heard anything, the sound was so imperceptible. His breathing seemed impossibly loud as he strained to pick up the scratch of stone on metal. Trying to hold his breath only made his heart pump louder in his ears, but then he heard it again. The trickle of pebbles over stone was unmistakable. Something was definitely moving. Mason's boots scuffed the floor as he shifted closer to the wall to get a better look.

Mason prayed. He begged God for a miracle. Ever so slowly the moonlight washed over the street. In the shadows Mason saw a figure crouched low to the ground. His fingers began to ache as they involuntarily throttled the hand guard of his rifle. He forced himself to loosen his grip, and his night vision picked up the unmistakable glow of light emanating from an optic. That was all he needed. He knew he had a target, but now he couldn't decide if he should take the shot. Mason was conflicted. Did he move or stay? Shoot or wait? It was an easy shot, but there was only one target. He didn't want to blow the element of surprise.

"Shit." He brought the rifle up and paused. In his mind the debate raged until he pulled the rifle down and moved for the stairs. He came out onto the street and quickly got his bearings before breaking into a trot. Every second he didn't have eyes on his target, there was a chance the figure could slip away.

Mason knew he needed to move south but couldn't find a cut-through and was forced to keep moving east.

Finally, he pushed through the opening of an alley. He stayed on the balls of his feet to muffle his footfalls while straining his eyes for any debris that would give him away. At last he came to the end of the alley and stopped before stepping out into the road.

The rising moon amplified his night vision, and the surrounding details appeared clear and crisp. His heart was beating in his ears, and he struggled to control his breathing. Mason judged that he was fifty meters from where he had seen the man, but there was no longer any sign of him.

Panic trickled down his spine like a drop of cold water. *Where the hell did he go?* A low hiss drifted from his left. He turned his head very slowly and peered down the street until he made out an arm in a doorway. The figure had moved across the street. Now he didn't have a shot. A rustle came from his right, and suddenly another figure emerged from the shadows.

Mason had two targets now. There was no way to engage both.

On top of that, he couldn't positively identify his targets. They could have been Barnes and Harden, or they could have been two hapless locals looking for something to steal. Either way he needed to be ready. Mason had to decide if he was going to wait until they met up or try to catch one in the open and hope he had time to pin the other man down.

He slipped his left hand into his kit, felt the metal pin of a frag, and slowly pulled it from the pouch. Mason moved it into his palm and waited for someone to make a move while keeping his right hand on the rifle, in case he needed to fire. Mason watched the second figure as he began inching his way down the low wall. Clamping the rifle against his leg with his bicep, he eased the pin out of the grenade while still holding on to the spoon.

The figure bounced up from the crouch and sprinted for the road. Mason released the spoon, which cartwheeled into the darkness. Suddenly he realized he couldn't make the throw with his left hand. Quickly switching hands, he took a tiny step forward and released his hold on the rifle. The weapon clattered against the brick opening of the alley as the frag arced toward the street.

Holding the trigger down, one of the men sprayed Mason's position, forcing him to duck back into the alley as the frag exploded, followed by a cry of pain. Mason picked up his rifle and shifted his angle as he moved out into the street and snapped off four quick shots. A body lay motionless in the street, but another burst of rifle fire sent him ducking back to cover. From his knees he prepped his last frag. Even though he didn't have a target, he tossed it out and hoped the shrapnel would find some meat.

The metal body clinked against the ground and bounced before exploding. Mason had to commit to the fight or risk losing contact with his target. Coming up from his crouch, he moved out of cover and hammered through the magazine as he twisted toward the doorway. Through the optic he caught a dark figure silhouetted in the shadows, and he squeezed the trigger as the reticle centered over the man's chest. Mason knew he had the kill shot but felt the trigger go slack as the empty bolt locked open.

He kept moving, all too aware that he was hung out in the open. He let the rifle swing free and rushed to pull the Glock from its chest holster. The man in the doorway moved to fire as Mason raced to get the pistol on target. The rifle's muzzle blast lit up the shadowed doorway. He felt the rounds hit his thighs and run up the front of his plate carrier.

Keeping the pistol on target as he pulled the trigger, Mason focused on the front sight, but he was falling as his legs crumpled underneath him. He landed hard behind a pile of rocks as bullets whistled over his head. Tossing the empty pistol away, he felt the blood soaking through his pants as he snatched a fresh mag for his rifle from his rig. Using his thumb to depress the magazine release, he ejected the empty mag with a flip of his wrist before inserting a fresh one. Slapping the bolt release with the palm of his hand, he rolled out and returned fire.

The rounds snapped across the street and slammed into the empty doorway. Mason couldn't believe that the figure was gone. Struggling to his feet, he tried to run across the road but collapsed after a step. Dragging himself across the ground, he kept his rifle up and ready to fire. But the street was empty.

"Shit," he yelled, and slammed his fist on the concrete. Using the rifle to push himself to his feet, he managed to hobble over to the body before collapsing in pain. Mason dragged himself until he was close enough to grab him by the front of his kit. It was Harden.

Harden was bleeding from his ears and mouth but still clung to life. Mason shook him and yelled, "Where the fuck is he? Tell me or . . ."

"Or what? I'm already dead." Harden spat blood down the front of his kit. He smiled and reached up to touch Mason's face. "I thought you were dead."

Mason slammed Anvil 7 back on the ground in frustration. He

could see vehicles coming down the street as he lay down beside Harden. The two men stared at each other, their blood staining the street.

"You can't stop him, can't you see that? You never could."

Mason propped himself up on his elbow to get a better look at his shattered legs. Ripping a tourniquet from his kit, he slipped it over his right thigh and cranked it down. It hurt worse than being shot, but the blood began to stop. He pulled himself closer to Harden and ripped his blowout kit off his left side.

Dumping it on the ground, he searched for another tourniquet. There was nothing but gauze.

"I'm not dying here," Mason growled as he ripped the sling from his rifle and looped it over his leg. He cinched it as tight as he could before dropping the magazine and forcing the takedown pin out of the lower receiver. Pulling the charging handle from the rifle, he stuck it through the top of the sling before tying a knot over the metal handle. Mason twisted the makeshift tourniquet until his left leg went numb. Taking the free end of the sling, he tied the handle in place and fell back on the ground.

Mason and Harden had made their choices. Both of them lived by their own code, yet somehow here they were. Staring into Harden's eyes, Mason could see the man's life slipping away.

"Was it worth it?" he asked.

"It was all I had," Harden whispered. Anvil 7 lifted his hand and placed it on Mason's chest. "Don't let me die alone."

He stared at the bloody hand. They had been brothers once, and now fate had them lying in a street bleeding out.

"Please," he whispered.

Mason took the dying man's hand and squeezed.

Ahmed appeared above him, and Mason freed his hand and pointed across the street. More men appeared. They lifted him into the back of the truck. Pain shot through his body, and he wanted to scream.

"Find his body," he yelled. "I hit him, he can't be far."

"Mason, please be calm. They will find him." Ahmed was holding his head in his hands.

"You have to find Barnes." Another man appeared. Mason caught a glimpse of a syringe and felt the prick of a needle. Abdul's voice echoed as he yelled at his men. Mason wanted to tell them something about Barnes, but he couldn't remember what. Or maybe it was something about himself. Either way, the drugs worked fast, and he felt the pain subside. It was finally time to rest.

CHAPTER 35

Washington, DC

NSA Cage checked his tie in the mirror before turning and walking over to his desk. He took a set of keys off the calendar and tossed them to Jacob, who stood smiling on the other side.

"I told you it would work out," Cage said as his old friend caught them in midair.

"Sir, the mission failed . . ."

"Did it?"

"Yes, sir, the bomb never went off, Barnes is dead, and Mason is still out there somewhere. Everyone is gone."

"But we're not. Sometimes a victory doesn't look exactly the way we expect it to."

"Yes, sir, but I feel like I let you down."

"At the end of the day, Collins is under investigation, and we are a step closer to our goal. While the rest of the country is playing checkers, you and I are playing chess. You have to keep that in mind and remember that this is just the beginning."

"It just doesn't feel right," Jacob said honestly.

"Jacob, I can promise you one thing: this is going to get much worse before it gets better, but we have to stay the course. Thomas Jefferson once said that 'the tree of liberty must be refreshed from time to time with the blood of patriots and tyrants.' Right now, that is our blood."

He stood staring at his aide, searching for any signs of weakness or hesitation, almost daring him to back down. Finally, Jacob looked up, his eyes burning with resolve.

"Sir, you know I will follow you anywhere."

"You say that now," Cage said before turning and heading for the door.

CHAPTER 36

Mason was dreaming about his old house. He was cooking dinner and waiting for his wife to come home. Suddenly the doorbell rang, and when he turned away from the stove, Tarek was standing there.

"I thought you were dead."

"Mason, we're all dead," he said with a smile. "Do you want a cigarette? It's a Camel."

"Yeah, that would be great." Tarek handed him a cigarette and lit it with a golden lighter. "I'm sorry I left you in the street," he said after taking a drag.

"That is okay, I was dead," the Libyan said with a smile.

"You wouldn't have left me," Mason said, ashamed.

"Ah well, who could know these things? It is not your fault that I am dead, but if you're not careful your food will burn."

Mason turned to see the dinner going up in flames. He looked for something to put out the fire, but his arms were so heavy and hard to move. The flames crept down the stove and across the floor, and Tarek laughed as the flames licked at his feet before crawling toward Mason, who was unable to move. The flames spread to his legs, and then he was on fire.

"Tarek, I can't move my legs, can you help me out?" The flames were spreading quickly, and he could feel his skin burning. The Libyan just looked at him and smiled.

"I'll see you again," Tarek said, and then he was gone.

Mason felt someone grabbing his shoulders and shaking him. He opened his eyes, and a man whom he had never seen before was holding him down. The man was dressed in white scrubs and was sweating as he tried to subdue him. Letting go of his shoulders, the man picked up a cord that traced up to an IV stand. He pushed the red button at the end of the line before dropping it on the bed.

Mason looked around, and he realized he was in a hospital of some sort. Zeus stood in the corner of the room, next to Renee, their faces covered in worry. Looking around, he eyed a pitcher of water sitting on a table next to the metal bed. It was too far for him to reach, but his friend walked over to the bed and poured some water into a plastic glass. Moving the straw to Mason's lips, he held it up so the American could take a drink.

It was the best water he had ever had. He drank the entire glass and felt his throat clearing up.

"Where am I?"

"You're in Cyprus."

"How did I get here?"

"We brought you here after you killed Harden. You've been out for a few days."

"What about Barnes?"

"We didn't find him. There was blood all over the place, and I don't think he got far, but they haven't found his body yet."

"You have to be kidding me."

Zeus shrugged and filled up the plastic cup with more water. He held it to Mason's lips and let him get another drink. The man was writing something on a clipboard and told Zeus not to let him have too much water.

"You need to try and be still. No more thrashing about."

"What are you talking about?"

"You had a nightmare. It really scared the hell out of me. I guess you just needed more morphine," Zeus said.

"So what's in the envelope, a check?" Mason asked Renee.

"It's from Mr. David. I think he's offering us a job."

"A job? Is she serious?" he said to Zeus.

"I cannot answer that, my friend, she won't let me see it, but after what you have done, I wouldn't doubt it."

"So, what's the job?"

"We can talk about that later. Right now you need your rest," Renee said sternly.

Mason looked down at his legs. He expected to feel something about the last few days. So many people had died because of him, and for what?

The American felt his eyes closing slowly. Like Barnes, it seemed that he was doomed to live until the war had finished with him. He tried to fight the drugs, because he was afraid of the dreams that were waiting for him. As he drifted off, a brief shadow crossed his drug-addled mind, and somehow he knew that this was just the beginning.

ACKNOWLEDGMENTS

First and foremost, I give all the glory to Jesus Christ for his grace and faithfulness, and for allowing me to work with John Paine, Bob Diforio, Matthew Benjamin, and the rest of the wonderful staff at Touchstone. Their tireless guidance, support, and patience took a dream and made it into a reality, and I am forever grateful.

I would also like to thank my wife, Amy, for believing in me when no one else did.

ABOUT THE AUTHOR

Joshua Hood graduated from the University of Memphis before joining the military and spending five years in the 82nd Airborne Division, where he was team leader in the 3-504th Parachute Infantry Regiment. In 2005, he was sent to Iraq and conducted combat operations in support of Operation Iraqi Freedom from 2005 to 2006, and from 2007 to 2008 he served as a squad leader in the 1-508th Parachute Infantry Regiment and was deployed to Afghanistan for Operation Enduring Freedom. Hood was decorated for valor in Operation Furious Pursuit. He is currently a member of a full-time SWAT team in Memphis, Tennessee, and has conducted countless stateside operations with the FBI, ATF, DEA, Secret Service, and U.S. Marshals.